The MOTHERS of Lovely Lane

NADINE DORRIES grew up in a working-class family in Liverpool. She trained as a nurse herself, then followed with a successful career in the health industry in which she established and then sold her own business. She has been the MP for Mid-Bedfordshire since 2005 and has three daughters.

By Nadine Dorries

NADINE DORRIES

The MOTHERS
of Lovely Lane

HEAD
of ZEUS

First published in the UK in 2017 by Head of Zeus, Ltd
This paperback edition first published in the UK
in 2018 by Head of Zeus, Ltd

9 7 5 3 1 2 4 6 8

A catalogue record for this book is available from
the British Library.

ISBN (PB): 9781784975197
ISBN (E): 9781784975081

Typeset by Adrian McLaughlin

Printed and bound in Great Britain by
CPI Group (UK) Ltd, Croydon CRO 4YY

Head of Zeus Ltd
First Floor East
5–8 Hardwick Street
London ECIR 4RG

WWW.HEADOFZEUS.COM

For my best friend, Alison,
and all mothers everywhere

Chapter 1

It was three weeks since the day of the accident that had rocked St Angelus and everyone who worked there to the core. Teddy Davenport, the most popular junior doctor at the hospital, boyfriend and true love of one of the most popular student nurses, Dana Brogan, had almost lost his life in a car accident. He'd been racing down to the Pier Head to collect Dana, who had just returned from a visit back to her family farm in the west of Ireland. From absolutely nowhere and without a second's warning, a young pregnant woman had stepped straight out into the path of his speeding car. Dana, sitting on her suitcase nearby as she waited for Teddy to arrive, had witnessed the whole thing.

In the days since the accident, Teddy had spent many hours in surgery, with patients and staff alike holding their collective breath, willing him to survive. He almost died a number of times. What saved his life was a resuscitation technique that had been newly discovered in America and was being pioneered at St Angelus by Dr Anthony Mackintosh. Every time Teddy almost succumbed to the shock of his injuries,

1

Dr Mackintosh brought him back, only for Teddy to leave them again within minutes. It was down to Dr Mackintosh and the heroic efforts of the orthopaedic surgeon, Mr Mabbutt, that Teddy eventually pulled through, and everyone knew it.

Through these darkest of days Dana was supported by her closest friends and housemates from the Lovely Lane nurses' home: Pammy Tanner, Victoria Baker and little Beth Harper. With Teddy now beginning his long recuperation on the male orthopaedic ward, she was beside him for as much time as she could manage. After nine hours on her ward shift, she routinely spent a further four hours at Teddy's bedside, with the permission of Matron, nursing him through the worst.

The accident and Teddy's near death had stunned everyone who worked with him or knew him. It even made the front page of the *Liverpool Echo*. There wasn't a nurse, porter or domestic at St Angelus who did not see the day of Teddy's accident as a turning point in the life of the hospital. It was like a catalyst that forced everyone to accept that it was now time to embrace the post-war world and the new NHS and all it brought with it. Taking the path of resistance, as Matron and some members of the hospital board had, was no longer an option.

Mr Mabbutt, physically and mentally exhausted after his many hours of orthopaedic reconstruction on Teddy, was vociferous in his views about the need for change. Once Teddy had left the operating table for the final time, the surgeon made it very plain that things at St Angelus could not continue as they were.

'I cannot go on operating like this, in these primitive conditions!' he yelled as he smashed the theatre's central overhead lamp with his fist.

Theatre Sister looked on in alarm as the huge concave metal structure swung wildly from side to side. She had stood at Mr Mabbutt's back during his most difficult operations for more than twenty-five years, anticipating his requirements and wiping his dripping brow, once smooth and youthful, now lined and craggy. No one dared refuse him anything, ever, so frequent and loud were his exclamations of 'bloody nurse', 'bloody patient', 'bloody mess' and even 'bloody sister', but she'd never seen him this angry.

'The bloody war was bloody over years ago. We have to have new theatres! We must update this equipment and we need more bloody trained staff, for God's sake. What is wrong with these people, these bloody do-gooders on the board?'

The newly qualified staff nurse, washing truly bloody dressings as Theatre Sister counted bloody swabs on to her trolley, burst into tears. Mr Mabbutt terrified her. Never more so than when he was shouting, and, like everyone else in the vicinity, she was petrified that the overhead light would crash on to the floor if he banged it again.

'It's like operating in a bloody field hospital here! I thought I'd left those days behind. The NHS was supposed to improve life, not make it more complicated. I want a bloody new theatre. We all need a new theatre or half of the people who come in here to be operated on will die. It's bloody astonishing Dr Davenport wasn't one of them. Get me bloody Matron – NOW!'

Mr Mabbutt's shouting and cursing could be heard all the way down the stairs and along the hospital corridor. A group of walking wounded, sitting on ladder-backed chairs in casualty, waiting to be seen by the gentle Dr Mackintosh, raised their heads from their copies of the *Liverpool Daily Post* and looked at each other in mild alarm.

But Matron had known Mr Mabbutt for decades and his profanity and bad temper had little impact. She was more than used to it. She ruled the roost and as only she and Mr Mabbutt knew, he was more scared of her than she of him. It had been many years since she had needed to reprimand him for his behaviour with a junior nurse. Engaged to be married, he had been summoned to her office and read the riot act. The result was that Mr Mabbutt changed his ways. In return he had been guaranteed Matron's absolute discretion, a promise Matron had never broken. Nonetheless, Mr Mabbutt did not want ever to be reminded of how he had almost lost the love of his life, to whom he had now been married for many happy years. He never wanted to push Matron over the edge. His guilt was her secret weapon and that meant she was almost the only person in the hospital who could deal with his rages. On this occasion, however, she decided to send for Dr Gaskell, the longest-serving and most senior doctor in the hospital and the man she trusted most of all.

Twenty minutes later, Dr Gaskell made his way to the consultants' sitting room. Mr Mabbutt had calmed down slightly by now, though not noticeably to the new young housekeeper who looked after the sitting room. 'Get me my tea and some toast – now! I haven't eaten for ten hours,' he snapped at her.

The housekeeper almost jumped out of her shoes, then retreated into the kitchenette to do his bidding. The consultants were revered beings and almost worshipped by the hospital staff. They brought life into the world, they saved it in moments of crisis and, eventually, they signed it back out again. It was hardly surprising that these particular men in white coats were accorded a status which could only be described as godlike.

'Dr Davenport is alive and that's a bloody miracle,' Mr Mabbutt said to Dr Gaskell as he sank into an armchair. 'Especially as we don't even have one of those new ventilators in the theatre. We don't have the drugs or lights or the new equipment the new hospitals in places like London and Birmingham have.' He snatched the plate of toast from the housekeeper and devoured it in three mouthfuls. 'I'm exhausted by the amount of work we now have to do. Have you seen how busy casualty is these days? Every day there's a broken bone for me to mend either from a fight or a car accident. It feels like every man in Liverpool is buying those lethal motor scooters and crashing the bloody things and it's me that has to put them back together again – in a bloody primitive theatre. We need a new theatre, desperately.'

Dr Gaskell listened and sympathized. Not so long ago he had considered retiring, but the medical advances and rapidly changing direction of the hospital under the new NHS had reawakened his interest. 'I totally agree, old chap. We must seize every chance we get and ensure St Angelus isn't left behind. It's the same in my field. They're already talking about the next generation of TB antibiotics to take over from streptomycin. Such progress I could only have dreamt of in my early days as a doctor. We must make the most of it while we can.'

A plan was hatched. 'Leave it to me, I'll have a word with Matron. There are ways to handle her, as you know. You have to pick your battles carefully, and in my opinion this one is very much worth fighting.'

The following morning, Dr Gaskell paid Matron a visit. He suggested that they move ahead with proposing to the

Liverpool District Hospitals Board that St Angelus urgently required a new theatre suite. 'We can lead the request together,' he said with a gentle smile. 'The board will surely be impressed by such a bold and progressive proposal.'

Matron flatly refused. 'Oh, well, I see!' she shot back. 'He has got to you too, has he? Mabbutt and the usual culprits? You aren't even a surgeon, Dr Gaskell. You are a chest doctor. You don't even use theatre very often unless you want someone to take a lung out. I don't understand why you are taking their side. We have a perfectly serviceable operating theatre. It's our maternity services that are suffering. They must take priority over surgery.'

Dr Gaskell wanted to bury his head in his hands. He had known Matron for all of his working life and her stubbornness was legendary.

'Matron...' He paused and took a breath before he went on. 'I am not saying that maternity should be shelved or ignored or is any less of a consideration. It is just that the old theatre is beginning to cause some serious problems. Problems we wouldn't want to read about in the *Liverpool Echo*, now would we?'

'I will not be bullied by Mr Mabbutt and be held answerable to his unrealistic demands,' she said. 'It is a poor surgeon who blames his theatre and it appears to me that is exactly what Mr Mabbutt and the band of merry surgeons he has persuaded to join him in his noisy little protest – including your own son, I might add – have decided to do. Oh, they have all been to see me, one by one, as well you know. But I remain resolute, I am afraid. The answer from me is no. Absolutely no. Maternity first.'

Matron felt let down by Dr Gaskell. Disappointed, even.

They had run the hospital together for more years than either cared to count, and through the most sombre and challenging days. During the week of the May Blitz, they had both worked on casualty around the clock and although that was now over ten years ago, it was a week that neither could forget. They had become the closest friends over their very long tenure at St Angelus and she hated having confrontations with him. These days it was unusual for them to disagree and when they did, it was often soon sorted out over a glass of sherry in her sitting room.

She rose from her chair and crossed the floor to Blackie's basket next to the fireplace. Bending down with the ease of a woman half her age, she stroked her dog's head, ran her fingers through the tuft of hair between his eyes and smoothed his quizzical brow. Blackie's job in life was to protect his mistress. He was blissfully unaware of his minute Scottie size and took on all comers he considered to be a threat to his beloved human.

'What does it matter to you anyway? You never go near the theatre block.' She ran her fingers over Blackie's eyes, which were closed in pleasure. 'You have other far more important concerns – leading the regional TB committee, for one.' There was now more pleading in her tone. She wished he would just give in to her on this without fuss or argument.

'It doesn't matter to me, Matron, not personally. I seem to spend most of my life in planning and committee meetings these days. And I have enough battles of my own to fight – keeping my patient list, for a start. The cheeky blighters on the board want me to hand over my patients to a new consultant, patients I have been caring for for over thirty years! A new theatre doesn't matter to me, but it matters to St Angelus.

And you are quite wrong, it has nothing to do with Oliver, although as my son spends half of his week operating in the theatre, his voice is a valid one, as valid as anyone else's.'

Matron raised her eyebrows. They both knew that Oliver Gaskell was in his position as consultant because Dr Gaskell senior was his father. Matron had no problem with nepotism. There was not a boy feeding the stoke holes or working as a porter's lad who was a stranger to the St Angelus family. The hospital thrived on taking care of its own. It had been obvious that Oliver Gaskell was a talented young man, if a bit foot-loose and fancy free. Matron wondered if Dr Gaskell knew of his son's reputation with her nurses. She was disappointed that, as the consultant for obs and gynae, he hadn't backed her in her quest for a new maternity department.

She sighed and stood up from stroking Blackie. 'Do you want some tea?' she asked as she smoothed away Blackie's imaginary hair from the front of her immaculate navy dress. 'Shall I call for Elsie?' She was desperate to change the subject. The two of them arguing like this was making her feel sick and uncomfortable. Contrary to rumour – a rumour that supported her reputation as a matron to be feared – she hated conflict.

However, Dr Gaskell was not to be distracted and, ignoring her question, he continued.

'It is the growing population of Liverpool, the patients, I care about. The people who are alive here and now, today, don't you see? And, yes, the women who need caesareans too. Maternity will also benefit from a new operating theatre. But we've so many badly healed war wounds and chronic injuries that we should be thinking about. Some of the operations carried out in those field hospitals may have saved lives, but ten years on and those men are still struggling. Our surgeons can help prevent some of them from enduring a lifetime of pain and chronic health problems. There is more damage to be attending to, Margaret. Our prosthetics clinic is full every single appointment, as you know. Every day. Doesn't that tell you something about the way things are?' He had used her Christian name, in desperation. Her eyebrows raised and he saw a smile almost reach her lips.

Matron pressed the brown Bakelite bell at the side of the fireplace to summon Elsie and then marched over to her chair and flopped down in an almost girl-like manner, crossing her arms before her.

Dr Gaskell had the distinct impression he was going to have to fight very hard to bring her on side. Harder than he ever had before. He let out a deep sigh as he crossed his fingers in front of his pursed lips. He would have to be slightly more imaginative than usual. Although something about her manner told him that he might have just taken the first fairy footstep towards getting his own way.

Matron set her chin at him. He looked up. Had he won? He dared to hope.

'I care about the women who are still giving birth at home and should be doing so in this hospital. Not just those who are being rushed in needing a caesarean section. The next grant should be spent on creating an efficient, lifesaving new maternity block. Maternal death is the biggest killer of young women in Liverpool, not appendicitis. We have to put an end to that and we can do, or at least we can make a start with a new maternity unit.'

Hope fell and crashed into his boots. 'But we have dedicated maternity and women's hospitals already in Liverpool. As a city, it is a provision of care we lead in.' His voice held a tinge of exasperation. He and Matron were the two most authoritative figures in the hospital and this was turning out to be the most difficult of power struggles.

'Yes, but not for the Irish diaspora who live around the docks. The only place they trust is St Angelus and besides, have you heard them? If you as much as mention visiting Mill Road Hospital, they almost faint. They are the most superstitious group of people I have ever known. We forget because we work and live amongst them how much that affects everything they do.'

Dr Gaskell knew this. He and the other doctors were continually trying to discredit the 'bottles' sent over from Ireland which some of their patients claimed had miraculous healing abilities. The latest competition for Dr Gaskell had been the urine of a goat that lived on a farm in Sligo and which apparently had magical powers. The only thing Dr Gaskell thought might be magical was the rate at which that particular farmer's coffers were filling up with money being sent from Liverpool for a bottle of the offending liquid.

'It will be a long time yet before those dreadful memories of the Mill Road bomb have faded,' Matron said quietly. 'All those mothers and babies dead. All those poor people they couldn't rescue having to be cemented over. You can't blame the women around here for not wanting to go near it. They refuse to deliver their babies in what is in effect a graveyard. And so they miss out on the best maternal care other women can enjoy. I just want the best for our women too.'

There was a moment's silence as both Matron and Dr Gaskell thought back to that horrendous time. The bombing on May the third 1941 had devastated the city and altered countless lives for ever. Mill Road maternity hospital had taken one of the hardest hits, killing mothers and babies, ambulance drivers, doctors and patients. So many were dead and the damage so bad that many bodies, including those of mothers with babes in arms, had to be limed and then cemented over. Men who were away at war, sustaining their own injuries on the battlefield, had no idea that back in Liverpool their homes were being bombed and their families lost. It was all still too much for words and as a result was barely ever mentioned. Except by the superstitious Irish community, who, when complications arose, still refused to attend Mill Road to deliver their babies.

The door to the small kitchen off Matron's sitting room caught in the breeze of the open window and banged shut as Elsie O'Brien, the housekeeper who looked after Matron's apartment, wheeled in a trolley of tea and toasted crumpets.

Hearing raised voices, Elsie kicked the brake on the trolley and decided to serve the tea as slowly as she could possibly get away with. This way she would hear more. Gather more gossip and vital information to pass back to Biddy Kennedy and the rest of the women in the St Angelus mafia. The mafia had an important job to do, looking out for the women and families from the dockside streets who worked at the hospital. They were the protectors of jobs, the feeders of children, first and last.

'I will pour the tea, thank you, Elsie,' Matron snapped.

Elsie's heart sank. 'I haven't buttered the crumpets yet, Matron. I'll just do that first.' She turned to Dr Gaskell, tried another tack. 'Oh, Dr Gaskell, isn't it awful about the accident and poor Dr Davenport almost dying.' She dabbed at her eyes with her handkerchief, but Matron was having none of it.

'Thank you, Elsie, I will butter the crumpets.'

Elsie almost grumbled out loud as she shuffled her way back to the kitchen, leaving Matron to serve her own tea. She would have to resort to positioning a brandy glass on the back of the kitchen door now to hear any more news.

Matron handed Dr Gaskell his cup and saucer and their eyes met. A calmness settled on Matron's vast sitting room as they both reflected on Dr Davenport's accident and the events of the past few weeks. The rain lashed up from the Mersey and beat against the windows, sending rivulets of tar down the blackened red-brick walls. Seagulls called out in the distance and the dark oak furniture gleamed in the reflected glow of the fringed lamps, testament to twenty years of devoted polishing by Elsie.

Dr Gaskell was one of the best TB doctors the country had ever known and the most respected consultant in the whole north-west of England. He was wily as well as sharp. As he sipped his tea he hatched a cunning plan which he hoped would outwit Matron, make her see sense and allow him to prioritize the new theatre above the maternity unit.

He looked about the familiar room, placed his cup and saucer back on the trolley and decided he would have one more go. He was going to have to drop the bomb. Her stubbornness was leaving him with no option.

'Look, Matron, I am also supportive of a new maternity unit, but we will only receive money for one or the other in this budget. I would like this to go no further, and I know it won't, but, you see, there are some very difficult problems we need to face. You don't need me to tell you that only a century ago this hospital was a workhouse. We are built almost on the river and as a result we have, er, problems to overcome.

It's more than just mice and water rats now, I'm afraid. These, er, *creatures* have to be dealt with and a pair of tomcats just won't do it.'

Matron placed her own cup and saucer on the trolley and he saw her hand wobble slightly at the mention of the loathsome, dirty creatures whose name he dared not speak. She knew what he was referring to. She knew everything. But it was something she refused to acknowledge. The cursed inhabitants of the Merseyside slums, the processing plants, the docks and the shops – and, it would seem, her hospital.

'Being so close to the Mersey, the old theatre block just isn't fit for purpose any longer. There was another subphrenic abscess on male surgical today. The patient had to return to theatre to have it drained and then the antibiotics will help to deal with it, but we both know that not so long ago that poor man would have died, more likely than not. Draining the abscess was all we had, wasn't it, Matron? That and intensive nursing through a high fever and prayer requests to the nuns at St Chad's that the poor blighted patient would survive. It's the third post-operative subphrenic abscess following abdominal surgery in as many months. Mr Davis is beside himself. He doesn't want this to reflect on his technique as a surgeon, and nor should it. Very soon the Irish will think he's cursed and refuse to be operated on by him.'

'We do not have those dirty little creatures in my hospital!' Matron was as close to raising her voice as she had ever been in all her years at St Angelus.

It did not go unnoticed and Dr Gaskell's eyes widened in surprise.

Her complexion had drained, her eyes had brightened and her body had stiffened. 'It must be down to Mr Davis, it's something he is doing wrong.' Matron picked up the teapot to refill their cups. The tea slopped over as she did so and when she sipped from her cup, she almost choked on her tea.

Dr Gaskell continued regardless as she removed her linen handkerchief from her pocket and dabbed her lips. 'Well, actually, it isn't just Mr Davis. The latest arrived following an appendicectomy. Mr Carter operated on that patient.'

He leant forward, picked up his own cup and saucer and sipped very carefully at his tea while he allowed that fact to sink in. 'We have a serious problem, Matron, and I think I know what might be causing it. There is only one way I can convince you of this. I shall return tonight after my supper at 8.30 p.m. and we shall inspect the theatre together. More crumpet, Matron?'

Matron looked very worried. He had her cornered, but she knew that there was no way she could refuse. He was up to something and she would have to play along. She returned to her tea, to play for time and give her a second to compose her thoughts.

At the sound of the word crumpet, Elsie appeared like a genie from a bottle. She popped her head around the door and into the room. 'Need more crumpets toasting, Matron?'

'Er, no, thank you, Elsie, I can't even manage this plateful.' Dr Gaskell had turned Matron's stomach with his talk of those dirty black creatures that she wouldn't even countenance speaking about in relation to her hospital.

Elsie looked bitterly disappointed as she retreated into her domain.

'All right then,' Matron said. 'I don't suppose I can refuse. Although, I must say, you are becoming something of a dramatist in your old age, Dr Gaskell.'

'Well, we shall see about that later, shan't we,' he replied as he allowed a smile to raise the corner of his lips.

Elsie had a spring in her step as she made her way to the greasy spoon for the domestics' morning coffee break. Even though Matron hadn't allowed her to listen in on the conversation with Dr Gaskell, she had still picked up some crucial snippets. She was met by the warmth from the cookers and the smell from the huge urns of milky coffee as she opened the café door. Seeing that there was no one at the food counter, she made her way over to it.

'How is anyone supposed to eat that bacon?' she asked the young girl who was serving. 'That's a tin of bacon fat you've got there – where's the meat?'

The young girl looked at Elsie with a resigned dismay that told her she had answered that question many times that morning already. 'Shall I put a rasher on your barm cake for you?' she asked.

'A rasher? You can't call that a rasher. I suppose you'll have to, but I'm only paying half price. Bacon meat is not the same price as bacon fat – go and tell the cook that. She has the fattest kids on Vince Street and we all know where the bacon's heading, don't we?'

The girl gave Elsie an imperceptible nod. Her mother and Elsie played bingo together. Embarrassed, she fished about in the tin of bacon fat, speared a couple of slices with a fork, laid them on a barm cake and passed the plate over to Elsie, who made to take her purse out of her apron. The girl looked around, checked that no one was watching and shook her head.

Elsie understood. 'Thanks, queen,' she said as she winked. 'You're a lovely girl. I'll tell your mam what a good'un you are.'

She let her unopened purse slip back into her apron pocket, then turned her head to glance around the vast room of scrubbed tables and wooden chairs. She was trying to locate Biddy, Madge, Betty Hutch and Branna – her usual cohort of domestics. But Hattie Lloyd, Dessie Horton's next-door neighbour, was sitting on a table near the counter and spotted her first. Elsie almost jumped as Hattie shouted out her name.

'Did you just pay for that bacon barm, Elsie? Didn't notice you open your purse.'

'Of course I did, you silly cow. What business is it of yours anyway? Your eyes are nearly as big as your mouth, what a pity they don't see too well.'

Elsie saw the raised hand of Biddy Kennedy and without waiting for a reply threaded her way through the tables to where her friends were sitting.

She slammed her plate down on the table as she pulled back her chair.

'I've got your coffee already,' said Biddy. 'I saw you coming in. What's wrong with your face now, Elsie?'

'Bloody Hattie Lloyd, that's what. She just accused me of not paying for me bacon barm.'

'And did you?' Biddy picked up her cup and blew on the scalding coffee, sending milky froth scudding into the air.

'No, I didn't. I complained about the lack of bacon. If I pay for a bacon barm, I want bacon on it. She's over-made-up and over-opinionated, that one. God, she gets my goat. How dare she accuse me of not paying.'

Biddy nodded in agreement and as she did, she turned in her seat and glared at Hattie Lloyd. 'It is a disgrace and it's right out of order. You don't do your own down,' she said.

She pulled a packet of Woodbines out of her handbag and offered them to Elsie, who took one. There was a code amongst the women. Madge Jones never offered her cigarettes round nor took one from anyone. When she could, she bought the fancy gold-tipped ones from America, brought in on an American ship, and she shared them with no one. Betty Hutch and Branna McGinty rolled their own.

Everyone lit up at the same time and as matches landed in the overflowing central ashtray, Biddy leant her elbows on the table and spoke.

'I know we look after our own here, but I think the morning-shift cook in this place is taking things a bit far. She's cutting the meat off the bacon and taking it home, probably selling it and robbing us of a decent breakfast in the process.'

Madge nodded and Branna spoke up. 'For some of the women with more than a few kids, and God knows, there are enough of them working here, the bacon barm they have in the morning is all they have to eat all day, until they get a couple of 'tatoes in the evening or a bit of scouse. Someone needs to have a word.'

'I was thinking the same thing meself,' said Madge. She held up her plate, on which lay an open barm and two slices of translucent fat. 'It's a joke.'

'A job for Dessie, I would say,' said Biddy as she lifted up the top of Elsie's barm, peered inside and blew her smoke straight into Elsie's face. 'I'll have a word with him. She wants her son to be taken on when he leaves school next summer. There are rules and they can't be broken. She needs telling.'

17

'So, what's it to be, Elsie, new theatres or a maternity unit?'

They moved on to the next pressing subject quickly. The half-hour break always passed before they knew it and they needed five minutes to get back to their posts.

Madge grinned as she drank her coffee. Madge and Elsie were always in competition to demonstrate who had the greater access to information about the goings-on at St Angelus. It was a tightly run race. As switchboard operator, Madge's ability to both answer calls and take useful notes was crucial to the St Angelus mafia. After years of practice, she could sniff a useful conversation a mile off and knew exactly when to slip the plug back in when a light was still on, slowly. Elsie, on the other hand, had perfected the art of loitering with a duster or tea tray.

'Well, we don't know yet,' Elsie replied, 'but Dr Gaskell is up to something tonight. He's taking Matron to the theatre when it's dark to show her why something needs doing. I couldn't make any sense of what he was talking about to be honest. He said the hospital has to deal with worse things than mice.'

Betty Hutch raised her eyes from the rim of her cup. She only spoke when she had something of note to say. She had cleaned the old theatres most nights for the past twenty-two years and she instantly knew what Dr Gaskell was up to. 'It'll be a new theatre then,' she said.

They all turned to look at her as one.

'Do you think so?' asked Biddy. 'It's not like Matron not to get her own way. Dr Gaskell usually backs down.'

'Not on this, he won't,' said Betty. 'He will definitely win.' No one ever argued with Betty Hutch.

'Well, that's been a useful coffee break, I would say,' said Biddy. 'We've sorted out the cook and we know which way the wind is going to blow on a new theatre or maternity unit, which is something even Matron doesn't know yet.'

'That's not so unusual,' said Madge. 'Most of us know what's happening before Matron.'

Biddy opened her handbag to extract her cigarettes again. 'Has anyone noticed how tired Noleen Delaney is looking? Jesus, have you seen the cut of her? The woman is like a ghost.'

'I saw her leaving the hospital when I went to clock on this morning,' said Madge. 'I shouted to her, but she was miles away, didn't hear me.'

'She would have been on her way to St Chad's,' said Branna, who had not stopped eating for long enough to fully join in. 'She spends more time on her knees, that woman. And their Mary, she doesn't lift a finger, you know. She should be ashamed of herself. Gives her mother the runaround, and with all that Noleen has to do for their Paddy. Mary should be helping with the housework after school so her mother can get to bed during the day, but instead she's never out of Maisie Tanner's house, messing about with nail varnish and the like with Lorraine Tanner. The two of them, always eyeing up the lads, they are.'

'Paddy's a right grumpy sod. I'd have done for him meself if he was mine,' said Madge.

Biddy felt her temper rising. 'Did you expect him to return from the war cock-a-hoop because he left his leg behind? He's a moaner, I'll give you that, but not because of his leg. It's because he has no work. No pride to be found for a man with no pay. The fact is, we have let this go on for far too long. We should have acted sooner. Noleen is worn into the ground and it'll be an early grave she's heading for if we don't wake up and do something soon.'

Elsie struck a match and they all bowed their heads towards the centre of the table to take a light then nodded in agreement as they inhaled.

'I wonder if Dessie could help. There must be a job – something, somewhere, for God's sake – that a man with one leg can do?'

'Can he write?' asked Madge.

'How would I know that? I've never asked him to send me a bleedin' letter. I wouldn't have a clue. Don't no one tell Noleen we've been talking about them, though. She's too proud, that one. Mighty proud. She doesn't understand our ways. Poor woman looked like she was dead on her feet. Haven't passed a word to her for weeks. With her being on nights, I just never see her any more, and she never gets to the bingo since Paddy came home injured and that's been years now. She never asks for help, always gives the impression she's coping, but she can't hide the bags under her eyes and she's nothing but skin and bone. I blame meself. I must have been asleep, taken in by all her codswallop, I was.'

A scream pierced the air from the direction of the hot counter and they all looked over to see Hattie Lloyd almost throw her plate back over the counter. 'I'm not eating that disgusting… creature!' she shouted. 'It's still bloody alive. Look, its legs are moving.'

The room fell silent and everyone watched as the cook herself came out to retrieve the plate from the floor. The young girl behind the counter was unperturbed. Finding unwanted creatures in the food was a not uncommon occurrence. They frequented the darkest corners of the hospital too, from the kitchens to the porter's lodge. She made to fill another barm cake.

'I don't want it now,' shouted Hattie. 'It's put me off, it has.'

The ladies looked one to the other. No one spoke. Wry smiles were exchanged and then Biddy broke the silence and said, 'Ah, God bless her cotton socks. It couldn't happen to a nicer woman now, could it? Oh, look, here come the nurses on their break, we must be late.'

Pammy Tanner had breezed into the café with Victoria Baker and Beth Harper.

'I see Nurse Brogan isn't with them,' said Branna.

'No. And here's a bit of news,' said Madge as she placed her cigarettes back into her bag and snapped the clasp shut. 'You know how Matron's been allowing Nurse Brogan to look after poor Dr Davenport in male orthopaedics, after her own shifts? Well, when it's time for him to go home, she's letting her go and nurse him in Bolton, where he comes from. I heard Matron talking to Dr Davenport's brother on the phone – you know, Nurse Baker's young man. A solicitor, he is. Very grand. So Nurse Brogan won't be here, the poor love. She's going to be stuck at Dr Davenport's bedside for a very long time if you ask me.'

'Well, that will be a test of true love, eh?' said Branna. 'I'd kill my husband meself if I had to spend every day sat at the side of his bed looking at his ugly mug.'

'We all feel the same,' said Elsie.

'What are you talking about?' said Biddy to Elsie. 'You thought the world of yours till he fell.'

'Oh, Jesus, I don't mean mine – he was goodness itself. I mean her fat lump of a useless husband. I'd kill meself if I had to sit by his bed. I'm agreeing with her.'

Branna looked affronted. 'Eh, hang on...' She was about to

argue with Elsie, but Betty Hutch began to speak. This was such a rare thing, they all listened.

'Seems to me that maybe all is not what it seems there. Nurse Brogan may be grateful to nurse him through his worst days now, but it might be a different thing altogether in a few months, I'd be saying. She's one that will surprise us all, one day.' And without another word, Betty made for the door.

'What is she on about, Biddy?' asked Elsie.

They watched Betty's back as she retreated.

'I have no idea. She's deep, that one.'

And with that, they all returned to their posts with Betty's words ringing in their ears.

When eight thirty arrived, Matron was ready.

'I'll be back shortly, Blackie, once I've seen these non-existent creatures Dr Gaskell insists are taking over the hospital, indeed.' She gave Blackie a biscuit.

Blackie rolled on to his back, his four legs stuck straight up in the air in anticipation of a tummy tickle.

'Not now, Blackie. When I return from this ridiculous bug-hunting mission, then I will take you for a walk. Later.'

Blackie quickly resumed his sitting position, his ears pricked and forward at the sound of his favourite word, head tilted to one side.

The lights of Dr Gaskell's car filled Matron's dark sitting room as his Austin slowed to a halt outside the main entrance to St Angelus, directly below her apartment. The engine died and as his car door squeaked noisily open, she made her way down the stairs towards the deserted and shrouded WRVS tea stand, where she had arranged to meet him.

'Good evening, Margaret,' said Dr Gaskell as he removed his gloves and walked towards her.

'Honestly, you and your new-found modern ways. You have taken to calling me by my Christian name a little too often, *Dr Gaskell*,' she said emphatically, prompting a smile in return.

She was secretly flattered that he occasionally called her Margaret. It made him almost a friend, not always just a colleague. She found it hard to admit this to anyone other than herself, but she had no friends. Her job had been her only friend down the years. Her mother, her nurses, her hospital – they were her life. And with the recent loss of her elderly mother she now felt even more alone: she no longer had her mother to visit, to care for and to love. But even when her mother was alive, Matron still hadn't shared the sadness of the secret love she held deep in her heart. Sister April had walked out of the hospital gates to join the Queen Alexandra nursing corps during the war and never returned, and Matron had never spoken of it. Her secret was her cross to bear. It guaranteed her a lonely, friendless life because a friend was by definition someone she had to be honest with and if she couldn't share the truth about who she was and what set her apart from every other woman she knew, what was the point?

As they walked together towards the theatre block, they passed Jake Berry, the under-porter, Elsie's son-in-law, wheeling an oxygen bottle towards the children's ward.

'Is it all quiet in theatre, Jake?' asked Dr Gaskell.

'Oh, it is Dr Gaskell, sir. Matron. All quiet on casualty too. Fingers crossed, eh, that I haven't spoken too soon.'

'How's Martha and the baby, Jake?' asked Matron.

'They are both doing fine, thanks. The delivery went well. Biddy Kennedy did the job for us. It was all good.'

Matron frowned. Biddy was an excellent housekeeper at the school of nursing, but no matter how many babies she had delivered, she was no midwife.

'I'm so pleased for you, Jake. But, please, if Martha becomes pregnant again, bring her in here, nice and early. Hospital really is the safest place to have a baby and there's no need to travel up to the maternity hospital. We have equipment here to help, and proper pain relief that neither Biddy nor anyone else would have at home. Not to mention the expertise the nurses can provide. Or at the very least, get one of the new district midwives to attend her.'

Jake didn't know what to say. His Martha had insisted she deliver their baby at home. Like most of the other women in the dockside streets, she wouldn't go near the Mill Road hospital. But Matron was his boss. Or rather Dessie was, and Dessie answered to Matron.

He raised his cap. 'Aye, I'll try, Matron. But perhaps you could have a word with her mother.'

'I did, Jake. If I told Elsie once, I told her a hundred times. The problem is, for people like Elsie and Biddy, the old ways are best. Elsie said to me that if Martha was sick, she would bring her in, but in their eyes, pregnancy is a condition, not an illness. What they don't see is that it can very rapidly become a crisis. We can do things here that save lives.'

A look of alarm crossed Jake's face. 'I'll do my best, I promise, Matron.' He lifted his cap once again and hurried towards the main entrance.

'That was a bit previous, if you don't mind me saying, Matron. She hasn't got over the birth of the first child yet,' said Dr Gaskell when Jake was out of earshot.

'I'm well aware of that, thank you. But we need to get the

24

word out. We've seen a huge rise in the birth rate in the last few years, as you know. Husbands and wives are making up for lost time, it seems. You mark my words, young Martha will be pregnant again very soon. The fifties are shaping up to be all about babies, Dr Gaskell. This post-war NHS, this massive number of post-war babies, they will give it all a name one day. And right now maternity is the fastest-growing service out on the district as well as here in St Angelus, which makes it yet another challenge we have to step up to. The number of appendectomies hasn't altered on account of the men being home again, but the number of women at risk from maternal death is rising fast and that is why I want the maternity unit first and foremost.'

Dr Gaskell wasn't about to argue with Matron. Besides, he was soon to give her the shock of her life. If the consequences weren't so serious, he would have grinned at the thought of it.

They both fell silent as they approached the theatre block. There was an atmosphere of foreboding as they moved into the dark, narrow stairwell. Dr Gaskell had called in earlier in the day to practise what he was about to show Matron. Of course there had been no scurrying actors on his stage in the middle of the day. Pale and watery sunshine had shone through the skylight and was its own disinfectant, but now...

'Are you ready?' he asked her as they stood outside the theatre doors.

'As ready as I will ever be,' she said.

A frown of disapproval crossed her face as a feeling of trepidation and a cold, creeping fear settled into the pit of her belly. She rested against the cold painted brick wall. It felt damp, even through her cape. She was wearing her uniform, as always, and she nervously checked the silver buckle on her belt. Needless to say, it was perfectly positioned in the centre.

'I'm about to switch the corridor light off, Margaret. Don't be alarmed. I will be back in a few seconds.'

Matron watched as he walked back down the corridor towards the light switch. As she heard it flick, the windowless corridor was thrown into deep blackness. Dr Gaskell waited for a moment to get his bearings and with no other noise to distract her attention, Matron could not ignore the unnerving sound in her ears. It began slowly from behind her. It was in the walls, a scurrying, rumbling sound... No, it was under her feet, coming from below.

She almost gasped in relief as she heard Dr Gaskell begin walking back towards her.

'Don't move,' he whispered. She felt his warm breath on her face even though she couldn't see him.

'Oh, for goodness' sake! You made me jump!' she yelped.

She instinctively began to brush her skirt and rearrange herself, an automatic reaction whenever she felt vulnerable. Dr Gaskell waited for her to finish pushing her belt from side to side and smoothing her skirt. Once she'd settled, he gave her no further warning. With one hand he took one quick second to fling open the operating-theatre door and with the other hand he speedily reached across the wall and flicked down the switch for the central overhead light. One, two, three. That was all it took.

Matron's hand flew to her mouth, but not before a scream had escaped her lips as she jumped sharply backwards, into the shadows.

Before them, thousands of startled cockroaches scattered and scuttled and nosily moved as one towards the perimeter walls of the theatre. The black floor receded, revealing the original white-tiled one below it. Within no time at all the shifting, scuttling blackness had disappeared under the skirting boards and back into the walls.

Matron looked as though she was about to faint.

Dr Gaskell got straight to the point. 'And that, Matron, is why post-operative subphrenic abscesses are popping up all over the wards, threatening the lives of the patients we operate on, and why we absolutely must have a new, sealed operating theatre. Not having one is putting lives and the reputation of this hospital at risk on a daily basis. Including the lives of our own doctors. It is something most people who work here know about, but no one is talking about it. You know yourself that Dessie has tried everything short of a hand grenade to sort the problem out. The "little problem", as you sometimes call it, is everywhere. All over the hospital. It is an old workhouse; short of knocking the walls down and rebuilding, there is nothing we can do. The little blighters are winning the battle. Cropping up everywhere. The entire workforce of this hospital will be looking to you and me to work together and sort this out, and that, Matron, that is what we must do.'

Dr Gaskell's wily manoeuvrings did the trick. The plans for a suite of new operating theatres at St Angelus were approved by the LDHB in record time. Two months later the new theatres were nearly ready to accept their first patients.

Chapter 2

Three months later

'Did your man find his other leg, Noleen?' Biddy Kennedy shouted across to the opposite side of Arthur Street, without any apparent consideration for those still asleep at that early hour of the morning.

Noleen Delaney failed to reply. She was lost in her own deep and tired thoughts as she hurried along in the half light towards St Chad's. Her head was set against the wet early-morning breeze which flew up from the Mersey and whistled down Arthur Street, slipping into the bedrooms and kitchens of the blackened red-brick houses along the way. Noleen's thin, cold hands were thrust deep into her pockets, her mind busy with the tasks of the day ahead. The soles of her shoes were so worn that she felt every chip of stone and discarded cigarette butt she trod on; they dug into her painful, corn-covered feet as she scurried along.

The night was reluctant to release its grip on the dockside streets. Morning fought to throw the first shaft of light and pierce the gloom, and the cobbled roads glistened beneath the street lamps, freshly washed from the heavy rain that had

fallen during the night. The clear plastic cover that Noleen
had tied over her headscarf to protect herself from the rain as
she left her night shift at St Angelus had now slipped down
and hung like a hammock across the shoulders of her thin
coat. It flapped in protest as it strained at the damp string
ties, chafing her neck. She had resettled the cover on her hair
twice already and there was no point bothering again. She
abandoned any attempt to return home dry. What hair the
wind didn't claim, the mist would flatten against her scalp
before she had laid all her sinful thoughts and deeds before
God, on her knees in St Chad's.

Biddy frowned and placed her wicker basket down on
the pavement. 'Noleen, wait up, would you.' She hurriedly
slipped her front-door key, tied to the end of a long piece
of string, back through the letter box and then slammed the
door shut. 'Noleen, wait!' she called out, but again there was
no response.

The air was filled with the sound of the first tugs of the
morning blowing their horns as they made their way out to
the container ships that had been bobbing at the bar overnight. The tugs would lead them, steady as she goes, through
the thick grey river mist that rested in a lazy haze on the
surface of the dirty water and safely into dock. By the time
the first tug had completed its journey, the klaxon would have
sounded, calling the men from Arthur, George, Stanley and
Vince streets to the docks. Their boots would thud across
the cobbles and down the worn sandstone dockers' steps
to the stand, and there the men would wait, hoping to be
chosen to help unload one of the vast, cold, filthy holds of
jute, wood or flour for an honest day's pay.

Noleen's thoughts had settled and, aware of someone

requiring her attention, she looked up, mildly confused, as Biddy asked yet again, 'Did your man find his other leg, Noleen?'

Biddy had startled Noleen. She was running late. Being late for the priest was something she feared only slightly more than being late for Matron and her night-time cleaning shift at St Angelus. She was usually safely within the confines of St Chad's for early-morning Mass before the day workers had begun leaving their homes for the bus stop and the hospital, as Biddy was doing right now. Noleen, suddenly aware of her chafed neck, untied the string under her chin and shook the plastic headscarf, soaking her bare legs as she did so. She took the string ends, one in each hand, snapped the plastic cover shut as the folds concertinaed together, and stuffed the useless cover into the pocket of her coat.

'Wait while I check the key,' said Biddy. Slipping her hand through the slim brass letter box, she jiggled the key around, satisfying herself that it was hanging in the right place. She always left her house via the front door, but she never returned that way, preferring to come home via the entry and in through the back door, which was never locked. The back-door key had been missing since the night the bomb hit George Street, but Biddy wasn't the slightest bit concerned about that. There wasn't a single family for as far as she could walk, or further still, that she didn't know. The key was left dangling on a piece of string in case anyone should have sudden need to get into Biddy's house through the front door.

'Oh, will you and him never give up about him finding his bloody leg,' said Noleen, a hint of exasperation in her voice. She removed one of her hands from her pocket, shook her head and vainly attempted to push her washed-out pin curls back to life. 'I wish he would find it. Holy Mother of God, how different my life would be then, eh?'

From different sides of the street, they both looked up towards the sound of a sash window being raised. It was Elsie at number seventeen.

'Trust you two. It would take you only a minute to have the whole street awake.' Elsie spoke down to them at a volume far louder than either Biddy or Noleen had used. Her still dark hair was perfectly coiffed and curled atop her thin face and was crowned with a halo from the single light bulb behind her. 'Biddy, I'm coming down now. Keep one foot on the kerb if the bus makes to go without me.' She slammed down the sash and the curtain fell back into place before Biddy had time to scold her for making the loudest noise of any of them.

Biddy checked that her headscarf was fastened under her chin as tight as she could bear and that her coat was buttoned up, then she picked up her basket and with one hand across her rotund belly, her coat buttons straining, she bustled her plumpness across the cobbles and on to the opposite pavement to speak to Noleen directly.

Elsie had a point about the early hour, not that Biddy would ever admit it. It might not yet have been 6.30 a.m., but that made no difference to the two friends. The time of day was irrelevant when the opportunity for a natter arose.

'Will you two ever stop giving out to each other?' Noleen chided with a wry smile as she nodded towards Elsie's bedroom window.

'Not if I can help it,' said Biddy. 'Where would be the pleasure in that now? You've got to have a bit of fun in life, haven't you. Blimey, Noleen, I feel like I haven't seen you for months. I've almost forgotten what you look like. Sure, you're like a bat. You only come out in the dark. And how is himself and his leg?' She didn't draw breath.

Noleen's husband, Paddy, had returned from the war minus one leg. It had been almost entirely blown away and, unbeknown to either Paddy or Noleen, the surgeon had struggled to retain a useable stump. The first ambitious attempt had been thwarted by the onset of bubbling, putrid, gas gangrene and the second attempt had been touch and go. Live or die. Paddy's ability to walk had been secondary to saving his life. His blood loss had been profound and the damage to his gangrene-infected tissue, nerves and vessels was severe.

Biddy had been one of the first women to arrive at the house when Paddy was medically discharged home. She turned up with a plate of food and a welcome, and since that day, Biddy and Paddy had maintained their own running joke.

'Where's your leg gone, Paddy?'

'What leg, Biddy?'

'Your missing leg, Paddy. That one there. Look, it's gone.'

'Jeez, I must have lost it. Have you seen it, Biddy? Will you keep an eye out?'

'No, Paddy, I'll keep me eye just where it is, 'cause I'm not careless like you, ye flaming eejit.'

The joke altered with each meeting and telling but always ended with both Biddy and Paddy laughing. Hearing her Paddy laugh was a very rare pleasure for Noleen these days, and she was grateful to Biddy for cheering him up, however briefly.

'I work nights, Biddy, 'cause I can get more hours in that way. Helps with home and the kids and it's a bit extra in the money.'

Most of the night cleaners at St Angelus were mothers who slept during the day. Like all the other dockside women, during the war Noleen hadn't known if her husband would return from his regiment. She had been desperate for work and willing to take anything to avoid having to travel to the munitions factory. Few of the night cleaners managed to sleep more than three hours a day for five days of the week and many of them quickly fell away through illness brought about by lack of sleep and relentless hard work. Many became patients at the hospital they had once cleaned by night. But Noleen was different. Somehow she had carried on. And instead of cramming all her hours into four nights instead of five days, she worked six nights on overtime and only took the one night off.

'Are you away to Mass?' Biddy knew the daily pattern of Noleen's life as well as she knew her own. There were no secrets on the dockside streets off Lovely Lane and the question was purely academic. Noleen would never miss Mass, nor even be away from St Chad's for longer than twelve hours at a time because, despite how difficult her lot was, she still gave thanks to God each and every single day for her good fortune. And that included the love of a good man who had been returned home, albeit not in one piece.

'Sure, I only have to look around me to see a house where no husband or father has returned at all. Why would I be complaining now?' was her set reply every time a neighbour said to her, 'You are a good woman, Noleen, you have a lot to be putting up with.'

Noleen had no time for misplaced sympathy. ''Tis not me who deserves your pity,' she told Father Brennan every time he tried to comfort her. 'Oh, no, not at all. From our own street we can see the bombsites filled with the rubble covering the places where our friends died with their children in their arms. What can be worse than that? I won't be wanting no sympathy from no one, thank you very much.'

Her own children climbed and played on those same graves of ashes and dust, day after day. The walls and stairs of houses identical to their own had been razed to the ground and whole families Noleen and Biddy had once known wiped from the face of the earth in a scorching, siren-filled second. It was this which made her feel gratitude in her darkest hours. The streets closest to Liverpool's docks had suffered during the Blitz and they were the survivors, the keepers of memories. She would not allow bitter tears to fall down her cheeks. Noleen was one of the lucky ones and she would never forget it, never stop saying thank you. She would forever count her blessings, one of which was a husband with nothing more than a missing leg.

'Bless and praise your loving grace, merciful Holy Father, there for us in our hour of need and always,' was Noleen's final prayer twice a day at Mass and then once again as she closed her eyes before sleep claimed her. Noleen never forgot.

In truth there was another reason why Noleen preferred to work nights. She would never confess it to anyone, but she hated going to bed. As she clambered off her stiff knees, slipped under the old army blankets and tried to sleep, a desperate feeling of dread would trickle down her spine like iced water against her burning skin. Sometimes it was the cold sweat of fear for what might have been. It covered her entire body, making her nightdress stick, her heart thump and her breathing quicken. The horror they had all witnessed on their very own streets and down on the docks came back to her.

The noise of the sirens and the shouts filled her head and the blood rushed and pounded in her ears. When the morning klaxon rang for the dockers, it sounded far too much like an air-raid siren; it made her skin prickle.

Recently, though, the fear had taken another shape. It had form. It was ghost-like and present with her in the room. Dark, black and silent. It crept in and slowly pressed down upon her when her mind was between wakefulness and sleep. She sensed it slither in and move towards her, and within seconds the beads of fear and perspiration would break out on her top lip and fan across her body. Her heart raced and banged against the sides of her bony chest, like a bird trapped in a cage. She felt as though she would suffocate with the pressure, lose the ability to inhale her own breath, as it slowly built and tightened.

She knew she was being warned about something and whatever it was, it was too horrific, too awful, to acknowledge. She had no way of knowing, was this her personal anxiety robbing her of a normal life or ghosts warning her of the future?

To try and ward off the worst of these bedtime terrors, she had taken to sleeping during the day on the settle in front of the fire, with Paddy in the chair opposite, watching over her. It was not the thing to talk about the war, about the losses or the hardship. All that had passed was meant to have been forgotten, and for Paddy, beset by his own demons, remembering was the last thing he wanted to do. When Noleen's terrors came, he would be alerted by her anxiety, which made her thrash around on the settle. He would slip his arm around her and whisper into the back of her hair, 'There, there, don't be worrying now. We are all here, safe and sound. Nothing is going to happen to any one of us. No more wars or bombs, and I'm not going anywhere. No use to anyone. No more disasters. We are all safe and sound. Shhh. Doesn't the man on the radio say so often enough? Hasn't Churchill said so? Shhh.'

As he stroked her arm and soothed away her fears, Noleen would whisper her prayer. It was all she had in her armoury. And then slowly, like a receding tide, her nameless, shapeless terror would ebb and fade from the room, leaving her like a limp, wet rag until a fitful sleep finally came.

Paddy had taken it upon himself to reassure her about all that was before them. But how could she tell him that she was being warned and she didn't know by whom or how. That her fear was not so much a product of the past but a foreboding about the future? If she told him, he would think she was losing her mind.

Paddy was not going away, ever. There would be no wars, there was no danger, how could there be? Didn't Paddy give her chapter and verse every day regarding everything the great and good were saying on the news? Didn't he read the newspapers from cover to cover and repeat to her the relevant bits every morning when she arrived home, smelling of Lysol and mops? The bits that backed up his own opinions and prophecies for a future of peace and harmony.

Sometimes, as she removed her coat while he repeated to her every word from the morning news bulletin, she wanted to scream at him, 'Shut up. Shut up. It doesn't help. It's not another war I'm worried about.' Instead, she would restrict herself to the occasional comment, just to reassure him that he wasn't talking to himself. 'Is that what they are saying now? Well, didn't Chamberlain come back flashing a letter saying peace in our time? We believed him, didn't we, and he was wrong. Why does this man know any more?' It was always men. But unlike some of the other women living in the shadow of the war on some of the poorest streets in Liverpool, Noleen never complained. She bore her lot with stoicism and efficiency established within a framework of strict routine and order. A routine that compelled her to attend Mass at St Chad's twice a day as Biddy, standing across Arthur Street from her on this dark morning, well knew.

'Have you ever known me to miss Mass, Biddy?' Noleen retorted. 'I was on my knees when I was in labour with our Finn. He almost popped out in the confessional. I am away to the early Mass, as always. Will I be saying a prayer for yourself, Biddy? Being the sinner that you are and as you hardly ever seem to get there yourself?' Noleen smiled a rare mischievous smile.

'That you could,' said Biddy. 'You could ask him to save me from having to risk my life every morning standing with one foot on the bus and one foot off, hanging from the pole like a fecking eejit, while lazyitis Elsie swigs the last of her tea stood at the sink and I keep the bus waiting for her. She thinks I don't know! Look at her, here she comes. Watch! Would you look at that. She doesn't even have her bag in her hand. I'm telling you, before she gets to my door, she will remember and run back. Watch her, see.'

Noleen, amused, waited and watched. Sure enough, Elsie stopped dead in her tracks, put her hand over her mouth, turned on her heel and ran back towards the entry shouting, 'Wait for me! Hold the bus, Biddy,' as she went.

Noleen began to laugh. 'You are a right pair, you two are. I'd say she's even more distracted now that she's a grandmother. She can't stop talking about that baby. And you the godmother too. No excuse not to be at the baptism on Sunday, Biddy.'

'I wish to God there was, Noleen. Father Brennan has never forgiven me since the day I told him I wished my husband had never come back from the war. It should have been him had the one leg, not your Paddy. That way, the bastard could never have run off with the Belleek tea set and me purse.'

Despite herself, Noleen chuckled. Biddy's irreverence, to be frowned on in any other woman who lived on the dockside streets, was tolerated with humour.

'Father forgives everyone, Biddy. He has to. You know that. Don't take against him. You may need him to pray for you in the hour of your salvation.'

'Oh for the love of God, I was only kidding, Noleen. You have gone mighty serious these past few months. Why don't you come down the bingo with us on your night off this week? You're in need of a good night out, I would say. Paddy won't mind. You might even win enough to treat the kids. Go on. Try. Last month I won enough to take a trip back home to Ireland.'

'I can't, Biddy. It's bad enough leaving Paddy on the nights I have to go to work. He goes mad with his own company, he does. The pain is bad for him sometimes, especially if he tries to put too much weight on his stump. The prosthesis near kills him. Hard as iron, it is.'

Biddy had often noticed Paddy's false leg, abandoned, leaning up against the kitchen wall in Noleen's house. It looked anything but comfortable, a heavy contraption of leather-clad wood and cold, sharp metal.

'If I come and speak to Paddy meself, would that be of

any help, Noleen? We have a great way between us, me and Paddy.'

Biddy was the only woman who had never said to Noleen, 'At least he came back,' and for that Noleen was grateful. Others had made that sort of comment on an almost daily basis, for no reason other than as a release for their own anger and pain of loss. Without any need for words, Biddy had always given Noleen the unmistakable impression she understood exactly what Noleen had to cope with.

She could see the strain of managing a job, a family and a husband in constant pain crouching in Noleen's eyes. In the past ten years Noleen had aged twenty. Her once almost jet-black hair was shot through with silvery white. Her skin was pale and lacklustre with a radiance similar to that of dirty bread dough and only the clear sparkling blue of her Irish eyes betrayed the fact that she was still not yet forty, a relatively young woman.

Noleen shook her head. 'It's not just leaving Paddy that's the problem, although that is hard enough. 'Tis the money. I just about make ends meet, you know that, Biddy. I don't have to tell you. Heavens above, you've helped us out often enough before Dessie took our Bryan on as a porter's lad. Half a crown on a few hours out at the bingo is just out of the question. I wouldn't sleep with the guilt.'

Biddy frowned. 'Aye, and you get little enough sleep as it is and that's a fact. And I bet Matron was on at you even worse than usual last night, wasn't she? With the big opening of the new theatres coming up so soon now. Seems no time at all since those theatres were just a set of plans. Did Matron and Sister Pokey have you mopping them again? There'll be nothing left of that nice new floor by the time everyone's finished cleaning it. Obsessed, they are. Matron inspects it every day. I asked Elsie, is she losing her mind or what?'

'No, not me. I was on the main corridor, but we all went up to take a look. Very posh it is. Sister Pokey was already there when I left this morning. She's ever so excited. Betty Hutch says that if Dr Davenport hadn't nearly died in the old theatre, after his accident, the new theatres would never have been built. She says his death and his miraculous coming back again was a wonder of God's making.'

'Does she now?' Biddy sniffed and looked towards the bus stop. 'Well, there might be some truth in that. 'Tis a fact that he died on the table a few times, they say. A young doctor like that.'

Noleen knew that there was nothing went on in St Angelus that Biddy didn't hear about, but Biddy was an old hand at gathering power as well as information. She neither confirmed nor denied.

'Anyway, you get yourself to Mass and then to bed, woman. You look wiped out.' They both looked towards St Chad's as the bells altered their tone to a single peal, tugging at Noleen's conscience and pulling her to Mass.

'Have you thought of asking Dessie if there might be any easier work coming up at the hospital? Something with a bit more money?' asked Biddy. She failed to mention that she had already voiced her concerns to Dessie and that he had promised to pop in. Biddy knew all too well how pride was Noleen's only fault, so when Dessie did call to visit, Noleen would have no idea it was Biddy who sent him.

'I can't. Dessie was good enough to take Bryan on, bless him. I don't want him thinking I'm ungrateful. He calls in to visit Paddy regularly as it is when I'm at work. Our Bryan is loving working up at St Angelus. Dessie owes my family nothing. I cannot be asking him for no more favours, Biddy, and don't you be asking on my behalf either. Bryan may be man of the house when it comes to earning, but Paddy and me, we still have our pride, you know. Are you listening to me, Biddy?'

Biddy appeared distracted. She was looking back down the street for Elsie. 'Wouldn't dream of asking him if you didn't want me to, Noleen,' she said. She dismissed the conversation with a sniff and a wrinkled nose as she craned her neck to catch sight of Elsie. 'Here she is. Here's the granny. Wonder what her excuse will be this morning?'

'Does she need one with her new grandson? Poor Martha and Jake must never get a look in.'

'It's me who never gets the look in,' said Biddy, affronted. 'I've knitted for him, I even delivered him, and all I get is a quick hold when he's crying and then it's back to Granny Elsie once the wind's up and the smile is back on his face.'

'Well, if it's a child you're wanting to be looking after, there's plenty in our house. You can borrow our Mary for a start,' said Noleen. She lifted her hand to wave goodbye and headed towards St Chad's as the nuns began to leave the convent and file in through the church gate.

Elsie marched on past Biddy with her handbag swinging to and fro, her eyes never leaving the bus stop. 'You gab so much, Biddy, we could have missed that bus.' She raised her bag to wave down the bus. 'Thank goodness I'm here.'

'You won't be for much longer if you don't shut up,' said Biddy as she shuffled behind her and they took their seats.

'What did Noleen have to say? Any news?' asked Elsie as she took her cigarettes out of her bag and offered one to Biddy. The air was already a thick blue haze of cigarette smoke and the bus was filled with the sound of striking matches and chesty coughs and the smell of damp wool.

'Nothing other than she was on her way to Mass.'

'Never off her knees, that one. They'll be worn out and good for nothing by the time she reaches forty, and what has she got to show for it, eh? She prays the most and has the least. Mind, I suppose she has more than most to deal with. Not many would put up with that nark, Paddy, the way she does.' Elsie snapped the lid of her lighter shut and let it slip back into her handbag as she pulled hard on her cigarette. 'Imagine, I nearly forgot me bag, me cigs, me purse and everything. I'm going doolally since our baby arrived.'

'Going? You went a long time before that. Listen, you can say what you like about Paddy, but I'm worried about Noleen Delaney, Elsie. That woman has a hard life. They barely have two ha'pennies to rub together in that house and yet she still manages to keep going with a smile. It's all down to Noleen and the lad Bryan and he's only young. There's four more below him needing to be fed.'

Elsie regarded Biddy through narrowed squinting eyes as her cigarette smoke stung and they began to water. 'She called in to our Martha's last night after Mass to see the baby and she crossed his palm with a sixpence. Our Martha tried to stop her, but she wouldn't have none of it. She's a good woman. She deserves better luck than she has and that's a fact.'

Biddy wiped the steam from the side window to clear a view as the bus moved away. Both women watched as Noleen made her way under the arch of St Chad's, her refuge. The only half hour of the day when she allowed hope to make an appearance in her life.

'There but for the grace of God go all of us,' whispered Biddy. Turning back to Elsie, she lifted her cigarette in the air. 'Oi, you've only lit your own, you daft bat.'

'Oh, sorry, Biddy.' Elsie undid the clasp on her handbag and delved inside to retrieve her lighter.

'There is one mystery in this world I will never understand,' said Biddy, 'and that is, how the hell does Matron put up with you?'

'Oh, don't say that, Biddy. That's awful.' Elsie looked downcast.

Biddy felt mean. Elsie lived in her own world of mild confusion and chaos, but for all that, she was a hard worker and Biddy knew well the reason why Matron put up with her. It was because Elsie looked after her with devotion and unswerving loyalty. Without question, Elsie made Matron's life a whole lot easier.

'Don't say what? What do you mean? You're too thick-skinned to take offence at anything. What's up with you?'

'Oh, I don't know, Biddy. With the new operating theatres opening and all the talk of a new hospital and everything, I feel like things are about to change, don't you? I don't like change. I don't. Nothing changed in the war. The bombs kept dropping and we kept working, you know, doing the same thing every day. A pair of old boots like you and me, there won't be a place for us, will there, if it all changes. And it's all such hard work, keeping up. I'm not sure Matron is going to stick around much longer now that her mother is dead. Dr Gaskell, he must be seventy if he's a day. I reckon he's only hanging on for Matron so that they leave together.'

Biddy fished around in her coat pocket and took out the exact change for the conductor, who had almost reached their seat. 'Don't be such an eejit, woman. They will only leave St Angelus in a box, the pair of them. They are St Angelus, those two. They won't be going anywhere and as long as they are there, we are too.'

The conductor had reached them and, half swaying, he leant on the back of the seat in front of them and put out his hand for the money. Neither woman said a word and both dropped two copper coins into his hand. He slipped the coins into his leather saddlebag, wound the handle on the side of his ticket machine and handed them two grey tickets before moving on to the passengers behind. He pointedly said not a word to either of them and hadn't since the night he'd offered to buy Biddy a drink in the Irish Centre and then walk her home. That was the day after her Mick had finally done a runner.

'Well, I know one thing,' said Elsie. 'A smile might crack on your man's face the day we do retire.' She nodded in the direction of the conductor. 'He's never forgiven you for turning him down.'

'He must have been bloody joking.' Biddy snorted in derision. 'I'd just got rid of one man, why would I want another?'

Elsie was going to reply that the man she got rid of had done anything he could to avoid a day's work and had run off with her Belleek tea set and her full purse, whereas the man on the bus had taken their fare every single day, rain or shine. He would have been quite a different kind of man. But Elsie didn't dare. You picked your moments to point out the error in Biddy's ways, and this was not one of them.

Both women turned their heads once again towards the window and looked out, each thinking about the past. The brakes on the bus squealed as they rounded the corner and the masts of the ships in the docks reached out from the blackness of the Mersey like fingers on the hand of a drowning man. The bus trundled away from the dockside and on up towards the steep incline that led to the hospital and Lovely Lane. The black glass eyes of windows shut tight in sleeping houses reflected the light from inside the bus and mirrored back the two women with their powdery pink cheeks and pale white faces, headscarves tied under their chins, each deep in her own thoughts. They looked on as shop workers pulled open their shutters and a very portly lady struggled up the steps to a processing plant and did battle with the huge mortice locks on the door. The dockside traders were attaching their flat-back trailers to the horses as the dockers' railway thundered overhead, transporting the early risers up to Clarence Dock.

Biddy dropped her cigarette onto the floor between her and Elsie and extinguished it with her shoe, feeling the heat of the stub penetrate through to the ball of her foot. She fought for something positive and reassuring to say to Elsie, to them both, but nothing came. There was truth in what Elsie said. Change could be just around the corner and the prospect of life on a post-war pension in a damp house was bleak. Biddy had spent years avoiding thoughts of the future. She preferred not to think about what must surely lie ahead and, if what Elsie said was true, might be coming sooner than she would like.

*

Whilst Noleen said her Hail Marys in St Chad's, back in Vince Street Paddy Delaney sat on his backside on the top stair, contemplating the journey down to the kitchen.

'Da, you all right?' asked Bryan, the first of the Delaneys to rise. He stood on the step behind him.

Bryan shared a bedroom with his brothers, Finn, Jack and Cahill, and their one sister, Mary, who was the only person in the house to have a bed of her own, behind a curtain suspended on wire across the end of the room. It was an arrangement that gave the budding teenager Mary the privacy she desperately craved but did nothing to reduce the number of arguments she had with her siblings, much to Noleen's dismay.

'Aye, I am, lad. Would you get the bottle from by the side of the bed for me? I don't want to spill a drop and have your mother fretting.'

'I will, Da. Go on, you go down first.'

Bryan stood at the top and waited as his father bounced down the stairs on his backside one step at a time. He asked the same question he always did. 'Shall I get the crutch, Da?'

The answer always came back the same. 'That useless thing? No.'

Bryan asked the same question as he could think of nothing else to say or do when he saw his father's body stiffen with the pain of the effort. He would never accept Bryan's help to get downstairs.

Bryan walked into his parents' bedroom, across the immaculate wooden floorboards that his mother scrubbed on her hands and knees once a week, without fail and regardless of how tired she was. He picked up the bottle his father used in the night.

In the room stood a tall chest of drawers that he knew had belonged to his grandmother and a ladder-back chair against the window. The net curtains were pristine, and the window they covered gleamed. The brocade curtains were darned where the moths had made their mark, but every summer they blew on the line.

Bryan appreciated every little thing his ma did for their family. He only wished Mary, his sister, would too. As he turned to leave the room, he glanced back at his father's wooden leg leaning hopelessly against the chair. It was made of oak and from the polished leather-bound top hung a blood-stained bandage. His father's wound opened every time he strapped the prosthesis on to the stump of his leg to heave himself out of the house to look for work. He still needed the crutch when the leg was strapped on as the set-up was unwieldy and his gait unsteady. They had tried everything, including cutting up blankets and binding them in crepe bandages to use as wadding, but nothing helped. The doctors had saved Paddy's life in the field hospital, but they hadn't put a stop to his suffering.

As Paddy heaved himself into his chair by the side of the fire, Bryan placed his hand under his father's arm and helped him sit. Without a word, he pushed the cushion down behind his back. The pain in Paddy's leg was lessened if he sat forward.

The two of them moved smoothly through the father-and-son motions of the morning. No words were spoken. Neither so much as coughed. Silence caused no offence. Paddy pulled the crocheted patchwork blanket over his knee to hide the offending stump and Bryan handed him the rinsed-out bottle to place down by his left side, nearest to the fire and away from view. The fire poker and coal bucket sat on the grate within his reach.

'Is is raining?' asked Paddy. He rarely made it outside, other than to sit on a chair in the street at the side of the front door. As a result he had become mildly preoccupied with the state of the weather.

'No. Looks like it did in the night, though. The yard is still wet. You can sit out later if you want, Da. Be a bit chilly, though, I reckon.'

Once his da was settled, Bryan brushed the ash from the grate into a bucket, placed the kettle he had filled the night before on to the range and visited the outhouse himself. As his da had used the bottle since coming downstairs, he took that with him as he went. On his way back indoors, he stopped in the cold scullery for as little time as possible for his wash and to clean out the bottle in the stone sink. He filled up the copper boiler and lit the gas below so that it would be hot and ready for his mam when she returned from Mass.

Paddy leant forward and began to rattle the embers with the long poker. This was one job he could manage from the chair. A pewter chest sat alongside him, on which rested the coal bucket. The kindling chest was always filled to brimming the previous night by Bryan, before he went to bed, and Paddy could easily manage both. He threw the kindling on the fire, waited for it to catch and then, using the tongues in the bucket, threw the coal on lump by lump.

A few minutes later, when Noleen came in through the back door, the kettle was whistling and the fire leaping and that was just how Paddy wanted it to be.

'Would you look at that?' she exclaimed as she shook off her coat and hung it on the nail on the back of the door. 'Aren't I the lucky one. Is Bryan in the scullery?'

'He is, scrubbing up. You know what Dessie is like with his

drill. He makes me laugh with his inspection of the porter's lads every morning. He thinks he's still in the army, he does.'

'Whether he does or not, we have a lot to be grateful to Dessie for. Besides, I think it keeps standards up. I mean, would our Bryan ever polish his boots like that if it wasn't for Dessie and his inspection? How was last night? How have you been?'

Noleen asked her husband the same questions every morning, knowing full well he would never tell her the truth.

Paddy leaned over to the big Roberts radio and the kitchen filled with the sound of static and voices lost on the airwaves as he tried to tune it. 'I've been grand. The bed was cold and I missed you, but nothing new there.' He grimaced. 'One of the kids must have touched this last night. How many times have I told them.'

'Was Lorraine Tanner around here last night?'

'Aye, she was. Her and our Mary were doing each other's hair. Lorraine asked me twice where Bryan was, she's definitely sweet on him all right.'

Noleen sighed. 'Well, she's wasting her time. Our Bryan has eyes for no one, just doesn't seem to be interested in the slightest. Says he has no time for girls and would rather play pool with the lads.'

'Girls, they are a different breed today, don't have a clue about anything,' said Paddy. 'I asked Lorraine was she going to follow Pammy up to St Angelus and train to be a nurse and do you know what, she said she would rather be a doctor like Pammy's boyfriend, Anthony. Imagine that!'

Noleen smiled. 'Well, I bet Pammy's doctor boyfriend didn't come from dockside streets like Lorraine. It was a big enough deal when Pammy was accepted to be a nurse. That's typical of Lorraine Tanner though. Never short of confidence, that one. Gets it from her mother.'

Noleen removed the whistling kettle from the range and poured the boiling water on to the same leaves she had used yesterday. Placing the lid on the teapot, she walked over to her husband and kissed the top of his head.

'And I missed you last night, even though you are a grumpy old bugger,' she whispered into his hair.

As she raised her head, her hand lingering for just a moment to stroke the back of her husband's neck, the back door burst open and Bryan marched back in. He was scrubbed and clean, smelling of coal-tar soap and with his red hair damp and smoothed back and flat against his head. He had a clean urine bottle in his hand.

'Here you go, Da,' he said as he placed it down by the side of Paddy's chair.

'And here's your cosy,' said Noleen as she took the knitted cover off the side of the range where it had dried overnight. Paddy had insisted on having one to save their Mary the embarrassment of seeing his bottle half full should she ever come to the side of the chair.

Five minutes later, Noleen had made the pobs, softening the bread with watered-down milk. She sprinkled them with sugar and placed them in the oven. Sugar was still on ration, but the black market around the docks ensured that no one went short of tea or sugar. A chest of tea lived in Biddy's scullery so that everyone in Arthur, Stanley, Vince and George streets could fill up their caddies once a week. The bizzies would never suspect a woman like Biddy of fencing from the docks. It was the homes of the militant men they raided, not respectable Biddy. Once a month, at Biddy's behest, a fresh tea chest arrived in her scullery and the old one was taken away.

It was because of the docks, the black market and St Angelus that the families on Lovely Lane and around the Dock Road managed to survive on their meagre wages. The hospital staff helped one another when the opportunity arose. Nothing was wasted. The previous evening, Noleen had been in the process of slapping dough down on the table when Bryan walked through the door. With a grin on his face, he'd extracted a long roll of greaseproof paper from the pocket of his donkey jacket.

'What the hell is that?' asked Noleen, drying the flour from her hands with her apron and covering the space from the table to Bryan.

'It's sausage meat, Ma. Cook from the ward 3 kitchen gave it to me tonight. She said you could make some sausage rolls out of it.'

'Are you kidding me?' Noleen's face had lit up. 'I can that,' she said. 'God bless Cook. Pass it here quick. Paddy, throw some more coke on the range to get the heat up.'

'I hope Cook hasn't given you that out of pity,' said Paddy, his voice loaded with suspicion.

'Well, if she has, Da, she's feeling sorry for a lot of people today because she gave something to nearly everyone. She said it will go off by Sunday if it isn't cooked and eaten.'

Bryan turned his back to his da while he hung up his coat, but Noleen caught his eye. She knew her son better than anyone. He might be able to kid his father, but not her. Bryan was the only person the cook gave sausage meat to, and as she rolled it, she silently thanked her for it. If Paddy had known, he would have said, 'Go and tell Cook to take her pity elsewhere, we don't need it here,' but the fact was, they did need it. They had next to nothing and Cook knew it. Noleen had to keep their heads above water. The house had to be spotless and a meal prepared each evening. The floors had to be mopped, the nets whitened, the step donkey-stoned, the range blackened and the windows cleaned more often than those in any other house. Noleen wore her fingers to the bone and when Paddy or Bryan remonstrated with her, it was always the same reply. 'We might not have anything, but no one will know it. I won't have my home or my family looking like we are down and out. My house will shine brighter than any other and that's the way it will be, Paddy. We will wear our pride in the shine on the windows, not hidden in churlish words.'

Paddy never argued with Noleen. They had their different ways of coping with what had become their lot. She scrubbed, he complained.

Noleen settled herself in the chair opposite Paddy with her tea, ready to savour the five minutes' rest before waking the other kids for school. 'The best five minutes of the day, this is,' she always said to Paddy. 'Me and you and our Bryan. Before the others are awake and crashing around and before Mary storms in giving out about something that someone else has that is better than anything we can buy.'

Bryan sat at the scrubbed wooden-topped table and fastened the laces on his boots. Then he began brushing the toe caps. 'Why is it the best, Ma?' he asked. For Bryan, with his siblings still sleeping and he the only one to be a part of his parents' morning conversation, it was special for him too.

'Your mam has just left confession, Bryan. She feels fine for the next half an hour, until she finds something to feel guilty about, and then she won't feel quite so good until she's been to confession again. Either that, or me and you, we're her favourites, 'cause our Mary drives her mad.'

Bryan and his father exchanged a smile as they both heard the bedsprings above them creak. 'Speak of the devil,' said Paddy.

'You know she's complaining that the bed we boys have is too big and doesn't leave her enough room?' Bryan said.

'Well, it wouldn't be our Mary if she wasn't complaining, would it?' Paddy blew on his mug of scalding tea.

They both looked over to Noleen for a response, but there was none.

Bryan stood up and, untwining his mam's fingers one by one, removed the teacup from her clasped hands and placed it on the range next to her. Her head had lolled to the side and her face flared orange in the reflected heat from the fire.

Paddy's heart almost melted with the love he felt for his wife. The glow from the fire had erased from her face the years of hard work that had robbed her of her youthful looks and at that moment she appeared just as she had when they'd first met. He'd carried that image with him during the years he was away from home, fighting in the war. His Noleen, with Irish sunlight glinting from her hair and a smile on her face.

The love of and for his wife had kept him going through the darkest, most agonizing hours since he'd returned from the war. Stuck in his chair with his useless stump, with Noleen out working and the kids sleeping, he often thought about throwing himself into the Mersey. A peaceful, watery grave seemed at times preferable to the daily pain and humiliation he was forced to endure. He had planned it in his mind so many times. How he would stagger down to the floating landing at the Pier Head and in the dead of night, once the last ferry had sailed, slip under the chain fence and into the cold, dark, welcoming water. Just like so many others had before him. But it was the responsibility he had towards his children, the good will of his neighbours and more than anything his love for Noleen that stopped him.

'Go and get the others up, lad,' he whispered as he gazed across at his wife. 'Let your mam sleep. Tell Mary if she makes one squeak she'll have the end of my slipper across her backside.'

Bryan made for the door that led to the back stairs. 'What, the slipper you never use, Da? The one that belonged to the other leg?'

Paddy winked. 'Shhh, listen while I tell ye, and don't tell our Mary. Sister Theresa called in last night while your mam was at work and you were out playing pool. Finn has an exam today and she said he needs a good breakfast. Full of praise for him she was. Said he has promise and that he's a clever lad.'

'Finn? He is clever, Da. He will definitely pass. Clever people make a lot of money and we could use a bit of that. He can have some of my breakfast too and pay me back when he's rich. Did Sister Theresa say if she thought he would pass the exam?'

Paddy's shoulders heaved as he silently laughed. Then he flinched with pain and cupped the end of his stump with both hands.

Bryan stood motionless and waited until his father's pain had eased and the tightly clenched lines of agony had softened on his face.

'Don't be daft, Bryan. Finn won't pass the exam. There's no chance of that. Our kind don't pass anything other than the gate man down on the docks when they're lucky enough to clock on or the bizzies checking for knockoffs in their old army rucksacks when they come back up. Our kids do well enough at St Chad's. Mother Theresa sees to that. She never gives up, does she, not even on the likes of the Ryan boys. Jesus, God the Father gave up on them a long time since, but not Sister Theresa. St Chad's is good enough for Finn, not Waterloo Grammar School. Who ever heard the like?'

'Let's give him his big breakfast anyway, though, eh, Da, and just do what Sister Theresa says.'

'Aye, but shhh, let your mam sleep. Don't say a word. She has enough to worry about without fussing over Finn and an exam he's never going to pass. And even if he did, it would be no use to neither man nor beast down on the docks.'

Bryan wanted to say to his da that no boy from the grammar school ever worked on the docks, but he let it pass.

He had no need to go upstairs to wake the kids as Mary emerged at the foot of the stairs and went to barge past him on her way to the back door.

'Move, Bryan, I need the lav.'

Paddy put his finger to his lips and nodded towards Noleen.

'Is she sick?' asked Mary with a note of alarm in her voice.

'No, Mary, just exhausted, as always.'

Mary was thirteen and it was impossible for Paddy to look at her without seeing the face of her mother as she had been as a young girl. It wasn't just that Mary had inherited her mother's dark hair and bright blue eyes, unlike the boys, who had their father's bright red thatch. It was in her flinty defiance, her determination that her life would be different and that she would one day be away from Lovely Lane and not just to another street on another dock. 'I won't be living around here. It'll be a nice grand house for me on Princess Avenue, just you wait and see,' Paddy had heard her say at least once a week since she was out of nappies.

'Sister Theresa says Finn has an exam today,' Mary whispered, glancing at Noleen. 'She says he needs a good breakfast.'

'Jesus, is there anyone the woman hasn't told?' said Paddy. 'Will everyone in the street be knocking on us to tell me to give Finn a good breakfast?' He looked irritated, which both Bryan and Mary knew meant that the pain was worse than usual this morning.

'I'm only passing on the message, Da. Don't bite me head off,' said Mary.

'Mary, don't tell your ma, I don't want her worrying. Finn won't be passing any exam, it's just a waste of time. I wish Sister Theresa had come to see me and tell me about it first, before every bugger else, but of course I'm the useless man with one leg. No one wants to tell me anything.'

Bryan and Mary exchanged a look. Their da's mood swings had been worse of late. 'It's like he hates himself sometimes,' Bryan had said to Mary.

'I won't, Da, but Finn will pass, you know. Everyone in school thinks he's clever. I won't tell Mam and Finn won't either, you can count on that. He can't remember to put his underpants on before his trousers some mornings. And by the way, Bryan, you may as well know, just in case you hadn't noticed, Lorraine Tanner fancies you.' And with that, Mary left the house and made for the privy before the others came down.

Unperturbed, Bryan removed the pobs from the oven

as Paddy, convinced that Noleen was now in a deep sleep, fiddled with the radio dial once more.

'Lorraine Tanner, eh? Your mother and I were just talking about her when you were in the scullery. Jesus, her mother, Maisie, now she was a looker before the war. Never went out the house without her stockings painted on. Made your mother laugh, she did, because she was always staining her legs with the used tea leaves. If Lorraine is anything like her mam or their Pammy – a great nurse she is, they say – you should have a think, lad.'

'Behave, Da,' Bryan whispered with a hint of irritation as he tried to set the hot dish on the surface with as little noise as possible. 'She's still in school, she's just like our Mary and she drives me mad.'

Bryan had noticed that Lorraine had been spending a great deal of time around their house, but his head was full of other things, like looking after his da, and when he did manage to step out in the evenings it was with the porter's lads from St Angelus, usually to play pool. Only then did he stop worrying about the money and the kids and the house, when he had drunk a pint of Guinness and knocked up a good score.

The outhouse door banged shut and Mary came back in.

'Looks like our Mary has decided to wake the Ryans too,' said Paddy.

'J.T. Ryan is up in court soon, Da. Ma said she wanted to go and see Mrs Ryan herself this morning. Should we wake her and remind her?'

'Not on your life. I don't know why she gives that woman the time of day. They are nothing but a family of villains. 'Tis only your mother and Biddy Kennedy ever bother with them. For a family of thieves, the mother has nothing. Poorer than the church mouse she is. What's the point of it? Seems to me that those who live by the book have more comfort in life than those who thieve do. Even in this house, and I'm not even working and nor will I ever be, more's the pity.'

Bryan ignored the note of self-pity, which was becoming a predictable feature of conversations with his father these days. 'They say he will go down this time, Da. He's been up before the magistrate too often to get off.'

'Good riddance. They all need to go down for a long time. The only decent one is the youngest, Lorcan, and he'll probably turn out just like the rest.' Paddy was warming to his theme. 'Their father was a good man, a brave man, and he looked after that woman. She was always a bit simple. Came from out on the bogs, past Sligo way. The women think she was an inbred, there was enough of them out there. He was already here, she came over when she was still a kid and he looked after her. God knows what would have happened to her if he hadn't. He took a bullet for his boys when he died, but, Jesus, there was not one man wouldn't have wanted him alongside them going into battle, I can tell you. He was the bravest. God alone knows what has happened to those lads. Their father will be turning in his French grave.'

Bryan listened carefully. His da told him a different story about his war experiences every single day. He began to spoon the pobs into bowls.

'J.T., he wanted to work at the hospital, Da, but Dessie wouldn't take him on. Said he hadn't the time to be counting the sheets in and out on the laundry deliveries. Said he couldn't trust him. Lorcan is the last, but I don't think he's the worst.'

'Oh, not yet he isn't, but he will be, Bryan. He'll have learnt all the tricks of the robbing trade from his big brothers, despite Sister Theresa going soft in the head over him and keep wanting to give him a chance. Your mammy, she has a soft spot for Lorcan too. They will be sorry, so they will, but there's no telling women like your mother and Sister Theresa. They will have to learn the hard way.'

'Everyone says Mrs Ryan has powers, Da. She can make bad things happen to people if she wants.'

Paddy snorted. 'The only powers that woman has lives on a shelf in the press. It gets mixed with a bit of water to make it last longer and she has a glass on a Saturday night. Powers indeed. I've never heard the like. Now, there are women around here who have been blessed with powers all right, but not that simple old soak.' He turned back to the fire. 'Mind you, if I think of it, maybe she does now – the power to hoodwink your mother and Biddy Kennedy and Sister Theresa and that's a fact.'

As Bryan began to dish up the breakfast and call Finn, Jack and Cahill downstairs, Paddy leant his head against the back of the chair and allowed his gaze to sink into the flames of the fire. This was a rare moment of contentment. Noleen was safe and sleeping. The house was running in military order. Behind him came the sounds of the scullery in use, the chink of spoons being placed in bowls and the gentle simmer of the copper boiler as it warmed. All was as well as it could be with the Delaney family. If only I could get out of this flaming chair, he thought to himself as the familiar anger rose like bile in his throat. He pictured the washing, sitting in a pile outside their bedroom door, waiting to be placed in the copper and fed through the mangle. 'I may as well be dead, the fat lot of use I am,' he muttered.

'Shut up, Da.' Bryan's voice was stern.

When his father began to slip into the depths of melancholy, Bryan's patience began to wear thin. He knew it upset his mother and he would risk a row with his father any day to prevent her from fretting. His da's moods could flip in an instant and Bryan could spot the signs a mile off. It usually happened late at night, when Dessie or one of the others had called in with a jug from the pub for him. Unused these days to a drink, the effect on Bryan's da was often as though he had drunk double the amount and his monologue of despair would begin.

It was during these moments, and only then, that Bryan felt his own anger and despair bubbling up. Because for him too there was no way out. He could never leave his mother alone to deal with his da, stuck in the chair for ever more, unable or unwilling to move. That would be his job, always, to protect his ma. The likes of Lorraine Tanner could move on and look elsewhere. He had his ma to care for and his siblings to help raise and there was no time in his life for anyone or anything else. While his father was trapped in that chair, Bryan was the breadwinner in the Delaney house and that was how it had to be.

'That's loads of pobs for me, Bryan, you loony!' Finn half yelled as he raced over to his place at the table.

Paddy couldn't help but smile as he turned and looked at his second son, who was rubbing his hands together.

'Look, Da, our Bryan's gone mad.' Finn began to laugh and Paddy put his fingers to his lips.

Seeing his mam sleeping, Finn was instantly mortified. 'I need the bog first,' he whispered to Bryan as he ran on tiptoe out of the door to the outhouse.

No matter how low Paddy felt, if Bryan didn't manage

to snap him out of it, one of his other sons would always unwittingly drag him back from the depths of his own self-loathing and make him laugh.

He smiled and drank his tea. What a morning and the light wasn't even fully up yet and everyone with their fanciful thinking, that Finn could pass an exam and Lorraine Tanner had ideas about their Bryan. He switched the radio off. He would let the news go. Better that Noleen rest. Nothing was as important as that. Noleen let out a long sigh as she sank further into sleep. Paddy wouldn't tell her about the exam when she woke. It would only be another thing for her to worry about. She'd told him that she'd been the last into Mass this morning because she'd been chatting to Biddy Kennedy. She must have missed Sister Theresa. Thank God for that or she would have known and been worrying herself sick about something that was never likely to happen.

'Tell you what, Bryan, throw a rasher on for Finn – for all of them, or Mary will give out. Then when he fails the exam we can tell your mother we set him up right and good.'

'You'll have to explain the missing rashers to Ma,' Bryan said. He took the bacon out from under the wet cloth on the cold shelf in the press and threw the rashers into the hot griddle pan on the range. The air filled with the spit and sizzle of meat and still Noleen slept.

Paddy sat back in his chair, took the top off his bottle of tablets, put one of his painkillers in the palm of his hand and, tipping his head back, gulped the last of his tea and threw it down the back of his throat. What did it all matter? It was just a few bloody rashers. No Delaney had ever even sat an exam, never mind passed one and that wasn't likely to change anytime soon. It would take more than a rasher and a big man's breakfast to bring that about.

Over in Arthur Street, Maisie Tanner had experienced a more noisy than usual morning. Lorraine was becoming more difficult by the day and her raging battles with her younger brother, little Stanley, were getting louder and more physical, involving the throwing of inanimate objects, usually shoes, rulers, or as was the case this morning, an ornament.

'Eh, eh, what are you up to?' Maisie grabbed the miniature statue of Our Lady from Lorraine just as she was about to throw it at little Stanley's head. It had been a gift to Maisie from Sister Theresa. 'That's mine, that is, thank you very much. How dare you!'

'Will you tell him, Mam? I know he has nicked my hairband. I know he swapped it for a bag of ollies and if he didn't, where did he get the money from for those ollies and where has my hairband gone?'

'Oh, I don't know, do I, love. I'll get you another on the market when we go. Stanley, where did you get those ollies from? You didn't take Lorraine's hairband as a swap, did you?'

'No, I didn't. Who would want her stupid hairband? The ollies belong to Finn Delaney. He gave them to me. He said he can't play with them today because of the exam.'

'What exam's that, love?' asked Maisie.

Lorraine, as always, was quick to answer. 'It's the eleven-plus. If you pass it, you get to go to Waterloo Grammar. I'd love to have passed that,' she said.

Little Stanley looked incredulous. 'No you wouldn't, because the grammar school is full of boys and they would hate you,' he shouted.

'No they would not, they would be lucky I was there. Anyway, Stanley, stop it.'

Maisie was close to exasperated. 'You stop it, Lorraine, both of you. It's too flaming far away, that school. Make sure you don't pass any exam, do you hear, Stanley. St Chad's was good enough for your da and me, it's good enough for you lot too. After all, our Pammy only went to St Chad's and look how well she's doing.'

'I won't, Mam, I promise. Finn might, though. He's clever,' said Stanley.

'Finn Delaney? Clever?' Maisie's voice rose two octaves as she spoke Finn's name. 'You have to be joking. He doesn't even know what his own name is half of the time. I've never known a kid like him before. Not an ounce of common sense. Even his own mam gets fed up with him, and she has enough on her plate. Forgets to eat sometimes, he does, she told me. Got no idea what's what. His head's always in a book. No, he's got no chance. No one around here has.'

'Mam, I'm going to call at the Delaneys' for Mary.' Lorraine was slipping her coat on.

'There's a change, Lorraine. Is there any reason why you spend more time in the Delaneys' kitchen these days than you do in your own?'

Lorraine had the good grace to blush. 'Mam, Mary is my best friend, that's why I go there. She has to help her mam a lot with all they have going on and her mam working nights.'

'Don't give me that, Lorraine. I gave birth to you, I know you. I think your attraction down at the Delaney house has more to do with their Bryan than your mate Mary.'

'Mam!' Lorraine almost shouted. 'Don't say that so little Stan can hear.'

Maisie wrung out her dishcloth and began clearing away the detritus of the Tanner breakfast table. She piled the bowls in the sink then took a packet of cigarettes out of her apron pocket. It might only be eight thirty but her hair was neat – hard from six days' application of Get Set hairspray – and her lipstick fully applied. 'Don't be daft, love, I won't. But I am right, aren't I?'

She leant her back against the range and, tipping her cigarette packet upside down, tapped the bottom until one fell out. She lit it on the flame from the pilot light. Blowing the smoke upwards, she said, 'Look, love, all I would say is take care. You are only young. Bryan has a lot of responsibilities and he is keen to get on. I don't want you to be having a broken heart.' She blew her smoke into the air.

Lorraine placed her school books into her wicker basket. 'Do you like him though, Mam?'

'Lorraine, I've changed his nappy and wiped his nose enough times, of course I like him. I like all the kids around here. We are really just one big family. It's not that. You are still at school and he is working now, up at the hospital, and he has his da to look after. I just don't want you to go getting hurt, that's all. Have you told Mary?'

Lorraine nodded.

'Well, love, if I can give you any advice, it is this, never let a fella know you fancy him. Even one who pushed your pram when you were in it.'

'Oh, God, he didn't, did he, Mam?'

'Of course he did. We used to put you and Mary next to each other and send Bryan off to push you up and down Vince

64

Street so we could get the washing done. Play hard to get, it's the only way.' Maisie turned back to the sink to flick her ash down the plug hole and looked out of the window. 'Oh, here we go, your hairband is walking up the path. I bet little Stan swapped it for little Finn's comic. Now let's see what a good mate Mary Delaney is.'

Lorraine looked up from her basket and out of the kitchen window, into the back yard. 'Stanley!' she screamed at the top of her voice, as Mary Delaney walked in through the back gate, proudly wearing Lorraine's hairband.

Chapter 3

Lorcan Ryan, nicknamed Rankie by his peers at school on account of how badly he sometimes smelt, had been taught that to survive you needed to know how to thieve and how not to get caught. His elder brother, J.T., had drummed this into him for what felt like his entire life. But now J.T. himself had got caught stealing a motorbike from Water Street. Unfortunately for him, the bike ran out of petrol before it reached the Pier Head. The owner, a fit young solicitor, gave chase and successfully both repossessed his bike and prosecuted J.T. for theft.

Lorcan had taken more than his fair share of beatings from his brothers as, no matter how many jobs they took him on or how much they taught him, he always ran away. Lorcan did not want to thieve. He did not want to let Sister Theresa down.

Today was the day of J.T.'s hearing. Lorcan had loyally accompanied his mother to the courthouse and they'd been sitting waiting on the limestone steps outside St George's Hall for hours. 'J.T. said he will be back out in an hour, Mam,' Lorcan had told his mother at 9 a.m., but it was now gone twelve.

The cold of the steps seeped through into their bones until Lorcan felt he would turn into stone himself if his brother didn't return soon. He was dressed in nothing but a thin jacket and his mother wore the shawl he couldn't remember ever seeing her without, indoors or out. As they sat and waited, his mother cried and then cried some more. Lorcan tried to persuade her to return home and wait for J.T. there. But it was no use, a fresh fall of tears appeared on her face each time he even suggested it. Mrs Ryan seemed impervious to the cold but Lorcan could barely speak, his teeth chattered so loud.

Unable to bear waiting any longer and feeling as though he couldn't think straight because he was so cold, Lorcan made his way into the vast interior of St George's Hall. He almost yelped as the warm air hit his face. A large fire burnt in a grate the size of their front room, but it was not something Lorcan was allowed to enjoy for long.

'Oi, what are you doing in here?'

His eyes were fixed on the flames of the fire and he knew the question was aimed at him before he even turned around.

'I'm looking for my brother, sir. J.T. Ryan.' Lorcan was as polite as if he were addressing the priest.

'Get out of here! Go on with you! Out.'

Heads wearing bowler hats and wigs turned from their business and regarded Lorcan as he stood and wrung his threadbare old cap in his hands. He felt his face flush with embarrassment.

'Don't be loitering around here and don't come back inside, you scruffy article,' the policeman shouted.

Lorcan turned and ran back out of the huge doors. He was confused. If he and his mother hadn't seen J.T. enter the building themselves, he would have doubted that he was even in there. He didn't tell his mam that the policeman had almost bitten his head off. She appeared to be unaware that he had even moved. Her tears fell unabated and Lorcan knew the source of her despair was the fact that J.T. was the only one bringing money into the house. Even though J.T. didn't have any kind of a job, he made regular money somehow, which paid the rent and kept a roof over all of their heads.

As more hours passed, Lorcan grew hungry and desperate. His mother's crying had turned to a low moan and he knew something had to be done and soon. She was becoming delirious.

He noticed a surly-looking boy come out of the courthouse, a boy he knew to be a friend of J.T.'s, no older than seventeen. Lorcan had seen him once before, at the end of their street, talking to J.T. He was one of the Bevan boys, with a far worse reputation than any of the Ryans. They lived in the Dingle and ran their own neighbourhood. Lorcan had seen him only last week, huddled under the lamp-post, skulking around the bins in the entry. When Lorcan had asked who he was, J.T. had hit him across the head. 'Shut your feckin' mouth and don't ever ask me that again,' he'd said as he walked into the house and banged the back door in Lorcan's face.

The Bevan boy stared hard at Lorcan now and Lorcan instinctively moved closer to his mother, feeling a need to protect her. The boy stopped still for a second, as though about to speak, and then, fixing his cap on his head, gave Lorcan a menacing smile before he ran down the steps.

Lorcan guessed that he must know what was happening to J.T. if he had been inside the courthouse. Maybe he had spoken to J.T. and had a message for them or some news at the very least? He considered running after him, but he decided against it. Hardly a week went by when the Bevan boys weren't mentioned in the *Echo*. He would rather shiver all day than speak to a Bevan boy with a dirty face, bruised knuckles and dark, menacing eyes.

As he watched the boy's retreating back, it dawned on him that maybe he would have to pick up where J.T. had left off. He might have to speak to the Bevan boy. Find out what it was that J.T. did to pay the rent. That might be his only future.

'What do we do, Mam?' he asked. 'Can I get a job yet? I'm fourteen now, aren't I?' His mam wasn't sure exactly when his birthday was, but she'd mentioned it last week and Sister Theresa at St Chad's had baked him a cake to take home from school.

His mother appeared not to have heard him. 'Oh, Lorcan, what do we do? Where has J.T. gone? They haven't sent him down, have they? What will we do?'

Fear gripped Lorcan. He felt as though the bottom was falling out of his life. The woman who was supposed to hold it all together was crumbling into the steps of St George's Hall and he had no idea where to turn.

As the light of the day faded, he knew something was badly wrong. His instincts told him that this time his brother would be put away for a very long time. But still they sat on the steps and waited, hoping beyond hope that J.T. would appear around the corner and throw his cap in the air shouting, 'I got off. I got off with it. The bizzies can't get me,' as he had so many times before.

The street lights fired up and men in bowler hats and carrying cases began spilling out of the hall and down the steps.

But there was still neither sight nor sound of J.T. The policeman who had shouted at Lorcan strode past, calling goodnight to a colleague in the courthouse, his head bent, cape flapping around his shoulders in the wind. Lorcan, swamped with relief at seeing someone who might know something, forgot the policeman's earlier hostility and stepped into his path. He didn't even have a chance to utter the words 'Excuse me' before the policeman laid into him.

'You still loitering around here, are you?'

The policeman glanced over Lorcan's shoulder towards his mother, who was sitting rocking with her shawl held against her mouth, too exhausted now to cry. Lorcan was concerned that she had eaten nothing that day. Neither had he. She was almost crazy from the cold. Lorcan began shaking, this time with fear.

'Your good-for-nothing brother was taken down hours ago. He got five years in Walton and good riddance if you ask me. He should be kept off the streets for ever. Thieving little beggar. And if I see you in here, you had better watch it, lad. I've got the Ryans marked.' He turned to address Lorcan's mother. 'Oi, you,' he shouted. Mrs Ryan was so lost in her own misery, she didn't even acknowledge him or look up. 'This is a public building. If you don't get yourself up off those steps in two seconds, I'll arrest you for soliciting. Do you hear me, woman?'

Tears he could not prevent rushed into Lorcan's eyes. He shuffled backwards, away from the policeman and towards his mother, and took her elbow. They had to get away from there. Lorcan could sense danger. He had to get his mother up off the steps, fast, and away from St George's Hall. There was no doubt now, J.T. would not be coming to join them and would not be returning safely home. Lorcan could no longer allay his mother's fears and unless they were to be homeless, he would need to find the Bevan boy and ask him what it was J.T. did to bring home the money he did.

'Come on, Mam, we have to go. Come on, please,' he said. 'He's gone now. They've taken him in the van to Walton.'

Lorcan's mother surfaced from her grief for just a second and her eyes met those of her son. Her skin had turned a deeper shade of tallow and the shadows of bloodless grey around her mouth had darkened as the day progressed. It seemed to Lorcan as though her bloodshot eyes were sinking further into her skull.

'Gone? How long for? Do we wait? He knows I'm here, he told us to wait here, Lorcan, we can't go. What will we do if J.T. doesn't come back? We have to wait, Lorcan.' His mother's voice rose and took on an edge of despair and panic. 'There's nothing at the house, Lorcan. Nothing. Not a penny.'

It was the policeman who answered her. 'He was given five years, you effing bog jumper,' he shouted. 'Now get yourself off those steps right now. Do you hear me? Or I will blow my whistle and there will be another Ryan spending a night behind bars. The jail will be full of bloody Ryans at this rate. You filthy Irish, the lot of you, you should have been left to starve to death. Famine, my arse. Why didn't you all just die in your own country, eh?'

Lorcan instinctively took a step towards the policeman, to ward off his words and try and stop them from adding to his mother's pain. He noticed that the policeman's moustache was speckled with spittle and his eyes were bulging. He was fired up with hatred and anger and it was quite clear he was all set to take it out on Lorcan and his mother.

'Take a step nearer to me, lad, and you will be sharing a cell with your brother, have you got that?'

Lorcan froze. What would happen to the house if no one was there? They would lose it. They had been behind with the rent so often and had been warned so many times. One more late payment and the harbour board would have them evicted. He nodded automatically. He was used to words of hatred. The only people who were ever kind to him were Sister Theresa at St Chad's and Biddy Kennedy and Mrs Delaney. No one else had any sympathy for the Ryans of Vince Street. His brothers' reputation had gone before him, tainted him, caused people to dislike him before he had even opened his mouth. By the time Lorcan arrived, he had been pigeonholed as a bad apple and someone not to be trusted. Ever since his older brother had stolen from the church and fled to America, they'd been known as a bad lot. Lorcan had worked out for himself that the route to survival lay in submission and silence. He never challenged anyone, hardly ever spoke. That way he had managed to survive his first fourteen years unscathed and out of the hands of the bizzies.

Lorcan pulled at his mother's arm. But with the news that J.T. had been sent to jail for five years, she'd descended into a fresh torrent of tears and unrestrained wailing. It was no use, he couldn't move her.

The policeman was true to his word and Lorcan jumped in fright as his whistle rang out, piercing the air. The next he knew, his mam was bundled off inside the hall and he was left alone on the steps, tearful and panicked. What should he do now? Who would help him?

Shivering and sobbing, he tried to think straight. There were two women who would help him: Mrs Delaney and

Biddy Kennedy. Mrs Delaney he thought might be sleeping because he had seen her at Mass that morning and she had spoken to him and he knew she'd been working a night shift at the hospital. 'Are you away to school now, Lorcan?' she'd asked him as they walked out of the door. She always had a kind word for him, unlike some of the other women, who regarded him as they would vermin. She had once told him, 'If you need strength to help you through the day, Lorcan, Mass in the morning is the place to find it. I wish I could get any of my kids to come with me.' Because he didn't want to let down a woman who was nice to him, he went to Mass whenever he woke in time. He hadn't wanted to tell her that he wouldn't be at school today but at the courthouse with his mother. He was too ashamed.

He raced down the court steps and headed for the Dock Road, sprinting all the way without stopping. He had a number of choices. The first was the priest. Father Brennan wouldn't slam the door in his face, nor would Sister Theresa, but he was too embarrassed to go to either. Biddy. He would go to Biddy. He ran straight to her house, praying all the way that she would help.

'And, where is your mam now, Lorcan?' Biddy asked the unkempt and dirty boy as he sat at her kitchen table and drank from the mug of tea she had given him while she fried him potatoes and buttered the bread.

'The policemen, they all came from nowhere, Biddy, and they took her away into the hall and she didn't come back out.'

Biddy didn't like the sound of that. She picked up her mop

and banged on the wall of her kitchen. Two minutes later, Elsie came running up the back path.

As soon as Elsie saw Lorcan sitting at Biddy's table, she frowned. 'What's he doing here?' she asked, without even addressing Lorcan.

'He has a name, Elsie. 'Tis Lorcan, as you well know, and he lives on our streets. Go and fetch Dessie for me. We have a bit of trouble with the bizzies.'

Elsie didn't even raise her eyebrows. She had lived amongst the Irish community since the day she'd married and she'd seen at first hand how they were often despised and maltreated. She had stood in shock and shaken her head at the signs in the windows of boarding houses on Scotland Road. *No Blacks. No Dogs. No Irish.* Trouble with the bizzies for her neighbours was nothing new.

'What do you want me to go down the entry to Dessie's for?' she said irritably. 'I'm helping our Martha to bath the baby. I'm not running around after a Ryan. Give you Irish a bad name, they do. Send him on his way. You don't want to be associated with the likes of them. They hang about with the Bevan boys from the Dingle. There's talk everywhere that J.T. was sent down today for a long stretch. They bring shame on those of us who live around here. Bring us all down with them, they do.'

'Elsie, I will not be turning Lorcan out. I'm feeding him because, in case you hadn't noticed, he is still but a child and he hasn't eaten all day.'

Elsie wrinkled her nose. 'Aye, and one who hasn't seen hot water for a very long time either.'

Without another word, Elsie left the room and Biddy needed no further confirmation that she was off to do as she was told. Minutes later, Elsie returned with Dessie in tow. Although she had a new grandson to bathe, her curiosity prevented her from going back to her house just yet.

'I thought you said you had a baby to bath?' said Biddy.

'Oh, I did. I'll have missed out, he'll be all tucked up in bed now. So, what do you need Dessie for then?'

Biddy ignored her, but Elsie knew that if she waited around, she would find out soon enough.

'Dessie, I've sent Lorcan out to the scullery and I'm putting the copper on. If his clothes don't fall apart when I'm washing them, I should be able to get them dry enough overnight in front of the fire for him to wear tomorrow.'

'Why is he here, Biddy? What's going on?'

Dessie had taken off his cap as he entered Biddy's kitchen and now, sitting at her freshly scrubbed table, he accepted the cup of tea she slid across to him.

'Emily is getting my tea ready,' he said, grinning from ear to ear.

Biddy couldn't help herself, she grinned with him at the mention of Sister Emily Haycock, the director of the school of nursing at St Angelus and her boss. 'Who would ever have thought it, eh?' she said as she pulled out one of the chairs and sat next to him. 'My boss getting your tea on. Well, all I can say is you deserve each other. Two such good and kind people should be together, Dessie. 'Tis only because you are both such eejits that you weren't together sooner.'

Dessie grinned again. He was often plagued by a similar thought. How he had worshipped Emily from afar for so long and how they could have got together years earlier if he had only had the courage. 'Well, we are making up for lost time.' He winked at Biddy.

'I'm very aware of that,' said Biddy. 'But isn't it time you were making an honest woman out of her? You will have Father Brennan banging on the door before long, Dessie. He won't tolerate sinners in his parish, you know that. Oh sure he won't. 'Tis only because you do so much for so many around here that you have got away with it for so long, you know that. But what you don't know is that Sister Theresa is on your side and fighting your corner every time one of the mealy-mouthed from around here sucks her gums, has a bitch or drops a bit of poison in his ear. Be careful, will ye?'

Dessie looked serious. 'I will, Biddy. It's all in hand. Father Brennan's already had a word. You know I will do the right thing.'

'Good. Now, we have more important matters to be dealing with. J.T. Ryan went down.'

Dessie rolled his eyes in response.

'Yes, he did, and that's not the worst of it either,' she continued. 'They put Mrs Ryan behind bars too. She got herself mighty upset. Lorcan couldn't move her from outside St George's Hall. Waited all day on the steps, they did, in this weather, and not one of them inside had the decency to come out and tell her or Lorcan what had happened. It's the bizzies, they've taken Mrs Ryan into a cell, only for tonight I would be thinking. I doubt they will put her up before the magistrate in the morning. How could they? Is it a criminal act to be brought down with the grief when your son is taken away? But, Dessie, just in case, had you better go to the courthouse in case they do and stand for her? She's not been all there for a long time, now, has she? Jesus, she wasn't there before, and it's a whole lot worse now.'

Dessie had once been a good friend to the Ryans, trying

hard to do right by their late father. But the older boys had shunned him and gone their own ways, forgetting their father and ignoring Dessie. Mr Ryan had been widely liked, respected for his values, his honesty and his work ethic. He had served in the same regiment as all the other local men during the war and Dessie had mourned his loss, just as he'd mourned the loss of the others, not least for the widows and children they'd left behind.

Even simple Mrs Ryan remembered the day half the women in the neighbourhood walked to Lime Street to see the men off. Later, she'd asked, 'How did he die, Dessie? Was he in pain? The telegram said he fell in action.'

'That's right, Mrs Ryan, he fell,' Dessie had said, never revealing the circumstances or the details.

From the day Mrs Ryan got the dreaded telegram, she began to slip. She told anyone who asked her that Mr Ryan, as she always referred to him, had died because he fell in the war. Mrs Ryan also fell, into a chair, and had barely risen since. She lived in squalor, with ashes from the fire around her feet and fags in her hand. Her dishes piled up, her nets turned grey and her windows greased over and she seemed to neither notice or care. For all that, she never appeared unhappy. She often sang to the fire. Talked to the fire. Slept in front of the fire. Like lots of the women at the docks end of Lovely Lane, she had long ago given up her bed to her sons as they had grown. And these days, even though there was only herself, J.T. and Lorcan left, she remained by the fireside, rarely setting foot outside of her own kitchen.

Dessie rubbed his hands through his hair. 'God in heaven, what will happen to her and the house now? How old is Lorcan?'

'He's just turned fourteen,' said Biddy. 'Or so he thinks. The government will know sure enough when it comes to stopping the widow's pension. You know the rules, it stops when the last child reaches fourteen and can go out to work. If Mrs Ryan's mind hasn't already gone altogether, it surely will when she realizes she's to lose what money she has. The lad will be expected to find work.'

'Shall I put the kettle on to top up the pot?' asked Elsie, sensing this was going to be a long discussion. 'I've made jam tarts next door, shall I fetch them? The jam's from a ship that came from Hungary. Don't ask me where that is. The people must be starving all the time if that's what they call the place, but they do make good jam.'

Neither Biddy nor Dessie answered. Both were contemplating a war widow's life without support. The life of a woman who had given birth multiple times and spent her useful years in the house cooking and cleaning for others, only to be deserted when her job was done and it was time for someone to look after her.

Biddy knew that life only too well, and Dessie was equally aware of the repercussions. As head porter at St Angelus he felt a responsibility to try and do something for the fatherless homes. The war and all he had seen drove him to try and make something worthwhile come out of it and that was why he ran the porter's boys like a regiment. It was to honour his men, his friends, the lads' fathers, and to uphold their values and all they had given their lives for.

Two pots of tea and a plate of black-market tarts later, it was decided that Lorcan would be taken on as a porter's lad at St Angelus.

'I've heard it all now,' said Elsie. 'We are taking on vagabonds and thieves, are we? Not sure what Matron will have to say about that.'

'She won't know, Elsie,' Dessie replied curtly. 'She leaves that to me. And besides, you can't tar Lorcan with the same brush as the rest of the family. I knew his da, remember. He was a great man if ever there was one. The mother isn't the sharpest knife in the box, never has been, but 'tis a fact that house began to fall apart the day her telegram arrived. I don't think she ever got over it. Some might say that given the melancholy that infected her, she didn't do a bad job. It's not as if she ended up on the corner of Scottie Road like some from around here. Lorcan has brought himself up. He's a lad who has studiously stayed out of trouble and Noleen Delaney told me once, he's a regular at Mass.'

Elsie looked suitably contrite. Dessie sounded very angry. He had the ability to alter his tone enough to convey any message without raising his voice, and he was definitely cross. She rose and began to clear the plates.

'His clothes are falling to bits,' said Biddy. 'Even with a coat on, Matron will notice if he comes to work dressed like that. He was always the scruffiest kid on the street. If it wasn't for Sister Theresa, he would never have owned a pair of shoes.'

'I've noticed that before today, Biddy,' Dessie replied. 'Who hasn't? The lads will have something fierce to say, never mind Matron. Some of them might even think they can drop their own standards if I let boys like Lorcan start in the state he's in. Send him to the back gate of St Angelus at four tomorrow. I should have everything organized by then. You know, those Ryan lads, if they had come to me before they started thieving, I could have shown them a different life.'

Biddy raised an eyebrow. It was J.T. Ryan who replenished

her tea chest and she knew the brothers had a pact never to steal from those, like her, who used the black market. But the black market had never been enough for the Ryans and so they fell in with the Bevan boys, an association that had led them all the way to jail.

Dessie picked up his mug and drained the tea before placing it back on the table with a bump and continuing with his theme. 'Always talking about getting to America, those Ryans,' he said, 'and every one of them an out-and-out thief. You know the eldest went missing on VE Day? Came to the street party and then disappeared after he had filled his pockets with food, broken into the convent and lifted the money from Sister Theresa's desk drawer.'

Elsie wriggled on her chair, keen for vindication. 'Everyone around here knows that, Dessie,' she said. 'Isn't that enough to make you think twice? You've gone soft in the head, both of you.'

'No, Elsie, it's the right thing. Give Lorcan a chance. Get him some decent clothes, fill his belly with food, find him a job, a reason to hold his head up in society, and if he wants it, he will become a transformed character, you mark my words. And with God's blessing he will keep away from the Bevan boys.'

'Aye, with God's blessing.' Biddy crossed herself as she rinsed the empty teapot under the tap. 'Because those Bevan boys are the root of all evil and they are too often around here.'

Minutes after Dessie had taken his leave, Elsie made to follow him. 'Right, I'm off to me own house. Be careful, Biddy. I think Dessie might have made a mistake this time. No good ever came from a Ryan boy and if Lorcan is involved with the Bevans, it could come back to bite you. Matron won't tolerate a bad'un at St Angelus.'

'I know that, Elsie. I'll be keeping a close eye on him.'

The sound of Lorcan rinsing under the tap in the scullery filled the kitchen. He'd been in there for ages, no doubt scrubbing hard at several weeks' worth of grime. The back door slammed as Elsie left and for a moment, clutching the teapot in her hands, Biddy stood and stared at her own reflection in the window above the sink. She had been lonely for a very long time. Finding clothes for Lorcan, washing his hair, sorting him a job with Dessie, feeding him, had all had an effect. Her eyes filled with tears. Once more, she was needed, just when she had thought no one would ever need her again. She had mothered her boss Emily Haycock half to death until she had fallen in love with Dessie. But Emily was a grown woman. An independent woman. Lorcan was just a boy. A shy, cold, hungry boy and his 'Thank you, Biddy,' had pulled at her heart. She would do more than look out for him, she would fight for him and he would not let her down, of that she was sure.

The following afternoon, as Lorcan Ryan left the porter's lodge at St Angelus with Dessie's words ringing in his ears, he couldn't stop himself from smiling. The two green pound notes Dessie had given him crinkled in his pocket and brushed against his leg. He'd never had such cargo in his pockets and he nursed the notes as carefully as if they were two unexploded hand grenades. If he hadn't been carrying the heavy brown-paper parcel tied with string in his arms, he would have held on to the money with both hands, for fear of it falling through one of the many holes in his pockets. With every few steps he took, he turned his head and looked back to make sure that the notes hadn't slipped out on to the path behind him and that he wasn't just imagining the scratching of the unfamiliar green paper against his bare skin.

Dessie had issued his instructions in a fair but firm tone.

'Go first to the wash house for a full bath, and scrub your hair again. Biddy has done a good job, but it will take a dousing of hot water to get your colour back and the way Matron likes it to be, Lorcan. Tonight, go to Biddy's. She has a nit comb and will give it a good comb through. Keep putting your head under the water until it runs clear. I have already been and spoken to the women at the wash house. It's all paid for and they'll run you a full hot bath, not the couple of lukewarm inches that most people get. I paid for double carbolic soap as well, so don't waste it, Lorcan, use every shaving.'

Lorcan didn't know what to say, and so, as he always did when in doubt, he looked at his feet and swallowed hard.

'I picked you up these clothes and boots at Chan's up on Scottie Road.' Dessie held the brown-paper parcel out and dropped it into Lorcan's outstretched arms. Chan's was a well-known high-end pawnbroker's. They only sold on shoes and boots that they had re-heeled and re-soled in house so that they made a top price. 'It's a pair of boots, two shirts and two pairs of trousers, vests, a waxed seaman's jumper, underpants, a new cap and white hankies. I insist that every porter's lad carries a clean hankie in his apron pocket and on the Monday inspection I check every one, so don't think you can get away with not having one.'

Lorcan looked shyly up at him and hugged the parcel to his chest.

'If you have trouble getting anything washed at home,

Lorcan, go and see Biddy. She washes on Sundays. She told me to tell you, she will drop whatever you have in the boiler for you and no doubt give it a run over with the hot iron too. Biddy wants to help you, Lorcan, so don't look a gift horse in the mouth. In return, make sure you help her out and put her own washing through the mangle, fill up her coal bucket, clear the moss away from the outhouse roof slates. The things Biddy struggles to do herself. She likes to keep the place smart.'

Dessie knew that a nice house, a clean house, was not something Lorcan was used to. 'Say, "Yes, Dessie," please, Lorcan.' His voice dropped and became more gentle. 'That way I know you understand what I'm asking of you.' He could see bewilderment etched on Lorcan's face. 'Just so I know. It's something you will have to say a lot at work, especially on inspection day.'

'Yes, Dessie,' said Lorcan in a clear and definite voice as he lifted his head and looked up at his new boss. He sounded very much as though he was aiming to please. He quickly lowered his head again, his eyes never leaving Dessie's gleaming boots. Boots he had often seen marching up the entry, making him feel mortally ashamed of his own.

Dessie was one of the few men Lorcan knew who had known his own da and still mentioned him. Lorcan had been too young to remember much about time spent with his father. What he did recall was a blur. A ride on a pair of shoulders from a man in uniform who was so tall Lorcan had been able to see over the entry walls as he was jogged up and down along the cobbles. A man who smelt of shoe polish, gunpowder and leather. But he did remember the boots that shone like Dessie's and the sounds of the leather being cleaned.

The spitting, and the polishing back and forth, and watching from his mother's lap in front of the fire as he was hushed into sleep by the repetitive, rhythmic brushing.

Biddy had told Lorcan that Dessie made the porter's lads line up in the yard and have their boots and attire inspected before every shift. Everyone knew about the military manner in which Dessie ran his workforce. Only Dessie was unaware of his reputation as the regimental sergeant major of St Angelus Hospital.

'Good lad. Right, here's two pounds. Spend some of it on food to keep your mam going until your payday. Now that you are fourteen, she will lose her widow's pension. Keep a few pennies by for yourself, for some boot polish and for your breaks at work. On Friday nights all the lads go to the Irish Centre with their pay packets, but they only have two, three pints at the most. Any lad who drinks his pay packet away doesn't have a job come Monday. Have you got all that, Lorcan?'

Lorcan was now nodding furiously. Two pounds? He swallowed hard. He could barely believe what he was hearing, but he responded on cue. 'Yes, Dessie. I've never been to the Irish Centre. I don't...' His words trailed off. He thought that Dessie was thinking he was like his brothers, who had never been out of the pub. He looked down at his boots.

'Don't let me down, Lorcan. If it wasn't for Biddy, I don't think I would be taking you on. Your brothers have a bad reputation. I'm risking a lot of flak for trusting you, but I knew your da, he was a mate, and I'm trusting that you are of his blood and that you'll take after him. You have a lot to thank Biddy for. And you keep away from the Bevan boys, do you hear?'

Now, on his way to the wash house, as he made to turn into Clare Street, Lorcan saw walking towards him the same Bevan boy he had seen at St George's Hall. There was a purpose in his step and he was heading straight for Lorcan. Lorcan's stomach churned. There was no doubt that he had been waiting for him, had probably been following him.

'Rankie Ryan! God, would you look at the state of you. I've a message for you. I'm Kevin Bevan. I'm the Bevan boy that has the brains. I carry the messages, organize the jobs and I have a big message for you my lad. What's in there?' He poked his fingers into the brown-paper parcel and stared at the string tied in a neat knot.

Lorcan's heart began to hammer in his chest. If this boy took the parcel, took his new things, how could he explain himself to Dessie? And, more importantly, to Biddy, who had put such faith in him and persuaded Dessie to take him on.

'Answer me, what is it?'

He now prodded the parcel so hard, Lorcan staggered back a few steps, but he was saved by the wall from falling backwards. His mind raced as he gripped the parcel harder. He could not lose this. No one had ever given him anything before. This was his own and this hideous, leering boy could not take it from him. It was his.

Kevin Bevan's face came closer to Lorcan's. He could see the whites of his eyes shining and smell his putrid breath.

'It's the dirty washing,' he stammered. 'I'm taking it to the wash house.'

Kevin Bevan's nose wrinkled. 'The wash house?' He immediately lost interest and moved straight to the purpose of his search for Lorcan. 'The message is that you have to take your brother's place on the jump-over.'

'The jumper?' Lorcan frowned. The Bevan boy might as well have been talking in a foreign language.

'The jump-over, you stupid git. Where you jump over the counter in the bank and rob the money from the drawer. Then you jump back over and leg it. Your brother said we could store the tools under the floorboards in your house.'

Lorcan was none the wiser and stared at Kevin's boots. They were dirty, black and tied with brown laces. It occurred to Lorcan that if Kevin knew that there were boots in his parcel, he would most definitely help himself. He remembered J.T. telling him that the mark of the Bevan gang was the brown laces in black boots and he had said it with pride. 'I'll have earned the brown laces soon,' J.T. said. 'The next job and I'm done.' The parcel weighed heavy in Lorcan's arms and he willed himself to keep on holding it up and to not move.

'Your brother wanted a bike to get away on after he had done the job,' Kevin Bevan continued. 'Said it was too much money and the bag would be too heavy to be sure his legs wouldn't buckle under him. Thought he would be able to do more than one jump-over if he got himself a bike. Wanted to get away, he said, to America. Then the stupid eejit got caught. That's what he was up to, nicking the bike, but us Bevan boys, we still want the job done. It's an order. And J.T., he's sent you a message from Walton.'

Lorcan's head shot up. How could J.T. get a message out of Walton? No one had been to see him. That was impossible.

Kevin Bevan continued. 'He says you now have a debt to him, that the responsibility falls on you and that you are to do what I say and none of your nonsense. He says you're as good a runner as him, so we will be calling on you to take his place.'

Lorcan stared at the mud-spattered boots and didn't answer. It was the truth: all the Ryans were good runners, and Lorcan was the best of all of them. What tools did he mean?

'Are you going to answer me or what? Jesus, are you as stupid as your feckin' mother? No, you won't do,' said Kevin. 'What the feck is J.T. thinking about? We need someone who has a clue what's going on. You Ryans, you aren't all you're cracked up to be if you ask me. Living on your family's reputation, I'd say. What you doing anyway, carrying around dirty washing wrapped up in paper, you big girl.' He smacked the parcel with his hands and it almost fell out of Lorcan's hands.

'I won't be doing no jump-over.' The voice that said the words didn't sound like Lorcan's and even he was surprised. 'Tell my brother I have a proper job now, as a porter's lad at the hospital, and I won't be doing no jump-over. I'll be looking after Mam and the house.'

Silence fell. Lorcan was terrified. He wondered if Kevin Bevan was about to hit him. But instead he roared with laughter.

'We don't want you, mate. You're a big girl. Doing the bleeding washing. What use are you to us? I'll find someone who knows what a jump-over is, but that's your brother cut out of the job. There won't be a penny. You can deal with the consequences.' Kevin Bevan walked away. 'Not a bleeding penny to your house,' he shouted over his shoulder.

Lorcan turned slowly and watched as Kevin retreated. His knees began to tremble and his hands shook. His mouth felt dry and he swallowed hard. He could not believe what he had just said, and what was more, he was still standing. Kevin Bevan hadn't hit him, he had laughed and walked away.

Lorcan felt the two pounds burning into his leg and thought of Dessie. He couldn't let Dessie down. Dessie was trusting him and no one had ever done that before. The entire time Kevin had been talking to him, he had been terrified that he would check his pockets for money. Now that the coast was clear, he began to run, with the parcel in his arms and faster than J.T. ever had, all the way down Clare Street. His heart was pounding, and not just from the sudden exertion. He knew that when his brother found out what he had done, there would be trouble. But Lorcan didn't care. No one had ever shown the slightest bit of care for him. He had lived his life trying to be invisible, different from his thieving brothers, unnoticed, and as a result, no one really knew Lorcan and Lorcan knew no one. Now, because he had run to the home of the only woman in the neighbourhood who had ever given him the time of day, he had new friends, Biddy and Dessie, and he would rather die than let either one of them down. He thought what Biddy's reaction would be if he told her about the jump-over and he knew, without a second's delay, that she would be both bitterly disappointed and horrified.

Warm and clean from his hot bath and wearing his new clothes, Lorcan made his way back from the wash house to his own house. He felt so smart and proud, he could barely keep the grin from his face. All the way, his hand kept straying up to his new, slightly oversized cap, feeling the rough finish of the tweed, and not a single hole to poke his finger in. He had never known a prouder day in his life.

'Are you there, Mam?' he shouted as he entered the kitchen.

'I am, Lorcan, is that you?'

Mrs Ryan was sitting in her chair as though nothing had happened and as if having spent a night in a police cell was a regular occurrence. On the table stood a plate of crumbs and the remains of a fish-paste sandwich. Someone had brought her food and lit the fire. He guessed it was Biddy, but the house was filthy and she wouldn't have stayed long. There were lice in the house, the sores on his legs told everyone that. Biddy had probably been on her way back from work when she called in. He knew Elsie didn't like his mother, had no time for lazy women, but his mother wasn't deliberately lazy, she was simply befuddled and confused and sad for a lot of the time.

Lorcan had lived with dirt all of his life and had never really noticed it, but after having sat in Biddy's kitchen, he could suddenly see how bad their house was. His mam didn't appear to understand what to do or that being the dirtiest family on the street brought shame and made people look down their noses at them. People had looked at Lorcan with pity or disgust in their eyes for all of his young life.

'I have money for food, Mam. I'll be going to the shops now, what will we have? Fried 'tatoes and rashers?'

He looked at the table. On a broken dish sat the remains of some rancid butter and there was a stack of dirty plates smeared with food that was weeks old. He smelt the familiar putrid smell of maggots, writhing away in the food waste that had been thrown under the sink. He couldn't even ask Biddy to come and help his mam, as good as she had been to him. Having seen the inside of Biddy's house, he felt shame like he had never experienced before. The filth in his house was too much for a woman of Biddy's age to take on and even if she wanted to, she would struggle to get the other women to help her.

Tomorrow would be a new start for Lorcan down at the hospital. Tonight, though, he would try and do something with the house. Finding a brush in the yard, he began to pull the rubbish out from under the sink where his mother had let it pile up for months.

'I thought you were going to the shop?' said his mam from deep within their only armchair.

He looked at her face and thought that at least there was some colour now.

'What time will J.T. be home?' she asked.

Lorcan didn't answer.

'I am off to the shop, Mam, and I'm going to buy some Aunt Sally to clean the floor when I'm there. But first I'm going to get all of this into the bin and then I'll call to the chip van for speed and get us some chips and a saveloy.'

Once he'd brushed the floor and piled all the rubbish and maggots out into the yard, he decided to push as much as he could into the old metal bin and put a match to it. He would mop the floor later on. Resentment towards his mother, a rare feeling, all but filled him, but it vanished as quickly as it had come. Lorcan loved his mam. There was something simple about her and she needed him now. He had to protect her. Biddy would help him if he asked, she had made that clear.

'I've got work, Mam. Dessie is taking me on down at the hospital. Did he tell you that when he brought you home this morning?'

His mother looked at him confusedly. 'No, he didn't say anything.'

Lorcan knew that Dessie would have told her when he'd fetched her home from the cells. Kept her informed. But she had already forgotten.

'Well, now, isn't that grand. Isn't that just grand that Dessie has taken you on.'

Lorcan placed a cup of tea in his mother's hand. 'I'm off to the chip van now, Mam.'

As he made his way down the back path, he heard her talking to herself. She had already forgotten that he'd said he was on his way out and it seemed that she had no recollection of having spent a night in a cell. For that at least, Lorcan was grateful.

He threw a match on the rubbish in the yard and waited for the flames to catch and burn high. He had already decided to call into Biddy's and ask if could he buy her something from the chippy, as a thank you for helping him out. Yesterday he was a boy still at school. Today he was a man, about to start work.

Sister Theresa had not objected to his leaving when Biddy had taken him down to the school. He had got the impression she was relieved that there was a better path for him to follow than that of his brothers. She had always been kind to him. He had heard her on more than one occasion talking to the other nuns and comparing him favourably to his brothers. They had all been brought up the same. Like his brothers before him, he was dirty and not very bright, and the hunger in his belly often made it hard for him to concentrate. The potential that another Ryan might steal from the Lord was always there. Sister Theresa knew that and yet she had never once held the sins of his brothers against him.

He poked the fire with a stick and as he watched the green smoke rise and the rubbish burn, he knew that his life was about to change. As he smashed the stinking rubbish down into the flames, he vowed that he would never work for any of the Bevans. He would never let Dessie and Biddy down.

Chapter 4

The nurses from the Lovely Lane home walked purposefully up the road towards St Angelus. Today was special and every person who worked in the hospital had been eagerly anticipating it. It was the official opening of the new operating-theatre suite, a dedicated block of prefabricated units that had arrived on the back of a number of trucks and threw into sad relief the soot-stained buildings that made up the remainder of St Angelus. The nurses were excited at the chance to finally get a proper look at the new theatres, which were sealed from floor to ceiling and kitted out with every mod con. There would then be several days of familiarization as the transition from the old theatres was completed.

Much to their surprise, Pammy Tanner, Victoria Baker and Beth Harper had all been placed on operating-theatre training together. They were the undisputed favourites of Sister Emily Haycock, who'd told them, 'I cannot think of three nurses I would rather have for the trainee nurse allocation. If Nurse Brogan were here, she would be with you too.'

Dana Brogan was in Bolton, where she was ensconced in the Davenport family home, caring for Teddy. Her job now, as Matron had informed her, was to assist in the rehabilitation of a very impatient and stubborn young man. Matron had sent her off with her blessing. 'We are going to need that young man back as soon as possible. I consider sending you with him to be a way of ensuring he eats and exercises well and does not do anything foolish to hinder his recovery.' She had paused and raised her eyebrows as she looked at Dana across the top of her reading glasses. Her unspoken message was crystal clear, that this assignment was work, not pleasure. 'Of course, it's a decision made possible by the fact that Dr Davenport's brother also lives at home.'

Dana had been delighted. It would have been hard to bear if some other nurse had been sent to care for her Teddy. However, it did mean that she was not able to share the placement on theatre with her closest friends.

'I am afraid, though, that you won't all be together at the same time,' Sister Haycock had told the other three nurses. 'There will be a mix of nights and days.'

They were standing in her office, waiting to hear the rest of her news, which would confirm whether or not the rumours flying around the hospital were true.

'Theatre Sister is in charge of commissioning the new operating theatres, and who better than my three star trainees to work with her. You all have the measure of her and know the drill, and what's more, Matron agreed with me.'

Oh God, no. That single thought ran through three brains in succession. Theatre Sister had a reputation for being firmer than most.

'Nurse Tanner, we may need you to float between the new theatre suite and casualty until everything is up to speed and we have a full operating list on the go. But I'm sure you won't mind that one little bit, will you?' She flashed a brief smile at

Pammy. 'I know it won't be easy for you all, but I hope you understand that I am trusting you and bestowing the honour upon you of being the first group of second years ever to be placed on theatre.'

The nurses grinned, this time with pride. All doubts about having to work with Theatre Sister were dispelled. After all, she can't be as bad as Sister Antrobus.

Emily beamed back at them. She'd been doing that a lot lately. It was a poorly kept secret at St Angelus that Emily Haycock and Dessie Horton were in the throes of a grand, passionate love affair the like of which few had witnessed before, even in a much younger couple, never mind a pair who were both past thirty.

It was thanks to Nurse Tanner's mam, Maisie, that the two had finally got together. Dessie had worshipped Emily from the porter's lodge for years. He had seen her walk past every morning on her way to the school of nursing until one day he finally made his move. Emily and Maisie had known each other from when Emily had lived in George Street. She lost her mam and younger brothers in the bombing. Only her stepfather, Alf, survived, because her mam had sent him out of the house to find Emily just moments before the house took a direct hit. Emily had grieved deeply from that day, but since she'd fallen in love with Dessie, a difference had come over her.

Everyone could see what pleasure they took from each other's company; they found it difficult to contain their feelings in front of their workmates and neighbours. But this outpouring of new love had begun causing problems for Father Brennan and his parishioners down at St Chad's. So much of a problem, he had asked Dessie to stay behind after confession.

'You know what I'm going to be saying, don't you, Dessie?' Father Brennan had said, and Dessie had had the good grace to look embarrassed. After his frank confession, he certainly needed to.

'I know, Father, of course I do. I'm just scared of rushing her and it's the practicalities, they get in the way. She was living in a room in the hospital, next door to Sister Antrobus... I had to take her in.'

Father Brennan waved Dessie's words away with his hands. 'You don't need to be explaining to me, Dessie, you have just done that in your confession. But you are causing a bit of a fuss around here. I have women complaining to me and I can only quieten wagging tongues for so long. Think of Emily, she will hear it all soon. Hattie Lloyd never stops giving out.'

'Don't worry, Father, I know what has to be done.' And, Dessie did, he just needed to be sure Emily would agree.

Pammy Tanner blushed because Emily Haycock, madly in love herself, now instantly recognized it in others. She had been covertly referring to the fact that Pammy was dating Dr Mackintosh, the casualty registrar. Despite her best efforts, Pammy grinned inanely every time anyone mentioned him. Not a day went by when she didn't look at him and find herself unable to believe her luck. He was bumbling and kindly, not flash or full of himself like many of the medical students. And he was not even remotely like Oliver Gaskell, the consultant on obs and gynae, whom Pammy loathed.

Pammy had made the dreadful mistake of falling for the dashing Oliver Gaskell at her first ever doctors' dance. She had very quickly learnt the lesson of many nurses before her, a lesson she now shared as often as she could. 'New consultants think they are more important than God himself. They think they can wrap any nurse around their little finger. Don't let them, I tell you! The moment they put a stethoscope around their necks, some of them change into monsters who would break your hearts in a flash.' Pammy said this to every new probationer nurse who came on to any ward she was working on. Some listened, most did not.

'You can't keep putting everyone off him,' Beth had chided her only the day before. 'It makes it sound as though you're bitter. Stop doing it. See the way that poor probationer has just looked at you?'

The two of them were making up a bed together on male medical.

'Nurse Harper…' Pammy stuffed a feather pillow into its case far harder than was necessary. 'Have you forgotten poor Nurse Moran already?'

Beth looked sheepish as she smoothed her hand over the bed and began to fold back the top sheet to the regulation eighteen inches. Something they could now all do by eye alone to the nearest quarter of an inch. 'Pass me the rule from the trolley,' she said, trying to change the subject. 'I want this turndown to be exact. Sister is in a bad mood today and knowing my luck she will measure it.'

Pammy reached her arm behind her, lifted the eighteen-inch rule and almost slapped it, a little too hard, into Beth's outstretched hand. 'Don't change the subject, Nurse Harper. Besides, you haven't been using the rule for weeks, we all know your turndowns are near perfect. Go on, answer me then. Nurse Moran, where is she?'

Beth looked uncomfortable. The hospital had been alight with gossip only weeks before, that the hapless Irish probationer nurse had fled from the nurses' home in the dead of night. She had not been heard from since.

'She was last seen outside the doctors' residence,' said Pammy, 'asking everyone who went in or out to fetch Oliver Gaskell and tell him she desperately needed to speak to him. In tears, she was, and did he come out and see her? No, he did not, despite the fact that he was in his room, hiding, like the mealy-mouthed, yellow custardy coward he is. And my poor Anthony had to pick up the pieces. He said she was a wreck but determined to get the boat back home to Ireland. Took her in the car, he did, with her case, down to the Pier Head so that she could catch the midnight boat. He wanted to take her to Matron, but she wouldn't go. She cried so much, he gave up and took her where she asked, but you mustn't tell anyone. Anthony could lose his job if Matron found out. Awful, it was. Anthony feels terrible. She promised him she would write to let him know she got home OK and bless her, he stopped worrying the day the letter arrived. Everyone thinks she was pregnant and do you know what that means to a girl from the country in Ireland?'

Beth snatched the pillow from Pammy, who was almost holding it to her chest.

'Anthony said those poor girls usually flee over here, to escape the punishments heaped on them, but Nurse Moran, with no one to talk to other than Oliver Gaskell and God himself, ran home. The poor kid. That's why I warn every probationer I can. And you, Nurse Harper, you should do the same.'

The bed head crashed against the frame as Pammy released the catch without grace in the midst of her agitation. Conversations which included the mention of Oliver Gaskell made her blood boil.

'But we don't know she was pregnant,' Beth remonstrated.

'Oh, for goodness' sake, why else would she have scarpered in such a rush?'

'I suppose you must be right.' Beth lifted the fob watch on her apron and glanced at the time. 'Thank goodness, coffee time. Saved by the urns.'

Pammy walked around to Beth's side of the bed as Beth smoothed the counterpane and the pillows to perfection. Their job was finished and for a second she linked her arm through her friend's.

'I'm not having a go, Beth,' she whispered as she looked around. It was a sin to address a nurse by anything other than her surname. Even the pair of twin sisters working at St Angelus had to do the same, much to everyone's amusement. 'I just don't want to see any other poor nurse taken in like I was. I think he could be dangerous. He's nothing like his lovely da.'

Beth nodded her agreement. This at least was true. Every nurse in St Angelus adored the kindly, fatherly Dr Gaskell. It was difficult to adore him more than his patients did, however.

As Pammy said the word 'dangerous', a thrill had run through Beth and for a brief second she closed her eyes as her tummy flipped. She didn't say a word to Pammy. Instead, she kept her gaze down. Beth was the quietest of the group and she was quite convinced the others didn't even consider that she might want a boyfriend of her own. But she had her own secret and Pammy was the last person she would ever want to share it with.

Pammy squeezed her arm. 'Look, I know you haven't had a boyfriend yet and it's hard to understand, but we nurses have to stick together and look after each other, don't we?

We have a responsibility towards the probationers, knowing what we do. And trust me, Nurse Harper, I know him. I'm right on this one.'

Beth looked up at Pammy and smiled. 'I know. Don't worry, I will warn all newcomers well away from the handsome and charming but extremely dastardly and dangerous Oliver Gaskell.'

Pammy grinned and wagged her finger. 'And don't ever forget the dangerous.' She laughed and gave Beth a playful push.

The two friends walked towards the ward doors where the nurses on first coffee break were waiting, cloaks hugged close to keep out the draught in the long corridor, impatient to head off down to the greasy spoon.

On this important morning, as they made their way to the new theatres, their previous day's conversation regarding Oliver Gaskell was entirely forgotten, by Pammy at least. Not so much by Beth. Pammy's words had haunted her the previous night and kept her awake for hours as she tossed and turned.

'So, it is true, Theatre Sister did walk out,' said Victoria, interrupting Beth's daydreaming. 'Apparently she was furious when it was suggested that her old theatres had to close down, but no one knows why. Stormed out of Matron's office, she did.'

'Well, she must have been seventy if she was a day. Mind you, I'm not sure who is the worst, the old theatre sister or Sister Pokey. They will have to appoint someone new, Pokey can't look after casualty and the theatres, although I suppose she's been alternating between the two for long enough now.'

The girls walked on in silence as Pammy prattled away.

The morning was bright and breezy. Winter was in the air and the fallen leaves had turned to mulch, quieting their footsteps as they went. Pammy changed the subject to her Anthony. 'We're off to the pictures later this week,' she said. 'He's only got four nights off all month. It's really not fair.'

It was no surprise that the steady, pragmatic and caring Dr Mackintosh appealed to the firebrand Scouser Pammy. He was the perfect balance to her scatty and chatty nature. There were no sides to Pammy. No game playing or secrets. 'Our Pammy, you'll never have to wonder what that one's thinking. She's more down to earth than a graveyard shovel,' her father Stanley often said.

Dr Anthony Mackintosh loved Pammy's openness and frankness. He loved her whole noisy, chaotic, happy family, and he especially loved her mam, Maisie, who fed him dinners like he hadn't tasted since he left Edinburgh when he qualified as a doctor. As an only child, the son of a son of the manse, raised in a lochside village of twenty-three inhabitants, he had embraced the bouncing Tanner home without any problem whatsoever. Having endured years of isolation and loneliness, when he looked at his bubbly, cheeky, beautiful Pammy, he couldn't believe his luck.

As the girls stood on the kerb about to cross the road, a familiar van pulled up beside them. The passenger window was down and the girls ducked to look inside. Jake, Dessie's deputy porter, was driving, and Bryan Delaney was in the passenger seat.

'Morning, nurses,' shouted Jake. 'Are you off to the new theatres?'

'Yes, we are.' The girls had stepped off the kerb and gathered around the passenger window.

'Well, let me tell you, the men from the *Echo* are up there with a big camera, so give them your best smiles, nurses!'

'You have a flamin' cheek, Jake – we always wear our best smiles, don't we, girls?' Pammy placed her hand on her head and smoothed her hair back under her cap as she spoke.

Perfecting her appearance was a preoccupation of Pammy's, although Beth would have argued that it was one every girl in Liverpool seemed to share. They all seemed to Beth to be leagues ahead of girls from the army stations she'd grown up on. She envied their attractiveness, style and shrewd quick-wittedness. It was a fact, the girls in Liverpool were more beautiful than any she had seen in any city anywhere. No wonder sailors wrote haunting songs about them.

Beth was standing beside Pammy and she smiled at Bryan. She didn't notice the colour rise from under his shirt, race up his neck and blend into his hairline.

Victoria picked up her fob watch and glanced nervously up the road. 'We are going to be late and it's Sister Pokey in charge this morning,' she chided as she stepped back on to the pavement.

'She is that, Nurse Baker.' Jake ducked his head to better see through the window. 'She's been there since half past six. Sister Haycock sent Biddy over to help and she's been driving her mad.'

'Oh, bloody Nora,' Pammy exclaimed. 'Thanks for warning us, Jake. See you, Bryan.'

Pammy and Beth stepped back on to the kerb and ran the few steps to catch up with Victoria, who on the mention of the name Sister Pokey had decided to set the pace and carry on walking.

'Our Lorraine can't stop talking about Bryan Delaney,' said

Pammy, turning to watch the back of the van disappearing towards Lovely Lane. 'I'm going to have to see if I can do a bit of me mam's matchmaking there.'

'Ah, that's so sweet,' said Beth. 'Lorraine has grown so quick. I've noticed the change in just these two years.'

'She's growing too fast. Most of the girls around the docks are well married with a couple of kids by the time they're nineteen. I'm regarded as a spinster. The wedding in St Chad's on Saturday, she was only sixteen. Mam doesn't want that for our Lorraine. She wants her to come to St Angelus like me and get qualified. God, I am so nervous about today!'

'Me too. I'm terrified about theatre,' said Victoria. 'It's my first time working with Sister Pokey. And I can't imagine what it'll be like with people being cut open all the time. What I enjoy most is talking to the patients, but unless we're helping the anaesthetist, I can't see we'll ever get to talk to a patient who's awake.'

The wind was stronger as they turned the corner into the road that led to the rear of the hospital. They made their way towards where the gates had once stood, before they were removed for the war effort. All that now remained were rusty tears on two large mounds of red sandstone, testament to the size of the ornate iron gates that had served to prevent people escaping, in the days when the hospital had been a workhouse.

'I'm the opposite,' said Beth as she pulled her cape tighter across her front. 'I can't wait. I have always felt that theatre was my calling. I wouldn't worry, though, Victoria. Sister Pokey is just looking after the opening and the first few weeks, so I heard Mrs Duffy say.'

Mrs Duffy was the housekeeper at the Lovely Lane home

and although not an official member of the St Angelus mafia, she always seemed to be one of the first with the news.

'They must have to appoint someone else soon. Mrs Duffy told me last night, Pokey wants to be back down in casualty as soon as she can. There's a staff nurse too, remember. She's been on theatre for years. The most exciting thing we will get to do is washing blood-stained wellies and instruments.'

The girls groaned as one.

'Oh, I do really get that, Beth,' said Pammy. 'Feeling like theatre is your calling. It is funny, the idea of the patients being asleep. To be fair, the patients are great, it's the relatives that drive me mad. Have you noticed how the fellas on men's medical will be smoking their fags and gabbing away in the day room, messing around, being a right pain in the backside with all their barmy, smutty jokes, and yet as soon as visiting time comes around, it's into bed with a wan face and groans of pain, all for the benefit of the flamin' wives. Then they come running into the kitchen or the sluice and blame us.'

'Oh, I know,' exclaimed Victoria. 'Give me strength. If you had seen the queue outside Sister's office at visiting time last night. A line of worried-looking wives asking, "Have you got a painkiller for the old man, Nurse? He's in agony, he is. Says he's been asking for hours but no one's been to give him one." It drives me to distraction. I told one sucker of a wife just before I left, "Has he not had any painkillers? In pain now, is he? That's most odd because only half an hour ago he was following one of the probationers around the ward offering to help her give out the drinks. He was more interested in which nurses' home she was living in than asking for pain relief."'

'You did not!' gasped Beth.

'Oh yes I did. No one blames me for leaving a patient in pain and gets away with it. It's just sympathy from the wives they want. Pathetic, if you ask me. And to think, some of them were away at the war, fighting. You would never believe it.'

'Well, I don't think Teddy Davenport was like that when he was a patient on orthopaedics,' said Beth. 'And we know his relatives, Victoria, don't we? They'd have got an earful if they'd tried.'

The girls began to laugh. Teddy would become Victoria's brother-in-law as soon as Victoria had sat her finals and her wedding to Roland Davenport could be arranged. She had grown up near Roland and Teddy, in a village near Bolton, and had known them since they were boys. The Davenports had been the Bakers' solicitors for several generations and it was Roland who handled the affairs of the almost bankrupt Baker Hall estate following the tragic death of Victoria's father. Roland supported Victoria in her desire to honour her late mother's memory by completing her nurses' training before they got married.

'Oh, here we go, the doctors are out and off to work,' said Pammy.

They all slowed their steps as a group of doctors dashed out of the door of the doctors' residence and made their way down the path towards the main hospital entrance just ahead of the nurses. One had a slice of toast in his hand which he ate as he walked. The others were talking amongst themselves, white coats flapping about them in the breeze.

Oliver Gaskell was at the front, chatting away, a gaggle of junior doctors close to his elbow and hanging on his every word. Beth glanced at Pammy and Victoria. Both had steadfastly turned their faces in the opposite direction. Pammy to make a point, Victoria in solidarity. Certain that neither was looking, Beth turned and fixed Oliver Gaskell with her eyes. She wanted him to look at her without immediately losing interest and searching for a more attractive place to rest his gaze. To regard her as someone worth a second glance. Look at me, please. Just notice I exist. She almost closed her eyes as she willed him to turn his head and look across at her.

As if he could hear her thoughts, Oliver Gaskell lifted his chin and looked straight over. It wasn't unusual. He couldn't help himself. He made a point of checking out every nurse in the hospital. Always in search of a new victim.

Beth's heart began to flutter like a bird trapped inside the cage of her breast, but she betrayed not a hint of it as, without smiling or acknowledging him, she held his gaze. The blood began to pound in her ears and she felt almost faint with the effort.

An expression of bemused interest swept across Oliver Gaskell's face. He furrowed his brow and, looking at Beth, he grinned, lifted his hand and pushed his dark, overly long fringe backwards.

Beth did not smile back. Instead, she dropped her gaze and turned her head towards Victoria, as though the brief exchange had never taken place. 'Do you know when Dana and Teddy will be back from Bolton, Victoria?' she asked. Her voice wobbled slightly, but neither Pammy nor Victoria appeared to notice.

'I'm not sure,' Victoria replied. 'I'm travelling up to see Roland when I'm off-duty later this week. As you know, Dana and Teddy are staying at the Davenport home with him, but he and I are going to sneak off and stay in my house. That's the beauty of living in the country, no one will see him coming in and out, and Dana and Teddy won't have to worry about the neighbours thinking they are alone together. Roland's going to give the housekeeper some time off. Although God only knows what the neighbours would think they were up to – Teddy is only just walking unaided. It's going to take for ever to build up his leg muscles after the accident. To be honest, I'm not sure he has a muscle left on him. The wastage was quite a blow for him, apparently, when the plaster casts were taken off. Dana says there's more meat on a butcher's pencil than there is on Teddy's legs.'

'His muscles will have wasted away from all that time lying in the hospital bed when he was on traction,' said Beth. 'It's a common enough complication. The physiotherapist gave Dana all the exercises he had to do before they left.'

Beth was the clever one of the group. She took her studies seriously. As the daughter of an army major, she had spent her life travelling from camp to camp and strict routine had become her means of survival. Each homework assignment from the school of nursing was completed before the other nurses in Lovely Lane had so much as put their teacups down, extinguished their cigarettes and changed out of their uniforms.

'Matron has been amazing, letting Dana go to Bolton to look after him,' said Pammy.

'Well, he is a St Angelus doctor,' said Beth. 'We do look after our own.'

'Yes, but she is his girlfriend and there are no parents at his home, are there Victoria?'

Victoria nodded as she pulled her cloak across her front and gripped it tight. 'You could have knocked me down with a feather when Matron agreed to it,' she said. 'I think it might have something to do with Roland being there – the big brother, and him being a solicitor. She probably thought that he was suitably strait-laced and would keep an eye on Teddy and Dana.'

She grinned and there was a knowing twinkle in her eye. She and Roland had decided that three years until she finished her training was far too long to wait to enjoy the more intimate side of their relationship. They had cast aside the convention that there should be no sex outside of marriage. With no parents alive herself, Victoria was more than aware that if Matron, or even Mrs Duffy, the housekeeper at the Lovely Lane home, knew exactly how intimate she and Roland were, they would faint before her eyes. It helped that after Victoria's father had died and the estate had been sold, she had been left her own home, the former dower house, not far from the Davenport family home where Roland and Teddy lived.

'That's rich, considering the two of you,' said Pammy with a wink.

Beth was quiet. In affairs of the heart she had no authority. She felt excluded from what were now daily conversations between her friends. Dana, Victoria and Pammy were all happily dating and when the four of them were together, she felt like nothing more than a bystander as the talk always quickly turned to discussing Teddy, Anthony or Roland and the complicated ways of men.

'And what about you and Dr Mackintosh, eh, Pammy?' Victoria asked, raising an eyebrow.

Pammy shrieked at the sheer audacity of the suggestion that she and Anthony had taken their relationship to the next level. 'We haven't done it, Vic, honest to God. Me mam would kill 'me if I had, and when she finished, me da would start. Besides, I'd be terrified of getting caught. Aren't you worried?'

'Golly, no, not at all. Roland is very careful. He tells me he has it sorted and as his brother is a doctor, I totally trust him.'

'Does he jump off at Edge Hill?' Pammy looked fascinated as she waited for Victoria to reply.

Now it really was Beth's turn to speak. She had no idea what Pammy was talking about. 'Edge Hill? What does that mean? That's the train station before Lime Street, isn't it?'

'Sorry, Beth.' Pammy placed her hand on Beth's arm and threw her a pitiful glance.

Beth hated the way they began any conversation about their boyfriends or their relationships with the word 'sorry'.

'That's just it. Roland is, er, getting off before Lime Street.' Pammy and Victoria looked at each other, their eyes twinkling. Both ignored Beth. 'Not being from Liverpool, I had no idea what that even meant until I heard the charge nurse on male medical discussing it with a patient who had had a vasectomy.'

'Really?' said Pammy. 'If you're a Catholic, like me, there's no other choice.'

'Well, it's working just fine for us too,' said Victoria. 'He hates using a sheath, says it's like having a bath with his mac on.'

Pammy and Victoria both began to giggle.

'That patient on male medical,' interjected Beth, 'he had a dozen children. That was why he was an in-patient. Oliver Gaskell said that if his wife were to have another baby, it would kill her. Jumping off at Edge Hill wasn't working too well for him,' she said triumphantly.

'Beth!' Victoria and Pammy both spoke at once. 'Are you sure?'

The girls had learnt much in their time at St Angelus but still had a way to go in the ways of life and men.

'Oh yes, I'm sure all right. If I were you, Victoria, I would tell your Roland that it's time to take his bath with his mac on.'

Pammy and Victoria stopped dead in their tracks, mouths open as Beth walked ahead.

'I'm sure the problem was that he wasn't considerate enough, not doing it properly. Not really that bothered if his wife became pregnant. My Roland has a great deal of self-control and is extremely considerate towards me. He would never let me become pregnant before we were married.'

Victoria half ran to catch up with Beth.

'You both need to have that, really. The self-control. You can't leave it all to the man and, well, my Roland is very intelligent, he knows exactly what he's doing. He would never be happy with just heavy petting. Neither of us would, Beth. I'm a modern woman and I'm not a Catholic. I just don't believe in waiting for marriage so that I can do what I want to do.'

Beth simply smiled at Victoria. She wasn't as convinced about this jumping off at Edge Hill method of birth control as Victoria appeared to be.

The main entrance of the hospital and the red sandstone steps up to the new theatre units were now in sight. Pammy decided to change the subject. 'I miss Dana. I wish she was here for the new theatre opening,' she said.

'Me too,' said Victoria, grateful for the relief from Beth's scrutiny. 'Who would ever have imagined that we'd even be having this discussion? Sometimes I wake up and feel as though it isn't real. If I feel like that, Dana must feel ten times worse. Poor Roland, he doesn't even like to go to work and leave Teddy, even with Dana in the house.'

'How long until Teddy's back to work, do you think?' asked Pammy. Now that the doctors were ahead of them, she was scanning their backs for a glimpse of Anthony.

'Well, you won't believe this, but he says he's going to be back on duty in two weeks.'

'No way! That can't be right.'

Victoria now had all of Pammy's attention. 'No, I don't think so either, but it's what he says. He's adamant. To be completely honest, it's more than his legs that are giving Dana a problem. That's the main reason why I'm going up there this week. Dana says things aren't right. I'm not sure what she meant, but when I was talking to her on the phone last night, she began to cry and when I asked her to explain what was up, she couldn't. All she kept saying was, "Don't let Teddy know I said anything," which would be jolly difficult anyway, because she barely said a word and what she did say didn't really make any sense. She was really very distressed. I wasn't going to tell you both, to be honest, not until I came back, because it might all be about nothing at all. But the more I try and persuade myself of that, the less convinced I become.'

'What? What do you mean? Why haven't you said anything before now?' said Pammy.

'What do you think it is? Is she all right?' said Beth, who had missed Dana the most.

The four girls were close. They had begun their nurse training on the same day, they lived in the Lovely Lane nurses' home together and they knew each other's secrets. They had been through the worst ordeal following Teddy's horrific car crash and it had brought them all as close as it was possible for friends to be. The twenty-four hours following the accident had felt like a living hell to them all and they still could hardly believe that Teddy, the joker, the vibrant, noisy, cheekiest doctor in the hospital, had very nearly lost his life. Until Dana was back amongst them and Teddy was back at work, they couldn't properly move on from that horrific night and return to normal.

'I don't really know, Beth. She was almost too upset to be making any sense at all. She just kept saying I wasn't to say anything to any of you. I talked to Roland straight after – she hadn't said anything about not telling him – and he said he'd heard Teddy snapping at Dana during the day, and that Teddy was acting like a man with a death sentence over his head, not a man whose life had been saved and who was improving at a rate of knots. Apparently, he has lost all his happy sparkle and become a very morose and miserable person. Anyway, I will tell you more on Saturday, when I get back.'

'Poor Dana, I bet she's missing us,' said Pammy. 'Make sure you get back as quick as you can on Saturday. All the way to Lime Street, Vic, no jumping off.' She nudged Victoria in the ribs. 'Vic, if we need to get ourselves over to Bolton on our off-duty days, you just tell us. Do the trains go out as far as where those animals covered in white fluff live? Oh, what are they called? You know, the woolly-backed things?'

Victoria chose to ignore Pammy's running joke about Bolton being somewhere on the edge of the universe.

'D'you hear, Vic? Dana's our mate. If she needs us, we should be there. You tell her, if she wants anyone to take a few days off and pay a visit, we will be there.'

'That's nice, Pammy, but it will be difficult, because I'm not supposed to say anything,' said Victoria anxiously. 'You know how private Dana can be. I don't want her thinking we've been discussing her.'

'As if,' said Pammy with a hint of indignation in her voice. 'I'll just ring meself and ask when she's coming home. Tell her we are all missing her. Like we are. It's not a lie. Me mam asks me every time I go home how Dana is and when she's coming over for a roast.'

'Well, I'll tell her that,' said Victoria. 'Dana loves Mrs Tanner and her roasts. Who doesn't? They're famous. Matron was asking me about them only the other day.'

'Was she?' Pammy's eyes opened wide and she almost choked on her words as Victoria began to laugh. 'Oh you, you got me there, eh, Victoria. Not bad for a woollyback.'

As the girls laughed and joked about, Beth lost track of the conversation and looked away. From the corner of her eye, she sneakily watched Oliver Gaskell as he turned through the main entrance and towards gynae on ward two. The girls were heading in the opposite direction, towards the new operating theatres. Beth's beating heart had almost stilled, although her mouth felt dry and her skin hot.

Pammy would roast her if she could read her thoughts. Beth, the short dumpy one who wore glasses. Beth, the one no one talked to about men or love or sex or marriage. Beth, the one everyone assumed would one day be the spinster matron among them, the person everyone wanted to be godmother to their children, because they admired and pitied her all at the same time. Beth, who had never even been kissed. What am I doing, she thought to herself. He's the Casanova of the hospital. The man Pammy despises. The doctor everyone knows is a heartbreaker. So why, as his reputation gets worse by the day, does he have this effect on me?

Oliver Gaskell held the door open for one of the junior doctors and at the last second, before he let it swing shut, he turned his head and caught Beth looking at him. He grinned. He was well used to the effect he had on nurses and he loved it. His charm worked every time. Even on the short, dumpy ones who wore glasses. He winked and waited for Beth to smile back at him.

He had kept a low profile since Nurse Moran had disappeared. He had spent weeks being the first to the post table in the sitting room at the doctors' residence, ready to remove the numerous tear-stained letters she had written and burn them on the fire before anyone else saw them. He didn't want anyone thinking he was more of a cad than he actually was. Anthony Mackintosh had told him that there had been a great deal of gossip flying around the hospital and the last thing he wanted was for either his father or Matron to hear it. He was the golden boy in both of their eyes and that was the way he wanted it to remain.

To his surprise, Beth ignored him. She didn't even blush. Instead, she simply turned towards Nurse Tanner and continued her conversation. But not before she had lowered her lashes and thrown him the briefest glance of disdain. He felt slightly miffed. There was no way he was losing his touch. That was absolutely not the case. Was it? Only yesterday he'd had one of the probationers glued to his side in the pub all evening. Maybe it was time to get back in the saddle now that the Nurse Moran fiasco had died down. That was exactly what he would do. He'd chat up the overly keen probationer today and offer to take her out for a meal. That always worked. Nurses' pay was so low, they couldn't resist a free feed.

Despite his intentions to fuel his ego and charm yet another unsuspecting nurse, he couldn't help wondering which ward little Nurse Harper was working on. He might have to turn back and give her the benefit of his smile once more. She must have not seen him. It couldn't be right that she hadn't smiled back. He was a consultant, for goodness' sake. Every nurse smiled back at a consultant. Especially him. They didn't just smile. They blushed, their eyes shone, their hearts raced and they were putty in his hands. He could see it in the flutter of their fingers, the fixing of the hair, the licking of the lips, the wiping of damp palms on skirts. Maybe she was just miserable and didn't know how to smile. Yes, that must be it, he thought. She's a stranger to happiness and that was something he knew how to fix in a flash.

The swing door shuddered back and forth behind him. He stole one last backwards glance as the three nurses sprang up the steps to the new operating theatres and a man with a camera shouted, 'Give us a smile, nurses. Go on, queen, please.'

Beth, Pammy and Victoria turned to the camera and beamed and he couldn't help noticing that Beth's smile was the brightest. As they laughed and joked with the cameraman, a new desire for conquest sparked inside Oliver Gaskell. He felt mildly resentful of what the man with the camera, wearing a shabby coat and a cap, had just achieved, where, for the first time ever, Oliver Gaskell had miserably failed.

Dana Brogan stood at the window of her bedroom in the Davenports' house in Bolton as the driving rain pelted the glass. It was not yet 9 a.m. and she thought of her friends, who were starting their day in the new theatre block without her amongst them to share all the excitement. Her red hair was reflected in the glass and her blue eyes stared back at her, blurred by the rivulets of rain on the outside of the leaded pane. The drops that gathered on the window mirrored those that ran down her cheek. She gazed out at the moors and the grey-brown rocky outcrop rising in the distance and thought longingly of the rolling green fields and bogs of Ireland's wild Atlantic coast, where she had grown up.

'Dana!' Teddy called from the room below. 'Dana!'

'Coming. Just getting my cardigan.' Dana quickly wiped her eyes, moved to the dark oak chest and heaved open a heavy drawer. She retrieved the navy woollen cardigan her mother had knitted to keep her warm on night duty and held it to her face. She was homesick and miserable and the person she wanted most in all the world right now was her mother.

'Dana!' Teddy shouted again.

'Coming.' Dana didn't hesitate. Slipping her arms into the cardigan, she raced to the door.

'Oh, for goodness' sake!' She almost shrieked the words as she ran to where Teddy was standing and grabbed his arm. 'You've almost pulled those curtains down from the pole. Why didn't you wait for me?'

'Because, Dana, I have to walk. I have to get back to St Angelus. I can't get the use of my legs back by sitting in a chair. You can't just disappear and leave me like that when I need you, Dana.'

She led Teddy across to the leather wing-back chair he had made his own since he'd been discharged from hospital. The seat was higher than the others in the drawing room and easier for him to get in and out of. The room had been furnished by his mother in 1920 and very little had altered since. Even though both their parents were now dead, Roland and Teddy hadn't bothered to change anything. Roland was waiting for when Victoria and he were married and he could let her take over.

The curtains were a heavy green velvet and Dana looked up in dismay at the one Teddy had been clinging on to for support, which was now half hanging off the end of the pole. Almost ignoring his comments, she said, 'Oh, Holy Mother of God, I'll have to get up on the chair and fix that now. Roland won't be pleased.'

'Who cares what Roland thinks?' Teddy snapped as he flopped back into the chair. 'It's my house too. It was left to both of us.'

'Yes, but, Teddy, Roland lives here all the time…' Dana's voice trailed off as she felt tears spring to her eyes once again.

She was glad Victoria was coming later in the week because she didn't know how much more of this she could take. Teddy had transformed from a loving, happy man to one who was surly and taciturn. This was not the man she'd fallen in love with. It was as though he was angry with himself about the accident. She had tried to talk to him about this.

'It wasn't your fault, you know, Teddy. That girl, she just ran out in front of your car. There was nothing you could have done.'

Instead of being grateful for her words of reassurance, he almost bit her head off. 'I know that, Dana. I was there, remember.'

She had almost lost her temper as she replied, 'You should be happy you are alive, Teddy, not constantly shouting. We all thought we were going to lose you on that awful night and I have been here with you day and night ever since. Feeding, washing, tending, nursing and caring for you, Teddy, but all you do is complain and snap at me.'

His only response had been to turn his head to the fire and sulk. It was a full day before he spoke to her again.

At least she had Roland to talk to. He had lived in the house alone, other than when Victoria visited, since Teddy had commenced his medical training in Liverpool. Dana was close to him. He was Victoria's fiancé and she knew they would all be friends for life. This morning, before he left for work, he'd chatted to her in the kitchen as she prepared Teddy's breakfast.

'Dana, I hope you don't mind me saying, but you are looking quite tired at the moment. Don't let Teddy push you around, will you? I know he is quite keen to get back to work, but as I have often heard you say, healing can't be rushed.'

'Oh, I don't, Roland.' Her words were weak and even she didn't believe them. 'It will take him a while to get back to himself. I'm sure he will soon, though. He just needs lots of tender loving care. Let me make you some tea and toast before you leave.'

'No, you won't, Dana. That is why we employ a housekeeper. You have your own patient to look after and that is quite enough. Look, when Victoria's here, why don't we all go out to the hotel on the top road and have a nice dinner. Why don't you suggest it to Teddy while I am at work today?'

Dana's eyes lit up and she fought back the tears of gratitude. 'What a lovely idea, Roland. Won't that be nice. It will be the first time the four of us have been out since, oh, I don't know, it feels like for ever.'

In the drawing room, Teddy sat alone, waiting for Dana to bring his breakfast to him. He had made it down the stairs unaided that morning. Mabbutt will be pleased, he'd thought. I must make sure he knows. It was time to phone Dr Gaskell senior and get himself back into work.

The thought sent a shiver of guilt down his spine. Before that day arrived, he would have to tell Dana his secret. About the black brooding cloud that hung over him. About the awful thing he had done and how the crash was obviously his punishment for the selfish way he had behaved. The kinder Dana was, the more she did for him and the more selfless and caring she became, the worse his guilt.

He looked up from the chair as she carried in his tray. Her red hair was bobbing up and down. It had grown over the weeks and it suited her. Made her look older, more sophisticated. She was no longer the naïve young girl who had stepped off the boat from Ireland with a list of instructions from her mammy. She looked at him and smiled her beaming, trusting, so-in-love-with-him smile.

'Roland is off to work,' she said. 'I made him some breakfast too. Victoria phoned after you went to bed last night, and do you know, the girls have their first day in the new theatres today. It must be so exciting for them, don't you think?'

Teddy looked into her smiling eyes and her innocence made it all so much harder to bear. As she poured his tea, only one thought filled his mind. She has to know. I have to tell her. The pain stabbed at his heart because his Dana was as proud as she was loving and kind, and the moment he confessed his terrible crime, his unforgivable sin, she would leave him and then it would be over. Before he'd had the time to tell her that he was hers – an idiot, a fool, a stupid man, but an idiot who would love her always and for ever, should she want him – it would be over.

Chapter 5

Lorraine Tanner and Mary Delaney had been firm friends since the day a young girl from one of the dockside families had laid them next to each other in the same coach-built pram, along with two others at the opposite end, to be walked up and down the street.

'Can I take your baby for a walk, Noleen?' was a line Noleen and every young mother heard at her back door within days of giving birth. Groups of girls as young as seven competed to fill the first battered Silver Cross coach-built pram of the day. They would traipse up and down the back entries, opening back gate after back gate and calling through to the women, who were invariably standing at the kitchen sink, until enough babies had been collected.

Mothering was a game to be played before learning to read. Live babies replaced the dolls and toy prams their parents could never afford to buy. The girls would rush to collect the best-dressed babies, those with knitted bonnets or pram suits to ooh and aah over. No one wanted to push the poor babies in clothes that were over-washed to a greyness and resembled rags. There was no fun to be had if there were no curls twisted with fingers and aided by a bottle of Goldilocks from the chemist. White leather reins were rubbed in Blanco, the chrome on the pram polished and its wheels cleaned and rubbed with the pride and tenderness of a chauffeur tending to his Rolls Royce.

Recently, however, Lorraine had discovered another compelling reason to place herself in the Delaneys' kitchen. That reason was Bryan Delaney, whom Lorraine had also known since the day she was born. But Bryan was now all grown up. Being a porter's lad and working for Dessie at St Angelus, he had prospects, or so her da had said.

'He's a clever lad is Bryan, not following his da down to the docks. Not that Paddy could unload a hull ever again, but still, you never heard of a porter's lad being killed by a crane, did you? And he doesn't have to make his way down the steps to the stand every morning wondering does he have work on the docks or not.'

Stanley Tanner did indeed have respect for Bryan, and pity for Paddy. Like his daughter, he came round to the Delaneys' as often as he could, to see his mate and try to keep him cheerful.

Paddy hated the pity. It was in the eyes of the men he'd once called his friends and workmates. The boys he had gone with on Saturday afternoons to watch Everton play when they were at home, the friends he'd gone out for a drink with on Friday nights. Before the war. These days he was less than welcoming to visitors, especially the men he had worked with on the docks and served with in the war.

'It's just that he really feels it, it has him frustrated, not being able to work or get out. It's his pride,' Noleen would say apologetically as, embarrassed, she escorted Paddy's visitors out. She'd wring her hands in her apron in anxiety, afraid they would not call back. 'I'm so dreadfully sorry. You will come again, will you? It's just that he's in so much pain, it makes him grumpy and grouchy, and when it's not the stump, 'tis his pride that hurts.'

This evening Noleen found herself having to apologize for Paddy's behaviour once again. It was her night off and she'd come back home after evening Mass to find Stanley Tanner in her kitchen and Paddy barely speaking to him.

'Don't you be worrying,' Stan said to her as she stood at the back gate to see him off. 'There but for the grace of God go all of us, Noleen. There's a lot of them just like Paddy who have returned from the war with a lifetime's reminder. God bless him. He was fighting to keep us safe, Noleen, and everyone remembers that. Paddy copped it, we didn't, and for that we should all do what we can. I don't take any notice of him and neither does anyone else. He's turned into a big nark all right, but you know what, he can't knock me away. I'll be round again next Saturday morning with the paper as usual, to see what he thinks and put a bet on the gee-gees for us both. That's if he stops being all holy and afraid of Father Brennan and lets me put one on for him.'

Noleen was too proud herself to say to Stan that this was part of the problem. Paddy didn't have a penny to put on the horses. It wasn't that he was being the good Catholic he pretended he had become when Stan called around. Or that he was afraid of Father Brennan and what he would say if he knew. It was more that the money was earned by Noleen and so, even if they had any to spare, Paddy wouldn't spend a penny of it.

She came back in from saying goodbye to Stan and walked over and sat on the arm of Paddy's chair. She slipped her arm around his shoulders, knowing full well that he found it more difficult to be grumpy with her when they were touching.

They touched a great deal. On the one night a week when they did lie in bed together, Noleen imagined they were young again. That it was before the war. She would lay her head on Paddy's shoulder, pull his reluctant arm around her and curve herself in to the length of his body. Placing her hand on Paddy's belly, she'd feel the soft skin around his navel, unchanged, the same fine hair to thread her fingers into, the same neck to kiss.

Her eyes would be closed, her body yearning, but Paddy always eventually pushed her away. First he'd shrug off her hand and then he would turn his face and within seconds he'd fall asleep. He had taken to wearing a pair of old pyjamas in bed, one leg tied into a knot halfway up. He didn't want her to have to look at his stump and the end of his stump was so sensitive that even the slightest brush of the bed sheet against where the stiches had once been sent sharp arrows of pain shooting up his leg.

Noleen couldn't bring herself to ask him why he wore the pyjamas or why he no longer made love to her. She didn't care that he had only one leg. He was her Paddy, the man she had loved and married when they were just sixteen. She would roll over and bury her head into the pillow to hide her burning tears of frustration and disappointment, unaware that facing the cold stone wall, Paddy's silent tears fell too.

'You are pushing all your old mates away with your stubbornness, love,' Noleen said now as she tried to squeeze up next to him on his chair. 'Especially Stanley. Why are you doing that? You could do with someone to talk to in the evening when I'm at work.'

'I don't need anyone to pity me,' Paddy snapped. 'I need no one other than my wife and my kids. That's enough for me.'

Noleen grimaced and stood up again.

'And besides, they don't want to come. They all have better things to do with their lives than to sit here and look at me. What do I have to say? Nothing. Where do I go, eh? Nowhere. I'm nothing and no one. Not any more.'

'They come to talk about the football, more like,' said Noleen as she cleared away the mugs of tea. 'No one, least of all a good man like Stan Tanner, comes out of charity, so less of the complaining now, do you hear me? I won't be putting up with it and neither will the kids. Besides, look what Stan brought with him, and you didn't even have the grace to take one.'

Noleen held out a plate of biscuits, freshly baked by Maisie that morning.

With one swoop of his hand, Paddy knocked the plate clean out of Noleen's grip and the biscuits flew across the floor. Within seconds, the Delaneys' dog was the best-fed animal on the dock streets.

'Well, you will wait a long time before I pass you another plate of biscuits, you ungrateful beggar.'

She picked up the broken plate and threw it into the bin. As she did so, she sighed. There was one man who might be able to help and she'd decided already that she would try and have a word with him tomorrow. Dessie Horton. He was the only person Paddy did have time for. They had served together during the war and fought side by side. They had a mutual respect that was born from shared experiences, about which they would never speak in front of Noleen, and rarely even to each other, it seemed. Dessie solved every problem around the dockside streets and Lovely Lane. But as she looked at Paddy, she wondered if this might be the one time Dessie would fail.

Dessie was a hero to local families. Not only for his bravery but for the way he ensured that all the posts for porter's lads at St Angelus were filled by a boy from a family where the father had fallen or was too injured to work. Bryan had been offered a job by Dessie on his fourteenth birthday and it was because of his income that all the Delaney kids had shoes to wear for school.

As it was, Noleen didn't have to seek out Dessie down at the hospital. He called at the house less than an hour after Stan had left them.

'I was just passing and came in for a warm and a cuppa,' he said. 'I know there's always both waiting for me here.'

Noleen smiled. 'Well, only a stupid woman would argue with that as both are true, especially for you, Dessie.'

Even Paddy smiled.

'I hear life has taken a turn for the better for you, Dessie. With a certain young lady from the school of nursing.'

Dessie made to protest as he removed his scarf.

'Oh, don't even bother trying to deny it. It's the talk of every house from here to Bootle. Get you, Dessie Horton, you big Romeo! Well, good on you. It's about time. Ignore all the wagging tongues and I'll tell you, if I hear anyone giving out, they'll get the sharp end from me.'

Dessie hung his donkey jacket up himself on the back of the door with a, 'No, I'll do it, it's heavy,' as Noleen tried to take it from him. He frowned as he did so. Some of the women were beginning to talk openly about his and Emily's living arrangements and his biggest worry was that somehow Matron would find out.

'And how's life down at the hospital? Is it the Mersey you see when you look out of the window of the porter's lodge, or is it the butterflies and cherubs you see flying past?' Noleen grinned as Dessie blushed. They went back a long way and no one could be more happy for him than Noleen was.

Dessie took the tea from Noleen as he settled himself down at the table. 'Oh, you know what it's like, everyone's running around like headless chickens. The new theatres have been opened. Matron has invited more dignitaries than you can poke a stick at. A whole week of it before they even use a knife for the first operation. Has the MP coming next, so she does. She's up to something, but do you know, for the first time ever, no one knows what. Not even Elsie.'

Noleen gasped. 'Well, fancy that. Elsie is usually the first to know. But surely Madge has an idea? Nothing gets past Madge.'

'Well, it has this time. It's all change everywhere, Noleen, and not just up at the hospital. Has Liverpool gone mad or what? They are building new roads, there's talk of new houses. Whole estates going up out in Speke and Kirkby. A new gasworks being built towards Seaforth for the coal extraction and yet here there are still bombsites all over the place and the houses are falling down. Wouldn't you think the government would want to look after those who are here first?'

'They are, Dessie. When those new estates are built, they will shift us into them. Our little community, it will be broken up and we will all lose touch with each other. Awful it will be. We should count our blessings while we can,' said Noleen. 'I was speaking to a patient at the hospital who lives off Scottie Road. They still don't even have lavvies in some of the houses. And the flats on Clare Street, one toilet per half landing, they have. Mrs Green remembers them being built. The first council houses they were supposed to be. At least we have our own outhouses and sculleries, Dessie. I'm not complaining, but as God is my judge, they won't let us stay.'

Dessie frowned. Noleen was not the first to say this and like many others, he could not imagine living anywhere else. He set his clock by the bore on the Mersey, the klaxon on the docks and the sound of the kids playing in the entry, being called in for tea.

'No, she leaves all the complaining to me,' said Paddy with a wry smile, speaking for the first time from his chair in front of the fire. 'Never stops giving out to me, she doesn't, and everyone around here calls her St Noleen. If only they knew.'

And for the first time in weeks, Noleen and Paddy laughed together.

After three cups of tea, a potato farl upon which Noleen insisted on spreading the last of the butter, and a great deal of conversation, during which he told them all about Emily, Dessie took his leave. Noleen walked with him down to the back gate. It was a cloudless night and the skyline above the roofs was dotted with smoking chimneys and twinkling stars. The two of them were bathed in the marmalade lamplight that reflected over the entry wall from across the adjacent street.

Noleen stood on the step, leaning against the wooden gatepost with her hands thrust deep into her apron pockets. 'Well, I can't say your visit wasn't welcome, Dessie,' she said. 'I have something to thank the good Lord for in the morning. I was planning to pop into the porter's lodge to see you tomorrow. Fancy, my prayer tonight was answered and I had barely just asked it. See how God works, Dessie? Paddy will have been glad to see you.'

Dessie didn't want to tell her that it was the mysterious ways of the mafia, or more accurately, Biddy, who had sent him there, not a prayer at Mass. He looked down at her lank hair, tired skin and heavy eyes. 'You look worn out, love, are you managing all right? You seem a bit down.'

His voice was loaded with concern. The dark shadows under her eyes were always there, but tonight she had struggled to raise her weary voice to speak. He had seen right through the laughter of their conversation.

Dessie's kindness made the tears spring to Noleen's eyes, but she quickly blinked them away. Noleen never cried. She was afraid that if she did, she might never stop. She had to stay on the treadmill, keep going every day, all day, and in her case all night too. With a deep sigh, she checked down the entry that no one was walking along the cobbles before she spoke. Even though the entry was empty, she swallowed hard and hesitated, still minded to dismiss his concern with a breezy lie. But then, with her eyes gleaming, she squared her shoulders and looked directly at him.

'I don't know which way to turn, Dessie.' She looked back down at her own hands.

For the briefest moment Dessie laid his hand on the top of her arm and said softly, 'Tell me, Noleen. I might be able to help.'

She took another deep breath before she looked straight up at him and held his eyes as she spoke.

'I'm run ragged with trying to work and look after Paddy and the kids. And it's not that I want him to do anything, although God knows, there are things he could do to help – there is more our Mary could do too, she never lifts a finger, so she doesn't. It's just that I'm worried that he's disappearing, my old Paddy. He's fading away before me eyes and I'm frightened. Don't get me wrong...'

Her eyes widened in alarm and guilt. She felt wrong, confiding in Dessie, but now she had started, she knew she wouldn't be able to stop.

'The thing is, he does try, he really does try, Dessie, it's just that there's no hope. We don't talk about the future any more. You know what me and Paddy were like before the war, we were always savers and had our big, grand plans. Paddy was always a grafter. I knew no other like him. It's why I fell for him in the first place.'

A shy smile lifted the corners of her mouth as for a fleeting second an image of a younger Paddy crept into her memory.

'He couldn't get down on the docks fast enough and he didn't hesitate to sign up. But now we have nothing to plan for, nothing to talk about because all we do is exist on my wage and Bryan's. I worry sick about the future. I love him with all my heart, Dessie, I'd have been just as glad to see him back with no legs at all, and he loves me. I see him changing, though. Every day it gets a bit worse. He's been too long sat on the same chair in front of the fire. Too long waiting for me to come home from work. He doesn't feel like a man any more. I know that's what it is, he just doesn't say it. It's the lads too. Jack, Cahill and Finn, they miss out on so much. Cahill tore another hole in his shorts today and I almost screamed at him and that's not me. It's not me, Dessie. I'm not a fishwife. I'm not one of those women who complains that I don't want my kids having to share shoes for school like some of them do. Oh God, would you look at me now. I am. I'm turning into a Dock Road shrew.'

She lost her battle with the tears, which were not far from the surface, and they tumbled down her cheeks and dripped from the end of her nose. Her breath shuddered with sobs she was reluctant to let go. She did nothing to stop them this time. It was Dessie's kindness, his perceptiveness and understanding. It broke down her normally rigid barriers of self-control and no matter how hard she blinked, they would not be stopped.

Dessie held his arms out to her. He instinctively wanted her to come to him, to accept his affection, rooted deep in the years they had lived side by side and grown to care for each other.

She surprised herself as she willingly fell into them. She let her tears soak into his donkey jacket. She felt the rough texture prickle against her cheek, and the smell of Lysol, oil, coke and smoke and all that was St Angelus filled her nostrils.

For the first few minutes he let her cry and drain herself of the years of pent-up tears and hurt. Then he spoke.

'I know, love. It's hard for a lot of women around here. I'm not going to tell you that you should be grateful because Paddy returned, but that doesn't mean that the day he came home he brought an easy life with him. It must be tough for you both.'

He had seen many women on the streets around Lovely Lane cry, but Noleen had never been one of them. Biddy had been right. When is she not, Dessie thought as he glanced up at the moonlit sky. The Delaney family needed help and he would have to think hard about a way to provide it without causing offence to either Noleen or Paddy, the proudest people he knew.

Yet again he said a silent prayer of thanks to Matron for

having given him the power to do what he could to help those families who had suffered most from the war. It was as if she had known from the outset that St Angelus could do much more than heal the sick. Matron had appointed Dessie as head porter when he returned from the war, almost before he'd had time to take his boots off. The bond between them was close. She respected the double row of medals that had gleamed before her when she called him to the hospital and she had been more than happy to grant his one condition. That he should be allowed to employ whomsoever he needed to work as a porter's lad or help him run the hospital. It would be his domain alone.

He wondered, should he talk to Father Brennan or Sister Theresa about Paddy? They were both, like himself, trusted faces in the dockside streets. The last refuge when all else had failed, when the bailiff knocked or the landlord complained. They helped out at times of crisis, supported families, held their hands through the worst – deaths, illness, poverty – before moving on to the next call for help. But Biddy hadn't gone to the church, and she would have if she had thought it was the answer, despite her stand-off with Father Brennan. She had called for Dessie and he would never question the wisdom of Biddy. He suspected that what he could do for the Delaneys might be of more practical use.

'Look, Noleen, the lads and I, the veterans, we are all meeting down at the Silvestrian on Friday. It's being organized by Stan Tanner, it's our regimental anniversary. Friday was a special day.'

Noleen didn't ask what was so special about it. The men had their own post-war secrets and rituals and the women didn't interfere.

'He won't have any choice but to go,' Dessie continued. 'I'll put Stan and Maisie Tanner on the case. We'll make him go. Let's make that the first step to getting him out of the door. We can do it together. He's happy with you and the kids, Noleen, it's the rest of us he has a problem with. He thinks we are laughing at him, he said that to me. What a load of baloney. Where does he get it from, eh? I've never heard anyone say a bad word about Paddy, before the war or after.'

Noleen's voice broke as she spoke, full of relief that Dessie didn't think her a fool. That he understood. 'He hears you all walking down the entry, on your way to work and it eats at him.' She lifted her head and extracted a handkerchief from her apron pocket. 'I know he's a good man, the best father any kids ever had, and you know it, but try telling him that. I don't know, Dessie. I swear, if I didn't come home every morning stinking of Lysol and with a pay packet in my hand on Fridays, he would doubt I was cleaning up at St Angelus. I swear to God he would think I was carrying on. He has no faith left in himself. Thinks he's a burden to everyone, that everyone is against him. He needs a job, but I can't think of a single thing he can do. He's wearing me down, so he is, but I can't let him even see that or say anything to him, because it would just make everything worse.'

Dessie caught Noleen's eye. This was the first indication that all was not well between the couple he had known for as long as he could remember. A man newly in love himself, he suspected that things were not as they should be in their personal life. Biddy's words rang in his ears. 'If everything's all right in the bedroom, downstairs takes care of itself.' He had heard Biddy say that so many times. As far as he knew, Noleen had never complained to any of the women.

They were the strongest couple he knew and he had just assumed that, despite what had happened, they would survive Paddy's injuries without any problem.

He let out a deep sigh. 'Let's get him to the Silvestrian on Friday, so he can remember what good craic his mates can be, what he's missing out on by being a miserable old moaning bugger sat at home. And then I'm going to put my foot down. He has to join us for our regular pub night on Fridays – he hasn't been for months now – and for a game of darts. He needs his arm to throw an arrow, not his leg. I'm sorry, Noleen, I think we've all given up on him a bit too soon, but he's a stubborn sod is your Paddy. I do have an idea of something he might be able to do at the hospital, but I might need to speak to Matron about it first. I don't want to tell you what's on my mind yet, just leave it with me. I'll collect Paddy at six for the Silvestrian, you just get your Mary to make sure he is ready. Tell her Uncle Dessie will have a word or two to say to her if she isn't pulling her weight. It's about time that one took some of the responsibility from your shoulders.'

Noleen half laughed as she folded her hankie and wiped her eyes. 'God bless you, Dessie, you've no idea how stubborn he is. You've always had more luck with our Mary than me, but I tell you, she's as stubborn as her father, listens to no one. God bless you for trying all the same, and for coming up with a plan. I can't begin to tell you, I can't. But he's still a wonderful father and a good man. My kids have never known the buckle of his belt, unlike many other kids around here.'

'I know that, Noleen. I've worked with my lads long enough to be able to tell which of them come from good homes and Bryan is one. Anyway…' Dessie looked down towards his own house as he spoke and, looking herself, Noleen saw the fleeting figure of Emily Haycock, hugging the black shadow of the wall across the top of the entry towards Dessie's back gate. 'Let me get him out on Friday. Don't you worry, Noleen.'

'I can't help it, Dessie. I see the man I knew disappearing before me very eyes and it scares me so much. Him having a bit of a laugh with you lot would be a great start. What would happen if I was sick? Who would look after the kids, the house and our Paddy? The worry drives me mad.' Her voice rose in panic again.

Noleen knew the answer to all of her questions and the answer haunted her daily. It would be left to their Mary. Their only daughter, who couldn't wash a dish without Noleen having to re-wash it, because surely, one day, Lorraine Tanner would grow up a bit, get her way and Bryan would notice the beauty before his eyes and he would be gone from them.

Dessie put his hand out and gave Noleen a gentle pat on her arm. 'Shhh, nothing is happening to you. Nothing, Noleen. Nothing is happening to anyone. Everyone is safe. We are all doing the same thing, making ends meet. Struggling from one week to the next. It's life around here, how it is, but you, you have it harder. Still, haven't you got the best friends anyone could want, all living on your doorstep, and don't they all worry about you and want to help? This do, on Friday, 'tis a free bar, so don't worry about the cost. Stan is inviting all of the porter's lads along with the vets, most of them lost their fathers in the war, and your Bryan will be there. He needs a night out too. The war is long over now, it's about time everyone started to enjoy themselves again. We've all for-gotten how to have a bit of fun, a laugh. Call me fanciful, but I get the feeling that life is going to get easier soon. Just you make sure your Paddy is ready for me to get him down there.'

Dessie was now the one speaking faster. It was obvious he was anxious to leave, although he tried his best to hide it.

Noleen wanted to say that she didn't have a cat in hell's chance of getting Paddy to agree to go, but she could see there was somewhere else Dessie wanted to be. He left with a wink and a smile. 'We will all help, not to worry,' he said as he raised his hand and turned towards his own home.

Noleen felt as though the weight of the world had been lifted from her shoulders. Whether it was the good cry, the promise of help, the warm hug or the reminder of the friends she knew she could depend on, she didn't know.

I'm getting old, she thought to herself as she watched Dessie walk down the entry and disappear into the night. And you are getting brazen, Dessie. Living over the brush like that. Ah well, you are just a man like all the rest, she reminded herself. There wasn't anyone who worked at St Angelus who wasn't expecting Dessie Horton and Emily Haycock to announce that they were engaged any day soon. Even with all the good will of the hospital workforce, they couldn't continue as they were for much longer. No one believed that Emily could keep sneaking up and down the entry and in and out of his house in the dark before Hattie Lloyd blew and kicked up a fuss.

Before she made to step back into her yard, Noleen took a glance down the entry and almost jumped out of her skin in surprise.

'Flamin' hell, Lorcan, you scared the life out of me. What have you done to yourself? Your head, 'tis shining like a Belisha beacon.'

There was genuine amazement in Noleen's voice, as a boy she barely recognized stood before her. She had never seen his face not covered in dirt. She had assumed his hair was a dirty auburn and yet here he was, his freckled skin scrubbed white and gleaming and his hair so red it was practically glowing beneath the sulphur street light.

Lorcan grinned from ear to ear. 'Dessie has taken me on at St Angelus, Mrs Delaney. I'm working as a porter's lad now.'

'With our Bryan?' There was a hint of surprise in Noleen's voice. She had always like Lorcan, had a soft spot for him. He sometimes slipped into the pew next to her at Mass and his catechisms were word perfect. He was the only Ryan she had known to attend Mass of his own volition, but then Lorcan had a lot to pray for.

'What's that you've got there?' She gestured towards the pole Lorcan held in one hand and the brush head he held in the other.

Without any embarrassment whatsoever, Lorcan lifted his head and said, 'Mrs Delaney, I'm trying to brush the kitchen, but the brush head keeps flying off the end of the pole and I can't get it to stay on. I've been to Mrs Kennedy's, but she's at the bingo. Do you know how I can get it to stop flying across the kitchen? I kept putting it back on, but I nearly knocked me mam out, so I had to stop.'

Noleen didn't know whether to laugh or cry. He was so serious, so earnest, but the thought of the brush head flying and little Lorcan trying his best to fix it made her smile. She also felt the faintest flutter of jealousy, which she quickly sent on its way. She would love a night at the bingo. Lucky Biddy Kennedy. Despite what Father Brennan said about gambling being a sin, she would still go. Sure, the man wasn't always right about everything and besides, she could always confess the following morning.

'I'm just on my way back home now, I don't want to bother anyone else. I'm going to make the tea when I've finished the floor.'

'You are brushing the floor *and* making the tea?' Noleen couldn't keep the astonishment from her voice. 'What are you making, Lorcan?'

The Ryan house was the talk of the neighbourhood. Jokes were created and circulated as a result of Mrs Ryan's simpleness and the dirtiness of the house. One of the lads from the regiment had visited Paddy only the previous week and passed his own comment, having walked past the Ryans' stinking back yard to reach the Delaneys' house. 'Even our dog wouldn't eat off her floors and he sleeps in the coal house,' he had said. Noleen had felt a pang of discomfort as he and Paddy had laughed. 'Aye, well, there but for the grace of God,' she had replied. Both men had looked up, momentarily confused. Neither understood her concern at another woman being laughed at. They passed no comment and instantly resumed their criticisms. She had wanted to throw the plate she was holding at Paddy and scream at him, 'When did you last wash a floor or clean a window or wash the nets?' But she didn't. When his friend left, it was on the tip of her tongue to say, 'Bye, Jack, your tea will be on the table when you get home and your sheets washed and changed. Did you do that yourself, did you?' But instead she smiled and sent her good wishes to his wife.

'Did your mammy ask you to brush up, Lorcan?'

Noleen was now curious. Bryan did a lot to help in the house, but that was because of their situation with Paddy and her working all the hours God sent. It was something that was kept quiet. Everyone assumed it was their Mary who helped Noleen, but not a bit of it. Bryan did the heavy lifting and it was all done in secrecy. He would rather die than have his friends know that he washed dishes.

Lorcan proudly set his chin at her. 'No, I do it all meself. I'm the only one at home now, Mrs Delaney. I have to look after the house and I don't care, I'm not a cissy and I like doing it.' Then in a much softer tone he added, 'Mammy, she's not very well today, Mrs Delaney.' It was almost by way of an apology, as though he was already beginning to regret having revealed to Noleen, mother of Bryan, that he undertook domestic chores.

Noleen knew it was a lie about Mrs Ryan being ill. She had seen Lorcan's mam slipping into the Anchor pub that afternoon when she'd been on her way to the greengrocer's. She bit her tongue rather than shame the boy. Instead, she reached out and took the pole from his hands. 'Come on, let's go and see what Paddy can do with this. He's a dab hand at fixing brush heads.'

Panic crossed Lorcan's face. 'Is your Bryan in?'

'I think so. Why?'

'You won't tell him it's me what's brushing the floor, will you? Say it's for me mam.'

Noleen shook her head in mock despair at his rapidly disappearing bravado. If only Lorcan knew. Her house would be closer to the Ryans' if their Bryan didn't pull his weight. 'Come on, you. In,' she said. She put her arms around Lorcan's shoulders and gently guided him towards the light spilling out into the dark back yard from the scullery door.

Ten minutes later, Lorcan was sitting on the threadbare rug in front of the Delaneys' fire, eating the last potato farl and drinking sweet tea.

Paddy rested the brush handle and the brush head on the coal bucket, which was wedged between his knee and stump, while he secured one to the other using a hammer and two long nails. 'There you are, lad, as good as new. The pole didn't split, thank God.'

Lorcan glanced up at Noleen and, placing his cup down, made to jump up.

'Sit back down, Lorcan, and drink up your tea, would you.' Noleen smiled at the boy. Bryan had already left to play pool with the other porter's lads, Mary was round at the Tanners' house and the boys were already in bed. They were alone in the kitchen and Noleen thought how peaceful it was and how nice to have Lorcan as a visitor. 'I cannot believe that in a month of Sundays our Mary would want to brush the kitchen floor. Your mammy, she's very lucky.'

Lorcan glanced in dismay towards Paddy, who immediately knew the right thing to say.

'Oh, aye. There's many a lad who wouldn't lift his finger to help his mammy, but they don't make great men.'

Noleen brought her own tea over and sat on the settle opposite Paddy, who held up the brush for Noleen to inspect.

'What do you think of that, eh? It'll be a long time before that brush head escapes again,' he said. 'When the brush wears down to the wood, lad, buy a new head and bring it here for me. I put them nails in and, if I do it right, I can get them out again without you needing a new pole.'

Noleen's heart lifted. Paddy was smiling. The simple task of mending a brush head, being useful and needed, had lit his mood as well as his face. She could hear the pride in his voice at having been able to help a neighbour in need.

'How are you finding work at the hospital, Lorcan? Does

our Bryan give you the runaround like he does me?' Paddy asked.

'Oh no, Mr Delaney. Bryan is my boss. He's teaching me what to do.' Lorcan's face was deadly serious.

Noleen laughed as Lorcan drained his tea. 'Stop quizzing the lad, Paddy. Go on, lad, off you go. You have to be up at six, so don't be cleaning all night, do you hear me? That's what I do for a living and there's not a lot of fun in it. We want better for you.'

For the second time, Noleen saw Lorcan smile as Paddy held the brush out to him. He took the brush and headed straight to the door. Just before the door closed, he turned back to them both and rewarded them with a grin.

'Thank you, Mr Delaney, for fixing me brush.' And then, in a second of silence, he was gone.

They both waited to hear the click of the back-gate latch before they spoke.

'Well, well, well,' said Noleen. 'What a breath of fresh air that lad is. See you, Paddy Delaney.' She waved her finger at him as she bent to retrieve Lorcan's cup and plate from the floor. 'I've always liked that Lorcan and he's proving me right.'

Paddy grinned. Lorcan had been a welcome distraction from his earlier mood. 'It's been busier here than on Lime Street station tonight. First Stanley, then Dessie and now Lorcan. I'm worn out.'

Noleen decided she'd try and make the most of her night off. She had a spare half a crown in her pocket from an extra night she had worked the previous week. 'Paddy, why don't I go and get you some fags and a few bottles of Guinness for us both now that lot are all in bed.'

She slipped from the settle on to Paddy's knee. Instinctively, Paddy turned his head towards the fire. There was a time when he would have leant back and pulled her down on to him and covered her face in kisses. Now, though, she felt his body harden and as he averted his gaze her heart constricted in pain.

'Probably best to save the money. Have an early night,' he said in a subdued tone.

Noleen's heart sank. Until tonight she hadn't cried for many years, but now that her tears had found a way to escape, they threatened to plague her again. 'Good idea,' she said as she wearily removed herself and walked towards the sink.

Any pleasure she had felt during the evening drained away, leaving her heart as heavy as a stone. Her shoulders slumped as she ran the taps into the enamel bowl in the sink. This time she didn't even attempt to halt her tears when she heard the door at the bottom of the stairs bang shut as, without another word to her, Paddy took the steps up on his backside, one at a time.

He would never agree to her spending money on his enjoyment. He would only do that if he had earned it himself. Not even a bottle of Guinness. It was beyond his comprehension that his pleasure was hers. That buying the Guinness, sharing it together, chatting and laughing like they used to, would make Noleen happy. Bring some light relief.

A mirror bound in faded yellow plastic hung from a nail on the wall next to her. It had once been Paddy's shaving mirror, in the days when he stood on two legs for such things. His face reflected back at her, not the Paddy of today but the happy groom she had married. The laughing, carefree man who had rejoiced with her every time she told him another baby was on the way. Paddy before the war. His reflection, distorted by her tears, was replaced with her own. Her bright eyes and wet cheeks shimmered and flickered in the reflected glow of the range behind. She thought of her marriage vows and the realization washed over her that there would be no more good times. No happy future. No more fun, laughter, carefree kisses or secret cuddles in the scullery when the children were around. Nothing to anticipate or look forward to together. No joy or let-up in the drudgery of their lives, until death did them part.

Chapter 6

'Well, what a performance this is all going to be,' Matron said to Emily as they hurried across the front of the hospital to the theatre block.

Emily didn't like to answer that it was a performance of Matron's making. The opening of the new theatres had lasted for days and Emily knew as well as anyone that Matron was not usually the sort to make a fuss of things.

'She is up to something,' Dessie had said as they'd lain in their illicit bed earlier that morning. 'I don't know what it is, but the St Angelus mafia is doing its best to find out.' He pulled himself up on to one arm and traced his finger down Emily's arm.

Emily laughed. It was an insider secret that Biddy and Elsie, Madge Jones the switchboard operator, and domestics Branna and Betty Hutch had saved the day on more than one occasion by being one step ahead of Matron. Or, more importantly, by being one step ahead of those who sought to take advantage of Matron and the hospital.

Only an hour later, Matron was now striding ahead of Emily with resolute determination. The fanned dovetail frill on the back of her cap was starched to within an inch of its life and her cape was draped perfectly about her, hardly moving as she walked with her brisk, neat steps. Even in the coldest weather, Matron would never be seen bunching her cape at the front for warmth. 'Standards, nurses!' was an exhortation she barked out more than a dozen times a day.

'I think a lot of people will be happy when today is over,' said Emily, as tactfully as she could.

There was no response other than Matron checking the fob watch on her perfect navy blue matron's uniform. Her silver buckle shone in the morning light. Emily, not in the school of nursing today, was wearing her sister's uniform and self-consciously gathered her cloak to the front. She had cleaned her own buckle last night with cigarette ash, damp newspaper and spit, but it had been so long since she'd last worn her uniform, it had needed more than one wipe over.

Matron was on a mission; this much Emily could detect. She tried again. 'It has been all go, hasn't it, and such a drag for you, Matron. First the opening with the press and the mayor, now the visit from the MP. It will almost be a relief for the staff to start the first full day list and get down to some proper nursing tomorrow. And to think, that was what they were scared of, before all the official visits started happening.'

'Yes, I must apologize to Sister Pokey,' said Matron sheepishly. 'I have made her task of commissioning the new theatres much harder. She has given the trained staff the afternoon off. She wants them as fresh as a daisy for the full list tomorrow morning. And once that first operating list has been safely and efficiently completed, I am determined that St Angelus will have a new maternity unit.'

Emily raised her eyebrows. 'How are you going to do that, Matron? Surely the board won't approve any more funding for at least another year after all this expense and hullabaloo. It was in the *Echo* a couple of nights ago. Did you see it? Everyone knows about the new theatre block now.'

'Of course I saw it. What a pain that was. Why couldn't we just open it and get on with the job? I didn't want all that fuss.' Matron seemed to realize she had snapped as she then continued in a softer tone. 'Look, I think that by inviting the MP to visit, I can use him, Sister Haycock, persuade him to give us another grant as soon as possible. I want him to see the new theatres first, and then I'm going to impress on him how a maternity unit had to be sacrificed in order for us to have the new suite. If he doesn't play ball, well then I have a story up my sleeve that I know he would not want to see in the newspapers about a hospital in his constituency. The new NHS won't want to be tainted by what I have to say. Not when his party is in government. Oh no, he wouldn't like that one bit. And do you know what the beauty of my little plan is, Sister Haycock?'

Emily was transfixed. She had never known Matron to be so animated. But then, Matron was a woman who was very used to getting her own way. Biddy had relayed to Emily a flavour of the tension that had ensued when Matron had been obliged to back the new theatre block at the board meeting. 'Sure, she's spitting feathers and chewing everyone's head off over there, so she is. Poor Elsie, she's a nervous wreck. Can't do right for doing wrong and when Dr Gaskell called in the other day, Elsie said he was as fast out the door as he had walked in and it slammed behind him. Now, what do you make of that then? That's not like him, is it?'

Emily had done what she always did and changed the subject. She took information in, she never gossiped out. Now, looking up at Matron, she could tell that Matron had taken her defeat over the maternity unit very personally indeed. She shook her head in wonderment at the bright gleam in Matron's eye.

'Dr Gaskell has no idea what I am up to, because I haven't told him. I'm setting off on this little crusade all alone because, mark my words, I know what they are all talking about in the doctors' sitting room. Oh yes, they want a new X-Ray unit next. Well, over my dead body, I can tell you that. These new consultants are all a bit too big for their boots and I swear some of them aren't even frightened of me.'

Emily couldn't help herself as she began to laugh. 'Oh, Matron, that is very funny. But let me tell you, I spent years being not just frightened but terrified of you! The nurses more than make up for some of the new consultants.'

The new theatres were now ready to swing into action the following morning. Although neither Matron nor Emily would admit it, both had loved visiting the unit every chance they got during the commissioning. Emily to see how her nurses were getting along preparing the unit and decommissioning the old theatres while keeping them running. Matron, to the puzzlement of all, to gaze endlessly at the sealed, pale green composite floor which neatly met the pale green tiled wall. Sister Pokey had become most concerned at Matron standing motionless as though her ear were glued to the wall. 'Er, is everything all right, Matron?' she'd enquired, only to be rebuffed with a very sharp 'Shhh.'

Everyone was enthralled by the shiny new steel equipment, the sterilizers and Little Sister steamers. They watched with interest as the enamel equivalents, which had served St Angelus well since 1915, made their way to the scrap merchant's via the porter's rubbish collection.

As Matron and Emily now passed across the porter's yard, Jake shouted a greeting and raised his cap. 'Morning, Matron. Everything is all good and ready, is it? We've been at it since six. There are so many oxygen bottles in the new theatres today, a national disaster couldn't drain them dry. And we've another delivery arriving before the weekend.'

'Thank you, Jake,' Matron shouted back without breaking her stride. 'Let's hope that doesn't happen, shall we. That's the last thing we need. Good to know we will be firing on all cylinders, though, and ready for whatever Liverpool's dockland community throws at us.'

Emily had to take two steps to each one of Matron's and still she was finding it difficult to keep up. It had been the talk of the hospital for days that Matron had invited the MP to visit. It was assumed that Matron was simply showing off, but, as Emily now knew, it was in fact because she wanted him to be on the side of St Angelus, fighting their corner from behind the scenes, over and above the hospital board.

'The second it was known that the MP was visiting, all the great and good from the hospital board past and present, even those from the old trust board, wanted to be here. Imagine if some of the equipment during the first operation list fails to work tomorrow – with all this attention, it will be our own little disaster after it being in the papers. We could do without the board breathing down our necks today. And Dr Gaskell demanded to be here too, even though he doesn't know what I'm up to. I couldn't fend him off yesterday. Make sure you don't breathe a word.' Matron placed a finger on her lips and her face was alive with intrigue and anticipation.

'Don't worry, Matron.' Emily almost placed a reassuring hand on Matron's arm but pulled back quickly. Matron's frosty manner had softened of late, but not quite that much. 'Dr Gaskell will never catch on and the MP cannot fail to be impressed. Sister Pokey had the nurses come in early to clean the theatres yet again. And I saw Madge on the main steps, she tells me that Cook had a bevvy of domestics running to and fro with glasses and cups and saucers earlier, to feed everyone up and keep them happy, just like you asked. The MP will leave thinking this is the best hospital on Merseyside and he will do his best, I am sure, to get every penny he can for us. I don't think many wards will be cleaned today, everyone is so excited.'

Matron grinned. 'I had to stop Elsie getting out the VE Day party bunting. Honestly, that woman. She wanted to string it along the front of the block. She thinks he's royalty. He may act like it, but I didn't like to disabuse her. Not one single operation performed yet and the floors have been cleaned half a dozen times as if there had already been a major incident. I had to tell her, it's the MP, Elsie, not the Queen. We want him to get us more money, not a medal and an OBE.'

'Heaven help us if the new Queen ever did come to visit, Matron. I think Elsie would put a mop and bucket in your hand, she's such a fan.'

'Well, it isn't something I shall be doing today, but I have been known to wield a bucket and mop, you know, Sister Haycock. I was a probationer nurse once. As was Sister Pokey. We can mop very well, along with the rest of them.' Matron looked up and almost broke her stride. 'Goodness me. A guard of honour at the bottom of the theatre steps. Would you look at the porter's lads. They are so smart, their late fathers would have been so proud of them all.'

Emily lifted her head and saw two rows of Dessie's lads

standing to attention. Dessie had told her that morning that he had managed to acquire new work coats for the lads, although Matron had initially complained about the expense. But Emily could see that Matron, having complained or not, was as proud as Dessie would be at the show the lads had put on. The new, long, tan-coloured coats were buttoned up to hide the shabby-looking clothes beneath.

'There's been a lot of Brylcreem used this morning,' Matron half whispered to Emily. 'And I have never seen the yard looking so clean. Not a scrap of coal dust or a used oxygen bottle hanging around anywhere. They must have mopped the cobbles. Oh, Sister Haycock, I do hope the MP is taken with us. I do hope he gets a sense of how dedicated to St Angelus everyone who works here is. You can't show that in a morning's visit. I can't explain it in words, it is something we need to impress without words, something he can feel.'

'Morning, Matron,' the boys sang out in unison as she approached.

Emily saw a look of appreciation flash across her eyes.

'Morning, Sister Haycock,' they sang out again.

Most of the porter's lads had begun work the day of their fourteenth birthday and some looked young for their age, not more than children. The older ones stood head and shoulders above them, clearly having benefited from the disciplined routine, the regular wage and the food from the greasy spoon.

'Goodness me, we really know how to put on a show at St Angelus, don't we. Morning, boys,' said Emily. 'Has the new chair of the board arrived yet, Bryan?'

'Yes, Sister Haycock. Half an hour since. Dr Gaskell has taken him up to the theatre. He had another man with him, too, from the LDHB.'

'Another man? That's very odd.' Matron's antenna was immediately alerted. 'Half an hour ago? They weren't due to arrive for another half hour yet. That means they are over an hour early.' She tutted. 'The Liverpool District Hospitals Board seems to be replacing its women members with men one by one. Would you believe it? They were all over us women like a rash when the war was on and there were no men around, and now they can't replace us fast enough. Righty oh, thank you, Bryan.'

Bryan almost saluted. He was desperate to be invited up into the actual theatre where the tour was about to take place. He kept asking Jake, 'Shall I take another bottle of the gas up? Shall I make another run to the autoclave? Do you need more dressings?'

From across at the lodge an hour earlier, he had seen Nurse Harper bustling in through the entrance. His heart had begun its familiar pounding at the sight of her and his mouth had dried. He just couldn't get enough of the intense pleasure and excitement he felt from simply watching her from afar. It was as if the very sight of her gave him an electric shock.

God, look at me, turn around, look. No, don't, don't look. His thoughts had raced and contradicted each other. Then, when she reached the foot of the theatre steps, she suddenly turned around as though she had sensed his presence and raised her hand in greeting. And he just stood there gawping at her, stupefied. He felt the blood rush to his face and then leave again as he almost passed out and by the time he had raised his hand in return, she had turned to continue into the theatre block.

He dropped the shovel on the floor and he knew, he could sense it, he could tell, she had laughed at him. Oh, not openly,

Nurse Harper was far too nice for that, but inside she must have been thinking, what a peasant that boy is, when he can't even return a wave. And she would be right, because wasn't it a fact, he had never been able to speak to a girl. Never tried to kiss one when he was at school, like all the other boys had. Had never had a gang of girls chasing him and chanting, 'Will you go out with our Sheila?' like he had seen the girls asking their Finn in the entry only yesterday.

The only girl who was interested in him was Lorraine Tanner and how could he take her seriously? He had known her almost his entire life. He didn't want a girl like their Mary, who didn't know one end of a washing line from the other, and Lorraine was Mary's best friend, so she had to be just like her. He would go half mad if he found himself stuck with a girl like their Mary. He had watched Nurse Harper from a distance, she was a worker. A good egg. Sister Haycock and Matron must like her if they trusted her to prepare the new theatre and greet the guests with Staff Nurse and all the rest.

His mood sank into his boots as he retrieved his shovel from the ground. His heart had now slowed to a steady beat and he resumed the hard, physical slog of shovelling coke into the cart.

Beth had made a special effort to arrive at theatre before anyone else. She had wanted once again to be the one to clean the huge central lamp in at least one of the two new operating theatres and there was always competition for that chore.

'Morning, Sister Pokey,' she called out as she removed her cloak in the staff room. 'Shall I start on the lamps?'

Sister Pokey looked up from her desk and gave no

acknowledgement or flicker of appreciation that Beth had arrived early. 'Yes, please, Nurse Harper. We can work outwards and finish in the dirty sluice.'

Beth's heart sank. It sounded like Sister Pokey had just allocated her all the cleaning. The old theatres hadn't closed yet. Not one operation had taken place in the new ones and yet Sister Pokey was acting as though a dirty op had already taken place.

Beth had been studying theatre procedure every night for the last week and had tried, unsuccessfully, to impress Sister Pokey. 'I take it, Sister, that once we are up and running, all the clean operations, the ones without infection present, or surgery associated with the bowel, will take place in the mornings, and operations such as the draining of abscesses will happen at the end of the list?' Even to her own ears that had sounded as though she was stating the obvious for no reason other than to impress. And Sister Pokey was not easily impressed. She had lifted her head from the notes she was writing, regarded Beth over the top of her glasses and said one cutting word in disdainful response. 'Obviously.'

On this early morning, Beth was surprised to see Biddy enter the dirty sluice straight after she did. Biddy never normally worked outside of her own domain, which was the school of nursing. But today was special.

'All hands on deck today, Nurse Harper. And close your mouth, you look like a fish. You have me to put up with today. Sister Haycock sent me over from the school. Matron is apparently in a flap regarding her very important visitor. The MP is coming and there can't be anyone with good hearing who doesn't know that between here and the Wirral.' Biddy dropped her voice to a whisper so that Sister Pokey couldn't hear her. 'They know the only one to make a decent cuppa around here is me, so you are stuck with me for the morning. But first Sister Pokey wants me to clean the step at the bottom of the stairs. What the point of that is, I don't know, with everyone running up and down. But apparently your man, he's arriving that way.'

Beth smiled, relieved to have Biddy there too.

Biddy leant against the long sink, one hand on her hip, the other on the handle of a bucket as she waited for it to fill with hot water. On the side of the sink stood a bottle of Lysol. The smell of it filled the room. Beth inhaled. She loved it. The smell that pervaded every hospital up and down the country and could turn grown men into a trembling lump of jelly. As she stood at the window listening to Biddy, she saw Bryan looking down in dismay at his porter's coat, which was covered in black coke dust. 'Oh, look at that poor Bryan,' she said. 'He's got coke dust all down his coat. He won't be happy.'

'Ah, well now, I reckon there's one thing that could make him happy all right.' Biddy grinned and Beth was intrigued.

'Oh, really, what's that?'

'Well, have you not noticed how he can barely take his eyes off a certain young nurse who works at St Angelus?'

Beth smiled. 'Oh, that's not so unusual,' she said. 'It happens all the time. Everywhere we go.'

'Well now, that's a surprise,' said Biddy. She had always had Beth down as one of the quiet ones. Mind you, she thought, aren't they just always the worst. How wrong can you be?

'I think it's the colour of her hair, it being so red and beautiful, and now she's grown it longer, it's even more eye-catching. How could anyone not notice her? And with Bryan being Liverpool Irish and her being from Ireland, I suppose there's bound to be an attraction. There's a lot of common ground there, isn't there?'

Biddy's face was almost contorted with disbelief.

'But I'm afraid he has no chance whatsoever. Dana only has eyes for her Teddy. And they will both be back very soon, we hope.'

Biddy took a long, hard look at Beth. She obviously didn't have a clue that she was the nurse Bryan was mooning after. 'Well, I don't think it's Nurse Brogan Bryan is after now,' she said. Using both hands, she clasped the handle of the bucket and with a grimace lifted it clear of the sink. ''Tis another nurse, not a million miles from here, he has his eye on and I reckon I could be looking right at her. And before you say anything, you could do a lot worse than Bryan Delaney. From one of the best families on Vince Street, he is.'

But Nurse Harper had already left the room and Biddy was talking to the back of the swing door.

Beth had already forgiven Sister Pokey for putting her back on cleaning again, although she was longing for the day when she could be a real scrub nurse. Inside the theatre, she pulled the shiny new lamp down by its chrome arm and then pushed it back up again. It could be tilted to the right or the left.

'Nearly as big as you, that thing,' said Biddy as she walked through, pushing her bucket along on a trolley.

No one had ever seen anything like it. Beth had spotted Mr Mabbutt the previous day doing just the same thing. She had wanted to shout, 'Oi, I've just cleaned that,' but Mr Mabbutt was a surgeon and she couldn't speak to him until he had spoken to her first. It was the way. Theatre protocol. 'It's a habit you have to get into,' Sister Pokey had told her. 'Surgeons need silence to think. Can't have mindless chatter around them when they are operating. Takes every ounce of their concentration. There are no patients to speak to and nurses shouldn't be chattering when there is work to do.'

Beth never chattered and she didn't reply. Pammy was working on theatre and everyone knew what a chatterbox she was. It was a relief to all that she would be floating between casualty and theatre.

Pammy arrived exactly on time at eight thirty.

'I wish I could just qualify now and never work anywhere else again, ever,' Beth said as they wiped down the new oxygen bottles Jake had wheeled up together with a pink chlorhexidine solution. 'I just cannot believe that we are going to be the first ever dirty nurses to work in the brand-new theatre suite.'

'How can you be so excited about being the dirty nurse?' Pammy said. 'Buckets of blood and bone, dirty wellies, and blood-soaked dressings to rinse and send to autoclave, that'll be our lot.' She dropped to her knees with her cloth. 'Were you all right last night on your own? I wouldn't normally have gone, it's just that it was Anthony's night off and with Dana being away, well, it was a bit difficult.'

Pammy had been out with Anthony Mackintosh the evening before and Beth had felt lonely in the Lovely Lane nurses' home with all her best friends away or out having fun. Victoria had gone up to Bolton to spend her off-duty time with Roland, Dana and Teddy, and Pammy had glammed up like only Pammy could and was out too. Beth had felt her single status come crashing down on her. She had confided this to the housekeeper, Mrs Duffy.

'Your day will come,' Mrs Duffy had told her, but Beth knew she was only being kind. There had been no sign, ever, that Beth's day would come. She was feeling very much left on the shelf, not least because the only man who interested her was entirely out of bounds.

'Oh, I was fine,' she told Pammy. 'I helped Mrs Duffy with the night drinks. The new probationers are going to give her the runaround, I can tell you. They have a lot more lip than we did when we started.'

'Well, I think they should get one or two of them on here in theatre. Honestly, Beth, we're going to get nothing but the rotten jobs. All the cleaning and sending away of the dirty equipment to be sterilized. I want to be stood at the surgeon's side, wiping the sweat from his brow, handing him the instruments.' Pammy sighed as she lost herself in the fantasy of being a theatre nurse, which they both knew was a million miles from the reality, at least until they had qualified.

'Biddy told me earlier that the staff nurses aren't even starting until the theatres are up and running.'

'Oh, marvellous,' said Pammy. 'Once they arrive, we'll be getting bossed around by everyone, not just Sister Pokey. All we'll be doing for our training month on theatre is the cleaning. What else have we done so far? I can't wait for when that's over and we can move on to the next stage, but it won't be any day soon.'

'It's not so bad,' said Beth, who was determined to love theatre. 'Sister Pokey said that once the theatres are fully functioning, we can escort patients back to the ward with the porters. Won't that be wonderful, handing over post-op patients from our care, back to the wards.' She looked dreamy eyed.

Pammy shook her head. 'Thank God Sister Haycock has let me run between casualty and theatre. I'd go mad if I had to spend all my time up here. I have to admit, the first time

I washed down these lovely green tiles and matching floor, I did think it was wonderful. But we've done them that many times now, I will scream if I have to do them again tomorrow. It's all very well for Pokeynose to keep saying, "Practice makes perfect, nurses," but I don't need to practise tile washing. I've been helping me mam wash our house since I could walk.'

'Has the MP arrived yet?' asked Beth. 'I can hear lots of muttering in the anaesthetic area all of a sudden. I hope he isn't late. The last trolley from the old theatre has come over now and we have to go and swab down the walls in there next and then that's it. The old theatre won't ever be used as a theatre again. The doors are officially shut as of this morning. Right now St Angelus has no operating theatre, you know.'

'Oh, blimey,' said Pammy with a hint of alarm in her voice. 'Let's hope all is quiet, then, on the Mersey front.' She stood up from where she'd been crouching as she'd wiped the bottom of a large black oxygen bottle and walked over towards the window. 'Tell you what, I'm looking forward to Victoria getting back. I can't get Dana and Teddy out of my mind. I'm dying to hear what's up with Dana.'

'Me too,' said Beth. She also rose from her squatting position, retrieved her bucket, walked over to the long flat ceramic sink and began to tip the dirty water away, being careful not to splash any on the rubber apron she was wearing over her uniform. 'It is funny to think that not that long ago Teddy was being operated on in the theatre which has closed down, isn't it?'

Pammy was looking out through the crack at the bottom of the slightly open frosted-glass window. She saw a long black car cruise to a halt before the row of waiting porter's lads. 'Quick, here he comes. The MP. Would you get a load of that fancy car. Right, quick, put the buckets away and let's take our places.'

Removing their rubber aprons, Beth and Pammy adjusted their hair and caps and made their way into the main theatre, just as Matron and Sister Haycock walked in through the door.

Matron turned round with a gasp of 'Good Lord, he's early,' and raced back down the stairs.

Pammy noticed a smile pass between two of the board members already standing waiting inside the main theatre. Her Scouse instinct told her that something was not quite right. The taller of the two men was doing all the talking. His hair was slicked back and his shoes were gleaming. It was clear he was ex-army and from the top ranks of the officer class. His whole manner screamed 'major'. Dr Gaskell had been talking to him but left him abruptly to rush down the stairs after Matron.

Pammy took up her position as had been drilled into her a hundred times. She tilted her head ever so slightly to one side to hear the discussion taking place between the two men.

'His office called my secretary,' the major was saying, 'and told her he had been invited. I thought, darn and blast the woman. We want this rat-infested heap bulldozed and a smart new central hospital built instead. It used to be a workhouse, after all, and something to do with the slave trade before that. Not a part of our history this city is proud of. There are more cleared bombsites in the city centre than we could poke a stick at. We have to mark out our patch now. Matron is up to something, mark my words. We need to be one step ahead, and Gaskell, he's past it now. A good man, the best doctor, but time for him to hang up his boots and let the younger generation take over, don't you think, what?'

What on earth are they talking about, wondered Pammy. She tried to catch Biddy's eye but was unsuccessful as Biddy tried to make herself scarce and head towards the boardroom, where she was due to serve the tea, but even Pammy noticed Biddy had stopped, dead still. She had heard him too.

The shorter man was now responding. 'It's on the table for government funding. The MP is supportive of the idea of a bespoke brand-new hospital, although he has a soft spot for St Angelus because his own mother was once operated on here. He keeps wavering. Anyway, my secretary, she's an absolute whizz, she contacted his office and gave them a different time, to catch old Matron off guard. I got Gaskell to come early so that I could have a word with him. By God, he's a difficult nut to crack, but I think we could, with a bit of persuasion, get him onside. Who do we know who's a member of the golf club at Gateacre? Because that's the place to work on him, not here.'

'Oh, absolutely,' said the taller man. 'I'll get that organized. We will approach him from all sides. A bit of a pincer movement, what. He won't know what's hit him. Offer him a position, do it on the golf course, naturally, not in writing. And then, when the deed is done and we've got the government to sanction building the new hospital and bulldozing St Angelus, withdraw the offer. Happens all the time. Needs to be done. In Liverpool's best interests.'

The smaller man raised one eyebrow. 'You know, it could always be sold off as a building. Used as a school or a factory. A sad waste of money and effort, though, opening this new theatre. It won't be in operation for long, hopefully.'

The men ceased talking and silence fell as they all heard the clippety-clop of footsteps mounting the stairs. Matron had decided to begin her tour in the central theatre. From there they would proceed along the upstairs corridor to the boardroom, where a feast had been laid out on the polished table.

Pammy finally caught Biddy's eye and a message passed from one to the other. But Pammy was unsure of what it was. Instinctively, she inclined her head and swivelled her eyes towards the two men. Biddy gave her an almost imperceptible nod and the faintest smile lifted the corners of Pammy's mouth as she strained her ears. She knew exactly what it was Biddy wanted her to do.

'Ah, good morning, everyone.' The MP had almost burst into the theatre and now took in the assembled company.

Matron began her introductions. Pammy and Beth were the last in the line-up. 'Good morning, everyone. May I introduce Mr Maximillian Marcus, our local MP and the minister for health.'

Everyone began to applaud, although Pammy was not quite sure why. He was yet to say anything. They had been given explicit instructions to clap at the end of his speech, not at the beginning. They had also been told during the rehearsal the previous day that Mr Marcus might ask any one of them a question during the round of introductions and that it was important that there were representatives present from every side of hospital life. Once again, Emily Haycock had picked out her favourites to represent the student nurses. After the introductions had been made, Mr Marcus would be shown round the theatre suite and then he would address the gathered crowd before he retired to the boardroom for tea with Dr Gaskell, the board members and some of the consultants.

Pammy's mouth dried as he approached her and she prayed to God that he wouldn't ask her a question. It was a prayer in vain.

'And, this is Nurse Tanner. She is from Liverpool and her family are your constituents, I believe.' Matron beamed and Pammy gulped.

For a second, she almost panicked and she wondered, should she curtsey or something, had anyone else? And then, noticing the change in Matron's expression, which was clearly asking, have you lost your tongue, girl, Pammy blurted out, 'Er, hello, sir,' and she bent forwards in the most ridiculous manner and dropped an impromptu curtsey as she shook his hand.

Mr Marcus grinned benevolently. It was a reaction he was used to. 'Ah, my constituents? Tell me, where do your parents live and do you live in at the Lovely Lane home?'

Pammy did the honours and dived in. 'Oh, I do, sir. And my family, we are from Arthur Street.' She was nervous she had spoken out of turn, said too much, but when she turned to Matron, she was encouraged by a big smile.

'Ah, Arthur Street.' Mr Marcus also gave her a big smile. 'And tell me, do you enjoy working at St Angelus? Which wards have you worked on so far?'

'Well, my favourite ward, sir, was ward one, female surgical. I really enjoyed working with the ladies and it was very rewarding to see them get better – well, most of them – and return home to their families.'

The MP's face softened. 'That is wonderful to hear. That really is.'

Now there's a surprise, thought Pammy. He is actually really nice.

'My own mother was a patient on ward one,' Mr Marcus said. 'Before the war. My father's friend, the best man at his wedding, actually, was the surgeon. Mr Williamson. She was under him.'

'Before Nurse Tanner's time,' interjected Matron. 'Mr Williamson was an excellent surgeon. But then so are all our doctors and consultants. We demand nothing but the highest standard here.'

'Oh, indeed, Matron. My mother cannot say enough good things about St Angelus. And about you too, Matron. She told me over breakfast only this morning, when I mentioned that I was on my way to see you, how all the nurses used to tremble with fear when your ward rounds approached. She also has the greatest regard for Sister Crawford, who if I am not mistaken, is still terrifying probationer nurses.'

'She is sir, every day. We are all scared to death of her,' Pammy blurted out.

Matron almost had to stop herself from expiring with glee. This could not be going any better than if she had written a script. He had also not let the cat out of the bag, which was that his mother and Matron's late mother had been life-long friends.

'And Matron. Nothing's changed then, we are still terrified of Matron, sir, it's just how it is,' Pammy spoke again and then immediately wished she hadn't as she caught a glance from Matron which clearly said, *Enough thank you.*

As they were speaking, Beth noticed from the corner of her eye that Oliver Gaskell had stepped through the double swing doors. Bryan Delaney then slipped in behind him, laid a covered enamel tray down on the table and backed out without being seen by anyone but her. She also noticed how

Oliver Gaskell had let the swing door bang back on Bryan, almost knocking the tray out of his hand. But none of that mattered – not his arrogance or his bad manners. Just to be breathing the same air as him, in the same room, made her pulse quicken and her face flush with heat. But Beth was nobody's fool. Before he had even spotted her, she had turned her face towards the MP, who was beaming at her in a very odd way. She realized that she had missed his question, having been so determined not to look at Oliver Gaskell.

He asked again. 'And you, Nurse, what is your favourite ward?'

This time, Beth didn't have time to answer.

Everyone froze in horror as the light on the board lit up and the buzzer began to sound.

Sister Pokey didn't waste a second. 'Out, everyone!' she shouted. 'That is the new emergency call board.'

The wall-mounted telephone began to ring and as Beth was the nearest, she was there as quick as a flash, at the side of the phone, slightly unsure how to pick it up as she had never seen a wall-mounted phone before. Putting the handset to her ear, she said nervously, 'Hello, Nurse Harper speaking. Theatre.'

A confident voice came back down the line towards her. The words were chilling. 'Hello, Nurse Harper, it's Doreen in casualty. We have a post-partum haemorrhage in casualty, really bad. The houseman is rather anxious and wants her in theatre. He is with the patient, said to tell you he has packed her as tightly as he can with gauze wick and dressings, but it isn't working. He needs Mr Gaskell to operate and try and cauterize the bleeding. He thinks she may need an emergency hysterectomy. We are just trying to locate Dr Gaskell senior to tell him we need the theatres.'

'Oh, he's here,' Beth blurted out. 'Just hold on, please, I will fetch him. They are both here.'

As Beth turned around, Sister Pokey was behind her. 'It is my job to answer the telephone, Nurse Harper. I am Theatre Sister, this is my domain. However, thank you. I was rather obstructed.'

Beth looked round to see the last of the backs leaving through the main doors and out on to the corridor, being shepherded by Matron. Dessie had appeared and was holding open the doors for Biddy, who was exiting with a trolley.

'It's a post-partum haemorrhage,' Beth said to Sister Pokey. 'They are sending her straight up. Doreen wants to speak to Mr Gaskell.'

Oliver Gaskell had made to leave by the stairs, too impatient to wait for the dignitaries to file out at their own pace despite Matron trying desperately to hurry them along.

Sister Pokey was never going to allow a simple admission, albeit one that was life-threatening, to derail her. 'Mr Gaskell,' she shouted. Shouting along with running was expressly forbidden except in the case of a haemorrhage and that was exactly what this was. 'We have an emergency PPH on the way up. Nurse Harper, we need to lay out the instruments, autoclaving towels, gowns, swabs, gloves, wellingtons and masks. Dressing packs, Harrison curved-lip forceps, three buckets, sterilizing tablets, Spencer Well's, boiling water, stirrups, speculums – all three, to be safe – Hartmann's solution and blood. We need blood… I will lay the operating equipment myself.'

Sister Pokey barked out her instructions and for a moment Beth froze. She felt fear grip her from the nape of her neck to her toes and she couldn't move.

'Yes, Sister.' She heard the words ring out in military fashion, but she hadn't spoken, it was Pammy, who had come up behind her and was none too gracefully prodding Beth in the back.

'Yes, Sister,' said Beth.

But Sister Pokey wasn't really listening. She was almost running alongside Oliver Gaskell to the theatre door to greet Dessie and Nurse Makebee from casualty, who were pushing a trolley. A sheet covered the trolley and Beth saw that blood had dripped along the floor in its wake.

'How old?' she heard Oliver Gaskell ask Nurse Makebee.

'Thirty-six, Mr Gaskell. She's an elderly primigravida. First husband died in the war. New marriage, husband is waiting downstairs. She tried to deliver a ten-pound baby at home, but her husband could see that things weren't going well and brought her in here in the side-car on his motorbike. The houseman used forceps in casualty, there was just no time to get her on to the ward. It was all pretty brutal. The houseman is on his way up to assist, sent me on ahead. He is just helping the husband. The poor man fainted flat out, smacked his skull on the radiator and has a head injury. Said he hadn't seen so much blood since '41...'

'Right, let's get to work.' Oliver Gaskell was efficient and focused as he pulled back the covers on the trolley. 'No point in removing the packing until we have her on the table. It isn't doing much, but it is definitely doing something. Buying us a few minutes at the very least. Hurry! We need blood. Nurse, run – and I mean run – and fetch the emergency blood from path lab. Now! Do you know where it's kept, if there's no one there?'

'Yes, Mr Gaskell. On the bottom shelf in the big fridge just as you go in through the door. I've fetched it before.'

Without another word, Nurse Makebee turned on her heel and ran towards the stairs. But she had no need to run any further as the houseman raced through the door carrying three bottles of blood in his arms. 'It's cold,' he said. 'Too cold.'

'Let me worry about that,' Oliver Gaskell replied tersely. 'Too cold is infinitely better than none at all.'

Trolleys rolled, oxygen bottles were wheeled into place, the anaesthetist arrived and everyone swung into action. The atmosphere was quite different from on the wards, Beth thought. It almost felt as if it wasn't really an emergency at all. Everything was so deathly quiet. No background chatter from thirty other patients. No nurses talking, trolleys trundling, curtains swiftly being pulled across. No domestics cleaning, bedpans clanging, phones ringing or visitors arriving.

The quiet was broken only by the sound of the anaesthetist shouting, 'God, where is the Pentothal kept? Oxygen, ET tube. Has this flow meter been tested?' He flicked a flow meter on the top of a blue gas bottle and Beth flinched. She had no idea what the answers were. 'Help me, I don't know where anything is in here. Has anyone tested the cylinders yet? Is there any Entonox? I went to the old theatres by mistake.' He seemed agitated.

Beth reached out, grabbed hold of the anaesthetics trolley she had practised loading and unloading earlier and kicked on the brake. She pushed the new chrome-and-green-leather stool towards the anaesthetist.

'Thank you,' he said as, without looking at her, he began pulling open the drawers and taking out the glass syringes, needles and glass phials. 'Where are the theatre nurses?' he asked as he began to draw up a syringe.

Beth picked up the tape, cut off three lengths and stuck them to the rail of the trolley for him to use.

'Thank you very much, Nurse,' he said and cast a quick glance around the theatre.

Beth swallowed hard before she spoke. 'I think the regular theatre nurses were given the day off after working so hard emptying out the old theatres.'

'Marvellous,' said the anaesthetist. 'Bloody marvellous. I hope you are up to it then, Nurse...' He dipped his head and over the top of his glasses glanced at her name badge. '... Harper.' Then he turned his attention back to the trolley and snapped the glass tops off three small bottles.

Oliver Gaskell was on his way into the scrub room and Beth could sense that at the mention of her name he had turned his head. The door to the room banged. The anaesthetist looked over at it and whispered to her, 'No time for me to scrub up, I'm afraid. We don't have long enough.'

Silence fell again and Sister Pokey barked out an order. It didn't go unnoticed by Beth or Pammy that she was as white as a sheet. It had been Sister Pokey's idea to let her precious theatre nurses have the extra day off as a reward.

'Nurse Harper, into the scrub room with Mr Gaskell. Help him with his gown and mask and make sure he has a towel and that his rubber apron is well tied at the back.'

Beth stared at Sister Pokey. She couldn't.

'Go, now!' Sister Pokey shouted.

She had no choice. She had to enter the scrub room. The taps were running and water was splashing all over the steamed-up mirror and the tiles as she walked in.

'Gown,' was the only thing he said, but his eyes were fixed on her in the mirror as she crossed the floor.

She took a deep breath, lifted her gaze and stared back. She knew where the gowns were, she had folded them and stacked them herself. 'Size?' It was a necessary question. She should have put a 'Mr Gaskell' and a 'please' on the end, but she felt that the familiarity and open appraisal of his stare had removed the need to follow convention. She just hoped he didn't think it had been her decision to help him in the scrub room.

'Large. Please.'

Beth thanked God she could reach the gowns. Putting her hand straight on a large size, she ripped open the autoclave paper and held the pack out for him to remove the gown with his sterile hands.

'You have no time to scrub up, but you will need to assist,' he said. 'Unless Sister Pokey is doing it. Just wash your hands in the chlorhexidine, very quickly. We only have a few minutes.'

Beth didn't reply but hurriedly washed her hands. As he turned towards her, she took the towel he held out and wiped them dry.

'Could you tie me up, please?' He turned his back towards her and before he had finished drying, he was out of the door and back into theatre. But not before he had looked her straight in the eye and left her in no doubt she had been noticed.

Sister Pokey was ripping open packets and letting the contents spill on to the trolley. The theatre instruments gleamed and were fanned out like place settings at a formal dinner. Pammy was with the patient, taking her pulse and blood pressure.

'Tie Mr Gaskell's face mask on, please, Nurse Harper,' Sister Pokey said.

Beth hesitated, but only for a second, and the only person

to notice was Oliver Gaskell. As she took the mask from his hand and fastened it, his skin felt hot beneath her fingers and then in an instant it turned clammy. He's nervous, Beth thought. She was nervous too. They had all been taken unawares. The atmosphere was palpably tense.

'Her blood pressure is dropping.' Pammy's voice cut through the air. 'It's been holding at one hundred over sixty, but it's just dropped to a systolic of eighty and I can't detect the diastolic.' There was a hint of panic in her voice. 'No, I've lost that now. It's lower.'

Pammy looked down at the woman. Her face was as white as the sheet upon which she lay and cold droplets of perspiration covered her face. Her hands were damp and cold and her eyes flickered open.

'My baby, where is he?' she asked Pammy.

But there was no time for Pammy to answer as the anaesthetist said, 'Quickly, here, please. Fast.'

The patient was lifted on to the operating trolley with little ceremony or dignity. The urgency of the moment took precedence. The sound of gas hissing from a tall canister filled the theatre and the anaesthetist placed the black rubber mask over the patient's face even before she had been eased into position.

'We can use this while you remove the packing and do what you can. I will never get a vein now,' he snapped. And then, 'She's in complete peripheral shutdown,' which was muttered more to himself than anyone else. 'I'm going to have to do a venous cutdown,' he said to Oliver Gaskell, who was pulling the light down by the long shiny chrome arm.

'Right, let's try this light,' Mr Gaskell said, reaching his hand up.

The air sizzled with static as the bulbs flashed into life and the room filled with the brightest light. Pammy was busy hooking up the new blood to a giving set, ready to hand to the anaesthetist who was struggling to find a vein to use and, looking at Beth, she shook her head in dismay. He was failing. Beth wondered who was the whiter, Pammy or the woman. Everyone in the room knew that the chance of this woman ever setting eyes on the face of her baby were almost zero. Suddenly the anaesthetist shouted, 'Eureka, pass me the cannula,' and without a second's hesitation, Pammy slapped it in his hand. Within seconds, the giving set was opened on to full and Pammy and Beth both watched in awe as the blood ran through on full, into the empty veins. Beth stood by Oliver Gaskell's side, holding on to a large kidney dish, waiting to receive the bloodied packing.

He took the forceps from Sister Pokey and began to tease away the end of the wick from the now congealed mess. 'No time to waste,' he said almost to himself. Beads of perspiration stood proud on his brow and his top lip. As the packing came away, the patient's blood fired out and hit his gown with force, pumping with the rhythm of her weakening heartbeat and filling the theatre with the familiar smell of metal. This was it. They were hovering somewhere in the void between life and death and in the splinter of a second, fate would make its call. Beth felt her own heart pounding five times as fast in her chest and she whispered a prayer. Please, God, save her. Without her knowing, Pammy had just done exactly the same. What else could they do? Oliver Gaskell would do his best, but if too much blood had been lost, if she was already in shock, if they couldn't get the cold blood in fast enough, if they couldn't find the source of the bleeding and stop it right now, if she had an adverse reaction to the cold blood, if it was her time… If fate was cruel.

The two young friends exchanged despairing glances, all too aware that between them lay a new mother, whose life was fading fast.

Chapter 7

Finn Delaney flew down George Street as fast as his legs would carry him – so fast that he slipped on the moss-covered cobbles in the north-facing entry. Landing on both knees, he skidded on for another yard or so before coming to an agonizing halt. His screams from the scalding pain ripped through the air.

Maisie Tanner was not far behind him. She was returning home from the butcher's, carrying potatoes and a scrag end of lamb in a string bag over her arm. 'Oh, Finn, come here, love. Are you all right?'

She dropped her bag to the ground and helped Finn to his feet, trying to restrain him from jumping up and down and yelling ever more loudly. Taking her handkerchief out of her coat pocket, she spat on it, held his arm, bent down and tried to take aim with her linen and spittle. His knees were crusted in black dust and blood began bubbling through the grit and grime in several places. It seeped through and slowly dribbled down his shins towards his long socks, which were now bunched in folds around his ankles.

Finn could not stand still because of the pain and he began hopping from foot to foot, screaming at the top of his voice. 'Mam! Mam!'

'You poor love, what a mess.' Maisie scored a hit with her handkerchief and managed to brush some of the compacted dirt away from one of the knees. There was no skin left beneath and the blood now flowed unhindered down his leg. 'We need the iodine on that, Finn. Oh Lord, where are our kids when you need them?'

Finn had stopped screaming for a moment and was looking at his knee with fear on his face.

'Come on, Finn, let's try and get you up. You haven't died, have you?'

Just then, Lorraine and Mary turned the corner into the entry, both running, having been alerted by the screams. The screams intensified at the sight of the girls approaching.

'Oh, thank goodness. Here we go, girls. Lorraine, take my shopping in and put it on the press. Start chopping an onion and peel those spuds. Mary, help me get your Finn home, he's in a right mess.'

Mary was alarmed both by the sight of Finn's blood and by the volume of his screams. Somewhere within, unfamiliar sisterly concern was stirring. 'Is he going to be all right, Maisie? He's not going to die, is he?'

'I doubt it, love,' Maisie said distractedly. 'Come here, Finn. Hold your breath. Oh God, look at the state of your socks. Hope your mam has a clean pair dry.'

A look of panic flitted across Mary's face, and if Maisie had had the time, she would have laughed. 'Oh, my giddy aunt. No, of course not. Of course he's not going to die.'

It suddenly occurred to Maisie that Noleen might not have any iodine in the house. Most did, but Noleen struggled more than most. 'Our Lorraine...' She lifted her head to project her voice over the back-yard wall. 'Lorraine, forget the spuds.

Get the iodine out of our bathroom cabinet and follow me down to Noleen's.' That's put me right out with the tea now, she thought. They'll all just have to wait.

The journey was slow. Finn was in agony and refused to put his weight on his poorly leg, so he hopped all the way. One hand on the entry wall, the other clinging on to Maisie.

Maisie tutted and huffed and puffed. 'Come on, lad, not far now. Nearly there. Another ten hops and we've made it.' If this had happened a bit later in the day, she would have knocked on the nearest back door and got one of the men to give Finn a piggyback home. But the klaxon was yet to ring. The men were still down on the docks and the air was still busy with the sound of cranes lifting the jute from the holds of incoming ships and the horns of the tugs that guided them in and out.

'How often do we tell you kids not to run on those George Street cobbles?' she said. 'They've always been treacherous. Even with no houses on one side, the sun never gets over that wall.' Maisie was referring to the houses that had taken a hit during the war and were no longer standing. The entry down the back of George Street was known as the rat run to and from St Chad's school for the kids who lived in Vince Street.

Finn wasn't listening. The pain in his legs was the worst he had ever known and his sobs, punctuated by 'Mam, Mam,' filled the air.

'Never cries for me, does he?' said Mary to Maisie, 'and I'm the one who's here.'

'There, there, love, we're in your entry now. Not far and then we're there.'

Lorraine had caught them up and held out a brown ribbed bottle for Maisie to inspect. 'Mam, is this it?'

'That's the one, love,' said Maisie as she comforted Finn in her motherly manner. They still had the entire length of the entry to walk and Finn knew it.

Mary looked ahead and noticed Lorcan slipping through the Ryans' back door. 'Lorcan, Lorcan,' she shouted. 'Here, would you give Auntie Maisie a hand?'

Lorcan pulled his cap tighter down on to his head, in case it should fall off, and sprinted towards them.

'Our Finn's cut his leg.'

Finn looked embarrassed. Suddenly the pain didn't feel so bad and he placed the foot of his injured leg on the ground. 'Shut up, our Mary. I'm fine. What did you do that for?' His face turned bright red as he tried to wipe away his tears from his dirt-stained face, mortified that Lorcan could see he had been crying.

Lorcan pretended not to notice. 'Come on here, Finn. Hup.' He bent over with his hands on his knees.

'Oh, isn't that smashing,' Maisie said. 'You are a good lad, Lorcan. Not like your lazy, thieving, good-for-nothing brothers. Finn, come on, hup, on Lorcan's back. I'll help.'

And before Finn could object, Maisie, Lorraine and Mary had lifted him up on to Lorcan's back, who, gathering Finn behind the knees, being careful to avoid the grazed fronts, linked his arms, shouted, 'Hold on!' and galloped down the entry towards the Delaneys' house.

'You wouldn't think that Lorcan came from the same parents as the other lads, would you?' Maisie said to Mary. 'Look how fast he runs. Mind you, they were all good runners, even with their arms full of knockoff stuff from down the docks. Never saw a Ryan break his pace no matter how much he was carrying. Could outrun any of the bizzies on the docks.'

Lorcan had disappeared into the Delaneys' house before she'd finished speaking and silence descended on the entry now that Finn was no longer screaming. All that could be heard was the rattle of the dark green chipped wooden gate as it clicked shut and the meowing of the hungry ginger tomcat who was staring down at Maisie from the top of the entry wall.

'Someone needs to shoot that cat,' she said. 'There must be a hundred of his little buggers running round the entry. Pulled my bin out of the wall last night they did.'

'Mam, I can't believe you just said that.' Lorraine looked upset. 'How could you? You had better go to confession and tell Father Brennan you said that, and if you don't, I'll tell him meself. All God's creatures, we are.'

Maisie sighed in exasperation. 'Out of my way now, Lorraine,' she said as the back door of the Delaneys' house flew open and a tired-looking Noleen ran into the yard, drying her hands on her floral wrap-around apron. Her hair was in curlers, under her headscarf, ready to be removed before Mass on her way to work.

'God in heaven, thank goodness you were there. Lorcan told me,' said Noleen. 'The lad's a prize idiot. There isn't a brain cell in his head. I tell him every day, "Finn, don't run down that entry."'

'I know, love. He's a boy, they just don't listen. I've brought a bottle of iodine with me, just in case you had run out and the chemist will be closed now.'

Noleen sat Finn on the wooden draining board in the scullery and pressed his head into her chest while she ran the cold water fast and tried to splash his knees to remove the grit. But every time even a drop of water went near his wound, he screamed the kitchen down. His snot smeared the front of Noleen's apron as he tried to escape.

'I'll make some tea,' said Maisie. Both women knew that once Finn was alone with Noleen and had had five minutes to adjust, he would begin to calm down.

As his sobs became pitiful moans, Paddy shouted from the kitchen, 'What's up, Noleen? Bring him in here.'

Twenty minutes later, the Delaneys' kitchen was full of wide-eyed children from almost every house in the street. This was a drama. Finn was sitting on the settle next to Paddy and Noleen was on her knees with a chipped enamel dish, white with a navy-blue rim, beside her. It was brimming with gritty, bloody water.

'Change that water, please, Mary,' said Noleen. 'Quick.'

Maisie was standing at the range, mashing the tea. 'Where's our Pammy when you need her, eh?' she said. 'We need Nurse Pammy here, don't we, Finn. She would have that knee fixed in no time.'

'I think I can manage cut knees, thank you very much,' said Noleen. There was a terseness in her voice, put there by concern for her son and the suggestion that someone else could bathe his knee better than she could. Pammy couldn't bless the water with tenderness and love, that was a mother's job.

Maisie caught the edge in Noleen's voice and glanced her way. Noleen immediately felt guilty. She had known Maisie Tanner all of her married life. When Lorraine had been born in the air-raid shelter, prematurely, Noleen had taken food to the house and helped with Maisie's mam, who appeared to lose her mind overnight, unable to accept the fact that half a street had been bombed, taking the people she had known all of her life with it. In the weeks that followed, Noleen had bathed Pammy and the boys and put them to bed while Maisie nursed little Lorraine as she hovered on the edge of survival.

'But I am really grateful to you for bringing him home, Maisie. And you, Lorcan. Aren't we, Paddy? I bet it's put you behind with your jobs, Maisie.'

Paddy passed Lorcan the plate of biscuits that was being handed around the silent, observant children. On the dock side streets, drama was a spectator sport. 'We are that,' he said. 'Your Pammy has really sick people to look after in St Angelus, Maisie, not a pair of knobbly knees like our Finn's. She'd be wasted on your knees, wouldn't she, lad? Knots on cotton, our Finn's knees are.' He was trying to make Finn smile and he succeeded. 'There you go, Finn. Feeling a bit better, are you now?'

Finn nodded reluctantly and gave his dad a shy smile. He wiped his dripping nose with the back of his hand and shoved a broken custard cream in his mouth. The kids from the street who were sitting watching him smiled in relief. Finn was going to live. None of them was yet aware that the worst was about to come.

'Are you ready?' asked Maisie with a wink to Noleen as she pulled the knitted tea cosy over the pot.

'As ready as we'll ever be,' said Noleen, who glanced at Finn. 'You ready, Paddy?' she asked, nodding towards Finn's arms.

The atmosphere in the room had taken on a new tension and the assembled children felt it. Concern crossed their faces as they looked at each other and then to Maisie. No more words were needed, something awful was about to happen.

Lorraine had been in enough scrapes to know what. But little Stanley, Maisie's son, had a shorter memory. He turned towards his mother, half a broken lemon puff in one hand and a garibaldi in the other. 'Ready for what?'

'What's that smell, Mam?' Cahill asked Noleen as he walked in through the back door and wrinkled his nose. 'Is our Finn dead? Mrs Murphy in the shop said he was dying with the pain.'

'Can someone tell me how that woman even knows?' said Maisie, exasperated. 'Here you go, love.' She passed the opened brown-ribbed poisons bottle to Noleen, who held a roll of cotton wool in her hand.

The assembled children inhaled in unison. Now they'd smelt it, they knew it, and the awful thing that was coming.

'Mary, Lorraine, would you come here and when I say blow, blow hard.'

Finn looked up and asked, 'Why, Mam?' As a boy who spent more time with books than playing football on the bombed-out wasteland, he had no idea what was coming.

'Cahill, you too,' said Paddy. He shuffled along the settle. Mary, Lorraine and Cahill stood to the side as Paddy placed one hand on each of Finn's shoulders and Maisie stepped forward and placed the palms of her hands on Finn's thighs.

'Just a little sting, Finn,' said Noleen as she teased the cotton wool into two, tipped up the brown bottle and turned the snowy-white pads a bright yellowy brown.

The clinical smell became stronger and filled the space. There wasn't a child there who didn't know what came next. The air ran from the room as, before Finn could object, each child breathed in hard.

'Get ready to blow, kids,' said Noleen as she placed the pads firmly down on to both of Finn's knees.

His screams were so ear-piercingly loud, they could be heard out in the entry. Fifteen children blew and blew into the air, not knowing why but aware that the blowing somehow helped with the stinging. Then silence followed as Finn fainted clean away.

Mrs Ryan was dozing in front of the fire. She had been dozing most of the day, on and off. She wasn't terribly sure what the time was and as she woke she looked around the room in a state of confusion. An aroma she was unused to hit her. It was the smell of cleanliness. The familiar stench of urine, smoke-stained curtains and a-dozen-times-fried fat had been replaced by soap and Dettol. The greasy grime on the windows had been cleaned away and the light shone through into the normally dark and dingy kitchen. The sink was clean and the table scrubbed, and the usual detritus of piled-up stale food, dirty dishes and newspapers had disappeared. She looked down at the floor and the quarry tiles beneath her feet were brown, not black.

Like the Mersey mist on a summer's morning, her befuddled brain began to clear. 'I haven't drunk gin today. Do I have any? Do I?' she asked herself.

She spotted her black woollen stockings, washed and hanging on the wooden clothes horse in front of the range. 'Ah, Lorcan,' she said out loud. Now she knew. It was Lorcan, that's who it was. And she remembered, he had been cleaning for days, or was it weeks?

The clock on the mantelpiece chimed and startled her, just as the back door opened. She couldn't remember the last time she had wound the clock. At her side, the range was freshly blackened and polished. She ran her finger along its top. 'Fancy,' she said.

Lorcan strode into the kitchen.

'Lorcan,' she croaked. 'Lorcan, would you look at the cut of you in yer fancy overalls and boots. Will you be buying me a jug of Guinness from the pub, lad? Have ye any wage yet?'

There was no reply. Mrs Ryan had completely forgotten that Lorcan had told her he would be playing pool at the Silvestrian. He had been beside himself with excitement that Jake himself had invited him. He'd told her all about it the previous evening.

'Mam, I told you. I'm away to play pool with Jake and the other lads from the hospital. I've been helping Mrs Delaney with her Finn. He fell and cut himself really bad, thought I might have to go back to work with him to the casualty, but he'll live. Mrs Delaney and Mrs Tanner fixed him up.'

He'd already told her a dozen times that he was going out, but she was only ever half paying attention. She was more interested in the cats who crawled out from under her chair.

'How did we end up with four cats in the house, Lorcan? For the life of me, I only remember us having one, I'm sure. Was it you? Did you bring them in?'

'I don't know Mam. They aren't ours.'

Only yesterday he'd had to clean up their stink outside. The smell of cat pee had stung his nostrils when he'd arrived home from work. So he'd gone out and thrown two buckets of scalding water over the back-yard cobbles. Now that he was working at the hospital, he knew from the other lads that Dessie could call round to the house at any time. What they hadn't told him was that it was the homes where Dessie felt the lad was not being properly looked after that got called at most frequently. Lorcan knew he would be ashamed if Dessie had smelt the yard. He was a working lad now and

Dessie believed in him, trusted him. This had imbued in Lorcan a new-found determination to clean the place up, now that his brothers were all gone. With the Lysol he had brought home from the hospital, and a lot of hot water, he would expunge the memory of his troublemaking brothers from his life.

'You should stop letting the cats into the house to settle in front of the fire. They are full of fleas.' He bent down, picked up two of them from in front of the hearth by the scruff of their necks, opened the back-yard gate and put them out into the entry. He knew asking his mother not to let the cats in was futile. They were kittens, only weeks old, and had already worked out that if they hung around the Ryans' back door they wouldn't get hit with a mop head if they tried to run in when it was opened.

Lorcan looked down at the wriggling bundles of orange fur in the entry and the sight tugged at his heart. 'Oh, here,' he said. Picking them back up, he returned them to the kitchen, fetched a bowl of watered-down steri milk and placed it near the hearth. He would have to make washing down the yard a regular thing. He would do it with his wash water when he got home, and he would try and get his mother to do the same. There had been a time, once, when his mam had been just like Mrs Delaney and Mrs Tanner, but when was that?

Mrs Ryan's face lit up. 'Did you clean the floor, Lorcan? Was it you?' She looked astonished.

'I did, Mam. I did a bit more when you were sleeping in the chair last night.' He had been cleaning every night, but this was the first time his mother had noticed.

'Well now, isn't that grand. What a good boy you are, Lorcan.' She leant forward in her chair, gazed down around her feet, clasped her hands in her lap in delight and studied the tiles as though the most beautiful tropical fish were swimming by. 'I used to do that, you know, Lorcan. Mop the floor.' Her voice became wistful. 'I don't think that floor has been washed since the day the telegram came. You know, the one about Daddy falling.'

Lorcan wanted to reply that he had guessed that was the case. It had taken him two hours and a large knife he had borrowed from Paddy Delaney to remove the thick layer of black grime.

'It looks so nice, I might give it a wash over meself soon. Keep it nice, like.'

Lorcan could hardly believe what his mother was saying. 'Would you, Mam?'

'Aye, Lorcan, I will. Help me get up out of this chair, will you. I don't recognize me own house. Isn't that just the thing now.'

She stood and Lorcan looked on nervously as she picked up each item on the press, examined it as though she had never seen it before and laid it back down. She held the figurine of Our Lady in her hand for the longest time of all and studied the plasterwork face intently. 'We bought this in Knock, you know, Daddy and me. Before you were born, Lorcan. We was full of the big ideas then, so we were.'

Lorcan thought now was as good a moment as any to make his suggestion. 'Mam, will you come to Clare Street with me, for a bath? I've been going myself.'

There was a long silence and Lorcan held his breath. His mam smelt bad. How could he turn things around unless she helped him? He wanted to show her that life didn't have to be the way she was living it. He wanted to bring a little of what he had seen at Biddy's and Mrs Delaney's house into his own, knowing in his heart that if he did, his mother might wake up from the melancholy that had seized her for so long.

She turned from the press and smiled. 'Aye, I might. Daddy used to go himself every Sunday night with the other men, while I bathed you and your brothers in front of the fire.'

She watched Lorcan pick up a discarded gin bottle from the hearth and put it away into a clean bucket he was obviously using as a bin. She looked around her house and she liked what she saw. It reminded her of other days, before she'd fallen into a gloom she'd found impossible to shake off. She had felt so overwhelmed that she had slipped under the surface of her own life, drowning first in grief, then in panic, unable to break back through. Most of her neighbours had coped, but she hadn't. She had fallen herself, in the midst of the bombs, just as her husband had. At times she had wanted to never get back up. But now she was emerging and someone was helping her and that someone was her own son.

Mrs Ryan looked into the expectant eyes of her son with his scrubbed-clean face and his combed-back hair. 'Aye, I will, Lorcan. I will. Let's go now, not tomorrow. Now, will we?'

An hour after Finn had recovered, Noleen was standing in front of the fire, peering into the mirror that hung above the mantelpiece. It was almost black with age and foxing, and a crack ran across the middle from when it had fallen off the wall when the George Street bomb hit. She removed her rollers one by one, placing them in the green lustre rose bowl she and Paddy had been given as a wedding present. The mantelpiece was the closest Noleen would ever have to a dressing table. Her lipstick, powder, hairspray, figurine of Our Lady and bowl of curlers served as ornaments. When she did her housework, they were all subjected to a quick flick with a damp duster, along with every other surface in the house.

The fainting Finn show was over, the audience had left and her family were settled into their familiar evening routine before she left for Mass and then work.

Paddy poked the fire and a shower of sparks flew up.

'Holy Mother, Paddy, you nearly burnt me legs. Can't you wait until I'm done? I will be two minutes.'

Noleen looked into the mirror. Mary was sitting on the floor at Paddy's feet with her ear to the radio as she twisted the dial.

'What are you up to, Mary?' asked Paddy, trying to hide his irritation. He hated it when the kids played with the radio. They could only afford a new battery every now and then. He had learnt how to give the battery a bit of extra life by warming it up on the range for ten minutes, but there was a fine art to knowing when it was the right heat without it then exploding in your face.

'I'm trying to find something that sounds like music and not old men talking,' replied Mary, in a huff. 'I don't want to hear people droning on all the time. War, drone, war, drone, drone, drone. We get enough of that from you,' she said, looking up at Paddy, who now smiled down indulgently and ruffled the hair on the top of his daughter's head.

Jack and Cahill were sitting at the table. Jack was reading a comic he had been given by little Stan, and Cahill was patiently waiting for him to finish so that he could read it next. Finn was lying on the settle opposite Paddy, reading a school book. His bright yellow knees were carefully arranged to be free of contact with anything other than the air, which was about all he could bear to have touching the throbbing, inflamed areas.

'How are your knees, Finn?' asked Noleen. Her comment was made through the mirror as, flinching and with her lips pursed, she tugged on a tangled roller. 'Has the Disprin worked?'

Finn looked up and nodded as his eyes filled. The truth was, the pain was almost unbearable. He turned his face towards his da, who saw his tears.

'Do you want a cuddle, lad?' Paddy asked.

Under normal circumstances, Mary, Jack and Cahill would have made much comment about Finn being a cry-baby, but as it was, they sympathized with him. Mary had brought her pillow down from upstairs to place under his head. Jack had offered him the comic first. Cahill had taken the boiled sweet that Maisie Tanner had given him out of her pocket and handed it to Finn with a grand statement. 'I want you to have it. I thought you were only going to have one leg left, like Daddy.' A look of horror had crossed Finn's face as he placed the sweet in his mouth.

Paddy propelled himself across to the settle and pulled Finn up and on to his lap, ignoring the pain in his stump as he did so.

Noleen's heart melted with pity as she saw the pained expression of her very serious son, who, under normal circumstances, wouldn't say boo to a goose. He usually had no idea of the time and needed to be reminded to eat and sleep. Tonight he could do nothing but stare at his book and flinch when he moved. She knelt down in front of the settle and placed her own hand on his back. She and Paddy glanced into each other's eyes and a look of tenderness passed between them. Both would gladly have taken on their son's pain. There was not a thing within their power that they would not do for their children.

'How many times have you been told not to run down that entry, Finn,' she said as she rubbed his back. 'The cobbles are covered in moss, it's lethal. Mrs Samson broke her hip just where you fell only a few weeks ago and she's still in St Angelus.'

'I know, Ma, but I had something to tell you.' Finn turned his head to face Noleen as he wiped the tears away with the back of his hand. For a second, excitement had flashed across his face. But it disappeared as quickly as it had arrived and he buried his head back into his da's chest to hide the fresh onslaught of tears.

'What was so urgent, Finn, that you had to run like a mad man, eh?' asked Paddy with a coaxing softness to his voice. 'Was it to tell me about the library opening on Waterloo Street, because, Jesus, don't we know about that already, you tell me every day.'

Finn muttered something, which neither Paddy nor Noleen could make out through the wool of Paddy's sweater.

'What's that, lad?' Paddy leant back, cleared his jumper from Finn's face and turned him slightly towards Noleen.

Finn sniffed loudly and Noleen took a handkerchief out of her apron pocket, spat on it and wiped his eyes and nose. 'Come on, Finn, you're killing me with the suspense. What was it you wanted to tell me? Are you in trouble in school? Have you been driving Sister Theresa to the end of her tether?'

Finn looked horrified at the mere suggestion that he might

have misbehaved in class. He loved Sister Theresa. He worked hard and wallowed in her daily praise. His tears forgotten, he exclaimed, 'No, Mam. Sister Theresa said I had to tell you that I passed the eleven-plus. She got a letter this morning and, Mam, you have to go up to the school because she has me a place at Waterloo Grammar where they have a room full of books and teachers who wear capes and hats and all the kids who go to that school, they become rich.'

A look of dismay crossed Noleen's face.

'They do, Mam, it's the truth. Sister Theresa, she told me. And Father Brennan, he said he wants to talk to you at Mass tonight. He said he was very proud of me. Sister, she wants to give you the list of everything I need so that I can start in September. She said I'm the first from St Chad's to get a place at Waterloo Grammar. Made up with me, she is.' The excitement had returned to his voice and eyes. For the moment his pain was entirely forgotten.

Noleen stared at Finn and then looked up at Paddy, her eyes pleading for help. She was confused. 'Are you sure, Finn? You haven't sat an exam, have you?'

'You passed it,' Paddy said in amazement as he leant back and gazed down at Finn. 'How?'

'I don't know, Da, I just did.'

'What exam?' asked Noleen again. 'You knew, Paddy?'

Paddy looked embarrassed. 'I did, but I didn't think he would pass it, did I. How was I to know?'

'Are you sure, Finn? You aren't lying to me, are you? Because if you are, I will march you into Sister Theresa's office myself tomorrow,' said Noleen. 'You might have sore knees at the front, but it'll be a hot bottom at the back if you are lying to me. I won't have it.'

Finn struggled to sit upright. 'No, Mam. No, no.' He sounded desperate to be believed. 'Ask Sister Theresa if you don't believe me. She wants to see you up at the school.'

Noleen's heart had dipped like a stone. If Finn was to attend Waterloo Grammar, he would need shoes, books, a uniform, not to mention the bus fare every week – it was much too far to walk. It was impossible. It could never happen.

'Well, Finn, that's unexpected, that really is. You're a clever lad, that's for sure. But the Lord alone knows how we're ever going to pay to get you there.' She shot a worried look at Paddy.

Finn began to cry again.

'There, there, don't cry, never mind,' said Noleen. 'It's not the end of the world, is it? I'm sure there's something can be done. You can't help it, can you.'

Every penny was spoken for. Unlike her neighbours, she had no five shillings a week to put by for the Christmas club at the butcher's. She wished to God she did. There was often not enough to make it through until Friday. 'It's not the end of the world,' she said again, almost to herself this time. But as the room fell quiet once more, it felt to her as though that was exactly what it was.

Emily Haycock sat at the table in Dessie's kitchen writing out a very long list. The kitchen was exactly the same as the kitchens in every other house on Arthur Street. Exactly the same as the one in the house on George Street where she'd been born and had grown up; the house that had been bombed into the ground while her sick mother and young brothers were still inside. As she looked about Dessie's kitchen, it occurred to her that falling in love with Dessie had been made even easier because moving into his house had been like coming home. From the bedroom window she could see the place where her old home had once stood. The wasteland remained untouched, covered in rubble, used as a football pitch by the children of Arthur and Vince streets. It echoed daily to the sound of children playing.

The old scullery, which contained the Belfast sink and a copper boiler, opened off the kitchen, close to the back door, and in houses with no children was used only on washdays. In every house it took the same number of steps to get from the back gate to the back door, across the same sets of cobbles, via the same black wrought-iron latch on the same dark-green painted door. She had moved from home to home.

The only other downstairs room in the house was the parlour, facing on to the front street. A room Dessie had not even used once since he had returned from the war. Emily had changed all that, insisting that in the evenings they close the curtains, light the fire and make a home of the room whose walls were covered in tea-coloured wallpaper adorned with fading brown peony roses. A standard lamp stood by the leather armchair, with tassels and fringes stained by nicotine to the same colour as the brown peonies. Dessie's parlour was now used more frequently in a single week than the parlours on any of the nearby streets were in a whole year.

The brown staining was down to the fact that the house hadn't been decorated since the day Dessie had moved in with his late wife in 1935. The kitchen walls were equally as bad. They were painted in a coffee-coloured gloss to about Emily's shoulder height, and then up to the ceiling it was cream-coloured gloss. Or at least it had once been cream.

Even though she had washed the walls down, twice – the second time to remove the brown rivulets left from the first time – it had made little difference. From the centre of the ceiling hung a brown corded rope wire supporting a desultory bayonet light bulb. The lino on the floor had worn away in most areas, revealing either black lino or the quarry tiles beneath, but Emily could just make out that the design had once featured a large pattern of golden autumnal oak leaves against a dark brown background. She looked down and sighed. 'You are disgusting,' she whispered. 'Autumn leaves look good on trees, not on the kitchen floor.'

She laid down her pen and sat back in the chair just as Dessie walked in wearing his trousers but no shirt. Since Emily had moved in, he'd taken to having his evening wash down in the scullery instead of the kitchen. He flopped into the threadbare bottle-green chair in front of the range and as he bent forward to lace up his boots he glanced over at her.

'Is that another list?' he asked. 'Will it be joining the other dozen or so on the press? I've never known anyone who can make as many lists as you.'

Ignoring his question, Emily pointedly looked around the room. 'Dessie, have you seen the state of this kitchen? When we do marry, were you actually thinking of carrying me over the threshold into this?'

Dessie looked affronted and followed her gaze around the kitchen. 'Why, what do you mean? What's wrong with it?' He didn't give her the chance to reply. 'Oh, I know what you're on about. It's those brown walls. Well, let me tell you, there's a reason I did them in gloss, it's so you can wipe them down. You just watch, on the weekend I'll give those walls a good scrub and they'll be as good as new, they will.'

Emily's heart sank. She had been dreading this. How could she complain about the state of the house without sounding mean and ungrateful? But it had to be said or nothing would be done and it was just too depressing to live with.

She had not lived in a home of her own since the night of the bomb. The accommodation at the hospital had been a huge improvement on her digs in Sefton Park, but it had been furnished. She had carried three battered leather cases around with her from pillar to post, waiting for the day when she could unpack her belongings in a place she could genuinely call home. And soon this would be it. But it was so unprepossessing, and what was more, it had been decorated to the taste of Dessie's late wife. It would never properly feel like her home until it had her own stamp on it.

'Dessie, I have washed the walls already, twice. You know this.' Standing up, she smoothed her plaid woollen skirt, adjusted the waist and moved over to Dessie's chair. She tugged down her jumper and mentally made a note that she would need to start acquiring some new clothes. She guessed her skirt was as old as the lino and only marginally more attractive.

'What's up, my lovely queen?' Looking up, Dessie sat back, put his arms out to Emily and pulled her down on to his knee. 'What's that look about, eh, eh? What's up?'

His stomach churned. He had not seen her look unhappy since they had got together, not once. Was she having second thoughts about being with him? About moving to his humble home on Arthur Street? Fear gripped him and his heart raced. If she was having second thoughts, if she was about to leave him, how could he live? How would he go on? If he looked to a future without Emily, he could see only blackness and despair, a gaping void. He was desperate to make things right. In the manner of a man unused to happiness and terrified of losing it, he asked, 'What is it, Emily? What's up? What's wrong?'

Emily curled up in his lap and laid her head on his chest. Deploying the gentlest of tones, she said, 'Dessie, I was rather hoping that we could redecorate the house throughout. Give the place a new coat of paint, some new lino, wallpaper in the bedroom, and some new chairs and nets.'

She nearly fell off his knee and on to the floor as he sat bolt upright in the chair.

'Are you kidding me?' he said, sounding alarmed. 'When I decorated this place in '35, I did it to last for ever. I didn't think I would have to do it again.'

Emily almost laughed at the look of outrage on his face, but she steadied herself and grabbed the arm of the chair. 'Dessie, for goodness' sake. I haven't asked for the walls to be papered in gold and we have enough saved up between us. I know you decorated it, but you didn't decorate it for me, did you? It was for someone else.'

Dessie pulled her close to his chest and slumped back into the chair. How could he have been so insensitive? Every woman needed a home which reflected who she was. It was part of what made them tick; one of the reasons they loved it when the travelling salesmen came to the door, as they did almost every day now, selling Hoovers, electric irons and ready-made curtains. This dull room was my wife, he thought as he looked around. It was as if the scales had just fallen from his eyes. What man ever had any say in how a home was decorated or run anyway? And objecting would not be the route to an easy life. His purpose now was to make the woman he loved happy. To love, cherish and honour – these were the promises he was about to make. Soon, soon, he would ask her to be his wife, and more than anything in the world, he wanted her to say yes.

'Emily, you are right. We have to get cracking. Let's choose the paper and paint at the Sunday market and let's go mad and get a runner for the stairs.' A grin spread across Emily's face. 'And we can have one of those fancy cabinets and a fridge. Jake has a fridge, why shouldn't we have one? He's my deputy and he has a house better kitted out than mine. Though he did win on the pools, mind.'

Emily jumped off Dessie's knee, returned to the table and picked up her pen and list. 'Everyone will have a fridge soon, now the price is coming down. And you get a bit of extra work space on the top. Biddy has a fridge and keeps her bread crock on top of hers. We both have enough saved up, you know. English Electric are doing some lovely ones at Blacklers. I've already been to have a look.'

Silence fell between them for a few seconds. Neither wanted to add that the reason they had money saved up was because there had never been any children, on either side. Dessie's wife had also died on the night of the bomb in '41 and from that day on his pay had remained untouched until he was demobbed in '46. After which he went straight on to work at St Angelus. Emily had never been married to anyone or anything other than her job.

'You know what this means, don't you? No more putting the jelly out on the back step overnight with a pan lid on it, waiting for it to set.' Emily's heart was fluttering at the excitement of it all.

'Well, won't that be the thing, eh? But do you want to do all that before we get married? It would add six weeks on, if you ask me.'

Emily landed back on his knee and threw her arms around his neck. Her thoughts were running away with her and she wasn't listening. 'You haven't even asked me yet. I might not say yes. I expect a proper proposal you know. Down on one knee.' Dessie began to kiss her, but she pulled away. 'I can ask Maisie if she will help me to run up some curtains for the parlour too, she's always been good with a needle. I don't mind the furniture that's already in there, Dessie, but we can get some new knickknacks and ornaments and things. I've a few of my own things in my case.'

She was too embarrassed to tell him that over the years she had added to her own bottom drawer. A tea towel here, a set of sheets there, aware that even if she didn't marry, one day she would have to fend for herself.

'Emily, listen. You are still sneaking in and out of the back door and avoiding Hattie Lloyd's curtain twitching. If we do the house up, it will delay the wedding. Can't we just get married first so that you can walk in and hold your head up high without having to pretend you didn't stay the night. When I carry you over the threshold, it will be straight up the stairs and into our bed. We won't be studying the wallpaper.'

Emily bit her lip as she thought hard. Dessie was right. Life wasn't so comfortable at present. There were a number of women who had turned their heads and tutted in the street as she had walked past and said hello. She would never tell Dessie that. She didn't want to be a problem to him and she knew he would be hurt. No one had done more for the young lads and families around there than Dessie had. It was only the prestige of her position at the hospital that stopped people from commenting out loud and within her hearing, and not everyone refrained. She had overheard Hattie Lloyd over the back-yard wall discussing her with someone only the other day. 'It's a sin, living over the brush like that, it is, Hattie, and not fair that you should have to live next door to it. You should complain to Father Brennan, he'll have something to say about it.'

Biddy had hinted any number of times that Emily should try and be a little more discreet. 'You don't want to go getting on the wrong side of the women around here, you know that. They live by the Bible and Father Brennan. Between the father and Sister Theresa, no one puts a foot out of place. They rule us all – well, all apart from the Ryans, and look what has happened to that family. Father's word is stronger than any law.'

Emily knew she was playing with fire. She was not a churchgoer, although she nursed a desire to be married in the church she had known all of her life and where she and her two little brothers had been christened. She felt in her heart that being married in St Chad's would mean that they would be there too, in spirit and memory. They were her family, all she had, and they were always in her thoughts. She had to include them in the big events of her life because they should have still been there with her. And she knew they were, somewhere.

Neither was Dessie a strict churchgoer and never had been. 'I go often enough to keep Father Brennan from banging on the door,' he had once told Biddy, and left it at that.

'Dessie, if we get married in the church, it will take for ever to arrange. I will need a dress. The cake will take a month to make and as for bridesmaids and bridesmaids' dresses, suits and all the rest of the paraphernalia... I want a nice home and I want to be your wife. Given my ripe old age, we need to get cracking on both. We can get this house done at the same time as we make the arrangements for the wedding.'

She looked up at him. The passion of their lovemaking had removed all memory of the blushes that used to colour her face on a regular basis. Emily was no longer a late-blooming bud. She was a woman.

Dessie wrapped his arms around her waist and swung her round and round. 'Not so fast, Emily. There is something I have to do first. Let's talk tonight. I'm going to get my shirt on now and nip down to the Silvestrian. We're having a pool night tonight and I'm picking up Paddy on the way. I'm forcing him to walk on that crutch of his. I promised Noleen that I'd get him out more. First, though, I'm calling round to see Matron about a new job I want to create. I think I can get Paddy taken on as night watchman.'

'Could he do the job, Dessie?' Emily began to help him with his tie.

'He could. I've had a chat to Joe in the prosthetics clinic. He said for me to take Paddy in and he will take a look. He said they can get men sent home in wheelchairs walking now and so he should be able to work something out for Paddy. It will make the world of difference to that family if we can pull this off. He will bring home five times as much as Noleen cleaning at the hospital. Jobs around here go to families of the fallen first and to those who served second. Thing is, we often forget about the injured and that's my fault. But I have a little theory about Paddy. Give that man something useful to do and it will be a million times more effective than any amount of physiotherapy. It's a reason to walk he needs.'

Emily smiled and gave him a kiss.

'I'll get the bus straight back from the Silvestrian. Getting

Paddy on and off will be a laugh. Might have to throw him on my back. Will you be all right?'

'Yes, I'll be fine. I've got plenty to do. I'm going to pop down and tell Biddy about my plans for the house and talk wallpaper patterns.'

Dessie returned her kiss before heading out of the room and upstairs to fetch his coat. Then the door banged shut and he was away.

Emily looked around at the brown walls. I'll be glad to see the back of you, she thought. That was something she loved about Dessie. There was no dithering, no hesitation. He could make a decision and get on with it. He grasped life with both hands, which boded well for the future. They had wasted so much time, both of them, that every day now had to be worth two.

She could see yellow – bright daffodil yellow and white for the walls, with a bright yellow-topped Formica table and plastic covered chairs to match. She smiled as she buttoned her coat and fastened her paisley-patterned headscarf under her chin. Yes, she could envisage exactly how it was going to look. Slipping stealthily out of the back door, she failed to catch the waiting image of the Silver Cross pram, standing against the wall.

The night was dark and moonless, but Emily liked that. It gave her cover. She glanced up at Hattie Lloyd's bedroom window and saw the curtains lift and fall. God, does that woman never give up, she thought. She turned from their own entry into the adjacent entry that crossed along the bottom and made her way down to Biddy's back gate.

She smiled at the familiar sounds filtering over back-yard walls as she passed each house. Alongside the back gate to Jake and Martha's house she heard the persistent cry of a baby and the sound of adults clucking. 'Try putting his dummy in, Martha.' That was Elsie; Emily instantly recognized her voice. Music on the radio serenaded her as she walked past Madge's, but as she approached the back gate of the sombre and silent Betty Hutch there was not so much as the sound of a mouse scratching.

She came across company in the form of Lorraine Tanner and Mary Delaney chatting at the Tanners' back gate. They were deep in conversation and didn't hear her approach until she was near. She caught the tail end of it.

'What did he say? What did he say? Did he say he saw me in the shop?' Lorraine was demanding.

'He didn't say nothing, Lorraine. Our Bryan never does. He wouldn't have known who was in the shop. He's a lost cause. Only interested in his job and playing pool down at the Silvestrian. He's down there now.'

Lorraine looked crestfallen at Mary's words. She had tried every means available to attract Bryan's attention when she had found herself queuing in the shop behind him. She had coughed, shuffled her feet and even shouted out, 'Hello, Mrs Lloyd,' to Hattie Lloyd when she walked in behind her. Lorraine didn't like Mrs Lloyd, she asked too many questions, and saying hello to her had encouraged just that.

'Oh, hello, Lorraine. How's your mam, lovie? I see she's got a new jardinière in the window. Where did that come from? Did she go to the prizes-only bingo in Bootle? Was that all she won then? Or did she win something else too?'

Lorraine blinked. Her mother had indeed won the plant

pot at the prizes-only bingo in Bootle – she'd been over the moon about it – but she'd only put it in the window about an hour earlier. She had been waiting to buy the aspidistra for it first.

'I don't know, Mrs Lloyd, I haven't even seen it,' she lied. As she spoke, her eyes never left Bryan's back, willing him to turn around. But he didn't even seem to notice that she was speaking.

Hattie Lloyd had continued. 'Well, it looks very nice, it does. Tell your mam it has the Hattie Lloyd seal of approval. She must have got the full house of the night to win that, did she?'

Lorraine was irritated and regretted having attracted her attention. Hadn't she just denied all knowledge of the jardinière?

Hattie Lloyd was looking at Lorraine through narrowed eyes. She knew Lorraine was lying when she said she hadn't seen what was in the parlour window. Hattie had known something was going on earlier in the week. Maisie Tanner didn't wash the front nets two weeks in a row for nothing.

Lorraine was saved from having to reply by the arrival of another poor child into the shop, who now became the focus of Hattie Lloyd's attention. Lorraine dropped her wicker basket on the floor. Bryan shuffled his feet in the sawdust. Still no recognition. It hadn't always been this way. He used to tease her and mess about along with the rest of them, but since he had begun work up at the hospital he had become aloof, quiet. Grown up. It was true that the boys rarely spoke to the girls when they weren't in gangs, but Bryan had stopped hanging around on the wasteland and he no longer played football with the other lads while the girls loitered on the periphery. He was never down the entry with the gang and she barely saw him any more, unless she visited Mary in the Delaney house. She felt sorry for him. Everyone knew that he looked after Paddy and the kids and helped Noleen out, and she'd seen for herself that he carried a heavy load. It was that which made her heart melt and want to reach out to him.

She coughed loudly. No response.

'Eh, Bryan, are you going up the Silvie? Me da's already left. I'm following up now.' This was one of the porter's lads shouting through the shop door.

At last, Lorraine thought. Oh, God, at last. He turned around to answer. Now he would see her standing there waiting to be served. But he looked straight over her head.

'I will, aye. Later. I'll walk Mam to Mass first. My da's coming to the Sylvie too. Dessie is knocking on for him.'

Walking Noleen to work or St Chad's was not something Bryan was afraid to admit to. Every mam in the street was revered, feared and respected. What many a da achieved with his belt, every mam could do ten times better with the side of her tongue. Bryan would not mention that he had to clear up the dishes, fold the washing when it was dry, put the kids to bed and wash down the back yard last thing because their Mary did nothing to help.

His turn to be served had arrived and he turned around to Mr Shirley without so much as a glance at Lorraine and said, 'A pound of carrots, a Spanish onion and a bag of the broken arrowroot biscuits, please, Mr Shirley.'

Lorraine's heart had dropped into her boots. Half an hour later, she had run down the entry to speak to Mary.

'Did he not even say he had seen me stood there? Nothing? Are you sure?'

Mary was by now both bored and desperately uninterested in Lorraine's infatuation with Bryan. 'No, he didn't, Lorraine, but me mam did say this. She said, "Our Bryan's acting a bit funny, Mary, I reckon there's someone he's sweet on."'

Lorraine's mouth opened and closed. 'Oh, God. He did see me then. He's just pretending that he hasn't.'

'Evening, girls,' said Emily Haycock as she passed.

Lorraine, still in a state of near stupefaction, jumped in surprise as Emily emerged from the shadows. 'Oh, hello, Miss Haycock.'

It didn't matter how many times Emily came face to face with Lorraine, she could not help but recall the night in the shelter when Lorraine was born. How could she not – it was the night Emily had lost her entire family. Emily had brought Lorraine into the world. Hers were the first pair of eyes Lorraine had looked into. Lorraine had been born knowing, inquisitive and silent. 'She's been here before, that one,' said the neighbour who was helping her deliver the scrap of a child in the midst of bombs and sirens and cigarette smoke. And Emily couldn't help thinking that maybe she was right.

'Why, anyone would think that you two girls had a secret,' Emily said, 'chatting away in whispers out here.' She smiled and rubbed her hands together for warmth.

'Oh, no, not really,' said Lorraine. 'Our Stan's driving me mad and me mam, she always takes his side, so I've come out here to talk to Mary. No point in me going in anyway, until I can get near the scullery, and me da's got our lads stood at the sink.'

Mary smiled up at Emily as Lorraine spoke. She wanted to be Emily. Just the sight of her almost took Mary's breath away. Miss Haycock was groomed, cultured, special. She even spoke nicely, not with the peculiar half-west-coast-Irish, half-Scouse accent of so many on the dockside streets.

'Did you wanna come in and see me mam? Shall I shout her for you?'

'No, no, not at all, thanks, Lorraine. I'm off down to Biddy's. Say hello to Maisie for me though, if you will. Night, girls.' And with that, Emily disappeared, back into the shadows in the direction of Biddy Kennedy's house.

Mary sighed. 'Oh God, I love her. Isn't she amazing? Did you see her make-up and look at the cut of her coat. She's done that all herself, me mam says. Always been working. Kept herself and her da – went mad, he did, they say, is that right? And she got a good job and everything. I would die to be like her. Emily Haycock is a woman of standing. Don't know why you want to hang around our Bryan. You'll turn out just like me mam, slaving away in the kitchen. Cleaning up the hospital. I wanna be like Miss Haycock. In charge of me own life.'

'Ooh, get you, fancy pants,' said Lorraine. 'How would you pay the rent if you weren't married? Anyway, Mam says it won't be long until she's getting married now, to Dessie. So being footloose and fancy-free can't be all it's cracked up to be, can it, or she wouldn't be giving it all up so easy. Me nan used to say that she'd be left on the shelf. Not the marrying kind, and when I asked her why, she'd say, "She's seen things no one should have to see and it affects you." It affected me nan. She was doolally most of the time.'

The girls fell silent. The wisdom of the Tanners' nana was legendary, and not to be questioned.

As she neared the end of the entry, Emily became aware of another presence approaching her. 'Oh, hello,' she said as the figure moved closer. On the left was the older end of the street, where, following the Blitz, the war widows had been housed. Mrs Green's house was in darkness. Probably already in bed, thought Emily. She heard an owl hoot just as goosebumps spread across her arms and the fine downy hair on her arms rose. It was a man and he hadn't responded. Everyone who lived locally said hello to each other. Emily had grown up on George Street and knew most people. This man was not someone she recognized. He was wearing a jacket, for one thing, and it wasn't a scruffy one, she could make that much out.

'Hello,' she said again.

His footsteps moved nearer. He was wearing a hat, which again struck her as unusual. Every man and boy around there wore a cap; not one wore a hat. Emily noticed that the man appeared to melt into the wall, as though he was pressing himself as far into the shadows as he possibly could. And then he was gone. She turned around as surreptitiously as possible, but there was nothing to see. He had been absorbed by the night as quickly as he had appeared.

'Come on, Lorcan, you don't need to worry about money. Here, Dessie asked me to give you this.' Jake slipped a shilling into Lorcan's hand.

'What's that for?' Lorcan asked as he clenched his fingers tightly.

'It's to reward you,' he said. Look, Dessie has been mighty pleased with all the effort you have put in. Blimey, you haven't stopped. Here's a word of advice, though, from me. Calm down a little or you'll put the other lads' noses out of joint.

They won't be putting up with someone who tries to look better than they do. Everyone works hard for Dessie, no one needs to do more than anyone else. Do you get my meaning, Lorcan? They might think you are after a favour or something.'

Lorcan nodded. 'I'm not doing that, Jake. I just wanted Dessie to know I was grateful like, for the chance...' His words tailed off.

'I know that, lad.' Jake reached out, lifted Lorcan's cap clean off his head and slapped it back down again in a gesture of affection. 'So does he and that's why the man himself asked me to give you this. It's good you've come to the Silvie tonight, it'll help you to fit in like.'

Lorcan pushed the shilling down his sock and into his shoe. Jake didn't smile or comment. Many of the lads had more holes than pockets and did the same.

'Did I see you and your mam coming back from the baths tonight?'

Lorcan looked straight up at Jake. 'We were there. Mam says because there's only two of us at home now, we can use the tin bath in future. I'll have it on Sundays and when I'm coming out to work, she will have it then.'

'Good lad, Lorcan.' Jake was full of pity for the earnest young boy. He had been told a dozen stories that week by the other lads. How Lorcan had been seen by one of them from his bedroom window, burning rubbish, boiling the copper late at night, putting washing out in the dark. He had started his job and taken on the running of the house at the same time.

'We go to the Silvestrian or the Irish Centre every Friday, so you'll have a night off and enjoy a bit of the craic. Knock on the back gate for me at seven every Friday from now on. I'll walk up with you so you don't feel like a stranger. You're one of us now. But for now, that money from Dessie, it's to get yourself a jug and join in.'

Jake moved over to one of the pool tables and as Lorcan followed in his wake, he thought his heart would burst. He was one of them now. The St Angelus porter's lads; the closest bunch of workmates in Liverpool. He belonged to a team and not one of them had ever mentioned J.T. to him. He felt as though his life was slipping into place.

He had done his best to see that his mother was well looked after before he left the house. He was sure he was doing everything right and proper and that Biddy and Noleen would approve. But he still felt a twinge of guilt leaving her.

'Your potatoes and cabbage are on the range, don't leave it,' he'd told her. 'And here's some tea.' He had boiled the potatoes in the cast-iron pot and in the last five minutes had added salt and cabbage. When the cabbage was soft, he drained the water off and chopped the potatoes and cabbage up together until the cabbage was shredded finely. He then scraped a bit of butter over the top and browned it off. He was pleased with himself. Biddy had taught him how to make it. 'It's better with rashers and a bit of fat and butter and milk in it, lad, but when you have none, it'll keep the wolf from the door. It's even better the next day.'

Before he went out, he'd tried to get his mam to make use of the empty bed upstairs. 'Mam, you can go up to the room now, as there's only you and me. No need to spend day and night down here in your chair. Why don't you go up tonight?'

Mrs Ryan was sipping from the enamel mug of tea Lorcan had given her. 'Aye, I will, lad. Soon. I'll give it a go. God, now, isn't the place just looking lovely. Who did that?'

Lorcan swallowed hard. He couldn't tell from one day to

the next where his mother was in her mind. He wondered who she thought had done it. He had spent three hours scrubbing and cleaning after work every night until he was fit to drop, but he didn't mind. He was getting a good meal now, thanks to his money and being organized. Once he'd had a night's sleep, he was ready to go the next morning.

The place was indeed looking lovely. The only room he hadn't cleaned was his brother's. He had left that until last, but tomorrow he would be up there with the scrubbing brush, the Aunt Sally in a bucket of boiling water, and a cloth to wipe up the murky water with. By the end of the night, it too would be spotless. He would put the sheets in the copper boiler and hang the old army blankets over the line. Biddy had told him how to do that too. 'Beat the dust out of them and leave them to air, Lorcan. It doesn't matter if it rains and it's best to do it when there's a good frost. Wait until they are frozen hard and then bring them in to dry off over the copper boiler and in front of the range when you go to bed. That way the ice kills the bed bugs and any lice with the cold. Good as new they are after that. Then, when there's a hot day in the summer, you can give them a wash in the leftover water in the boiler, before you drain it away. But only on a hot day, mind. They take for ever to dry once they have soaked through. You can only fit two at a time on the line though.'

Lorcan had done exactly as Biddy had instructed with his own blankets and he was proud of his efforts. The sores on his legs were healing slowly and no new ones had appeared. He was winning the battle with the lice and the bed bugs. He had brought a tea chest home and turned it upside down to fold his shirt on and put his few things on at night so that they didn't have to lie on the floor.

'I did it, Mam. I've been doing the cleaning. Do you like it? And I've made you 'tatoes and cabbage on the range.'

'How would you have done that?' His mother looked into the pan. 'I'm after thinking that maybe you have a woman slipping in when I'm sleeping, Lorcan.'

Lorcan smiled. It was a rare thing. 'No, Mam, I haven't. Biddy Kennedy has been helping me.'

His mother reached out and grabbed his hand. Her eyes welled up with tears as she looked at her son. He was the only person she had left in the whole world.

Lorcan knew the look and the words that were about to follow. 'I'm not going robbin', Mam. I'm not like the others. I'm going to make our house nice and clean and I'm working in a proper job at the hospital. I'm going to work hard, Mam, so Dessie keeps me on. Jake told me that one day I might become an under-porter and that's enough of a wage to keep a home and a wife, he said, but I will just look after you, Mam, and anyway, we have enough now, don't we? We never need any of the others again. And even if they were to get out, I'm the man of the house, Ma. We don't need none of them. I can manage. We are respectable now, thanks to Dessie.'

Lorcan couldn't remember ever in his life feeling as good as he did today. He wasn't just wasting his words, it was true. He was the man of the house.

Mrs Ryan looked up into his face. 'Oh, don't be saying things like that now. We want them to come back, 'tis their home too. The place isn't the same without J.T.' She shook his hand in her own, hard, as though to shake it away, but kept tight hold.

Lorcan felt as though she had pierced his heart with a knife. 'The place isn't the same? No, it isn't, Mam, it's cleaner and we have regular food and it's better without J.T. He brought us nothing but shame. People talk to me now he's gone, and Dessie gave me a job.'

'Oh, shush, Lorcan. I never wanted them to go robbin', you know. They just wouldn't listen. Wilful they were, like all boys. Once they had a notion in their head about things, there was no stopping them. They went off the rails when your da fell in the war and I couldn't control them. Everyone said it was because I had all boys, not a single girl amongst you, and they needed a da, you know, 'twasn't their fault, Lorcan. Boys, oh sure, they do need a da and don't I know it. They all... well, they just got too strong for me, they wouldn't listen to a word I said, ran wild they did.'

Lorcan had vague recollections of arguments. A memory surfaced of J.T. hitting his ma and himself as a little lad trying to beat at his brother's legs with his clenched fists to stop him and then a hand coming down and swatting him away.

'It was hard, Lorcan. I couldn't stop crying for your da. I couldn't believe he wasn't coming home. It was like all the strength went out of me, and it just never came back. Do you know, Lorcan, when the klaxon goes, it has taken me all this time to believe that your da won't be walking through that door. I was sure they were wrong, maybe they had mistaken him for someone else and that he might be one of the missing ones. He's not, I know that now, but then I didn't have the notion to do a thing, not even get myself washed. I used to keep a nice house, I did, before your da left. They were bad days, they were. It's not your brothers' fault, you know. Don't think too badly of them. If I had been a proper mother to them, now, wouldn't it all be very different.'

Lorcan looked at his mam and for the first time he had an insight into how tough life must have been for her since their da had died in '42. But he also knew that, whatever the reason for her malaise, he was as good as an only child now. Her defence of his brothers almost took his breath away. Surely she would just slam the door in J.T.'s face if he ever turned up there again? He never wanted to set eyes on any of his brothers again. They could hang for all he cared. His job now was to make the name Ryan one that didn't cause people to sneer and curse.

He put on his cap and went to the bread bin for his money. His pride and joy, saving money. He made for the press, lifted the lid on the bread bin and put his hand inside. Disappointed, he pulled his hand back out.

'Aw, Mam, did you take the money out of the bread bin, did you?'

Mrs Ryan didn't try to pretend. 'Aye, I did, Lorcan. One day, it was, but I can't for the life of me remember which. Was it you what put it there? Did you put it there? Well, would you fancy that. I thought 'twas J.T. now.'

'Mam, you know I did. J.T. is in prison, Mam, and he's gone for a long time. It's just me and you now. It was for the shopping tomorrow.' He didn't say that he'd also wanted to take some for his night out with the porter's lads. He wasn't going to drink, but he knew he'd need some pennies for the light over the pool table. Jake had told him that. He let out a deep sigh. He would have to hide the money in his room from now on. And he'd have to start calling into the rent office on payday every week, on his way home from work.

Hours later, as she woke in the chair, it dawned on Mrs Ryan that Lorcan had said something about being out. Her head

209

seemed clearer. She was feeling more hopeful. She wiggled her toes and nudged the sleeping kittens off her feet, then stood to tip the scuttle of coal Lorcan had left on to the fire. As she straightened her back, she remembered the visit, from the man, after Lorcan had left.

'Who was he now? Was it J.T.? It was,' she said out loud. 'The man in the hat and the jacket? 'Twas J.T. It was. Sure, wasn't he looking fine in the fancy jacket.' But then she remembered Lorcan had told her J.T. was in jail. The memory of Lorcan leaving was foggy at first, but some light began to filter through. 'Oh, yes. It was J.T. He had wanted to keep something in the bedroom upstairs, now why was that? Should I be telling Lorcan?' No. He had told her not to tell Lorcan anything. 'Haven't I been good? I said not a word.'

She would do anything for J.T., keep any promise. He wasn't a bad lad, just a bit wayward at times, but hadn't he been the most beautiful baby? The most endearing toddler. Hadn't he been the one who caught her heart and wasn't she the only one who understood him? She did miss him. Lorcan never understood, always acting as though J.T. didn't exist, was not part of her flesh. Expecting her to turn him away when he returned. She was his mother, brought him into the world. She would give him anything she asked. And wasn't she good, she never told Lorcan where the money in the bread bin had gone.

She was muttering to herself as, for the first time in years, she climbed the stairs. They were so unfamiliar to her, she panicked for a moment and stopped her ascent, clinging on to the banister, believing she was in someone else's house. She heard a noise. In the yard, she thought, or was it upstairs?

'J.T., is that you?'

She clung on to the banister and continued to the top. Opening the door to J.T.'s bedroom, she switched on the light and looked around. It was cold and bare. She'd prefer to sleep by the warm fire, like she always did, but maybe it would be nice to lie down for once, just for a nap. She couldn't remember what it was like to lie on a bed, it had been so long.

There was a stale aroma in the room, of unwashed bed sheets and body odour. The bare light was reflected in the greasy window. The oak floorboards were now black with dirt and age. She smiled. The room smelt of her son. J.T. might not be there in person, but she could smell him. She lifted the sheet to her face and inhaled. Despite what Lorcan had said, if he were to walk through the door now, she would welcome him back with open arms. Lorcan would too. 'Oh aye, he would,' she said to herself.

She laid the sheet back down and smoothed it over, wanting to touch the place where her boy had last slept. The bottom sheet felt warm. She frowned at the bed and placed her hands on her hips. A small pile of J.T.'s clothes lay in the corner of the floor and a floorboard, sticking up from under them, caught her eye. 'Well, we've mighty strong mice now,' she said. 'I'll be putting the cats up here.'

Her eyes widened as she remembered what the young man had said to her. J.T., was it? Oh, why could she not remember? He was keeping something in here, for later. That was it. 'What was it?' she said out loud.

She thought she heard the back door. Moving to the bedroom door, she shouted down the stairs, 'Lorcan, is that you? J.T., is it you?'

No reply came back, but a ginger kitten leapt on to the bottom step.

'Oh, 'tis you. You scared the life out of me.'

She didn't like being upstairs alone in the house. A tinker had once called at the door and because she hadn't any money for the heather had told her in a menacing tone to watch herself up the stairs if she didn't want to be having an accident. She hadn't been up the stairs from that day to this.

She decided to investigate the floorboard and to take a look at what was under there. She lifted the corner and it came away with the ease of a paper bag as it slipped to the side. It was dark below, and she could see nothing until she moved and the glow from the overhead light glinted on something that was metal.

'What's that?' she said, curiosity getting the better of her. Falling on to her knees faster than she had for many years, she put her hand down inside and felt something long and cold and metallic. Lifting it clear of the floorboards, she gasped. It was a gun, and there were more just like it. They had shifted and clattered as she lifted the first one free.

Her mind was still struggling to make sense of it all when she heard a floorboard creak behind her. In the reflection in the greasy grey window she saw a man behind her, his hat in place and his arm outstretched. He looked faintly familiar. He was holding her poker from the side of the fire.

'J.T., is that you?' she asked, but she had no time to turn around or to think anything else before a blow across the back of her neck felled her.

As she lay there, speechless but conscious, all she could see was a pair of black boots with brown laces. There was the sound of floorboards being ripped up. A noise pounded in her head and she felt a pressure bearing down on her. She tried to shout for J.T., because hadn't he been there? But the words just wouldn't come. She tried to lift her arm, but it was as heavy as lead and no matter how much she tried, it just would not move. Then the blackness came, washing over her gradually. The noise faded and all she could think was, no one puts brown laces in black boots, do they?

Lorcan had had the best night of his life. It turned out he was a natural at pool. One of the dockers had shown him how to chalk up and hold his cue and Dessie himself had had a game with him. To top it all, he had walked home with Bryan, just the two of them, because Dessie had already accompanied Bryan's da back to the Delaneys'. They called at the chip van and Bryan bought them a bag of chips and a saveloy each. Lorcan thought that nothing he had ever eaten in his life had tasted so good. He had never been so happy.

He folded half of his chips back in the newspaper, but, unlike Bryan, he did not shove them into a passing bin in the entry wall but hugged them to him, keeping them warm for his mam to have on some bread and butter when he got indoors. He and Bryan talked all the way home and he could have whooped with joy. He was no longer an outcast because of his brothers. He, Lorcan, was already wiping away the stain and the shame they had brought upon his mother and himself.

'Do you want me to knock on for you tomorrow morning?' Bryan said as he lifted the latch on his back gate and looked back, waiting for an answer.

Lorcan's heart soared. 'All right. Thanks. I'll be ready.'

'Right, see you at half seven then, lad. Night.'

As he approached his own back gate, Lorcan almost skipped. He could see that it was open, and light was spilling out into the entry. This was unusual and the smile slipped from his face. The ginger kittens stood, half in the back yard, half out, looking up the entry as if waiting for Lorcan to return. Their ginger faces were illuminated by the kitchen light and they gave an anxious meow as he approached.

'What the hell…?' Lorcan sensed that something was very wrong. Seeing the back door open, and the door to the bottom of the stairs, he dropped the chips and ran inside, jumping up the stairs two at a time shouting, 'Mam! Mammy!'

As he opened the bedroom door, he found his mother. She was lying on the floor, her eyes closed, her mouth open. Falling to his knees next to her, Lorcan could see that she had turned an unearthly white. Thin strands of her silver hair were trapped in a small puddle of congealed blood. The air filled with his screams. 'Mam! Mam! Mammy!' Through his tears, it was impossible for Lorcan to tell if his mother was alive or dead.

Bryan, on his way to the outhouse to empty his da's bottle, heard Lorcan's screams. He'd heard similar cries many times before at the hospital, from visitors leaving casualty or the mortuary. He ran down the entry, leapt over the ginger kittens gorging on chips in the yard, and shouted to Lorcan. The concern in his voice made him sound more like any brother Lorcan had ever known.

Chapter 8

Beth's night shift had lasted for ever thanks to an emergency operation and she decided to walk down the back stairs and out of the rear entrance, the quickest way to Lovely Lane. Theatre had been unusually busy with emergencies and she had spent the entire shift feeling lonely and tired. There was something desperately sad about knowing that every nurse in the Lovely Lane home the previous night, which had been a Friday, was out with their boyfriends, at the pictures or in the pub, but she hadn't demurred when Sister Pokey had asked her to cover at the last minute when the day staff nurse had called in sick. 'I will make sure Matron knows,' she had said when Beth agreed. Sister Pokey was a good sort really, Beth thought. Not friendly or kindly, sometimes sharp, but nothing like some of the overly officious sisters on the wards. Especially considering she'd been nursing for almost forty years and had begun her training during the First World War, presumably never thinking she would have to nurse through a second war.

Beth had felt particularly bad for the older Irish lady, Mrs Ryan, who had been admitted as an emergency at about midnight. Not long after, Dessie Horton, the head porter, had turned up at theatre, along with the woman's son, Lorcan. 'He's one of my lads,' Dessie had whispered by way of an explanation. 'His older brother appears to have been fencing something pretty serious because the bizzies arrived at the house before the ambulance. One of them told me her lad has jumped from Walton. He's one of the Bevan gang. Mrs Ryan got caught by one of them coming to claim his loot. I'll come by and take Lorcan home later. The bizzies want to talk to him and the poor boy hasn't got a clue. I'm going to stand for him and make sure the bizzies know that.'

Beth knew who the Bevans were. She had come to hear of them within months of arriving in Liverpool. They were notorious and were named and shamed in the *Echo* on a regular basis. 'The lives some people lead,' she said to Dessie as she dropped two sterilizing tablets into a sink of hot water then carefully placed a kidney dish full of bloody forceps into it, followed by several glass syringes, one at a time.

'Is it me, or are the streets becoming less safe nowadays?' Dessie said. 'Feels like as the black market disappears, robbing is becoming the thing to do.'

Beth had known neither, having lived a sheltered life in army camps. 'I think it has more to do with the fact that while the war was on, there were fewer men around to cause trouble. The streets became safer and women stopped locking their doors. Women aren't burglars, they don't fight. They're more inclined to look after each other than try and blow each other's heads off.'

Dessie's mouth dropped open. He was taken aback by Beth's comments, but he couldn't argue with her, he had heard Biddy say something similar often enough.

The operation to relieve the pressure on Mrs Ryan's temporal lobe had lasted for four hours. Having never witnessed brain surgery before, it had made Beth queasy in a way no other surgery had. It was the sheer primitiveness of it. The slow drilling of the holes and the removal of part of the skull by joining the holes together and cutting a flap of the skull away using a small handsaw. The surgical expertise required was enormous, and the physical effort caused the surgeon to sweat profusely throughout.

'Do we have nothing more sophisticated than this?' she had whispered to Sister Pokey.

'Well, pardon me.' Sister Pokey peered at Beth over the top of her spectacles and her face mask. 'You don't consider that removing a section of the skull to prevent intracranial bleeding while being careful not to cause any further brain damage is in any way sophisticated, Nurse Harper? Why don't you just fetch some more swabs, please. Although if you would prefer to stay and advise the surgeon on a more effective way to save his patient's life, I am sure he would be most grateful to have you talk him through it.'

There followed a moment of silence, and then came the sound of the small hacksaw slicing through skull. The theatre was hot and the smell of blood and the bone dust filling the air made the normally stoic Beth feel nauseous. 'Yes, Sister,' she stammered. With her face as red as the blood on the surgeon's boots, she turned away.

'Nurse Harper,' Sister Pokey called to her as she retreated. There was a note of sympathy in her voice. 'It's desperate measures. She is unlikely to survive anyway, but it is worth a try. There are so many potential complications. The pressure could build up again. She could be left with brain damage, or a nasty post-op infection. Our job, though, is to assist the surgeon to the best of our abilities. And remember, her son is part of the St Angelus family, so we go the extra mile to look after him and see him right, however primitive the procedure might seem. Now, with those swabs, we will need at least a dozen sterile crepe bandages and six twelve-inch by twelve-inch soft lint pads. We have to dress the head like a balloon in order to protect the area of the brain no longer covered by the skull, to prevent any further damage and to keep any infection out.'

'Yes, Sister.' Beth now felt stupid in addition to being lonely, single and left on the shelf. As she counted out the fresh swabs on to a new trolley, she wondered whether this was it. Would the rest of her life be spent walking up the path from Lovely Lane to St Angelus, while her friends all moved away and married? While they had babies of their own rather than delivered or nursed other people's? She felt her friends drifting away from her already, even though they still had a while to go before finals. She had been so looking forward to theatre, but she had to admit that she missed the wards and even the buzz of visiting time.

As Beth made her way to the nurses' home after her shift, having delivered Mrs Ryan on to the ward with her head bandaged and padded, the only thing to put a lift in her step was the fact that Victoria would probably be back by now, with news of Dana. When she got to Lovely Lane she took the stairs two at a time and burst into Victoria's room without knocking. But the sight of Dana sitting on Victoria's bed with Pammy's arms around her stopped her dead in her tracks.

'Dana, what are you doing here?' Beth flung off her cape and then threw herself into Dana's arms. 'You aren't due back here for ages. Have you left Teddy behind?'

'No, she hasn't,' Victoria said. 'He has come too, even though he can barely walk. He's insisting on returning to work. Roland has taken him over to the doctors' residence and Mr Mabbutt is going over and will hopefully talk some sense into him. But as it stands, he thinks he is back on the ward on Monday.'

Dana erupted into a fresh bout of tears and Beth pulled her into her. 'There, there,' she said. 'Don't cry. Mr Mabbutt will tell him it simply isn't possible for him to return on Monday.'

'It's not just that.' Dana pulled away from Beth and blew her nose. 'He's not my Teddy any more. He's changed. I know he's not fully recovered, but I think going back to work might be the best thing. Roland said he might have been going out of his mind with frustration or something.'

Pammy turned to Victoria, who was standing by the sink. 'What do you think, Vic?'

Victoria looked paler than usual and tired. 'He's been like a bloody rude bear with a sore head, the worst patient I have ever met. I don't know how you stuck it, Dana. I think the sheer anxiety of having to put up with his temper this week has made me ill.'

'Oh, no, why?' asked Pammy. 'Was he that bad?'

'Either that or it's the car journey. I much prefer taking the train to Bolton, but there was no way Teddy could have made the journey on the train. He practically press-ganged Roland into driving us back. I'm not so bad in the front seat, but when you're in the back, as me and Dana were, God, all those lanes. And Roland drives so fast. Here, move over,' she said to Pammy. And, climbing on to the bed, she lay down. 'I just need half an hour to get my stomach back.'

'Well what a mess,' said Beth. 'Has Mrs Duffy fed you all?'

'She has kept us all a lunch in the oven,' said Pammy. 'It's shepherd's pie. Mrs Duffy said to eat it quick or the gravy will dry up.'

Beth's stomach grumbled loudly at the mention of food. 'Don't move,' she said as she jumped up. Her mouth was now watering and she could practically smell her lunch wafting up the stairs. 'I'm starving. I'll put it on a tray and bring up four forks, but I'm just going to my room to change first. Gravy for everyone?'

'Oh, stop, please,' groaned Victoria with her hand over her eyes.

'Oops, that'll be three forks then,' said Beth.

'Yes, but you had better be quick,' said Pammy. 'I saw Celia Forsyth hanging around the kitchen.'

'Don't move, anyone,' shouted Beth and in a flash she was out of the room and gone.

Dana moved to the sink and ran the tap to splash her face. As she dried it, she turned towards the bed and said to Victoria, 'Shall we tell Pammy?'

'What? What?' Pammy handed a mirror to Dana to check herself. 'Tell me. What?'

'I think we better had,' said Victoria.

Pammy flopped on to the bed and slapped Victoria on the thigh. 'Sit up. Tell me. What?'

'On the way back from the doctors' residence just now, after we dropped Teddy off, we saw Beth, but she didn't see us.'

'Well what's so unusual about that? Knowing Beth, she was probably head down and marching. I'm sure that's how her father taught her to walk. Do you think he shouts "Attention!" before he speaks to her?' Pammy laughed at her own joke.

Dana and Victoria exchanged nervous glances.

'You tell her,' said Victoria. 'I feel too goddam ill.' She placed her hand on her brow and closed her eyes.

'You are going down with something,' said Pammy. 'That's not travel sickness.'

Dana sat herself on the chair at Victoria's desk and using her two feet shuffled it closer to the bed. Putting her stockinged feet up on the bed, she said, 'I am so glad to be back here with you lot, I can't tell you.'

Pammy jumped up and kissed her on the cheek. 'We've all missed you, Dana. Me mam and our Lorraine too. But stop changing the subject and tell me, what is it?'

'OK, but you have to promise not to react, Pammy, or to fly off the handle. We have to make a plan and you only have a couple of minutes at the most to keep yourself together.'

'Oh blimey O'Riley, what on earth is it? The suspense is killing me.'

'Well, as we left the res we saw Beth with Oliver Gaskell. They were by the cedar tree on the corner at the back of the car park, and he was, well, oh my goodness, I don't know how to say this. You are going to go stark staring crazy.'

'What do you mean? Why would I do that?' Pammy sat up and looked from one to the other. 'What are you worried about? You know I cannot bear that womanizer. I bet you Beth was giving him a piece of her mind.'

Victoria snorted and Dana bit her lip.

'No, she definitely wasn't doing that, Pammy. Well, if she was, not in the way you might be thinking.'

'In what way? Flamin' hell, tell me.'

Dana took a deep breath, held Pammy's gaze and spat it out. 'Pammy, they were stood by the cedar tree and he was kissing her.'

'Oh my giddy aunt, no! No!' Pammy jumped to her feet and began pacing the floor, across to the window and back. 'How? Why? Oh no, no. How could she? Has she lost her mind?'

The door to the room opened and Beth came in, balancing a hot plate on a tea towel in one hand and some forks in the other. 'Oh no what?' she asked as she looked around. 'Has who lost their mind?'

'Nothing. No, nothing,' said Pammy as she threw a desperate glance towards Victoria.

'It's me,' said Victoria. 'She's saying "oh no" because of me. Because I'm ill and it's my first full day on theatre soon and I don't know what to do and she thinks I'm mad for worrying about it.'

'Really?' A frown crossed Beth's face. 'But don't worry, you are with me. It's hardly a drama. Trust you, Pammy, you always make a mountain out of a molehill. If you had a bit more organization in your own life, you wouldn't be so alarmed by minor matters in the lives of others. Now, Victoria, you obviously need a nap. A restorative kip to get over your car sickness. Mrs Duffy says everyone suffers from it with these new fast cars. She says that when you get to fifty miles an hour, and I bet Roland's car reaches that, it does something to your insides. She said they wobble about and it takes your stomach a while to catch up with the rest of your body. I think she may have a point, although it's more likely to be something to do with the inner ear.'

'Well, I see nothing has changed while I've been away,' said Dana crisply. She stood up from the chair and, glaring at Pammy, slapped her across the shoulders to stop her from staring at Beth as though she had landed from another planet. 'Beth laying down the law as always. You know, I've missed that, Beth. You keep us all in order. Always so sensible. Teddy should have had you looking after him, not me. Anyway, Beth, what's your news?'

Victoria sat up and concentrated on Beth. Dana pulled her chair even closer. Pammy dived over Victoria and sat cross-legged on the pillow. 'Yes, Beth,' she said, 'what's your news? Anything you want to tell us? Me in particular?'

Beth sat at the desk and filled her mouth with mashed potato. 'I'm starving. I haven't eaten for hours,' she said. 'You lot talk while I eat and then I'll tell you all about the new theatre and the brain surgery we had in overnight. Anyway, Dana, is Teddy back for good now?'

Beth had skilfully diverted the conversation away from herself. Just to make sure, she continued. 'Did you set any dates, Vic, while you were up in Bolton with Roland? The married nurses rule applies to student nurses, you know. Now that Matron is abandoning it, you could easily get married.'

'We won't plan the wedding yet,' said Victoria, 'it would be just too hard from here. No, like I said, I will pass my finals first. I am absolutely determined that when I walk down the aisle, it will be as Staff Nurse Baker. And then I'll know that if Mummy is looking down on me she can be proud.'

Beth had already zoned out. She found these sorts of girly conversations quite boring, but today there was another reason for her distraction and it was making swallowing her food difficult. She pushed her fork to one side and three pairs of eyebrows were raised heavenwards.

Over in the doctors' residence, Teddy's shouts could be heard along the corridor and all the way down the stairs in the doctors' sitting room. 'But I have to go back, don't you see? I've come back to Liverpool to return to work, not to sit here in this box recuperating.'

Mr Mabbutt thrust his hands into the pockets of his white doctor's coat and drew his thin, angular body up to its full height. He had been in and out of theatre all morning, dealing with yet more road accidents. His shiny bald head had turned an angry red to match his face and he glared at Teddy over the top of his glasses.

'Well, you made a very foolish mistake, Dr Davenport. What use do you think you can be to me in your condition? You can't walk without the aid of your crutch and you are in need of an X-ray at the very least before I can make any kind of a judgement. I told you, you have to let those bones knit over time and with due care. I absolutely refuse to let you back on the wards. It is not happening.' Leaving Teddy in no doubt, he turned towards the door. 'Good food, the gentlest exercise, hot Epsom-salt baths three times a day. That's what you need.'

Turning towards Roland, who had tried to remain invisible, he snapped, 'You can leave him here. He's fit enough for that and the housekeeper here is very good. She will make his meals for him and I can keep checking up on him. As soon as he is ready, I will let him back on the wards, but not before. Goodbye.'

And with that, Mr Mabbutt reached for the door handle. Just before the door closed on him, he turned back and said, 'Oh and by the way, Dr Davenport, Nurse Makebee asked me to pass on a message. She wishes to see you as soon as possible. She was in the office when I took the call telling me you were back and she knew I was on my way over here.'

He looked uncomfortable. 'I told her that it would be more appropriate to speak to that young girlfriend of yours, Nurse Brogan, but she refused. Said she would catch you in my clinic. Which reminds me, I'll send Dessie Horton or Jake over with a wheelchair to collect you for nine and we can get that X-ray done.'

Mr Mabbutt exited and headed down the stairs. Teddy watched him through the window as he crossed the car park to the ward block.

Throughout the meeting Roland had sat on a chair in the corner of the room without saying a word. Only now did he break his silence. 'Well, that was all very interesting,' he said. 'Are you going to tell me who Nurse Makebee is and why she is so keen to see you?'

Half an hour later, Roland walked into the pub and ordered a whisky and dry. He had to drive back to Bolton, but there was no way he could make the drive without something to steady his nerves first. He replayed the conversation, or the argument, more like, he had just had with his brother over and over in his mind. He had to keep telling himself that it wasn't a dream.

His brother was not the man he thought he was and Roland was reeling from the shock of it. Teddy had always been the charming, chatty one, whereas he was the more serious older brother. Nonetheless, he had assumed that they both held the same values, especially when it came to important issues like love and family. What he had learnt just now had shaken him to his core.

He tipped his head back and downed the drink in one.

'Another please,' he said to the barman. As he looked down into the dark amber liquid, waiting for the burning rush of the first one to subside, he went over Teddy's words in his mind.

'The day of the accident, when I collected Dana from the Pier Head, I realized I had made a terrible mistake. Done a terrible thing.'

The atmosphere in the room had suddenly felt tighter, as though the air had been sucked out. Roland knew that the wise thing would be to say, 'Don't tell me, I don't want to know,' but he didn't say that. Despite his trepidation, he had to know. However awful whatever it was might be, he had to know.

'Done what? What do you mean? Dana had been at home in Ireland, hadn't she?'

'Yes, Dana had been in Ireland. And while she was there, I spent my two-week holiday with Sarah Makebee.'

Roland leapt up from his chair. 'You did what?' he shouted.

Teddy stared at the carpet and continued doggedly with his confession. 'I'd bought the holiday as a surprise gift for Dana, but she was unmovable, cold as ice. She had to have her holiday back at home with her mammy and daddy, didn't give me a second thought. I got it into my mind that she was frigid. She wouldn't let me near her. But Sarah Makebee jumped at the chance of the holiday and so… she and I went on holiday as man and wife. But, believe me, Roland, I very soon knew what a fool I had been. And I knew that if Dana ever found out, I would never see her again.'

'What do you mean "as man and wife"? Did you sleep with this woman?'

Teddy snorted with laughter. 'Oh don't come the papist with me, Roland. You and Victoria have been sleeping together all along. The girls do talk, you know. Do you think I'm stupid?'

'But, Teddy, Victoria and I are engaged to be married. I knew the first time I kissed Victoria that come hell or high water I was going to make her my wife. I have sworn to look after her, to protect and cherish her. I respect her wish to qualify as a nurse and I wouldn't do anything to stop that. What does this... this Sarah Makebee mean to you?' He almost spat out the last few words. Unused to shouting, he was now storming backwards and forwards across the room.

Teddy remained in his chair. Although he wouldn't admit it, the car journey from Bolton had made his leg stiff and it was now painful after the flexions Mr Mabbutt had forced him to do in order to demonstrate his range of movement. Taking a deep breath, he looked up at his brother. 'She means... she meant nothing. She was just there and, I suppose, willing. Dana had gone away and I had this hotel and, anyway, Sarah Makebee has her own boyfriend. He's here now, he's a registrar.'

'Good God, the woman sounds no better than a common prostitute. Does she have no morals?'

'Of course she has morals, she is just a very modern, post-war woman, that's all.'

Roland looked down at Teddy with distaste written across his face. 'I don't know what's up with you, Teddy. I don't know how you could treat Dana like that. The way she has looked after you. Spent night after night on the ward when you were recovering. Day after day looking after you in Bolton. I take it that she knows none of this.'

'Of course she doesn't.' Teddy was angry now. 'I was on my way to pick her up and then ask her to marry me. I was full of guilt and remorse – I'm not a total cad, Roland. I knew what I had done was wrong, that I had made a mistake.

In a way, being with Sarah Makebee made me realize how much I missed Dana and how you can't simply replace someone you love with another person, just like that. I know what it means now, to really love someone. I couldn't get Dana out of my head, couldn't stop thinking about her. And then, I don't even know what happened, but don't think I have got off lightly, Roland, because this... this...' He jabbed his finger and pointed down at his leg. 'This is my punishment. This and the guilt I feel every minute of the day. Because every little thing she does for me, every kind word, is like being stabbed in the heart. It hurts, Roland, more than the leg hurts, and I cannot stand it any longer. How can I ask her to marry me now? I must have been a fool thinking I could. I cannot live every day knowing what I have done to her. It is unforgivable and that is the top and bottom of it. What I did is beyond forgiveness.'

'And so Dana must be punished as well? You have treated her very badly over these past weeks. It has been all I could do to hold my tongue. If that is how her life is to be, with you being vile to her because you aren't man enough to live with your own mistake, she would be better off without you. Are you going to confess to her?'

'Oh, don't be a bloody fool, Roland. Do you know Dana at all? If she knew what I had done, I would never see her again. I've never met anyone so full of pride. I swear, that would be it.'

'Are you at least going to tell this Sarah Makebee to keep away?'

'Of course I am. Obviously. It's not me that's asked to see her, is it? She has her own boyfriend. She won't want him to know about me, I can assure you. All she is worried about is that she has heard I am back. Terrified I will spill the beans and ruin her perfect little life and her planned marriage to her soon to be consultant boyfriend. But none of that makes any difference, Roland. If I tell Dana, she will leave, and if I don't, I have to live with the agony of the shame and the pain and the guilt. God, what a bloody idiot I was. I'm a coward when it comes down to it. I can't do that.' He shifted in the chair and grimaced, then looked his brother in the eye. 'God, Roland, I feel like a boil has been lanced by telling you. I am so glad you know. But before you say anything, please do not think that telling Dana is an option. Not unless you want me to say goodbye to her for ever. I need to see first if the guilt fades, once I'm well. See if I can live with myself, with her; if we can be happy.'

Roland hadn't replied. He knew what Teddy had said was right. Dana was full of pride. He had been amazed at the patience she'd shown while nursing his grumpy brother. He thought about how much he had enjoyed having her around the house and what a wonderful sister-in-law she would make. He had visions of his and Victoria's children playing with Teddy and Dana's children in the tree house at the home where he and Teddy had been born. But, as Victoria had told him so many times, he was just a big softie and he had been that way since the day his mother had died.

Now, looking into his drink, he felt burdened. It might have felt to Teddy like lancing a boil. To him it felt as though a huge weight had been placed upon his shoulders. Teddy had saddled him with a secret that felt like acid in his gut. He picked up the drink and just as he was about to down it, it occurred to him that he did have someone he could share this with. Victoria. He would tell Victoria and it would be a secret they could share together. Victoria had more integrity than anyone he had ever known. It was as if a light had been turned on and shone a way out of his misery.

'A burden shared is a burden halved,' he said as he lifted the glass and sank it in one.

Beth had cleared up the forks and the dirty shepherd's pie dish once they had all finished eating – all except Victoria – and was about to take them down to the kitchen.

'What's up with you? Have you ants in your pants?' Dana asked her. 'You've yet to tell me your news. What's been happening while I've been looking after the patient from hell?'

'Oh, not a lot really,' Beth replied cheerily. 'I've been mostly working in theatre,' she said. 'You know me, the only single one in the group. The workaholic, boyfriendless one, sat on the shelf.' And she shot out the door.

'Well, well, well,' said Pammy, 'would you credit the nerve of her. I don't know how I've kept my mouth shut.' She folded her arms and looked as though she would chew Beth's head off when she returned.

'Don't you *dare* say anything.' Dana wagged her finger at her. 'I don't want Beth thinking we were spying on her. Do you hear me, Nurse Tanner?'

'But you were, weren't you? Don't go getting all Irish pious with me.' Pammy scowled. 'I can't believe I am sat here having to pretend that I don't know one of my best friends has something going with the biggest cad in the hospital. And after the way he treated me?'

'Pammy, I was not spying on her. We were not. I swear to God. They weren't even trying to hide. Under the cedar tree, they were. All she needed was a flashing neon sign on her head saying, "Look at me, necking with Oliver Gaskell". But I swear to God, if you let Victoria and me down, we will fall out. Beth is the quiet one and she will not take kindly to being caught out.' Dana's tone was firm and brooked no nonsense.

'I just can't get over it. She knows how I feel about that man and she knows about Nurse Moran too. What's up with her? You know everyone thinks he got that poor Nurse Moran pregnant and didn't stand by her, and her being Irish too. I don't get you, Dana. You know what that meant for her. Has Beth completely lost her marbles?'

'Oh, don't you be talking now. Can't you answer that question for yourself? Sure, weren't you the one who was drooling after the fella when we first arrived? You couldn't get enough of him right from the off when we were probationers. It was Oliver Gaskell this and that, morning, noon and night. And besides, I'm not so sure Nurse Moran was pregnant. She was an awful clumsy person, but I can't imagine that. I know where she comes from and she would have had the fear of God about any such thing drilled into her by her mammy long before she came to Liverpool.'

'But, Dana, that was before I knew what he was like. He's a cad. He wanted to get into my drawers as fast as he could. The minute I told him me da would have his guts for garters, he didn't want to know any more.'

Dana sighed. 'God, I am so lucky. My Teddy knows the terror I have of getting pregnant outside of marriage. You're right about that, Pammy – there is no worse sin at home. I would probably never be able to go back and I doubt that Daddy would ever set eyes on me again. 'Twould just be the most awful thing and, you know, Teddy was so good, he really understood that. But that's why I don't think Nurse Moran was pregnant. If she was, Ireland would be the last place she'd run to. It may be the 1950s, but, believe me, pregnant girls over there go missing and are never heard of again. She may have been clumsy, but she wasn't stupid.'

Victoria propped herself up on to one elbow. 'Oh, honestly, why does everyone regard sex as though it's a danger not a pleasure? As if everyone gets pregnant the moment they have it. It drives me mad how primitive some people are.'

'Oh, Victoria, that's not fair, it is a danger. Go and ask any of the women in the unmarried mothers' home on Princess Avenue. They will tell you how easy it is to fall into sin and be punished,' Dana replied.

'Oh, for goodness' sake,' said Victoria, exasperated now. 'They got pregnant because they were stupid. They didn't take the proper precautions, that's all.'

'Are you feeling any better, Victoria?' asked Pammy. 'You sound it. You're talking about sex again, your favourite subject.'

'Pammy!' Dana almost squealed. 'Honestly. I was so looking forward to coming back, but now I'm wondering if I wasn't better off in Bolton. Everyone is so testy and rude.' She turned to Pammy to emphasize her point.

'Right, well, on that note, I'm going to take that nap,' said Victoria. 'I don't think the brandies we had after dinner last night have helped me very much, to be honest. I'm going to unpack and get my uniform ready for tomorrow,' she said.

'Ooh, brandy, get you,' said Pammy. 'You are so sophisticated, Victoria. I wish I could be a lady like you.'

Down in the kitchen, Beth dried the forks and put them in the drawer. She liked to clean up and help Mrs Duffy, and as pleased and excited as she was to see her friends, she was finding it difficult to be in the same room as them.

She had been on her way home, walking past the doctors' residence, when she saw that her shoelace was undone. She crouched down to tie it and was almost done when she heard Oliver Gaskell calling her name. She looked up, surprised out of her reveries about her lunch to come.

'Nurse Harper. You seem to be having some difficulty.'

Beth responded as quick as a flash. 'And you appear to be loitering. You startled me,' she said.

'Not at all. I was just putting my bike away, thank you very much, and I saw you as you came towards the back gates. Now there is someone who might fancy a meal at the Sunrise in Chinatown, I thought. I hear you have had a busy night in theatre. They do lovely banana fritters for dessert and I've yet to meet a nurse who can resist them. How about it?'

Beth hoped he hadn't heard the sound of her stomach groaning at the mention of banana fritters. She thought of Victoria arriving back at Lovely Lane and the promise of news about Dana. 'You have lots of experience of taking nurses there then, do you? I suppose that fits. No, thank you. You will have to find some other poor unsuspecting nurse, but not me.'

His brows furrowed and then he laughed out loud. 'I don't want to take anyone else. I want to take you.' He rocked on to the balls of his feet, leaning over her slightly. His dark, wavy hair fell forward and his eyes were full of laughter and mischief, studying her like a chess player to see what her next move would be. He didn't have to wait long.

'Well, you can't have me. I'm afraid I'm not one of your acolytes, Mr Gaskell. Now, if you will excuse me, I have to get along.'

For a split second she thought he looked irritated, angry even, but within a flash he was grinning from ear to ear. 'Nurse Harper, are you really turning me down?'

Beth looked back at him and raised her eyebrows. 'Well, if not wanting to have dinner with you is turning you down, then yes, I am. Dear me, it appears you may not be used to that. I'm sorry.'

But she wasn't sorry, she was terrified and her heart felt as if it was banging against her chest like a hammer. She pulled her cape across herself so that he wouldn't see her hands shaking. Her mouth was dry and she felt as though something was about to happen, as if she was at some sort of crossroads.

'Nurse Harper, can I just give you something to take with you. And then I would like you to think about it and when I ask you out again, sometime soon, you may give me a different answer. Would you mind?'

Beth looked down at his hand in his jacket pocket, thinking that he was about to extract something to give to her. But before she had the chance to say another word, he placed his arm across the small of her back, pulled her into him and kissed her hard. For the briefest moment the only thought in her mind was to let go, to forget the world and everyone in it. This was it, the moment. It was here and she had been waiting for it for a very long time. But something stopped her from yielding to him and she wrenched herself away. She was breathing hard, much to her annoyance, but she managed to compose herself. When she could trust herself to speak, she replied, 'Well, I don't think that is going to make me change my mind about anything, thank you very much. Goodbye, Mr Gaskell.' And then, before her knees betrayed her and she sank to the ground, she was gone.

Now, in the kitchen, as she thought about Oliver Gaskell's kiss, a thrill ran through her and made her stomach flip. She hugged the tea towel she was drying up with and pressed the tips of her fingers to her lips, the place where his lips had lingered only an hour before. What would be his next move, she wondered. And if she really wanted to tame and keep this man, what should be hers?

Chapter 9

Lorcan studied the intravenous solution in the glass bottle as, drip by drip, it seeped into his mother's flaccid white arm. Her breathing was steady and he hoped that was a good sign. He'd seen the nurse count her breaths in and out using her fob watch and then, seemingly happy with what she found, write a number down on the chart at the end of the bed.

He was alarmed by the volume of bandages and the size of her head, which was slightly elevated on a small pile of pillows. 'That's to keep the swelling draining the right way,' the nurse had whispered to him as she slipped another pillow underneath. On his mam's temple, a small stain of blood had leaked through the bandages and spread on to the crisp white pillow.

Lorcan knew his mother would hate the bandages. She panicked if she felt trapped. She didn't even like to be upstairs in the house alone and would frequently open the back door, even on the coldest of days. 'Just catching the air. Can't breathe in here,' she would say. He knew she would try to pull off the bandages and yank the drip out as soon she came to.

The nurse was so kind to him that when she spoke he thought she might be a real angel. As soon as she'd seen the look on his face, she had explained why there was such a lot of bandaging. 'Don't be worrying about the big bandages, it's just to protect the area where the little piece of skull has been removed. It looks really dramatic, doesn't it?'

Lorcan nodded. He still couldn't speak. At first it had been through shyness, and fear of losing his mam. Now it was because he was scared that if he tried to say anything, a single word, he would lose control. The demons that were running around in his head would rush out as soon as he opened his mouth. He knew that it must have been one of the Bevans who had done this to his mother and that it was something to do with J.T. Was it punishment for him having refused to take part in the jump-over? He wanted to kill whoever it was with his own bare hands. No words would escape him, but an anger, a ferocious red fury, burnt within.

'Look at you, you poor love.' The staff nurse was talking to him again. Lorcan knew she was a staff nurse because of her pale blue uniform; it was different from the pink uniform the student nurses wore. Jake had explained the ranks and uniforms to him on his first day.

The nurse slipped a thermometer under his mother's tongue and held her fob watch to time the minute. There was a waft of Dettol and something that smelt vaguely like flowers, but it was overlaid with a stronger smell that lifted up from the bandages and the blood. The nurse extracted the thermometer, shook it hard, placed it in a small enamel kidney dish filled with diluted white Dettol and wrote something else on the chart. 'I'm just going to get the sphygmomanometer to take her blood pressure again,' she said with another of her dazzling smiles, as if he would know what on earth she was talking about.

Lorcan lifted his gaze from his mother and through the narrow row of high-up windows he could see that night had finally turned into day. He had no idea of the actual time, but even though he had only worked at the hospital for a short period, the porter activity and the wicker baskets full of dirty linen being replaced by neatly folded and often still warm sheets and pillow cases told him that the new shifts had started. Lorcan had worked a whole day on linen duty just this week. Wards eight and nine were his responsibility. He had felt a huge sense of satisfaction at home time, leaving both linen cupboards stacked and stocked for the night nurses.

His mam sighed, distracting Lorcan from his thoughts. The nurse bustled back in and her presence instantly made him feel calmer. Her complexion was pink and powdery and her shiny blonde hair had been swept across her forehead and tucked under her frilled and starched cap. She was speaking and he focused on her lips as they moved.

'You sit down and I shall go and fetch you a cup of tea and a couple of biscuits, put you back on your feet. You must have had a terrible shock. You looked wiped out, you poor thing. We'll look after her for you and I'm on all day, I won't leave her side, I promise.'

Lorcan felt the breath he hadn't been aware he was holding leave his body in a rush. He wanted to get on to his knees and cry in gratitude for the kindness of the nurse he didn't know, answering the prayers he had no idea he had been saying. She didn't wait for him to reply but instead laid her hand on top of his for the briefest moment. It was warm and soft and damp from having been freshly washed, and it felt to Lorcan almost as though a real angel had folded her gossamer wings around him.

He had no idea he was hungry or thirsty until she reappeared with the steaming tea and the plate of biscuits. She left him alone to drink and eat, as if sensing that he would be able to do neither in her presence, and then seemed to know by instinct when he had finished. She came back in and checked his mother's drip was still flowing freely. He could hear in the distance the sound of crockery clanking, the far-off wheels of a trolley making its way along the main corridor and the hushed voices of two men; porters, he assumed. Then the telephone in the office rang out and filled the ward with its shrill, repetitive tone.

'I'll be back.' The staff nurse smiled as she left the cubicle. A moment later, she returned. 'That was our very own Dessie Horton. He said he will be here soon for you, Lorcan. He's going to take you home.'

Lorcan was touched that Dessie would do that and he felt stronger after the biscuits too. His hands had stopped shaking and he felt more composed. 'Will Mammy be all right? Should I not stay?'

The nurse smiled at him again. 'You can't, Lorcan, I'm sorry. Sister would give me my marching orders if she saw you here. You're not even supposed to be here now, really, but I know Sister won't get to me on her rounds for a wee bit longer, so we're safe for the moment.'

Dessie crept into the cubicle so quietly that neither Lorcan nor the staff nurse heard him. He was followed closely by the surgeon who had operated on his mother. The cubicle suddenly felt very small and full.

'How are you doing, lad?' Dessie whispered.

The surgeon walked over to his mother's bed and, picking up her wrist, held it with the tips of his fingers to take her pulse as he studied the watch on his own wrist. 'Amazingly, we managed to control the swelling pretty quickly,' he said to the nurse, who had picked up the chart from the end of the bed and was standing with her pen at the ready, awaiting his instructions. 'Her vital signs are steadying nicely.' The surgeon looked back at his watch. 'Perfect. Couldn't have asked for better than that,' he said as he laid her hand back down.

'Does that mean she will be OK, doctor?' said Dessie, instinctively posing the question Lorcan was too afraid to ask.

'Well, there may be some residual brain damage, I'm afraid, but we won't know that for a few weeks. As we can't see inside a skull, we can't tell what impact the bleed has had or which parts of the brain were affected. The X-rays simply tell us if there's been a fracture to the skull, and that isn't what causes the damage. For now we shall concentrate on nursing her through the effects of the surgery and getting her back on her feet. When everything has settled down we will conduct some neurological tests to assess the brain damage. If she makes it through the next forty-eight hours, and I think that is a very strong possibility, she'll live. I don't want to tempt fate, but I think your mother is probably a very lucky lady, Master Ryan.'

It was just too much for Lorcan to hear all at once. He had held so much in for hours that now he could barely control his reaction to the doctor's words. A loud, anguished sob escaped his mouth.

Dessie placed his hand on his shoulder and squeezed it lightly. 'Come on, lad,' he said. 'It's time to take you home.'

When they reached the main entrance, Bryan called out to them. He had been running and was out of breath. 'Dessie, Biddy sent me, the bizzies, they are at Mrs Ryan's and so is

Biddy. She says you are to take Lorcan straight there. Matron put a flea in their ear and sent them out of casualty. Told them they couldn't wait there and to come back when Mrs Ryan was recovered. Right mad with them she was.'

'Good old Matron,' said Dessie and he smiled for the first time that day. 'Right, Bryan, listen. You come with me to Lorcan's house. I'll stay until the bizzies have gone and then I'd like you to come back and stay with Lorcan tonight. I'm going round to see your da with some news this evening, so I'll help him with whatever he needs and you look after Lorcan. We don't know if whoever did this will come back.'

'I know, that's what Biddy said. The bizzies are talking to Emily in the parlour, Dessie. She saw the bloke in the entry. She's giving them a description.'

For a brief moment Dessie felt sick. What if whoever it was had attacked Emily instead, just for having seen him?

When they reached the Ryans' house, Biddy was in the kitchen, placing an enamel dish of fried potatoes into the bread oven in the range. She started talking before Lorcan had taken his coat off.

'Right, no messing about now, listen to me. Lorcan, the bizzies are in the parlour. Dessie, you take him in. Bryan, you get the first wash down in the scullery. I'm going to fry some eggs and there's a bit of smoked haddock poaching in some milk to go with the 'tatoes. Lorcan, how's your mammy now? Dessie, wash them hands, would you, you've no doubt been carting God knows what around.' She took in Lorcan's pathetic face as she spoke. There were white circles under his eyes from all his tears.

'The doctor says he thinks she's going to be OK.' Lorcan sobbed again.

Biddy put out her arms and Lorcan fell into them, burying his head in her chest.

'Well now, isn't that grand news. Whoever doubted it? I didn't. Your mother has had a hard life, Lorcan, she has survived worse. Now then, enough of this.' She held him away from her. 'All this is just an inconvenience to be got through and we will all come out the other side, none the worse. The Lord God will do his work. We got through the Blitz, didn't we?' She picked up the tea towel off the range and used it to close the oven door.

Dessie made no comment. No one ever mentioned the May Blitz. Not ever. Although they walked daily through the ruins of their former lives and over the graves of people they'd known and loved, no one ever spoke of it.

'What a difference you have made to this place,' said Biddy, changing the subject quickly before too many ghosts drifted into the room, bringing the memories of the smoke, the eternal dark, the dismembered bodies hanging from rooftops, the flames from the ship that took a direct hit, the relentless bombing raids on the streets and the bombs raining down on the docks, one of which had taken Dessie's wife. 'Clean as a whistle it is,' she continued. 'Goodness me, your mammy has a nice clean home to come to when she is discharged. Now, go on, into the parlour, and if those bizzies give you any trouble, come for me.'

Dessie winked at Biddy as he put his hand in the middle of Lorcan's back and guided him through. She was forgiven for her faux pas and the ghosts melted away.

'I'll bring you some tea in,' said Biddy. 'Both of you. No

more for the bizzies though, don't want them staying all day now, do we. Get them away as fast as you can, Dessie.' This was hissed in barely more than a whisper. Noise carried in a two-up two-down.

Just as the door to the parlour closed, Elsie dashed in through the back door, carrying a plate. 'I've made a fly pie for the boys,' she said. 'Used up the last of me currants.'

'Did you get them from down the docks?' asked Biddy.

Elsie ignored the question. 'Plumped up lovely with a bit of cold tea, they did. How is she, did they say?'

'She will live but may have brain damage,' said Biddy as she placed the fly pie on the press.

'Jesus, how would anyone be able to tell?' asked Elsie. 'She was away with the fairies as it was.'

'I have no idea, but would you look at the cut of this place and what a job this lad has done for his mother.'

Elsie looked around the floor. 'You know, Biddy, the last time I came in here, my feet stuck to the floor, it was that bad. I haven't been back since.'

'No, well, I've not been one meself for making the casual visit. None of us have. But now she's in hospital, we all have to, just as we would for anyone else. The lad needs us, Elsie. Time to marshal the troops. He's done a grand job with this place, but we can get an army in and we'll do better. You will see your face shine in this floor by the time we've finished.'

That evening, over in Vince Street, Noleen was on her way to St Chad's and then on to work when Dessie passed her in the entry. 'Oh, good to see you, Dessie,' she said. 'I got a message from one of the lads. How is Mrs Ryan? Is our Bryan at the house now? Is he helping young Lorcan?'

'He is, Noleen. He's a great help. I'm coming by to see Paddy, I have news for him.'

'Well, I hope it's good news. You know our Finn passed the eleven-plus? Have you ever heard the like? He has a place for the Waterloo Grammar. I can't send him there, Dessie. We have no money for that. If I buy him a uniform, the others will have to go without shoes.' Noleen's voice began to rise.

Dessie cut her off and spoke quickly. 'Well, that might be about to change, Noleen. I'm in to see Paddy with a bit of news. I have him a job.'

'A job? Doing what, where? Paddy can't work, Dessie. Who would take him on?'

Dessie laughed. 'Give me a chance, Noleen, would you. It's at St Angelus, a night job. Twelve pounds a week – good money. But, first I have to take him to visit Joe at the prosthetics clinic. Joe reckons he can work wonders and that Paddy shouldn't be in as much pain as he is.'

Noleen crossed herself. Twelve pounds a week would transform the family fortunes. 'That's the rent and the bills, the food, everything covered right there,' she whispered almost to herself, hardly believing it. 'Who has given him the job?'

'It's Matron. We have new rules to abide by with the coal deliveries. He will be a night watchman. I gave him a glowing testimonial. Didn't tell Matron what a moaning miserable bugger he is, because I wouldn't now, would I.' Dessie grinned, savouring the look on Noleen's face. 'Now I need to speak to Paddy, and soon, because if I'm not back home before lights out, Emily will divorce me before we are even married. Paddy starts his first night next Saturday and he gets double time from midnight until Sunday morning at seven when he clocks off, so there's a bonus in the first week. Jake will collect him and drive him in the van down to Joe at the clinic.'

Noleen had changed colour, both from the news Dessie was imparting and from exhaustion. He could see her mind working overtime, grasping for the right things to say.

'Well, whatever next,' she whispered, almost to herself. 'So much is changing so fast, Dessie.'

'It is that. But that's the way now, it seems to me. Do you not feel like we've all been in a dream since the war ended and now we've woken up all of a sudden?'

'Like we have all only just stopped grieving, more like,' Noleen replied.

Dessie couldn't argue with that, it was an explanation as good as any other.

'Noleen, I'm going to offer Paddy the job on one condition, that you take four nights a week off. Keep working at the hospital if you want to, but you have to go part time.' She made to object, but Dessie was having none of it. 'I don't have to tell you, Noleen, what a pittance you night cleaners get paid.' He sighed. 'It's because there are so many of you. The NHS hasn't been so good with its pay for you women, has it? Cleaners and nurses alike. It's a shocker, considering how you all kept the country fed and running in the war.'

As Noleen dared to think that she might be able to work fewer hours and spend more time in her own home, the thrill travelled through her and sent a flutter into the pit of her stomach. Was this too good to be true? Was Dessie about to tell her this was all a joke?

'And don't you be worrying about Finn. He will go to the grammar. Everyone is behind you on that. He's the first child from a St Angelus family to be offered a place and I'll tell you this, you know how competitive this lot are, he won't be the last. They'll all be trying to get their kids in there the minute Finn walks down the road in his smart uniform.'

It felt to Noleen as though Dessie was speaking in a foreign language. She wanted to discuss it some more, but the peal of the distant bell was calling her to St Chad's and Noleen never missed Mass. 'I have to go, Dessie.' The bell stopped ringing. 'Oh God, I'm late.' And without another word, she ran towards the church as though a devil chased at her back.

As Dessie entered the Delaneys' kitchen, a scene of domestic contentment met him. It occurred to him that this was Noleen's work – her perfect family, her domain – and that for Finn to attend the grammar was something new, beyond her control. When money was short, change was something to be feared.

Finn was lying on his front, sprawled out across the hearth with a book resting open on Paddy's only foot and his chin in his hands. As usual, the other boys were nowhere to be seen and Dessie guessed they would be out with the other lads, kicking a ball about in the dark out on the bombed-out wasteland. Mary and Lorraine Tanner were at the kitchen table painting each other's nails and a strong smell of solvent hit Dessie's nostrils as soon as he stepped into the room. Paddy had the *Liverpool Echo* spread out on his knee and next to him was a half-drunk cup of tea, Noleen's last act before she flew out of the door.

'How are ye, Dessie? Is it Bryan you are after, because he's over at the Ryans' house helping Lorcan.'

'I know that, Paddy, I asked him to go there. Finn, could you get any closer to that fire?'

Finn didn't flick a muscle. He was so engrossed in his book, he was oblivious to the fact that Dessie had even entered the room. The side of his face nearer to the fire glowed red from the flames.

'Hello, Uncle Dessie.' The girls spoke as one, but only Lorraine Tanner continued. 'How long is Bryan going to be at the Ryans'?' She was direct, as was the way with the entire Tanner family. But Dessie could tell this was no general enquiry. Lorraine was fast becoming a precocious teenager. 'Do you like me nails?' she said before he could reply. She held out her hand in the manner of a courtier waiting for it to be kissed.

'Yes, very nice. That's a good colour if you like rotting roses.'

'Rotting roses!' Both girls squealed.

Lorraine pulled her hand in sharply to re-examine her nails. 'That's Cutex pink shimmer, that,' she said, affronted. 'It's not rotting roses, who would wear a colour called that?'

Dessie winked at Paddy, who grinned as he winked back. 'Oh, your Uncle Dessie has always been able to wind you girls up, hasn't he?' Paddy closed the newspaper and folded it. 'You never learn, do you? Mary, do you think you can tear yourself away from the rotting flowers and make Uncle Dessie a cup of tea?'

'Do I...' Mary was about to protest, but she caught the warning look in her father's eye and thought better of it. 'When's our Bryan coming back?' she asked testily as she slid from her chair and with the ball of her hand pushed the kettle along the range to the hot plate, being careful not to smudge her newly painted nails.

Lorraine swivelled round in her chair, keen to hear the answer. She couldn't sit around in the Delaneys' kitchen much longer.

'You see, Dessie, if our Bryan was here, he would have made the tea and Mary could have continued with what she does best, which is very little, as you know.'

'Now, Paddy, that's not true. Mary is a good girl, aren't you Mary?' Mary grinned as Dessie continued. 'She just needs a few lessons on how to be a help to her mammy, that's all.' Mary's grin quickly turned into a scowl.

'That'll be the day,' said Paddy. 'But it's not our Mary's fault. I keep saying this, but Noleen, she's her own worst enemy. Thinks she's the only person who can do anything around here. Sometimes I'm glad I've only got one leg and have an excuse not to do anything because I'd only do it wrong. There's only one person Noleen doesn't have a go at in this house and that's our Bryan. Isn't it, Mary?'

Lorraine wanted to scream. Dessie hadn't answered the question.

Dessie gently pushed Finn's feet over with his boot and sat down on the settle opposite Paddy. Finn didn't appear to notice.

'It's something to do with birds, you know,' Paddy said as he inclined his head towards Finn's book. 'Swallows and Amazonians or something. Sister Theresa lent it to him. I don't know how he passed that eleven-plus. Our Bryan said that when he went to wake him up yesterday, Finn was sat up in bed reading that book and then he shouted at Bryan to get out of the water. Bryan was only stood in the room. He's not all there sometimes, our Finn. Anyway, how's Mrs Ryan? I hear she's through the worst.'

Dessie almost laughed out loud. Never in his life had he been the first person to impart any news, anywhere. Before he could ask Paddy how he had such good knowledge of Mrs Ryan's condition, Paddy went on to explain.

'Betty Hutch called in to tell Noleen on her way back from the shop and she heard it in from Madge, who was buying flour.'

'Ah, Madge.' Now she really was the first one with the news. 'The doctor thinks she will live, but she might have brain damage.'

'Jesus, how will they be able to tell?' said Paddy. 'You could get more sense out of mad Betty from the mission.'

'I know. Anyway, she will live and that's all that matters and all that Lorcan is bothered about right now.' Dessie dropped his voice to a whisper. 'Lorcan wouldn't have got to keep the house if anything had happened. The harbour board would have had him out within a week. It's a blessing in more ways than one.'

'What did the bizzies say?' Paddy lowered his voice too. 'Was it one of J.T.'s mates? He was a bad bastard, that one. If the father, God rest his soul, could see what those sons had turned into, he would swivel in his grave.'

'Aye, well, Lorcan isn't like any of them, so thanks be for that. It looks like it was one of the Bevan boys. There is more, though. J.T. has jumped prison. He was being transferred and he overpowered the two officers and did a runner. I told the police, all the Ryans are fast runners.'

'It wouldn't have been J.T. who attacked her... would it?' said Paddy.

'No, never. No son could do that to his own mother. No, the attacker was in the Bevan gear – the hat and jacket malarkey, big ponces that they are. Emily saw him and she could tell he wasn't from anywhere around here. She told the bizzies that. They said there is a man coming out that will take fingerprints in the house and then they'll be able to tell if it was a Bevan or not.'

Paddy shook his head. 'I've read about that fingerprinting in the *Echo*,' he said. 'They got a murderer in Toxteth with it. I'd like that job. What an interesting job that would be, catching fingerprints.'

'Well, now, I have news on that score,' said Dessie. 'I have you a job. It's at the hospital.'

Paddy raised his eyebrows and looked hard at his friend.

'We are moving on to night-time coal deliveries. It's crazy, but the corpy believes that the dust which becomes airborne during large deliveries can be a fire and health hazard, so now the coal has to be hosed down after each delivery. Which means we have to do it at night. I need a man to check the coal lorries in. I'm putting a lad on nights to hose down. Matron is a stickler for the rules and it has to be done. It's a sit-down job, twelve green ones a week, six times more than Noleen earns, and you start on Saturday, five nights a week. It's on one condition though, Paddy, that Noleen drops four of her nights, at least. She's been working five and six nights a week and it's been killing her. I swear to God that she'd work seven if we'd let her.'

Paddy threw his newspaper into the coal bucket and answered Dessie without hesitation. 'Well, you can keep it. I don't want your job. I was an engineer, not a night watch-man and I won't be taking it.'

Dessie was too stunned at the chilling tone in Paddy's voice to respond.

Paddy leant forward in his chair, his face flushed and his eyes glinting with a resentment Dessie had never before seen. 'You think I'm going to sit in a hut like a useless article while the men I grew up with work on the docks and get taken on from the stand on account of their strength and not much else? Because they weren't in the wrong place like I was? Because they came back in one piece? They aren't taken on for their brains, I can tell you. Most of them drink away half of what they earn. I may not have much to call my own while I am sat in this chair, Dessie, but one thing I do have is my pride and I won't let anyone take that away from me or my family. This is a made-up job and it better not be Biddy Kennedy and her interfering ways behind this, so help me God. You were a good man, giving our Bryan a job, and I will always be grateful for what you have done for him. But me, I don't need your charity, thank you very much. Mary, where's that tea?'

'You can put on your big hard-man act with anyone else, Paddy, but not with me, you know that, don't you?' Dessie shook his head in annoyance. 'I knew you before, lad, we all did. We faced the same here and over there. 'Tis a terrible thing happened to you, but there are many like you, getting on with life. You will see them when Jake takes you to the prosthetics clinic, if you'll let him. Now why don't you just straighten your bloody face for one night and let that wife of yours have a break. You never know, you might even enjoy working yourself.'

Lorraine left the table and moved over to the range, where Mary was pouring Dessie's tea. 'I'm off now,' she said.

Mary put the teapot down with a bang. 'What? No, you can't, your nails aren't dry and I thought you were going to put my rags in my hair for me after.'

'I can't, we've taken too long on the nails.' The truth was that Lorraine felt uncomfortable. Although Dessie and Paddy had been speaking in hushed voices, the atmosphere in the kitchen had chilled and Paddy looked angry. Lorraine loved Uncle Paddy, but she didn't like the moods and sulks he was prone to. 'I promised Mam I'd get home earlier tonight. She's been on her feet all day long, cleaning, and I said I'd do some of the flat-ironing for her.'

'Flamin' clean, cook, scrub, wash and flat-iron, it's all women around here do,' said Mary. She continued pouring the tea and almost missed the mug when she heard Lorraine's reply.

'Well, except for your mam, Mary. She does all that, and works nights at the hospital too. My mam says she doesn't know how she does it. She says the women at the bingo say that your mam is the unluckiest woman on the street. My mam said she really would be dead on her feet if she had to do everything your mam did all on her own. I have to pull my weight in our house, Mary, 'cause if I don't, I get it in the neck from me da. I used to think you were dead lucky and I was jealous of you, but I like helping me mam, really.' She turned to face the two men. 'Bye, Uncle Paddy, bye Uncle Dessie. No point in saying bye to soft lad on the floor there now, is there?'

Paddy looked up. 'Now, Lorraine, you cannot call him that any more. Jack and Cahill, they have changed his name to "the professor" now he's passed that exam.'

Lorraine laughed. 'Right you are. Night, Professor.'

Finn didn't stir from his book.

Lorraine made her way down the yard and left Mary staring at the closed door. Lorraine was going off to help her mam, and Maisie Tanner had never worked a day in her life, other than looking after her family. *Except for your mam. She does all that, and works nights at the hospital too.* Lorraine's words rang in Mary's ears. *Your mam is the unluckiest woman on the street.* She stared at the door with Dessie's tea in her hand as the words sank in.

Noleen fell to her knees on the prayer stool, placed one hand on her brow and closed her eyes. As she shut down the worries that plagued her, the familiar surroundings became all that mattered. The burning of the incense and the tick, tick of the swinging thurible as it clicked in time with the beat of her heart. The holy smoke that filled the air and drifted, waiting to carry her prayers heavenwards. The low, melodic chanting of the nuns that washed away her cares, easing her breathing to a steady rhythm. The footsteps of the altar-boy, the swish of his skirts; the fading tones of the organ and the smell of the wood. And the darkness, illuminated only by the flickering candles. The weight and worry lifted from Noleen's shoulders and she sighed. 'Holy Mary, Mother of God, be with us now, in our hour of need, and always.' She took her rosaries out from her coat pocket and pressed them to her lips.

Paddy has a job. She almost whispered the words out loud. Paddy has a job. Finn wants to go to the school. Dessie wants me to cut down my hours. She opened her eyes, looked to her right to the statue of Our Lady and whispered, 'What do I do?'

Father Brennan began to move about at the altar. She heard the coughing of one of the mothers from Charles Street in the row in front and glanced her way. Her coat was thin and worn, the shoulders damp and her headscarf frayed. She had lost her husband in the war and had looked ill for months, but like all war widows, all wartime mothers, she had no option but to carry on and work. With five mouths to feed, who could not? Once again the thought crossed Noleen's mind that the poor woman was not well. She promised herself that she would ask her if she was managing and if there was anything she could do to help. It would be hard because, like herself, all dockside mothers were proud, but Noleen would do it, before they left the church. She had been so long bemoaning her own plight that she had failed to notice others around her who were also finding life tough.

Tonight Noleen had a lot to be thankful for. She might be able to spend more time at home with her children, and Dessie had said that Finn really should go to the grammar. A cold fear squeezed her heart. She didn't know any family who had a child at the grammar, and wasn't that really what she was afraid of? She didn't know what to do. But Sister Theresa had said, 'We will do all there is to be done, Noleen. Just let the boy go and do his best because he has a gift for the learning and it's all he wants in the world. And if Finn isn't afraid of the tremendous opportunity before him, why are you?'

Noleen did what she always did when in doubt, she closed her eyes and prayed to the friend of all mothers everywhere. Sister Theresa is right, isn't she, she prayed. It's not a mother's job to hold her children back. And it's not as though I will be alone. I have the nuns and Father Brennan to help me. 'Holy Mary, Mother of God, be with us now and in our hour of need.' She kissed her rosaries again. The prayer I ask, you have already delivered, because you understood my needs before I knew myself. Our worries are over. Paddy can earn a regular wage and won't that just change everything.

There will be a life to be lived. She smiled. And 'tis all down to you, Holy Mother.

The nuns' chanting started to fade and Father Brennan's sonorous voice began to reach her. Noleen let his prayers seep into her soul. There was no better place to be. As all her problems melted away and the strength she desired to carry her through each day and night filled her, she smiled as she began to pray once more. 'Hail Mary, full of grace, the Lord is with thee; blessed art thou amongst women, and blessed is the fruit of thy womb.' Tears of love and gratitude for the mother of all mothers filled her eyes and her heart as she whispered, 'Thank you.'

Chapter 10

Victoria looked down at the three pairs of blood-covered wellingtons standing in the long sink and wanted to heave. Theatre was nothing like she'd thought it would be. 'I've yet to see a single patient, awake or asleep,' she grumbled to Beth. 'They don't even tell us what operation it is, we have to guess from the body parts being wheeled in through the door into the dirty sluice.'

Beth laughed. 'I've told you, all the operations are listed on the blackboard, with patient names, wards, surgeon, theatre number and the expected time of surgery.'

'What does that matter?' Victoria snapped. 'You have to be able to have two minutes to escape from this room to read it. The only thing we do up here is clean and clean. We are just glorified boot-washers, do you know that? Cleaners of blood and gore.'

Beth, usually the chirpiest and least complaining of all the Lovely Lane girls, for once agreed. She switched off the hot tap she was running into the sink and sighed. 'I'm not sure Sister Pokey is fully aware of my degree of competency,' she said. 'She does seem to prefer the staff nurses she has worked with for years. I do wonder sometimes if she wishes we weren't here.' She fastened her rubber apron at the back and reached for her rubber gloves. 'I live in rubber. I squelch when I walk.'

Victoria turned her head sharply and pursed her lips. 'Your competency, Beth? We are all as competent as each other, we started together, remember?' She sounded very unhappy and the tone of her voice put Beth on her guard. 'You always speak as though you are more qualified than the rest of us. I haven't seen much proof of that and I have worked with you more than the others.'

She pulled the tap handle on her own sink in frustration and while the scalding water ran through, she opened the metal container of sterilizing tablets and threw two into the sink. As they landed in the water and began to fizz, she placed the back of her hand under her nose and against her mouth. The faint aroma of the Yardley lilac hand cream she had slathered on that morning struggled to compete with the pungent smell of blood as the water hit the boots. Her head swam, her eyes watered, her mouth tingled. 'I'm sorry Beth,' she said. 'I don't mean to snap. I'm still not feeling very well.'

It had amazed everyone who nursed with Victoria how well she had adapted to her training. Being the daughter of Bolton's grand Baker Hall, which had been in her family for eleven generations until her late father managed to lose it, she was used to a life of privilege and comfort. Everyone had expected her to be the weakest of her group of student nurses, but she'd been the star, much to others' surprise.

'Oh, poor you.' Beth quickly dried her hands, walked over to Victoria and placed her hand in the small of her back.

Victoria had turned a ghastly shade of pale. Beads of perspiration stood proud of her brow, and her face powder, applied only an hour earlier, had begun to cake on her damp skin.

The loud hum of the suction machines in theatre, which had filled their room as they'd scrubbed and cleaned, had now become intermittent. 'The tonsillectomy must have almost finished,' Beth said. 'Would you like me to fetch Sister Pokey?'

Both girls were silent. The end of an operation meant only one thing. More bloody boots and aprons. Bloody swabs to be counted and dressing sheets to be rinsed before being sent to the autoclave. Enamel kidney dishes and instruments to be rinsed and submerged in the water with sterilizing tablets that stung and burnt their hands and arms where it splashed.

Beth's shoulders drooped. She had been holding her own feelings at bay, determined to say nothing, just get on with the job and put up with whatever Sister Pokey threw at her, but it had taken Victoria only a couple of minutes to break her resolve. Beth had wanted desperately to be on theatre, but as more than just a dirty nurse. She learnt nothing trapped in this small sluice room while all the action took place in the main theatre outside. She felt sick herself as the sharp metallic smell of blood filled the air. 'Let me open the window a bit more,' she said as she pulled up the sash. A cold blast of fresh air rushed in.

'Trolley coming through.' Sister Pokey's voice rang out as the swing doors pushed open. 'Catch,' she said as she pushed the first trolley through. The fresh air lost its battle with the instruments of surgery and a pair of freshly removed tonsils.

Victoria turned away from the sink to reach out her hand and stop the trolley, but it was no use. She failed to make it to the adjoining sink and promptly discharged the contents of her stomach directly at the feet of Sister Pokey. Victoria had always been the one with the weakest stomach. Vomiting at each new sight and smell associated with nursing had been her biggest challenge, but it was one she had eventually, with some difficulty, overcome. This had served only to further impress everyone as to how well she had adjusted to nursing, as though a sensitive stomach in an aristocrat was much more difficult to conquer. Pammy, born and bred in Arthur Street, had reinforced this myth as she had never so much as batted an eyelid at the worst sights and smells. But Beth, who had been present with Victoria through some of her more sickly moments, was aware that this latest moment of weakness was a dramatic event even by her standards.

Sister Pokey glanced down at her shoes, raised her eyebrows and looked back up at Victoria with an expression that bordered on disdain. 'Well, you had better make sure that's the first and the last time that happens,' she said. 'We have no time on theatre for nurses with queasy stomachs. It can take a week to acclimatize, even for a qualified staff nurse, but if by the end of a full week of shifts you are still like this, then I shall have to ask Matron to transfer you back on to the wards. Is that clear?'

Victoria continued wiping her mouth with the back of her hand, her eyes wide in alarm. Beth, meanwhile, scrabbled around with a cloth, trying to clean Sister Pokey's shoes. Neither could yet absorb what had just happened.

Oliver Gaskell walked into the room just as Beth got to her feet. 'Next case is mine, Sister. A nice straightforward salpingo-oophorectomy. She'll be in and out in less than an hour and I want to use clips, not sutures, so please make sure the gun is sterilized.'

'Yes, Mr Gaskell, right away.' Sister Pokey raised her hand to her hat to check it was on straight. Even Victoria, despite wanting the new composite floor to open up and swallow her, noticed the simpering tone of Sister Pokey's voice and the pink flush that rose to her cheeks.

'What on earth is going on?' said Oliver Gaskell as he fixed his gaze on Beth and took in her own embarrassment, standing there with an offensive-smelling cloth in her hand. 'Do you live in here, Nurse Harper?'

Both nurses saw the look that flashed across Sister Pokey's eyes. It was almost unheard of for a consultant to know the name of a student nurse and if he did, he would never mention it in a clinical setting. But Oliver Gaskell did things differently, and he got special treatment, even more so than the other consultants. At thirty-five, he was the youngest consultant in the hospital, and his dark wavy hair – the fact that he was the only consultant who actually had any hair – and his permanently twinkling dark brown eyes put almost every nurse regardless of age or rank into a tizzy. It was known that he had halted his training to serve in a field hospital during the war, and he was the son of the revered Dr Gaskell. The young man's authority, and the way he challenged the normal behaviour for a consultant, disarmed and distracted everyone, causing the ward sisters to trill, 'Oh, he's just a boy, he will mature and learn the ways.'

'Of course she doesn't live in here, Mr Gaskell,' Sister Pokey replied. Although his question had been directed at Beth, there was no expectation that she would reply when Sister Pokey was present.

'Well, it seems that way to me. I think it's about time Nurse Harper got to do some real work, Sister Pokey. I cannot for the life of me see what a nurse can learn in here. It's the other side of this door where the action takes place. Come on, Nurse Harper, scrub up, I want you to assist on this operation.'

Sister Pokey's face flushed a deep shade of red. 'But, Mr Gaskell, Staff Nurse is laying up already. She has your instruments...'

'Of course she does, Sister Pokey, because she knows exactly what to do, but it is about time someone else had a go. And besides, Nurse Harper did an excellent job when we had that emergency post-partum haemorrhage on our first day in the new theatre. That lady came back into clinic today, by the way, bouncing her little chap up and down on her knee. I told her to come back in for a hysterectomy just as soon as she finishes breastfeeding. Made it clear that we might not be able to save her next time.'

The room went silent as they all thought about the poor young woman that none of them had believed would make it. Beth beamed. A life had been saved, in here, and she had been a part of that. She saw Oliver Gaskell grinning at her and she quickly looked down and studied her shoes. She was the second nurse in two minutes wishing the composite floor would claim her.

Victoria, as ill as she felt, glanced from one to the other, looking for the slightest indication from Beth that this interaction with Mr Gaskell, his wanting her to assist, had been planned.

After what appeared to be an interminably long silence, Sister Pokey spoke. 'Well, this is most unusual and I am afraid you will lose a friend and a fan in Staff Nurse, who will have to change places with Nurse Harper, Mr Gaskell. But if you insist... Nurse Harper, scrub up, please.'

For a moment it looked as though Beth was rooted to the spot. Then, without raising her eyes from her feet, she said the words of obedience they all uttered a hundred times a day, 'Yes, Sister,' and, turning, began to untie her rubber apron.

'Jolly good,' said Oliver Gaskell. 'See you in the scrub room, Nurse Harper.' And in a flash he was gone.

'Staff Nurse! Staff Nurse!' Sister Pokey shouted, and without even addressing Beth or Victoria, she turned on her heel and went off to deliver the bad news.

'Did you know he was going to do that?' Victoria asked immediately she and Beth were on their own again. 'For goodness' sake, I feel like death and now I am going to have to work with that battleaxe of a disappointed matron-no-longer-in-the-making. She is the most unfriendly staff nurse I have ever come across, with a chip on her shoulder the size of a manor house. And they say the new ones are the worst – God alone knows what she was like when she was newly qualified because she's a right bitch now. She's built like the Tanners' brick outhouse and she has as much charm to boot. She's a bloody dragon, I swear.'

Beth didn't have the chance to reply before a voice rang out. 'Who is?'

They both turned around in horror to find Staff Nurse – eyes glaring through her tortoiseshell glasses, steel-grey hair scraped back into a bun, arms folded beneath her enormous breasts – standing behind them.

'You all right, Dana love?' asked Pammy in a soft voice as they entered the hospital grounds through the back gate and headed towards the wards. She gave Dana's arm a gentle squeeze. She had been waiting outside the doctors' residence while Anthony sneaked Dana in to visit Teddy.

Dana had been all smiles and chatter on the walk up. 'I feel a bit like Little Red Riding Hood, with this basket of goodies from Mrs Duffy, bless her. She made all this yesterday evening so that it would be fresh for him today. She is such a diamond.'

'I had to stop me mam from knitting him socks,' said Pammy. 'I said to her, "Mam, he's fine. Socks aren't going to make him better," but she would have none of it. "Oh yes they do, Pammy. Shows how much you know. You need to keep the blood warm in the feet for the legs to heal."' Both girls laughed.

'My mammy is the same. She only wanted to send food over from the farm. Would you get the cut of him? Every woman for miles fussing over him.'

Pammy became serious for a moment. 'I think it's because it's a miracle he's alive, Dana. It really is a miracle.'

Dana slipped her arm around her friend's shoulders and hugged her for a moment. 'A miracle performed by your Anthony and his resuscitation technique. And, don't you know, they are learning it in every hospital in England now.'

'I know,' said Pammy. 'We all have to go back into school for a day. Sister Haycock was telling me. Poor Anthony, he had to go up to London and explain how it works. Giving evidence, he called it.' She looked up at the doctors' residence. 'Right, speak of an angel and hear the flutter of its wings, here's Anthony now. He will sneak you up. Don't be too long, Dana, we can't be late.'

Since Dana had come back down from seeing Teddy and they'd resumed their walk into the hospital, Pammy had been barely able to get a word out of her. Her mood had totally transformed from what it had been ten minutes earlier.

Dana had breezed into Teddy's room all cheerful, but her smiles had fallen away even before she'd closed the door. He was a vision of misery, and it made her heart collapse with worry. She couldn't remember the last time she had seen him smile. He was sitting in the one armchair in his room, which had been placed close to the window, and he was staring out over the dark Mersey at the ships being unloaded down on the docks. Being high up in the building, he had one of the best views, even if only half of the ships' masts were visible, the remainder being shrouded in mist.

'Morning, you,' she trilled.

Teddy looked up and gave her a half smile before turning his gaze back to the window.

'Aren't you happy to see me?' she asked, only half joking.

'Of course I am,' he replied, although he sounded anything but.

Dana rested the basket on the table next to him. 'I have a bag full of goodies from Mrs Duffy, they will cheer you up. Are you in pain, Teddy?'

His response almost took her breath away. It was so sharp and sudden, as though he had been waiting for her to arrive so that he could snap. 'Of course I'm not in pain. I want to get back to work. I wouldn't be able to do that if I were in pain, would I? Flaming Mabbutt won't have it, though. Wants me to be trapped here for weeks on end, looking at the four walls in between bouts of physio. I know that the best thing for me would be to get walking around those corridors. Nothing will build up my leg muscles better than that. The man is driving me to distraction.'

'Well, he is the consultant, the one who fought very hard to put you back together again, and if it wasn't for him, you might not have even been able to consider returning to work. You said yourself, when he showed you the X-ray, that he was a genius to have repaired your legs, given the extent of the injuries.'

Teddy turned his face clean away, back to study the unloading of the *Cotapaxi*.

'At least you have interesting things to look at up here,' said Dana. 'You can see the ships. And you've all these books...' Her voice trailed off. She knew that nothing she said would make any difference and nor would he agree with her. There was only one thing Teddy wanted anyone to say. 'Anyway, I can't stay, Pammy is waiting outside. But look, Mrs Duffy has baked you a fruit cake and there's bacon sandwiches and they are still nice and warm. She has put in some fruit and a big steamed steak-and-kidney pudding, so you aren't going to starve.'

Dana flicked back the tea towel from the top of the basket to show him. He turned to look, attracted by the smell of the warm bacon, and Dana bent down to kiss him. It pierced her heart when he turned away and her kiss landed on his cheek rather than his lips. Standing up straight, she forced back her tears as a niggling thought tapped at her brain. But instead of letting it in, she asked, 'Are you sure you aren't in any pain, my love?'

'No. I have told you. No.' It was almost as though Dana were no longer in the room.

As she tiptoed down the back stairs, avoiding the housekeeper, she wondered how long it would be before he noticed that she had left.

'Dana, is something wrong?' Pammy, never one to mind her own business, tried again.

Dana shook her head. 'Oh, I'm fine, thanks. It is just a bit difficult seeing Teddy in such a miserable state. He is desperate to get back on to the wards. I'm going to be driven mad all day long worrying about him.'

'Well, we are both on casualty today. Sister Haycock is alternating us with Beth and Victoria on theatre. She's combining theatre and casualty as one long placement. So don't do your worrying alone, just give me a nudge if you want to talk. It must be really awful for you and Teddy. At least I have me mam just down the road. She wants you to come to ours for a roast on Sunday, by the way, if you can't get into the res to see Teddy.'

'I love your mam,' said Dana with a smile. Knowing she had support made her feel instantly less alone. 'She's my second mammy, don't you know. Will you tell her that? Do you know, I think theatre would be the best place for me. I'll be happy to be up there. I won't have to answer one patient or nurse after another with an update on Teddy's condition. Patients who are sleeping the whole time you're with them will do me just fine for the next month.'

Both girls laughed. Pammy thought that this moment of shared secrets might be a good time to mention something that had been on her mind. 'Dana, watch out for that Nurse Makebee on casualty, would you. She must have asked me a dozen times over the past few weeks how Teddy was. If her own boyfriend wasn't a registrar, I'd be worried.'

'Oh, I know. Don't worry, I have my eye on that one. Makebee asked Mrs Duffy too. You know, Mrs Duffy doesn't like her very much, says she keeps pushing at the rules and she's sure she's slipping out at night to meet her boyfriend. He's working at the Northern now.'

Pammy let out a sigh of relief. She had been worried about mentioning Makebee to Dana, but there was something about that nurse that made the hair on the back of her neck stand on end. 'Really? I never knew that. Good on Mrs Duffy for telling you. Poor Mrs Duffy. God, if Makebee is slipping out at night, that would worry her sick. She must have sent more food parcels for Teddy than she put together during the war.' She smiled. 'You know what? I have a feeling that soon Teddy will be back on the wards and all your problems will be over.'

'I hope so,' said Dana, 'because if things don't get back to normal soon, there is no way I am going to pass my exams.'

Beth pushed open the door of the scrub room and made to reach for a pack of theatre gowns for Oliver Gaskell from the shelf. Suddenly a hand slipped around her waist from behind, spun her round and removed her glasses.

'That's better,' Oliver Gaskell said as he placed his lips on hers and began to kiss her in a way that made her feel weak. Pulling back slightly, he looked into her eyes.

'What are you doing?' asked Beth, her gaze fixed on the door. She was terrified that Sister Pokey would follow her in.

'I'm doing what you have been wanting me to do,' he said. 'I could see it in your eyes. Do you mind if I do it again?' After waiting for the briefest moment, he kissed her again.

Beth lost all sense of reason or fear of being caught in the arms of a consultant. She had thought of nothing else but this moment since he had stolen his last kiss at the back of the doctors' residence, but this, here and now while she was on duty, was dangerous. If Sister Pokey or Staff Nurse were to find them, he would be instantly forgiven for his indiscretion whereas she would most likely be sent to Matron and then, without grace or forgiveness, given her marching orders. As she melted into his arms to the sound of voices just the other side of the door, one thought crossed her mind: she had forgotten to say no.

Chapter 11

Maximillian Marcus swung round in his leather chair and looked out at Big Ben, which had just struck twelve. Bang on time, his secretary walked into his office carrying a box of correspondence, her notepad and pen.

'Good morning, Miss Jackson. Pray tell me, what interesting letters have we received today?'

Miss Jackson had spent twenty-five years in the secretarial pool at the House of Commons, which was situated in the pit of the building, before being promoted by Mr Marcus. She was delighted with her position, even if she had no real understanding of his Liverpool docklands constituency, having herself never strayed far from the area between Earls Court and Westminster.

'You have a very busy afternoon,' she said as she sat and crossed her legs. Her stockings crackled as her sharkskin underslip slid across her knees. This morning she was wearing her dogtooth-patterned woollen skirt and a black twinset. Her tight curly hair was now more grey than the shining brunette it had been during the war years, and, like many women of her generation and younger, she had long since resigned herself to remaining a spinster. The removal of almost her entire male cohort to fight for King and country had put paid to her aspirations to become a wife and mother. These days it was the House of Commons that filled her time, and other people's lives provided her with all the gossip material she needed.

'But your correspondence is light today. It won't keep you from your lunch with the secretary of state for health.' Maximillian always lunched in the members' dining room when he was in the House of Commons. 'Now, what would you like me to do about that tiresome matron at St Angelus? She has written again to request your support for a new maternity unit. It seems that the Liverpool District Hospitals Board has outright refused to agree to one, following the opening of the new theatres there. It says that there are enough maternity beds in Liverpool already.'

'Really, is that so?' Maximillian opened the box on his desk, extracted a cigarette and lit it.

Miss Jackson coughed politely. She hated his smoking when she was in the office and had tried every method possible to let him know, short of actually telling him. 'Yes, and you know, the chairman of the board is really a very gracious man. He strikes me as the sort who would never take such a decision lightly.' She failed to mention that she and the LDHB chairman's secretary had struck up a close telephone friendship. Nor did she tell Mr Marcus that there had even been occasions when the charming chairman himself, the major, had telephoned her in person.

'I'm afraid, Miss Jackson, that my mother doesn't agree.'

'Really?' Miss Jackson sniffed and pushed her glasses further up her nose. As she had said at the lunch table yesterday to a whole group of Commons secretaries, some of whom had been there so long they looked as old as the building, 'If there is anything worse than working for an MP with a wife who has an opinion, it's one with a mother who interferes.'

'Yes, you see, my mother knew Matron's mother, so when she needed to be operated on, it was to Matron's hospital and care she went. And to Matron's credit, she has never uttered a word to anyone. Or even...' He swivelled round on his chair and pointed his cigarette straight at Miss Jackson. '... or even taken up my grateful offer to be of assistance should she ever need me. Until now.'

Miss Jackson had been about to transfer his every word to paper using her best Pitman's shorthand, but instead she was using her pen, held mid-air, to fend off his cigarette.

'And what's more, I have been given very clear instructions by Mother, which I shall be discussing with the secretary of state over lunch.'

Miss Jackson knew there was little point in arguing. However, this was the perfect excuse to place a call herself to the charming major. She had been simply unable to disagree with him when he'd shared his views with her. Why keep an old workhouse going when there were plans to build a lovely new hospital with every modern convenience? The major's telephone calls were the highlight of her week. It was so nice to have men back on the various boards again. The wives of servicemen who had filled the vacancies during the war had done a good job, but the men were back now and it was the responsibility of any woman with a shred of self-respect not to take a job that a man could fill. The men needed to regain their places in society and that was exactly how it should be.

Less than an hour later, Miss Jackson had dispatched Mr Marcus to his lunch and was simpering down the telephone.

'Oh, Major, I do hope I'm not bothering you. I think you said you were going out to play golf later this afternoon? I'm glad to have caught you as I have some news that you may be interested in.'

As she held the handset to her ear, she trembled. What she was doing was very wrong, but he had taken her for tea at Fortnum and Mason's, which was a great deal more than Mr Marcus had ever done. And besides, Mr Marcus often implied that she was a very lucky lady indeed when at Christmas he presented her with a half-dead poinsettia, a bottle of sherry and a Christmas card from his mother. No, loyalty very definitely had to be bought. As far as she was concerned, the major, with his attentiveness and his endless compliments about her ability, poise and style, had very definitely won.

Dr Gaskell lifted the clubs out of the back of his Austin 7. He didn't get to play as often these days. The rain bothered his bones and today was damp and cold. He was wise and wily enough to know that there was something significant behind the request for his company on the golf course this afternoon. He didn't trust the major and refusal to attend was not an option, not according to Matron anyway. He had popped into her apartment before he had left the office the previous evening. She had greeted him with warm sherry and cold words.

'Is this how we are to run this hospital now?' she had quipped. 'On the golf course, men together, playing power games? What matters more, who wins at golf, or who gets their own way when it comes to the running of St Angelus? Do enlighten me.'

'As you well know, this is not something I normally do,' he had responded. He felt wounded by the sharpness of her words.

'Yes, well, that's as may be. It appears to me as though my opinion counts for very little these days. Have you seen this?' She pushed a copy of the *Nursing Times* towards him. 'There are people who believe that there is no place for a matron in the NHS. That we don't have the right skills to run a hospital. How dare they?'

Dr Gaskell sipped on his sherry. He couldn't see into the future, but what he did know was that the world about them was changing very fast.

'No one seems to listen to me or even want to know my opinion. Everywhere I look, there are women being phased out of board positions, and even on the wards, to be replaced by men. Now that the board is almost entirely male, I am simply ignored, and meanwhile you are invited on to the golf course to talk about the future of the hospital I have run very successfully for a very long time.' Her voice was now raised and her eyes had begun to water.

Dr Gaskell's reply sounded feeble even to his own ears. 'Yes, but you know, all those men back from the war, they need to find work of one sort or another…' His words faded away. He was in danger of patronizing her, something he had never done before. 'Look, now that we've got the new theatres up and running so successfully, what we need to secure for you is your maternity unit. Never mind how we get there, it has to happen. If I promise you I can deliver that, would that make you happy? Would it concern you in the slightest who I met on the golf course if that was the outcome?'

A smile spread across her face and tears threatened. 'Of course I wouldn't mind.' She sighed and stared at the roaring fire in the grate. 'I cannot tell you why or how I feel this way, but in my heart I know that St Angelus is in danger. These men, they understand only numbers and accolades. It is all about recognition for them, not what is best for the hospital. I only know what I want to do for the women of the dockland streets and I don't care how it happens. I have no pride when it comes to saving lives.'

Matron's words rang in Dr Gaskell's ears as he slung his golf bag over his shoulder. The major waved across to him from the entrance to the club house. Do not leave this golf course without the promise of a new maternity unit, he said to himself, and he wasn't sure what felt heavier, the golf bag over his shoulder or the weight of his promise to Matron.

Chapter 12

Biddy rolled the pastry out on to her wooden table using a flour-dusted bottle, then flicked it across the top of the enamel pie dish containing the steak and kidney in gravy with a deftness that would have impressed the head pastry chef at the Grand Hotel on Lime Street. Noleen had been sitting at her kitchen table for over half an hour and although she had talked about everything from the weather to the price of fish, Biddy had a strong suspicion that there was something troubling her. She had to find a way to get it out of her before Noleen left her kitchen. 'And is that all the news ye have for me, Noleen? That Frank and Lita are thinking of selling the fish shop and retiring down by the coast. They've done mighty well for themselves, have they not. I remember the day they arrived, with nothing other than their little girl and a suitcase between them.'

'Thank God they did.' Noleen blessed herself with the sign of the cross as she spoke. 'They might have ended up with the rest of all those poor souls. What Hitler did to them...'

'They had family, you know. Frank's mother. I heard she made them leave her behind, said she would hold them up. They didn't just arrive here with nothing and no one, they had to let go of all that heartache, their entire past, and carry on with no idea of what would happen to her after they left her. And they had to start all over again.'

Like all conversations about the war, most was left unsaid. Biddy balanced the pie dish on one hand as she began to trim the edges of the pastry. 'I'm just glad they came here to us. We know what it's like, we had the famine. It runs through our blood, we understand what it's like to be strangers. I've always bought my fish from Frank and Lita.'

Noleen changed the subject. 'How is Mrs Ryan doing? Our Bryan never has a clue when I ask him. I don't think the lads talk much about anything other than football.'

Biddy let out a snort. 'And when was that ever any different? She won't be out of that place for at least a month; more, even. I've told Lorcan to move in here with me. Who do you think I'm making the pie for? I couldn't be bothered for meself. I told him, "I don't want you in the house alone, the bizzies haven't got that wicked man yet." If they had, they would have been back here to tell us and that's for sure. I said to him, "Stay here with me, would you now?"' Biddy lowered her voice to a whisper. 'You know J.T. is on the run? That's why I don't want Lorcan there. The bizzies are watching the place like a hawk. One of them is in Betty Hutch's back bedroom day and night. Betty hasn't said a word, but Hattie Lloyd, she sees them going in and out. No, I don't want Lorcan anywhere near the place. There is something gone on between the Bevan boys and J.T. and Lorcan needs to keep right out of it.'

Noleen smiled up at Biddy. She was in her element. A lost waif to care for, a bit of drama on the street, it was all she needed to make her happy. 'Is he tipping up?' Noleen nodded towards the bread bin, where every woman who lived near the docks kept her money.

'He is that. I didn't ask, mind. It was just there in the morning after payday. He's paid the rent on his own house too. It's a good job he gets it at the war rate. I was worried because if anything happens to his mam, the concession doesn't pass to him. The harbour board would throw him on the street within a week. But he's been no bother to me and I would take him in without a moment of hesitation. I'm telling you, Noleen, he's a good lad. He will never see the inside of Walton Gaol as God is my judge. Not even to visit his no-good brother when the bizzies finally get their hands on him.'

Lorcan hadn't needed to be asked twice to move in with Biddy. Once his initial anger had passed, he was as afraid as Biddy was of the Bevan boy returning, and when he heard that J.T. was on the run, he was scared stiff that his brother would come to the house and make trouble. Besides, at his own home there was no one making him steak-and-kidney pies for his tea. That was something that had never happened to Lorcan, as far as he could remember.

Elsie had much to say about this. 'Lorcan Ryan comes to stay and the fatted calf is brought out. What has he done to deserve this? Nothing, I would say. And aren't you worried? What if J.T. comes flying over your wall and wants to stay too?' She had asked Biddy this just as Biddy was slipping an apple pie into the oven.

'He hasn't done anything to deserve it, Elsie. It's just nice to have someone else in the house to bake for and I'm guessing that if J.T. did come to call, he would walk through the gate rather than jump the wall. But as the bizzies are everywhere, I don't think it's likely he's anywhere near here, do you?'

'He might be desperate, Biddy. He might need food or money. If he comes in here and tries anything, knock on the kitchen wall with the mop and I'll send Jake in. Look at those lamb chops! Well, you're putting the rest of us to shame. How can you afford lamb midweek, anyway? It's egg and chips in our house.'

Biddy took a deep breath. How could she explain to Elsie, the matriarch of an entire family, what being needed felt like? 'You don't have any idea, do you, Elsie? You run in and out of here with tales of your Martha and Jake and the baby and you give them to me second-hand so that I can be pleased for you, and I make no bones about it, I am pleased for you. You are a lucky woman, Elsie, but me, I'm not. I have no one and nothing and yes, I may be just an old woman making a right fool of myself looking after that lad, but I don't care.'

'You don't care?' Elsie was incredulous. 'The day his mother comes out of hospital, he'll be back down the road and he will forget you as quick as he will that apple pie you're making right now, mark my words.'

'Like I said, Elsie, I don't care.' And Biddy didn't. It might be the last time ever anyone would need her help and she was going to make the most of it.

Noleen had fallen quiet and was staring into her cup. A visit from Noleen was a rare event and usually far more enjoyable than a visit from Elsie. She was one woman for whom there really never were enough hours in the day. But tonight was her night off, at least. Just as Biddy was wondering where Noleen's small talk was heading, Lorcan walked into the kitchen, cap in hand, dust on face, fresh from finishing his shift and visiting his mother.

'Lorcan, you must have smelt your tea cooking. Into the scullery with you for a wash. I'm just putting the potatoes on.'

'Thanks, Biddy.'

Noleen looked up from her cup. A mother first and always, the plight of another mother was always a concern for her, as for any of the women thereabouts. 'There but for the grace of God' was a prayer uttered every time they heard of bills not met, bailiffs knocking or sickness striking.

'How's your mammy, Lorcan, is she any better?' she asked.

Lorcan flushed, as he always did when someone spoke to him. 'She is, she's awake, but the doctor won't let her get up yet and he says she's going to be in the hospital for a long time.'

'Well then, 'tis a good job you have Biddy here to look after you. Isn't she doing a grand job? You have landed on your feet here, Lorcan, and that must be a relief to your mammy, to know you are being taken care of.'

Lorcan hung up his jacket and made his way towards the scullery door without answering. He didn't want to tell Mrs Delaney it was he who did the looking after in the Ryan home or that it would probably be the last thought in his mammy's head, to wonder what he was eating or who was taking care of him.

It was a long time since Mrs Ryan had looked beyond the horizon of her own very small world. J.T. had always been her favourite and today, when he visited her, for the entire half hour she'd thought that he was J.T. No matter how many times he'd said, 'No, it's Lorcan, Mammy,' she'd replied, 'J.T., 'tis just grand to see you, would you sit down here beside me.' But he wouldn't tell anyone this, not Biddy or Mrs Delaney. He would keep it to himself.

Just before he left the kitchen, he turned back to Noleen.

'How is Mr Delaney, does he like his new job? Dessie said he's been taken on as the new night watchman.'

Biddy almost dropped her tea towel. She stared at Noleen. Noleen had not mentioned a word and yet this was the kind of news that once would have brought her running down her back yard. 'What new job?' she asked.

Noleen looked back down into her tea and Lorcan hovered, unsure what to do next.

'What job, Noleen? Is Paddy working? Isn't that the best news! My God, why didn't you tell me? Will Finn be able to go to the grammar now?'

Noleen put up her hand as though to protect herself from Biddy's words, which, if Biddy only knew it, were piercing her very skin. 'There is no job, Biddy, so there will be no grammar school either. Finn won't be going anywhere.'

'What? No job? But Lorcan just said...'

'Dessie, he told the lads...'

The look on Noleen's face cautioned Biddy. 'Lorcan, get into the scullery, now,' she said.

She didn't need to ask twice. Lorcan sensed that he had just said something very wrong and the scullery door closed almost before Biddy had finished her sentence.

Biddy pulled out the chair next to Noleen. The legs scraped along the floor and the screech sent an involuntary shiver down Noleen's back. 'Noleen, what the hell is Lorcan talking about?'

Noleen placed her cup on the table and looked Biddy in the eye. 'Lorcan is telling the truth. Dessie found him a job, as a night watchman, sitting in Dessie's hut at the hospital, checking in the coal lorries because the new rule says the coal dust has to be hosed, or something daft. But I wish he hadn't told the lads because now our Bryan will find out.'

Biddy instantly knew that this was possibly the very reason why Dessie had told the lads. 'Noleen, you aren't making any sense. Has Paddy not grabbed at the job with open arms? A watchman, doesn't he just have to sit in a chair and let the coal trucks in and out? Look, I'm no brain of Britain, but even I know all you need is a hand to write and a pen to write with. What in God's name is his problem?'

'The problem, Biddy, is that he has refused it. Says it's a load of baloney and it's a job Dessie has made up for him out of pity.' Tears welled up in her eyes. She picked up the cup to distract herself, saw it was empty and placed it back down on the table.

'Well, did you not explain that Dessie doesn't do that? He is too loyal to the hospital and to Matron. If he has offered Paddy a job, it will only be because there is a job. If Dessie was into inventing jobs, every man around here would be in work. What's up with him? And what about Finn? Did he think of him at all before he refused the job? Who does he think he is, Noleen? You are working every hour God sends and he's just sat on his big fat stump. Is the job still open to him?'

Noleen almost smiled at Biddy's automatic protectiveness, caring for Finn and immediately understanding the worry and resentment that had been niggling at Noleen since the morning Paddy had told her that he would be taking no job. Biddy's words warmed her and made her feel less guilty about the intense anger towards Paddy that she had kept hidden.

'He wasn't due to start until Saturday, so maybe Dessie is hoping he'll change his mind between now and then. But that is never going to happen, I can tell you. He's so stubborn, Biddy. I don't need to tell you that, you know what he's like.'

Biddy thought Noleen was about to cry, but she realized she was beyond tears. She was a woman whose life held few surprises and much hardship and she was immune to disappointment. Biddy wiped her floury hands on her apron, jumped out of her chair, whipped her headscarf off the back of the door and began to fasten it over her curlers. She had her coat on before Noleen had even noticed.

'Where are you going?' Noleen asked, surprised.

'I'm away to your kitchen, that's where.'

Noleen made to stand and follow her.

'Oh no, not you. You stay here and give Lorcan his tea. Take that pie out of the oven in ten minutes for me.'

'But...' Noleen was on her feet. 'I have to get the kids their tea, I have to come.'

'No you don't. No ifs or buts. You stay here. There's not a man alive who wants his wife to see him humiliated, no good ever came from that. Stay put until I get back and that's an order. I'll sort the kids their tea, Noleen.' And with that, the back door slammed.

Paddy hadn't moved since earlier in the afternoon and it was obvious to the kids that something was very wrong. Noleen had popped out to Frank and Lita's, or so they thought, and she had been gone for a very long time.

'Dad, when is Mam back? I'm hungry,' said Mary. 'The lads will be in soon from playing football and they will want their tea.' She was unprepared for the response she received from Paddy, not least because never once had he raised his voice to her.

'Why don't you get the tea, eh? How old are you now?

282

You should be doing more to help your mother and with looking after this house. Our Bryan does more than you and he's a lad. You should be ashamed of yourself.'

The blood drained from Mary's face as she stared at her da with her mouth open. As Paddy's only daughter and the obvious favourite of the pack, her laziness was a direct result of Paddy's indulgence; Noleen had never been in any doubt about that. 'Da!' she gasped.

'Don't you "Da" me. Why don't you try peeling a pan of 'tatoes for a change, instead of waiting for your mam to get in and do it. Who do you think you are, royalty? The bloody Princess Margaret?'

Mary rocked on her heels and had barely had the chance to catch her breath when the back door opened and Biddy stormed in.

'Mary, here.' Biddy opened her purse and handed Mary a half crown before the door had a chance to close on her back. 'Get down to the chip van for the tea. I could hear you two all the way down the entry. You'll be the talk of the docks soon, carrying on like that. Your mother's at my house helping me with Lorcan.'

'Thanks, Auntie Biddy.' Mary's face broke into a grin as she pulled on her coat.

'Go on, away. I'll put the plates on the range to warm. I haven't long, I've things to do at home.'

Mary was too excited about fetching the chips, a rare treat, to let the thought that was nagging at her take form. Why was her mother helping with Lorcan when they needed their tea?

When she had gone, Biddy almost threw the plates from the press on to the range. Then, sitting herself down on the settle in front of Paddy, she took a deep breath and looked straight at him.

'Woman of this house as well, are you now, Biddy?' he asked, his voice loaded with sarcasm, his head not moving nor his eyes leaving the *Liverpool Echo* he had flicked open on to his knee. He knew exactly why Biddy was there.

'Oh, I wish I was, Paddy, because there would be none of your nonsense with your high-and-mighty ways. Just who the hell do you think you are, turning down a job and forcing Noleen to work herself to the bones? Eh? Such a big man, you would put the fact that a friend tried to help you before the education of your son or the welfare of your wife? And Bryan, poor Bryan. Lorraine Tanner's mad for him, but he will never notice it because all the lad can think about is you. You and your bloody leg and what he can do to make your life easier. You are one selfish bastard, Paddy.'

Paddy inhaled sharply. He had known Biddy for more years than he could count and he didn't think he had heard her swear since the day her husband had run off.

'You, you would drive the Pope, the Lord himself and all the angels in heaven above to swear, you would. You do know what you are doing, don't you? With all the worry heaped on Noleen's shoulders and all the work she has to do, you will put her into an early grave. Aye, that's right. You'll be sat here staring into the fire expecting your kids to run around after you, but do you know what, Paddy, they won't, because when they know that you turned down a job so that their mother could work herself to an early death, they will be off and you will be left alone. All alone to stare into your bloody fire. You make me sick, you and your pity. Think you are the only man who came back from the war with a hard-luck story, do you?'

Paddy leant forward and made to speak. His face had flushed bright red and his eyes shone with anger, but Biddy didn't let him talk.

'Don't be trying to give me your pathetic excuses, because there aren't any. I'm ashamed I ever called you a friend, because no friend of mine would be selfish enough to treat his wife the way you have treated yours. I don't want to know you any more, Paddy. I don't want to help you or worry about you and I'm going to tell your wife she's a fool if she does. Your kids, they need to know what their father is really like, so I'll be telling Bryan meself. And as for little Finn, when he's down on the docks, risking life and limb, wearing his bones out before their time to make ends meet, God willing,' Biddy's hand flew to her chest and made the sign of the cross as she blessed herself, 'I'll make sure I tell him myself, "You have your da to thank for that, Finn."'

Biddy had been so angry, neither she nor Paddy had heard the back door open. They both turned to see Bryan filling the doorway.

'I already know, Biddy,' he said in a low voice. 'Dessie told us in the break today that Da would be starting as the new night watchman. I knew one was coming, I just didn't know it was supposed to be Da. I went along with it when Dessie said it, but I knew it couldn't be true or Da would have told me.' He looked directly over at his father and his eyes were filled with a mixture of hurt and loathing.

Biddy knew it was a look more powerful and more meaningful than any words she had used. She stood to leave.

Paddy said nothing and turned his face towards the fire.

*

All her anger spent, Biddy left the Delaney house without another word. She was shaking so much, her legs trembled as she walked. Noleen's frying pan had hung dangerously low and close and she knew that if she'd had to sit in Paddy's company for much longer, she might well have taken it down from the hook and hit him with it.

She squeezed Bryan's arm as she left and gave him a look full of understanding. It was down to Paddy now. The next half hour would be crucial, while her words stung and Bryan's shamed. She might have lost a friend for ever, but Noleen might have gained her husband back and that was all that mattered to Biddy.

As she crossed the entry back to her own house, she saw Dessie and Emily coming back from the bus stop, as bold as brass. Biddy was almost out of breath by the time she caught them up. 'Stop, would ye!' she shouted.

They both turned round and Biddy could see that they were weighed down with arms full of tins, brown paper bags and wallpaper.

'Hello, Biddy, what's up?' Dessie asked.

'Biddy, you shouldn't run like that,' said Emily, 'it's not good for you.'

Biddy placed her hands on her knees and caught her breath. 'It's not running that's bad for me. Having to put a rocket up the backside of a grown man who doesn't know any better is what's bad for me.'

'Are you talking about Paddy?' Dessie asked as he placed two heavy paint tins on the ground.

'I am. You told the lads about his job offer today, why did you do that?'

Dessie looked down the road towards the Delaneys' house.

'I had given up trying to persuade the stubborn bugger. I thought that maybe if I made it known that he'd been given the job, he would find it harder to be so obstinate, especially with their Bryan and the kids knowing. I was forcing his hand, Biddy.'

'Aye, well, you were right. Lorcan told me and I've said my piece. I've left him to Bryan now. So help me God, Dessie, it will be the last word I will ever speak to him if he doesn't take the job and that's a fact.'

'Well, we've all tried our best. It's up to him now.' Dessie bent back down to pick up the paint.

'What do you think?' Emily turned back a corner of a roll of wallpaper to reveal a cream paper with pink roses and green leaves.

'Now isn't that just gorgeous,' said Biddy. 'Will there be an announcement of any kind soon? I'm not sure I'm happy working for a woman who is so brazenly living a life of sin.'

'Has your name changed to Hattie Lloyd by any chance?' asked Emily as she raised her eyebrows and laughed.

From the derelict bombsite at the end of the road, the cry of 'Goal!' went up from a chorus of kids just as the street lights ignited. Mary, who was now escorted by Lorraine Tanner, came into view and the three adults watched as Cahill and Jack ran over. 'Have you got chips?' Jack yelled to his sister, forgetting about the football game now that he'd spotted the vinegar-soaked newspaper and smelt the chips.

'No surprise Lorraine Tanner is with them,' said Dessie. 'Makes right puppy eyes at their Bryan, though the lad hasn't got a clue.'

'It's not that, Dessie. Poor Bryan doesn't have a minute to notice or think about anything other than helping his mam, bringing in a wage, looking after Paddy and helping with the kids. He'll be drawing a pension before it dawns on him that he's let his life pass him by, and all he will have is an empty heart and a cold bed to show for it.'

Lorraine and Mary looked over and waved. Biddy raised her hand and waved back and as she did so let out a deep sigh.

Dessie had taken his leave. 'I'll take the paint and come back for the paper and paste. Wait there,' he'd said to Emily.

'I think I might attend Mass with Noleen tonight,' Biddy told Emily. 'I don't know what it is, but I have a bad feeling about something in me water, and it's not my pessary,' she whispered. 'Do you not feel it yourself? It's as though the winds have crossed.'

Emily shook her head. 'Biddy, what are you on about? You should be looking forward to the weekend. I'm looking forward to mine. I'm hoping Maisie will help me run up my new curtains.'

As Biddy walked back to her own house, she tried to shake off the feeling of foreboding that had wrapped itself around her like a probationer's cloak. She knew it related to Lorcan. 'Stop, will you, there's nothing going to happen to Lorcan,' she said to herself as she shook her head. 'Get a grip of yourself woman.'

She found herself wondering what her life would have been like if her Mick hadn't run off. There were more single women living in the streets than married ones, thanks to the war, and once again the image of Noleen's frying pan came to mind. 'There was just nearly one less,' she muttered, just before the Angelus bell rang out. Biddy blessed herself and gave thanks. Thanks for being a free woman, for her man having deserted her, because if he hadn't, her life would have been different. She would have had even less patience than she had now and surely to God, her and that frying pan would have been heading straight to Walton Gaol tonight.

Noleen was fastening her scarf under her chin as Biddy walked back into the kitchen. 'I'm off to Mass,' she said. 'How did it go?'

'Wait while I come with you,' said Biddy. 'And you won't be going home tonight, even if it is your night off. Best you stay here, let him calm down and ponder on his own stupidity. If you go back tonight, it won't do any good. Let him stew.'

For the first time in their married life, Noleen did not return home to Paddy. She slept in front of Biddy's fire on the settle and only at first light did she lift the latch on the back gate as quietly as she possibly could and made her way down the entry towards home.

Her heart was heavy and the image of Paddy on the day he'd been medically discharged came into her mind. He had been transported home from convalescence in a large house in north Yorkshire. The doctor had told her that they would have liked to have kept him for longer but that the demand for the beds was too high. Although not yet completely well, Paddy was fit enough to return home.

He was carried into the house on a chair by two female ambulance drivers and it took Noleen every ounce of her strength not to collapse with relief. They were unable to get him upstairs that first night, so some of the local women brought round army blankets and spare pillows and they padded the settle in front of the fire and turned it into a bed. In the midst of the chaos, the bowls of dirty water, the makeshift bedpan and the enamel urinal the ambulance drivers had left her with, Noleen wondered how she was ever going to cope.

As she tried to help him get comfortable, Paddy grabbed her hands and said, 'I'd have been better off dead. You would have been better off.'

Noleen felt a surge of anger and strength all at the same time. 'How dare you say that, Paddy Delaney? I'm run ragged here and you are telling me you don't appreciate what I'm doing? Do you realize that in the past week there have been two telegrams on these streets, about men who have died, who won't be coming home. Don't you dare say that ever again, do you hear me?'

Paddy had no reply. He knew the men who had died. They were in his own regiment, and his eyes filled with tears. All day there'd been a flow of neighbours in and out the back door wanting news of the regiment, of their own men.

Noleen dropped down on to her haunches and looked up at him. 'Paddy, it's hard now and it will be hard for a while, but we will get there. I just need to work out the best way we can manage. And we aren't alone, lots of the neighbours will help. Biddy Kennedy has already brought round the best cake you have ever eaten, hasn't she?'

He didn't answer but stroked her hair and seemed to feast his eyes on her face.

'Paddy, you may have come home without a leg, but you came home. And me and you, we will never spend another night apart, not ever, do you hear me?'

He cupped her face with his hands and kissed her, then pulled her into him so tight that she had to force herself not to yelp. 'I have missed you and thought about you and the kids every single day,' he said.

Noleen pulled away. 'And we have you, Paddy, and it was awful and it will never happen again, because you aren't going anywhere. We will never be parted again, never as long as we both still live, and isn't that wonderful?'

Paddy began to laugh through his tears and she through hers. It was a truly breathtaking thought, that after years apart through the worst of circumstances, Paddy was back in Noleen's arms and they would never, ever be parted again.

Now, as she walked up her own back yard, she thought about how much Paddy had altered since that day, and for the first time ever, she was nervous of opening her own back door. She decided that she would lay the breakfast table first and switch on the copper boiler and keep herself busy, and then, before the kids woke, she would run to Mass. That way she could keep conversation to a minimum. Besides, keeping busy was all she had.

As she hung her coat and scarf on the back door, she felt as miserable as she ever had, her thoughts lost down the worrying path of how she would cope with the days and years ahead. A voice broke through those thoughts and, looking up, she gasped and placed her hand on her mouth. She was speechless.

Paddy stood before her, wearing his false leg. She had forgotten how tall he was and it was a shock to her.

'I sent our Bryan to fetch Dessie last night. There's a new clinic opened at St Angelus and Joe, one of the men who works in there, does wonders with the legs, so Dessie tells me. I'm off to see him and I'm starting the job. It will be hard, but not as hard as it was when you didn't come home and I realized what a stupid eejit I've been. I don't deserve you, Noleen.' He wobbled slightly and placed his stick on the floor for support.

Noleen's heart filled with love and pride and an urge to protect him. She rushed over and placed her arms around him. 'How does it feel?' she asked.

'It hurts like I've been kicked in the leg by a horse, but Dessie says they have contraptions now that they put between the leg and the stump and they will make me a leather girth to strap up and around my waist so that I can move it forwards easier without it coming out sideways first and knocking the dog out. You better watch out, Noleen, I'll be winning the street races at this rate when we next have a fête.'

For the first time in as long as she could remember, Noleen burst into peals of spontaneous laughter.

Chapter 13

Victoria woke with a start, aware that something was very wrong, and sat bolt upright in bed. It was a big mistake and she only just made it to the wastepaper basket before she was violently sick. Kneeling on the floor, she cupped her head in her hands. She had never felt so ill before in her life.

Over the last few days she had thought she was improving and had even managed to eat supper last night. Roland had written to say he wasn't very well either and had taken to his bed for two days, so she'd assumed they'd both come down with the same thing. She was not a complainer. Having nursed people through the worst of surgery and disease, nowadays she had little patience for hypochondriacs who made a big deal of the slightest twinge or headache. She had never heard her poor mother complain once, and yet it turned out her mother had probably never felt well, according to the doctor, on account of the rheumatic fever she'd had in childhood. She had stoically carried on regardless and had helped to look after injured war veterans. Her sudden heart attack had stunned everyone.

'Never complain,' Victoria said to the mirror as she washed her face in the sink. For a startling moment it wasn't her reflection looking back at her but that of her mother. 'It's not the thing to complain, Victoria. No one likes a complainer. Big smile, best foot forward.' How many times had her mother said that to her – when she'd fallen off her horse, off her bike, out of a tree.

As she saw how pale her complexion was, Victoria decided it was time to consult a doctor. She would do so without fuss and without telling the others. She wiped her face dry with the towel. At least it was Sunday and she wouldn't have to face theatre today. As she folded the towel and placed it on the painted metal rail at the side of the sink, she decided she would speak to Pammy's Anthony. He would know exactly what to do.

A voice rang out. 'Only me.'

There was the usual early-morning tap on the door and Beth slipped into the room carrying the tea tray. Victoria had heard her steps on the stairs and had hurriedly whipped her towel off the rail and thrown it over the wastepaper basket. She'd picked up her perfume and squirted it into the air, then flung up the sash window to kill the smell. As the door opened she'd turned back towards the sink to brush her teeth.

'Here you go,' said Beth as she placed a cup and saucer at the side of Victoria's bed, being careful not to tip the tray.

Victoria turned briefly and saw that there was a letter propped up on the tray, but she felt too ill to even ask who it was from. 'Thank you,' she managed through a mouthful of bristle and toothpaste.

Beth appeared to be preoccupied herself and padded out of the room without another word.

*

In her own room, Beth prepared to open the note she had found in her pigeonhole when she'd gone downstairs to light the fire and make the tea before Mrs Duffy arrived. The front of the envelope was handwritten and she had traced the individual letters with the tips of her fingers as she waited for the kettle to boil. She now laid the tea tray down on her bedside table, drew back the curtains and allowed repeated thrills of excitement to run through her body as she teased herself, prolonging the moment when she would discover the sender's name. She studied the handwriting. It was wide and bold.

Snuggling back under her covers, she knew exactly who it was from. She sipped her tea and made herself wait a little longer. This was the normal Beth. The Beth in complete control, not the Beth who had danced with fire, twice.

Unable to bear it a moment longer, she tore open the envelope. Her heart beat faster at the pleasure of reading the words, which almost jumped out at her. She clasped her hand over her mouth to prevent a squeal of excitement from escaping.

You have driven me mad, ignoring me in this way. Why are you doing this? Can we please at least talk, or what am I supposed to do? I can hardly barge into theatre and ask you for a date in front of Sister Pokey, can I?

I will wait for you at the bottom corner table in the Lyons Tea Rooms this afternoon. I have seen the off-duty on the wall of the office in theatre and I know you are not on call today. I will be there at 1 p.m. The table is discreet. I only want to talk to you, nothing more. It is up to you. What can you lose? The worst that can happen is that you have a jolly good lunch ...

Beth had been invited to Maisie Tanner's for Sunday lunch, along with the others. As Pammy Tanner was the only nurse resident at Lovely Lane who lived in Liverpool, this was a regular occurrence. All the other resident nurses were working on the wards and would eat at the greasy spoon, otherwise they would have been invited to Maisie's too. They always returned to Lovely Lane with a new tin of goodies to share. Beth was enjoying having Sundays off. Sunday was not a routine operating-list day and theatre was only used for emergencies, so there was a skeleton staff. A consultant in St Angelus on a Sunday was a rare sight.

She would have to make an excuse to Pammy, Victoria and Dana, because there was one thing she knew for sure, nothing would keep her from going on this date. It was far too tempting, the chance to give the big man a bit of a put-down. Nothing would come of it, she knew that. Most certainly not. She would enjoy his company and hear what he had to say and yes, to him it probably would be a jolly good lunch, but he had never eaten at the Tanners' house, had he? And when the lunch was over, she would leave him in no doubt that she would never be a notch on his bedpost. She would not be the next in a long line of nurses to be pitied or laughed at. Pammy Tanner was on his list of hearts broken and she had never forgiven him, and then there were the rumours about the hapless Nurse Moran, which were just dreadful. He was a brute who was used to getting his own way and should be ashamed of himself. Beth should be disgusted with herself for even having allowed him to kiss her. What was she thinking, condoning his actions by agreeing to meet him?

And there was Pammy to consider. If Pammy were to ever find out she had even contemplated meeting him for lunch, she would lose her as a friend for ever. When it came to a choice between a man or a friend, the friend must surely win. A man could leave her at any time, for another woman, but Pammy would be her true friend for all of her life. A friend never left.

Nonetheless, as much as Beth tried to erase Oliver Gaskell's kisses from her mind, she couldn't stop herself from reliving the delicious sensations he had stirred within her. As she lay back on her pillow and sipped her tea out of her old country roses cup and saucer, two thoughts crossed her mind: that it was the best cup of tea she had ever tasted and that she would be safe to meet him, because unlike all the other nurses, she most certainly had her heart firmly under control.

'I feel so bad having to leave Teddy,' said Dana as she, Pammy and Victoria marched along the street towards the Tanners' house.

'Well, you didn't have to,' said Pammy. 'He was invited as well.'

'I know, but he is such a bear with a sore head, he knows he would be terrible company. And besides, he would never have agreed to being pushed down the street in a wheelchair.'

'I swear to God, Dana, you are a saint. Don't you think so, Victoria? Seeing as you've known Teddy since he was a child.'

Victoria raised her pale face and looked confused. Every

step was an effort for her, but she didn't want them to know. 'Think what?' she asked.

'Don't you think Dana is a saint?'

'Oh, I do,' she replied, without knowing why.

'Well, as I am on nights soon, I may see a bit more of him,' Dana said. 'Anthony said it will be easier to slip me into the res once it's dark. I'm floating between casualty and theatre.'

Pammy looked shocked. 'As long as my Anthony doesn't expect me to go sneaking into the doctors' res, my mam would kill me if she knew that.'

'Oh, I'm only going to visit on my way to work, for a chat. None of us are quite as sophisticated as Victoria and her wanton woman's ways.'

They all laughed and even Victoria joined in.

'Fancy poor Beth getting called into the hospital like that. She is always too obliging. I mean, I know she said she got a note from Matron, but don't you find that a bit odd, Matron writing to her?'

'She must have got one of the lads to deliver it early this morning.' Victoria linked arms with Pammy. 'The envelope was on the tray when Beth brought me my tea.'

'Well, get her,' said Pammy, with a tinge of jealousy in her voice.

As they opened the back gate to the Tanners' house and stepped into the yard, Dana and Victoria felt as though they had arrived home almost as much as Pammy did, so familiar were the surroundings and so warm the welcome.

'Come on in, come in,' shouted Maisie from the kitchen. 'Stan, the girls are here. Little Stanley, have you set the table? Lorraine, where are you? Hello, girls, hello.' She came to the back door and hugged each of the girls as they stepped through. 'Our Stan's just carving the meat, working up an appetite, he says, he's been desperate for you to arrive. Poor Beth having to work. I want you to take her a roast back in a pudding dish, I will tie it up in a tea towel. Pop it in a pan of hot water for her or in the oven. Keep it warm for when she gets in, poor love.'

Before the girls could answer, they were commandeered by the Tanner children, who bombarded them with questions. Victoria slipped into the parlour and, hoping no one would notice, sat on a chair to catch her breath.

Not two minutes later, Maisie walked into the room carrying a jug of apple sauce. 'Oh, Vic, are you all right, love? You don't look well.'

'I'm fine, thanks, just a bit under the weather. That smells delicious. I'm just checking on the table, I usually like to do it with little Stan, don't want him to think I'm shirking.'

'How long have you been feeling like that?' asked Maisie. 'Have you seen a doctor?'

'Oh, no...' Victoria had to stop for a second as she swallowed down excess saliva. Composed, she tried again. 'I don't need to see a doctor, it will pass.'

Ten minutes later, big Stan was standing waiting to relieve Maisie of a hot tray of roast potatoes and carry it into the parlour. 'Think our Victoria has got a bit of a cold, love, she doesn't seem too good to me,' he said.

'Really.' Maisie placed the tray in his hands. 'Well, I'll tell you what, that cold will have a name soon.'

Stanley looked directly at his wife. He knew that tone and it was not one to ignore. 'Is that so, love? What will that name be then?'

'Well...' Maisie poured the gravy from the meat tin into

the gravy jug. 'That all depends, Stan, on whether it's a girl or a boy.'

Stan's mouth opened and closed as he stared at her. 'What? You mean...? No, surely not. Are you sure?'

'You know what, Stan, you really are a useless article. How many kids do we have? Of course I'm sure, and this means trouble for Victoria.'

'Are you going to tell her?' Stan, shocked as he was, knew better than to disagree with Maisie. If she was telling him Victoria was pregnant, then she was, even if she didn't know it herself.

'Me? Well, I think I might have to because there is one thing I do know, that kid, she hasn't got a clue. She may have a suit of armour stood in her hallway and a coat of arms to her name, she may have big paintings and portraits of members of her family going back to the ark, but she has no mother to guide her and it's going to come as a shock to her when I tell her she's in the family way. It's such a shame she hasn't got a decent family. I hope if her mam is looking down on us, she'll think I have done a good job for her if I do tell her. Mind, if I was the one looking after her, she wouldn't be pregnant in the first place. And that Roland, such an accomplished young man, him inheriting his own solicitor's firm and everything. He won't have a clue either.'

Maisie set the meat tin back on the range and wiped her fingers on her apron. 'These kids, they are all for the modern world, but not one of them has any thought for the danger or the consequences. Father Brennan was on about it in his sermon this morning and you, Stan, you would know that if you had been awake and listening. I just hope our Pammy was taking note. And did you see the way that Paddy Delaney walked into church with Noleen? Wasn't that just great? The things they can do today. I mean, I know it's a false leg, but at least he can get about.'

As she finished speaking, the kitchen door flew open and Lorraine burst into the room. 'Mam, our Pammy says have you got Nana's smelling salts, it's Victoria, she's fainted.'

Beth left the nurses' home through the front door in her uniform and cape. The other girls had already set off for Maisie Tanner's. She shouted, 'See you tomorrow, Mrs Duffy,' and then hid around the back near the bins until the coast was clear. When Mrs Duffy had no new probationers to fuss over, she always took Sunday afternoons off. Beth knew she had already prepared a cold supper and left it in the fridge, just in case one of the nurses working on the wards didn't have time for lunch, which was not a rare occurrence. She had also left a plate of fairy cakes filled with butter-cream and dusted with icing sugar hidden under a tea towel in the middle of the table. The nurses always loved it when they arrived home to find that she'd baked them a special treat. With all her chores completed, Mrs Duffy soon made her way down the road towards the bus stop. Beth sneaked back into the nurses' home and quickly changed out of her uniform.

She arrived at the Lyons Tea Rooms ten minutes late; she'd timed it exactly. Once she reached the door, she decided she would wait even longer, so she walked back up the road and down again. Her stomach was fluttering, her mouth was dry and she had no idea why she was there. She had hated lying to her friends, but she hadn't been able to help herself. Seagulls screeched their warning overhead as she turned away from the door for a second time, but it was no use. Wild horses could have charged down Mount Pleasant in an attempt to drag her away, but in her heart she knew she would have fought them off. Oliver Gaskell had played with her mind and she had played with his. All that mattered now was the next step and who would surface from this afternoon the winner. As she battled with her emotions and the rising thrill of expectation, she knew that if she was to keep the respect of her friends, it would have to be her. At all costs, she had to win.

When Victoria opened her eyes, she was lying on the brown studded leather sofa in the Tanners' parlour. Pammy was sitting next to her, holding her hand and taking her pulse, and Maisie hovered over her, looking more than a little concerned.

'Well, hello,' said Pammy. 'You have decided to join us.' She smiled at Victoria as she laid her wrist down on the crocheted knee blanket she had placed over her.

Maisie took her cigarettes out of her pocket and lit up. As she exhaled, she said, 'Would you look at me, me hand's shaking. Me nerves are shot. Honestly, Victoria, between you and Finn Delaney, fainting is becoming quite the thing on this street. You haven't passed the eleven-plus or anything, have you, and forgot to tell us?'

As she spoke, Anthony came into the room, removing his coat and hat as he walked. Under Maisie's instructions, big Stan had stood at the end of the entry to meet him and have a quiet word in his ear. Big Stan had spoken quickly because racing up behind had come little Stan, gabbling out the drama. He had run alongside Anthony all the way to the house and was still beside him as he entered the parlour, both arms outstretched, catching the doctor's garments as he went.

The lad's face dropped now as his mam said firmly, 'Little Stanley, get back in the kitchen with me,' and grabbed his collar. Before she led him out, he stole a look at Victoria as she lay on the sofa. The beautiful Victoria, whom he adored in the manner of a puppy.

The fire was roaring up the chimney and had made the room too hot. 'Can you open the window, Anthony?' Pammy asked in almost a whisper as she placed the back of her hand on Victoria's brow and moved the crocheted blanket down.

Anthony did as he was asked and then with an expression of grave concern took in Victoria's pallor, her grey, watery eyes and her general lack of sparkle. He had only known her for a few months, but she was a bright, clever, fizzy personality and it was clear that something must be very wrong to have laid her so low.

He placed a kiss on the top of Pammy's head and for the briefest second inhaled the scent of her. With every day that passed, he loved her more. One day soon, he was going to have to tell her how much he loved her and wanted her to be his wife. He hoped that she felt the same way, because if she didn't, he had no idea what he would do. They had not been together as a couple for very long and yet the thought of life without his practical, cheeky Pammy was almost too much to imagine. He could barely remember anything of his life before she and her madcap family had taken him into their home and hearts.

'Pammy, could you fetch me a cup of tea and maybe one for Victoria, with some sugar in. The last cuppa I had was at nine this morning. If I don't get one soon, I might have to ask

Victoria to shove over and make room for me on there.' He grinned and nodded towards the sofa.

Pammy looked up at him and her heart instantly melted. He could have asked her for the moon and she would have tried her best to net it. 'On my way,' she said as she sprang up.

Anthony immediately sat down in her place.

'Have I ruined the dinner?' Victoria turned her face towards Pammy.

Holding on to the brass doorknob, Pammy swivelled back round. 'Have you hell. The kids are made up. They are all sat around the fire in the kitchen eating it on their laps and me da's had his at the kitchen table. Yours is in the range with mine and Anthony's. Da's gone back to the pub. Dana is being made to do a football jigsaw puzzle with our lads, she says she will be in as soon as she gets stuck. You've given me da a great excuse.' In a gentler tone, she added, 'Everyone is worried sick about you though, Vic. Nothing would make Mam happier if you managed a bit of dinner.' And with a smile she left to make Anthony his tea.

Victoria looked up at Anthony and her eyes filled with tears. 'I was going to come and see you tomorrow,' she said. 'I have been feeling so dreadful. At first I thought it was car sickness from when Roland and I drove Teddy and Dana back, but it hasn't gone away and now Roland has been ill in bed too, so I've been thinking maybe it's a bug or something. He doesn't seem to be as bad as me though. He probably thinks I'm exaggerating.' Her voice faded as she removed her lace handkerchief from the sleeve of her cardigan and blew her nose.

Anthony looked at her square on. 'Victoria, I think I know what is wrong with you. I would need to examine you to be one hundred per cent sure, but I can't do that here. And besides, you may wish someone else...' His words petered out and he sounded mildly embarrassed.

Victoria failed to notice. She dabbed at her face and looked at him expectantly. A flash of hope came into her eyes. 'Oh, what is it? Will it pass soon?'

'Oh, it will pass all right, but it will take its time.'

'Really? How long?'

Victoria was struggling to sit upright so Anthony slipped his hand under her elbow and, standing, grabbed the cushion from where Pammy had placed it under her feet and tucked it under her head. 'Is that better?' he asked as he plumped it and then helped her ease down on to it.

'Much, thank you.'

Anthony knew his next words would come as a bombshell. Pammy had dropped hints about the sort of relationship Victoria enjoyed with Roland. He knew of the decision they had taken not to marry until Victoria had sat her finals but also not to deny themselves the intimate pleasures that marriage would bring. Pammy had made it very clear that Anthony would enjoy no such pleasures with her and that she was very much keeping herself for the man she married. He could not explain why, but this thought drove him mad. He had to marry Pammy and soon. She had to be his and his alone and until that moment came, he could never be sure that she was truly going to be his, no matter what she said to reassure him.

'Here, sip this,' he said as he picked up the glass of water on the floor that he had just nearly kicked over. He assumed that one of the boys had been sent to fetch it when Victoria had fainted.

She lifted her head, took a few sips and then flopped back down again.

Anthony heard the kettle sing out enthusiastically in the kitchen. The sound of canned laughter on the radio and chatter filtered in, accompanied by the chink of crockery and the clang of cutlery. He knew he had about three minutes before Pammy returned with the tea.

'Victoria, I can see you have no idea what is up with you and so I just need to ask you one question, because I think I do.' He took a deep breath. 'When was the first day of your last menstruation?'

Victoria's cheeks turned pink and her eyes widened in alarm as she scrabbled to remember the date.

Anthony saw realization dawning and then he said, 'I'm guessing it was about six to seven weeks ago?'

Victoria held her fingers up and appeared to be counting. Then she nodded.

'Victoria, I believe you may be pregnant.' As much as Stan had insisted to Anthony that Maisie had never been wrong about this, Anthony would not make his statement any more definite without first having it confirmed via a urine test. 'To be certain, we will need a sample of your urine to send away for the Hogben Test.'

For a full fifteen seconds, Victoria lay there stock still without saying a word. Then she exhaled loudly and pulled a face. 'So some poor toad will have to have my urine injected into it, the poor thing?'

Anthony looked relieved. 'Well, at least you can smile. And yes, you're right: if you are pregnant, "some poor toad" at the testing centre will respond to the relevant hormone in your urine and will spontaneously lay a few hundred eggs.'

'I don't think I can make sense of it yet, Anthony. It's as if you've just told a patient in clinic and I'm simply the nurse waiting to squeeze a hand or offer a tissue.' Her voice dropped to a whisper. 'How long will it take for the results to come back?'

'About two weeks, usually, but I can try and hurry it along for you. As you probably know, we use the testing centre in Sheffield – although the way Matron is campaigning these days, I wouldn't be surprised if we had our own colony of *Xenopus laevis* toads at St Angelus before too long! It would certainly speed things up – and there'd be no more smelly accidents when the urine jars break in the post.'

Victoria wrinkled her nose in disgust.

The door opened as Pammy entered backwards, holding the tea tray out in front of her.

'Here we go. Tea for my lovely man and a nice sugary one for you, Vic, and then Mam is coming in with our dinners. Just think, we can eat in peace today, eh? No kids scrabbling around. Even our Lorraine has disappeared down to the Delaneys'.'

Victoria tried to smile, but she felt more like fainting than ever now, at the thought she might be pregnant.

While Pammy poured the tea and gabbled away, Anthony squeezed Victoria's hand. 'Phone Roland,' he mouthed to her as with the other hand he mimed dialling a phone and then putting it to his ear.

Victoria nodded, almost imperceptibly. She inclined her head in Pammy's direction and mouthed back, 'Don't tell anyone.'

Anthony sent her one word back in response. 'Never.'

'Here we go,' said Pammy as she stirred the sugar into

Victoria's tea and turned to face her. But as Victoria reached out to take the cup, her hand shook so violently that Pammy said, 'Oh, wait, hang on, I'll give it to you. You and me mam, you are both the same today. You need that sugar in your tea, miss. You will be much steadier once you have this and then your dinner down you.'

Victoria nodded. Get a grip, she thought to herself. No one must know. Smile. Drink the tea. Eat the food. Act normal. For the briefest second the image of her own mother came into her mind. It was summer and she was wearing her big billowy hat that she tied under her chin whenever the two of them pedalled off on their bikes, their baskets filled with dressings for the soldiers who had been medically discharged. The country lanes were perilous, full of pot holes and stones, and occasionally Victoria would fall off sideways and meet the road. Her mother would brush her down and straighten her skirts and then, looking her in the eye, she'd say, 'Right, there's my girl. All will be well, we must soldier on.' She would plant a kiss on the end of Victoria's nose and immediately all Victoria's cares and embarrassment at having taken a tumble would fly away.

As Pammy fussed over Anthony, Victoria looked into the fire. Despite its warmth, she felt the coolness of her mother's kiss on the tip of her nose. 'Soldier on,' she heard her whisper. 'Soldier on.'

Beth walked towards the corner table in the Lyons Tea Rooms with a confidence in her step that she truly did not feel. She was convinced that every pair of eyes had turned and was watching with disapproval as she passed.

He was already sitting at the table and rose to greet her as she approached. 'I wasn't sure you would turn up,' he said, and she noted that his voice sounded far less arrogant than it did when he was speaking as Mr Gaskell, obs and gynae consultant at St Angelus. 'Thought you might not be the person I had you down as. That you might have had second thoughts and bailed on me.'

'What kind of person would that be?' asked Beth as she removed her gloves, popped them into her handbag and placed it on the floor beside the empty seat. She turned back to scan the room.

'Don't worry,' he said, 'I've already checked. There is no one here from the hospital.'

Beth half smiled as he pulled the chair out for her to sit down. He had placed her so that she had her back to the room and could look out of the window, and he faced the other way. 'I chose this place on purpose,' he said. 'It's somewhere that people who work at the hospital don't visit, but it's busy enough that we won't be noticed.'

Beth nodded. 'That is very thoughtful. And do you bring all your young ladies here?' she said as she arched her eyebrows.

He looked suitably wounded. 'What on earth do you mean? I act like a gentleman at all times.'

'Really?' said Beth as she leant back in her chair and folded her arms. 'Would poor Nurse Moran testify to that?'

His face flushed, but before he had the time to answer, the waitress approached. Beth studied the menu. She was only halfway down it when, to her surprise, he began to order.

'Two steak Dianes,' he said, 'and a bottle of red wine. You only have one Bordeaux, so we will take that and—'

'Excuse me.' Beth's voice was clear and firm. 'I prefer to

choose what I eat myself, if you don't mind. I am very happy to pay for my own meal, if that's a problem.'

For a brief moment he looked affronted, then puzzled. 'Do you know what you want?' he asked, with a mocking grin on his face.

'Oh, I always know exactly what I want. No one decides anything for me.' She snapped the leather-bound menu shut and looked at the waitress. 'I will have the chicken chasseur, please.'

'And is the red wine acceptable?' he asked.

'Oh, certainly, a very good choice,' she said, sending him a beaming smile, which seemed to completely disarm him.

They passed the meal in amiable conversation, all things considered. Beth even managed to get him to open up about his work in the field hospital during the war. He also talked about his parents and his work, and then their chat came full circle, back to Nurse Moran.

'I would very much like to know what happened there,' said Beth.

'Look, I know what you are getting at, but I don't care what the rumours say, she was not pregnant, I can assure you of that. She was just not cut out to be a nurse and, frankly, she had so little confidence, she could barely function in a social setting. She became terribly clingy. Too clingy. And, in truth, I blame you lot in Lovely Lane.'

Beth almost laughed. 'Excuse me,' she said, 'I hope you can back that statement up with more than just your own opinion.'

'Oh, most certainly I can. She often told me she had no friends and that you all laughed at her. She said that she couldn't bear to sit in the lounge with the new TV because no one other than Mrs Duffy spoke to her, and that she had made a terrible mistake even coming to Liverpool. She couldn't get home to Ireland quickly enough. She was desperately lonely for home, where people were kind to her and she didn't feel so different and put upon. She often cried herself to sleep, apparently.'

Beth rolled her eyes. Every probationer nurse felt homesick at one time or another. It was something they'd all had to get through. Nurse Moran had just needed to toughen up, be a bit less sensitive.

'I felt bloody sorry for her actually,' Oliver Gaskell continued, 'and I was very intrigued to finally meet you, Nurse Harper, because she told me that you were one of the cruellest and that you laughed at her the most. She was afraid of you and your officious manner. I once said to her, "Nurse Harper looks a decent sort, have you spoken to her?" And she told me you had once shouted at her most severely. Anyway, she is happy back at home now. She was a mere dalliance. There was no intimacy between us, if that is what you are implying with that look. I just felt sorry for her. She has begged me to visit her, but I'm frankly just not that interested. I don't want to sound like too much of a cad here, but she was good for the old ego, you know, terribly doting and all that, and I felt that she needed the company. Frankly, I was worried about her. Loneliness can be a terrible thing.'

At that moment it was Beth who wanted to run away. She felt humiliated. The reason he had looked at her twice, dallied with her himself, was because Nurse Moran had complained so much about her. But she wasn't cruel, that was a gross injustice. She remembered how once, in the middle of an emergency when Nurse Moran had done something stupid yet again, she had snapped at her. They had all laughed at her. Her antics on the wards had become legendary throughout the hospital. Even the porters had seen her as a good sport to play their practical jokes on, and they had, often.

Beth felt as though a brick had landed in her stomach. Her face burnt red with embarrassment. She instinctively knew he was telling the truth because if there was any probationer who had arrived at St Angelus and looked as though she was a fish out of water and without an ounce of staying power, it had been Nurse Moran. As Beth folded her napkin, she recalled something Mrs Duffy had once said about Nurse Moran being terribly homesick. He was telling the truth. She knew it as well as she knew that she had just eaten a delicious meal. 'Oh, God,' she said as she looked down at her plate. 'I don't know what to say.'

Oliver removed his napkin from his lap and, folding it into four, placed it at the side of his plate. They had been talking for far longer than Beth had realized and there was now hardly anyone else left in the restaurant. The bottle of wine stood empty on the side of the table as if shouting out to them that it was time to leave.

'Goodness me, it's three thirty,' Beth said.

He seemed equally keen to change the subject. 'Yes, they are laying up for afternoon tea. I think they may want us to leave. But I would quite like the afternoon to continue – on a happier note and with no further mention of Nurse Moran. Now that I've had the chance to properly meet the famously officious Nurse Harper, I'd rather like to find out some more about this feisty, intelligent, challenging woman. What do you think?'

Beth was quite taken aback at his candour and before she

could stop herself she asked, 'What do you have in mind?' She could have kicked herself for sounding too keen.

'Well, the housekeeper at the doctors' res has gone. She only works half a day on a Sunday. The res will be empty, with everyone out. Why don't we take another bottle of that wine to my room?'

Beth watched his lips as they moved. The lips that had kissed her twice already. She didn't need to be asked if she wanted them to kiss her again. She took a breath and, betraying neither her racing heart nor her cascading doubts, she answered, 'Well, I am trying to think of a reason why not. However, being such an allegedly cruel individual, I'm not sure I deserve it.'

He raised his eyebrows and grimaced. 'I'm sorry, but it is the truth as she explained it,' he said matter-of-factly.

'Oh, I'm sure and I am stung by what you have said. However, I'm not going to mention it again other than to say that Nurse Moran was a bit of a dippy girl and yes, she did take some ribbing, from everyone, not just me. I am guessing that you have been a bit of a gentleman, saving her blushes. But the truth is, you are taking the blame in the most salacious way and you have to find a way to stop that because people are blaming you for the worst of reasons.'

'Beth… I'm not going to call you Nurse Harper any more because when I finally persuade you to slip into my bed, it will sound rather perverse.' She felt her stomach somersault and she wanted to reprimand him, but no words came. 'One thing I have learnt from working in this hospital is that all things pass. As soon as there is someone else to move on to – and there will be very shortly, no doubt – no one will even remember Nurse Moran's name.'

Beth knew he was right. 'Well,' she said, folding her napkin, 'I'm not sure I believe you now. It appears you make some fairly wild assumptions and get certain things very wrong indeed.'

He grinned at her, well aware that she was referring to his assertion that she would be slipping into his bed.

'The thing is, there isn't any gossip at St Angelus just now, so the story of you and Nurse Moran will run and run because there is no one else to talk about.' Even as Beth spoke those words a shiver ran down her spine. 'I think we should take the wine,' she added. She was going to need a bottle all to herself for Dutch courage.

Oliver showed no sign of surprise at her words as he beckoned the waitress. 'I shall go and pay then,' he said, 'and collect the wine.'

'Thank you,' said Beth. 'I will just pop to the bathroom.'

Washing her hands and looking into the mirror above the bathroom sink, Beth thought to herself, today, my girl, is the day you hang up your white socks, and you know it. You are going to lose your virginity. Victoria will no longer wear that crown. But when he tries to contact you after, you blank him, do you understand? This is the deal you make with yourself right now. Do you understand? Her eyes were talking to her reflection and burnt out of the mirror at her. Yes, she answered. Yes.

Emily and Dessie were struggling under the weight of their purchases from the Sunday market. Dessie carried two rugs, one under each arm, and Emily carried two brown-paper bags filled with ornaments and knickknacks for the makeover of Dessie's home. Bryan had come to help them and under his arm swung a wooden stepladder that almost felled nearby shoppers every time he turned to address Dessie and Emily. In his other hand, he carried a coir mat.

'Gosh, I'm gasping. Shall we call into the Lyons? It will be time for their afternoon tea soon,' said Dessie. 'How about it, Bryan? My treat for you coming to help. I would have had to borrow a pram from one of the women if you hadn't come.'

Emily could have cried with relief. The last thing she felt like doing right now was cooking a dinner when they got back home. 'It makes sense,' she said. 'That way we can just carry on quickly with the ceilings when we get back.'

'I'm going to do the ceilings,' said Bryan. 'You aren't allowed up this stepladder, Sister Haycock.'

'Bryan, it's Sunday, my name is Emily.'

'Sorry. It just doesn't feel right to call you that.' Bryan was so grateful to Dessie for having got his da the job at the hospital, he would have decorated his entire house single-handedly if Dessie had let him. Paddy had worked his first shift the previous night and Bryan had immediately noticed the transformation in his father's mood when he'd returned that morning. He knew that his mother would have an easier life now too and could do fewer night shifts and that was all down to Dessie as well.

'They do the best Welsh rarebit in there,' said Dessie. 'They put beer in it and it's on the afternoon menu.'

'Forget that,' said Emily, 'I want the chocolate Victoria sandwich cake with the chocolate glaze on the top.'

Bryan was standing the stepladder up on the pavement. He really wanted the Welsh rarebit too. But as Emily finished speaking, she placed a restraining hand on Dessie's arm.

'What's up, Emily, love?' He turned towards her, thinking she had changed her mind. 'There's nowhere else open, and you don't want to be cooking.'

'Look,' Emily hissed.

'Where?'

'There. Look who's leaving the Lyons.'

Dessie looked across at the entrance and there as bold as brass was Oliver Gaskell with Beth Harper on his arm. From his coat pocket protruded the neck of a wine bottle and in broad daylight he stopped, stooped and kissed Beth full on the lips.

Dessie and Emily waited while the two lovers passed, oblivious to their audience.

Neither couple was aware that Bryan had just died inside. His secret burning crush for Nurse Harper had been extinguished before it had seen the light of day. The one joy in his life had been seeing her at the hospital, watching her, imagining what it would be like to kiss her. It was almost too much to witness another man, the rake of the hospital, kissing her in public like that.

'Come on then, lad,' said Dessie to Bryan as they made to walk towards the entrance.

'No, not me, Dessie.' Bryan shook Dessie's arm away.

'What do you mean, not you? You aren't helping us without some reward.'

'I don't need any reward, Dessie. Anyway, Mam is cooking our dinner. Look, I'm taking this ladder back and the mat. Here, er, Emily, give me those knickknacks too. Dessie, put them in the string bag and hook them over the end of the ladder.'

There was no arguing with Bryan and in minutes he was off, walking down towards the Mersey with the two rugs trapped between the legs of the ladder and Emily's bag swinging off the end.

'What do you think of that then?' asked Dessie as they sat down at the table Oliver and Beth had just vacated.

'What, Bryan being such a good help or Nurse Harper and Oliver Gaskell?'

'Well, not Bryan. He's probably never ate in a café before and felt embarrassed. I never thought of that.' Long ago, before Dessie had plucked up the courage to tell Emily how he felt about her, he had seen her out with Oliver Gaskell, in a very smart restaurant in Bold Street. They had never spoken of him, but he knew his Emily well enough to know that he, Dessie, had been her first lover and as far as he was concerned would also be her last.

'I think only one thing,' said Emily. 'Beth Harper needs to be warned.'

'How do you propose to do that? This is out of the mafia's league. They will wish her well, they are a bawdy lot at heart, especially Madge.'

'No, this is not something for that lot. I can't leave this to Biddy. There is only one person I can trust with this information and that's Pammy Tanner. She is good friends with Beth Harper and she can put her straight. I am amazed that Nurse Harper isn't aware of his reputation. Although perhaps I shouldn't be – she's so smart and sensible, she probably just keeps her head down and only concerns herself with studying and work. She suits those glasses she wears.'

'She didn't seem too shy to me, out there,' said Dessie as he picked up the menu.

Emily had been staring out of the window as though expecting Beth and Oliver Gaskell to reappear. She looked down at the table and picked up a menu herself. 'I think she has probably been caught off guard. I just hope she has her wits about her and knows how to say no if he tries to go too far.'

'Oh, Emily, it's Sunday afternoon, they are probably walking down by the Pier Head for a stroll. It's one thing kissing in broad daylight, but... She is quite safe.'

Emily wasn't so sure. Oliver Gaskell had a bottle of wine in his pocket. No self-respecting young lady would ever be seen drinking alcohol outdoors. They were taking that wine somewhere. 'I would just feel much happier, Dessie, if Pammy Tanner knew. I'm going to speak to her tomorrow. Oh look, they are wheeling the trolley out and there's the chocolate cake in the middle.'

Dessie took his reading glasses out of his jacket pocket to read the menu. 'Let's hope I'm as lucky and the Welsh rarebit is still on the tea menu,' he said, Beth Harper and Oliver Gaskell now forgotten.

Oliver Gaskell removed Beth's glasses and laid them carefully on his bedside table.

'I can't see now,' she said nervously.

'You don't need to,' he replied and then he kissed her again.

Just as her knees gave way, he moved her backwards and lowered her on to the bed. He undid the buttons of her skirt and slipped it over her hips and down her legs and off with such deft speed that Beth lifted her head and gasped. She was determined to lose her virginity to this man. Victoria wasn't the only one who could manage that. But she was totally unaware of what would be involved.

He came back up towards her and kissed her ears, her neck.

She didn't care about anything any more. It was as though the real Beth Harper was still sitting at the entrance to his rooms and had not crossed the threshold. She had never known such an intense sensation, such pleasure. It was everything: her head swimming from the wine, the smell of him, the feel of the air on her naked skin, and then him against her, all of him touching all of her. All she wanted to do was respond to every kiss and every touch with greater passion and urgency.

He wanted her to be in control and so she lost her virginity not as she had imagined she would but astride him with him holding her hips, gently guiding her. And then he moved one of his hands on to her and she could bear it no longer as she crashed down on to him and let out a noise she was unaware she had made until he said, 'Shush, tiger, you will bring the other doctors running in with a stretcher, wondering what on earth is going on.' And instead of feeling embarrassed and shy, she collapsed off him and on to her side, laughing. He pulled her into him.

'Did you... make that noise too?' she asked.

'No,' he whispered into her hair. 'I'm afraid we will have to do it all over again.'

She pulled her head back and looked directly into his eyes. 'Really?' she asked, unable to keep the grin from her face.

'Oh, yes, really,' he replied. 'But only if that is what you want.'

Beth closed her eyes and breathed in the unfamiliar smell of sex in the warm room. She waited for him to kiss her and when he didn't, she opened them again. 'What's wrong?' she asked.

'I am waiting for your reply,' he said as he moved a curl of her hair away from her forehead.

'Oh, well, yes, I do want it,' she said. She wanted to say that she could not at that moment think of a day when she would not want it. Or a time when she would ever say no. But as he began to kiss her, she reminded herself that this was not how it was going to be. She would make the most of today, but she had made a promise to herself and it was one she had to keep. If the others knew where she was right now, they would never forgive her, especially Pammy. Her friends were everything to her, more important than any man. A man could leave you, a friend never would. A true friend was for ever. This was for one day only and she would enjoy every moment.

Victoria waited until the others were ready for bed before she headed to the phone in the laundry room.

'Are you sure you are going to be all right?' Pammy had asked her. 'That was a nasty turn you had today.'

'I am fine now, honestly. I feel much better, thanks. Look how much of your mam's dinner I have just eaten, it totally restored me. I feel as right as rain, honestly. I'm just going to give Roland a call. He knows I'm not well and he's a bit worried.'

'My mam's dinners would restore anyone,' said Pammy proudly. 'Beth should be back any minute now. I'll pop her dinner into the range to keep warm for when she gets in. I am wiped out, so I'm going to have a bath and then read my Evelyn Pearce in bed. I feel so bad for Anthony having to work nights again. He never gets a proper night's sleep, the poor man.'

'He thinks the world of you, Pammy. He's daft about you and he is the loveliest man.'

'Do you think so?' Pammy's eyes instantly brightened and

she clasped her hands together. 'You know, Victoria, it's so hard, isn't it? I mean, I do love him, I am sure of that, but how do you know?'

Victoria leant against the wall and folded her arms. 'Know what?' she asked.

'Well, whether he's the one. He's my first proper boyfriend and, you know, it's not like it is with you and Roland. I daren't, well, you know what I mean. If I got caught, me mam would never hold her head up in the street again. I just couldn't take the risk and do that to them, so how do I actually know? I might not like it when we do...' Pammy blushed and Victoria wanted to hug her.

'Pammy, I am no expert and all I can say is if you love someone, it's heavenly and natural and you have the best time. But I think you and Anthony are doing the right thing. If my mummy were still alive today, I think I'd be just the same as you are now. Roland and I, we have no one to answer to. No one really cares what we do, so it's different.'

'You lucky things,' said Pammy.

'No, Pammy, honestly, you are the lucky one. You have a wonderful mother and she is here and with you. You really are the lucky one.'

Five minutes later, Victoria dialled the number of the Davenport family home. It was a while before Roland answered and Victoria began to panic. But then the familiar click came down the line as Roland's voice rang out.

'Bolton 172.'

'Roland, darling, I need you to come back to Liverpool.'

'Well, I am happy to do that, but do you mean tonight? I am in court in the morning, you know that, or I would have been there today.'

'No, just sometime within the next, er, week or so, if you could. After court one night, maybe?'

'I will do what I can. I could see Teddy as well, cheer him up. I could stay in his room with him. Will you be able to come out for dinner?'

'Yes, probably, if I'm on the early shift in theatre with Beth. I do have something important I need to discuss with you, my darling.'

Roland sounded concerned. 'Can't you tell me now? Why the secrecy?'

'I can't, Roland. All I can tell you is this: on the drive here, please think very, very seriously about how much you love me.'

Roland began to laugh, but the phone at the other end clicked before he could respond.

Victoria had put the phone down, which was just as well as she only just made it to the bucket that was kept in the laundry room before she saw Maisie Tanner's dinner for the second time.

As Anthony donned his white coat in the changing room attached to casualty, ready to see to the first patients waiting, he smiled to himself at the events of the day. Maisie had cornered him in the kitchen when he had carried the plates out. 'Close your ears, little Stanley,' she had said and little Stanley had clamped both of his hands over his ears as Maisie had grabbed Anthony by the arm and pulled him into the scullery. 'Anthony, love, what do you think? Did big Stan give you my message? Am I right? Victoria may have fainted, but she's not ill, is she?'

'Well, fainting isn't normal, Mrs Tanner.'

'No, love, I know.' Maisie checked over her shoulder to make sure little Stanley wasn't listening. 'But it is normal when it's not an illness but a condition. I've known loads of women to faint when the quickening came.'

Realization dawned on Anthony. He knew that local mothers set great store by the quickening. It was the point when they believed the heart of a foetus began to beat independently, when the foetus became endowed with a life of its own.

'The quickening doesn't happen until around twelve weeks, but she looks like someone who's only two months gone.'

'How can you tell just by looking at her?' Anthony asked, failing to keep the incredulity out of his voice.

'Well, it's obvious. The morning sickness stops at twelve weeks, just before the quickening starts, and that one is still being very sick. I could smell it on her hair when I gave her the smelling salts. Eight weeks, I would say. And you call yourself a doctor.' Maisie tutted and shook her head. 'And you've told her, have you?'

Anthony nodded.

'That's for the best. The sooner she knows, the sooner she can tell her Roland and they can decide what they are going to do to get out of this mess they've got themselves into. And I'm warning you, Anthony, we won't have that sort of news darkening our doorstep, do you hear me?'

Anthony got the message loud and clear. 'Mrs Tanner, you are wasted in this kitchen, you should be working up at St Angelus. I don't know why we bother sending our patients' urine all the way to Sheffield when all that is really needed is for you to have a quick glance at them.' He grinned.

'Listen, son, I've been saying for years that I'm wasted in this house. That's why I was so keen for our Pammy to be someone before she becomes a mother, to do something with her life. Every day when I go to the shops, someone tells me something nice about what our Pammy has done down the hospital and I say to our Stan, well, you know, being just a mam wasn't a waste. Our Pammy might not have been a nurse if things had been different. I'm very proud of her, you know, Anthony.'

Anthony looked at Maisie wistfully and thought how much he missed his own mother. She had died before she had witnessed his passage from schoolboy to doctor.

'I'm proud of you too, love,' Maisie said.

Anthony's heart warmed. She was not his own mother, but he felt a growing love for her all the same. If Pammy accepted him for her husband, he would have the best mother-in-law and the closest to a mother of his own that anyone could wish for.

Chapter 14

Jake was standing at the back of the delivery lorry as he counted out the gas bottles being unloaded. 'Take it easy,' he shouted to the lads as they wheeled them down the ramp. 'We don't want any damaged thumbscrew valves. That gas is flammable, don't forget.' He turned towards the cab. 'Have you got the flow meters?' he shouted at the delivery driver.

'I have, they are safe up here with me.' The driver lifted his cap and slicked his hair back before replacing it and hanging his head out of the window.

Jake yelled out to Lorcan, who was wheeling one of the big bottles into the store. 'Lorcan, you know which ones are the oxygen, don't you?'

'Yes, Jake, they are the black bottles and they have the big white zero on the side.'

Jake nodded. 'That's a good lad. Just don't get them mixed up when you're storing them.'

A major delivery arrived at St Angelus every day. All day long, vehicles trundled in and out, demanding attention, and as the hospital became busier, Jake found they were all working much harder. Twice a week it was the gas bottles for the wards and theatres. Liverpool being on the banks of a river and under a perpetual blanket of smog meant that the medical wards were full of patients with bad chests, so the demand for oxygen was huge. Everyone knew that piped oxygen was on Matron's list of improvements. She'd already told Jake that a new maternity unit would lead the way and that she could then argue that the wards should be supplied at the same time. But she had to secure the maternity unit first and there'd been no news yet.

The deliveries of coal and coke came daily. The coke came directly from the gasworks and was delivered every night. It kept the stoke holes fired and the wards heated. The coal came direct from a city merchant's. There was an open fire at the end of every ward, where the more mobile patients sat during the day, and the buckets were topped up four times a day by the porter's lads.

In addition, there were morning and afternoon laundry collections and deliveries – the clean came in and the dirty went out – and then there were general stores, pharmaceuticals, fresh food and dressings.

Lorcan returned to the back of the lorry as Jake was checking off the nitrous oxide anaesthetic bottles with his clipboard.

'Here, Lorcan, you go around to the cab and get the flow meters. We ordered a dozen and I want you to check they're all OK. They gave us a broken one last week. Take them to the hut, check them and put them on the shelf marked flow valves.'

'Yes, Jake,' said Lorcan and he ran towards the cab.

'Here you are, lad.' The driver threw the packet of flow meters at Lorcan from the cab window. Lorcan was too slow and the meters landed at his feet. The driver leant out and looked back. 'Pick them up quick, you stupid arse,' he shouted.

Bending down, Lorcan scooped the valves wrapped in brown paper and string off the ground. He could hear a rattling sound inside the packet. 'But are they all right?' he asked.

'Of course they are. One or two might be broken, but you've plenty of spares. Don't say anything to miladdo back there or he'll make me drive all the way back to Widnes to get some more and it'll be docked off my pay.'

Lorcan was terrified. Telling Jake was exactly what he wanted to do.

The driver stared down at him. 'If you are thinking of doing that, mate, I wouldn't, if you know what I mean.'

Lorcan didn't know what he meant, but he knew what trouble looked and felt like and above all else, he was desperate for a quiet life. The driver looked mean. Lorcan's life was on the right track finally, his mam was improving and he was still living with Biddy, and the last thing he wanted was any trouble. He nodded, turned on his heels and ran to the hut. Once inside, he scanned the shelves and found the box marked flow valves. He took it down and saw that there were half a dozen or so already lying in the box. He opened the paper parcel carefully and to his surprise found that none of the glass tubes was broken. The rattling had been the loose peas inside the tubes which indicated how much oxygen was coming through. Everything looked intact.

He almost laughed out loud with relief as he lifted the box up on to the shelf, but his expression gradually turned to one of horror as, through the window, he caught sight of a familiar silhouette. A man with a beard was running away from the back of the ward his mother was on. Lorcan recognized the run. The man might have been wearing a hat and not a cap, but the distinctive long stride and fast pace were unmistakable. Lorcan knew that run all too well – he'd scampered in its wake a hundred times or more. It was J.T.

Lorcan would have struggled to identify his brother otherwise, as the bearded man in a smart suit and a hat, but it was definitely him. The sight of him made his skin prickle with sweat and he could hear his own heart pounding in his ears. He ducked down beneath the window, terrified that he might see him. What was J.T. doing there, at St Angelus? Was he looking for him? Maybe J.T. knew that Lorcan had told the police it must have been Kevin Bevan who'd attacked their mam. Maybe he was coming to punish him. Or perhaps he'd guessed that the keys to their house were in their mam's handbag, in the locker beside her hospital bed, and he'd come to steal them. The police had insisted Lorcan lock the house up in case either the attacker or J.T. returned; they had called in their own locksmith and even paid for it. Lorcan hadn't been back to the house. There had been no need.

He crouched there in the hut, frozen to the spot. He didn't know what to do for the best. Who to tell? What to do?

Then came Jake's voice, shouting, 'Lorcan, where are you?'

Over on outpatients, Dana stood patiently next to Teddy's wheelchair, waiting to see Mr Mabbutt. She was in uniform, so sitting down was out of the question. 'It was good of him to ask for you to come before outpatients is officially open,' she said.

She had left the Lovely Lane home early that morning, raced up to the casualty department, collected a wheelchair, steered it over to the doctors' residence and collected a complaining Teddy, who objected to being pushed through the hospital in full view of everyone arriving for work and the ward windows. Dana felt so drained from trying to pacify him and so exhausted from pushing him, it was as though she had already done a day's work before she had started. Teddy had kept his best face for his many well-wishers. They approached him with such obvious pleasure beaming from their faces, it would have been impossible for him to have remained grumpy for long.

'Well, would you look at you! You took the eyes right out of me head,' said Branna as she walked through outpatients on her way back from her break. 'Don't you be mollycoddling him now, do you hear?' she said to Dana before she left. 'Why do you think I will work only on the women's ward? Men, they make dreadful patients and you only have to listen to Sister on orthopaedics to feel sorry for her. Some of the men up there are in plaster casts for months. Try to give her hell, they do, and their wives are even worse.'

'They have my full sympathy,' said Dana with more than a hint of raw truth in her voice. 'I know exactly how they feel.'

Branna winked at Teddy to dispel any offence he might have taken at her comments. 'Dr Davenport, will you be back to work any day soon? The place isn't the same without you and your high jinx.'

Jake bounded over, abandoning a large wicker basket on wheels at the edge of the quadrangle of still empty wooden chairs in the waiting area. Within an hour, every chair would be filled and there'd be more patients leaning against the walls, waiting for a name to be called and a seat to become vacant.

'It took me nearly half an hour to get him here from the res,' said Dana to Jake. 'So many people are so relieved to see him in one piece.'

Suddenly a white-painted door flew open and Nurse Makebee popped her head out. 'Ah, there you are,' she said to Teddy, then threw Dana a less than friendly glance. Without asking Dana to help, she came over to the wheelchair and, kicking off the brake, turned Teddy around and wheeled him away.

'Shall I come too?' asked Dana, surprised.

'No need,' said Nurse Makebee. 'I can manage quite well.'

Dana felt slightly deflated. Teddy hadn't turned around as he left or insisted she should follow and now, with no obvious patient to look after, she felt slightly daft standing there alone.

'I'd watch that one if I were you,' said Jake as he walked back to the basket. 'She eats men for breakfast, or so they say. Not that I would know, mind. I have my Martha. If Nurse Makebee walked to work stark naked, I wouldn't notice, and besides, I'm just not important enough for the likes of her. Chin up, anyway, Dr Davenport is looking just great to me.'

A funny feeling settled in Dana's stomach. She felt unimportant, a spare part, used. She had done absolutely everything for Teddy since the day of his accident and now she stood there, hanging around outside while Nurse Makebee assisted Mr Mabbutt. A sad and mildly rebellious feeling settled in the pit of her stomach. To hell with it, she decided, I don't care if anyone sees me, and she flopped on to one of the chairs opposite Mr Mabbutt's room. Under the white door opposite, through the light slipping out from the brightly lit room, she saw the dark shadows from the wheels of Teddy's chair and the shuffling feet of Nurse Makebee next to it. She stared at the door and waited.

*

'Does she know?' Nurse Makebee hissed at Teddy on the other side.

Teddy almost sneered at her. 'Well, thank you for your good wishes, I must say. No, of course she doesn't know, but she may as well do. It is the worst situation to be in. All right for you though, isn't it. Does your fiancé know?'

She looked affronted. 'No, of course not, but he's not here any longer. He is back in London now. He only came for experience on chests with Dr Gaskell.'

'Well, bully for you. I suppose you have some other poor man in your temporary grasp now that he's gone.'

She had the audacity to smile at him, almost mockingly. 'Teddy, this is the 1950s, darling. I have no idea what my fiancé is up to and nor he I, but a girl can't be expected to live without the er, nicer experiences in life, can she?' She grinned and even Teddy, who called himself a liberated man, was shocked.

'Golly, you really have no shame, do you?'

Nurse Makebee opened his notes, extracted the outpatient sheet and clipped it to the front. 'Shame? That's a thing of the past,' she said.

'You should meet Oliver Gaskell, you two would be well matched,' said Teddy.

'Oliver Gaskell? Oh no. That man is all talk. He is one big puff of hot air. Likes to make himself out to be the Romeo of the wards. It's the reputation he loves. I'm afraid his actions don't match his intentions. Ran a mile, he did, when I suggested we went for a drink.'

'I find that hard to believe. He's never out of the pub and he has a different nurse on his arm every night.'

'It's all a performance,' she said matter-of-factly. 'Oh, I'm

331

not saying he doesn't date, I am sure he does, but, you know, he's just not fun enough. I like naughty boys, like you, Teddy. Anyway, never mind Oliver Gaskell, how are you feeling?'

Teddy almost groaned out loud. The fact that she felt his behaviour was more wanting than Oliver Gaskell's actually stung. 'Goodness, you sound like you might really care. Well, as you ask, I can't live with myself. I resent everything Dana does for me because, frankly, I don't deserve her, and yet I can't bring myself to tell her about us because the second I do, she will walk straight out of the nearest door. It's a living hell. Dana has morals and she lives by them.'

Unscathed by his words which had meant to embarrass at the very least, Nurse Makebee almost threw a gown at him. 'Here, put this on. Mabbutt will be here in a minute. We can't change what happened, Teddy. We had a holiday. You had a hotel booked, I had two free weeks, it was a shame to waste it. We had lots of nice dinners and sex and I read some jolly good books as well, and if I remember rightly, the books were a darn sight more interesting than the sex. You really do need to brush up on that technique of yours, you know. Even a peasant from the bogs like that one outside would have room for complaint. Look, we are both adults, for goodness' sake. It's not the 1930s, there has been a war, remember? Everything changed.'

Teddy grimaced, his face flushed with embarrassment. She had been his first. It wasn't supposed to be like this. He had been so stupid and he wished every day that the car crash had killed him. He didn't want to live with this guilt any longer. It was agony and to add to it, her words were cutting him like knives. 'Don't you see how wrong all that is? How wrong we were. War or not.'

'Oh, don't worry, Teddy. It will be another ten years before women catch on to the fact that we are equal to men and deserve equal freedoms and pleasures. Why do you think I am a nurse? Florence Nightingale was good at leading the way and standing up to men. Although I'm not sure she would have approved of going as far as I do.' She laughed and then added testily, 'Look, I need to know, are you going to be an idiot and confess to the bog jumper out there, or are you going to man up and get on with this, for both our sakes? If you confess, I'll have to watch my back as my fiancé might get to hear something and er, we are due to be married next June. You aren't the only person in this hospital who bears a grudge towards me. There are one or two nurses who are less than friendly.'

'I can imagine,' said Teddy. 'I've heard that your fiancé is very wealthy. Stands to inherit a very large GP practice in London, isn't that right? And a family estate in Buckinghamshire that's worth a few bob? Where does all your talk of liberation come in there, or doesn't it?'

Nurse Makebee looked stunned.

'You are just a sex-mad hedonist,' said Teddy. 'If you really were all you profess to be, you wouldn't be so horrible to that wonderful lady outside this door. You would want to stand up for her, for her rights. You would not behave so callously and do what you did. What we did.' He stopped. He was close to tears. He was the loser. He had zero defence for his own behaviour and he was guilty as charged.

The outer door banged open and shut and Nurse Makebee glanced over her shoulder nervously. Mr Mabbutt had arrived in his examination room.

'Look, Teddy, it would be best for us both if you just did the

right thing and protected me. I am the innocent party here.'
Her voice had taken on a whining edge and Teddy could see
that she was not as confident as she had been only moments
before. He wanted to shout at her, 'Innocent? Really? How?'

Teddy heard Mabbutt pick up the phone in the next room.
His murmured voice floated through. Nurse Makebee carried
on talking, faster and in hushed tones. 'My reputation would
be damaged, while yours, as a man, obviously only stands
to be enhanced.'

'My reputation would be enhanced? How? As an unfeeling,
uncaring cad? My life is ruined. I love her and I have nowhere
to go with this. And now you, with all your big talk of
liberation, want me to protect you so that your wedding to
a wealthy man goes off without a hitch? What about Dana?
What about destroying her world, what about us and the life
we imagined would be ours, what about that?'

Mabbutt's footsteps could be heard shuffling around the
desk.

'She doesn't need to know, you stupid man, and what she
doesn't know won't hurt her. What we did is in the past. Forget
your conscience, grow a pair of testicles, get on with your life
and stop your pathetic "I can't live with myself" nonsense.
It's self-indulgent and, by the way, very unattractive indeed.
You are lucky to be alive after your accident. Try thinking
about that. If you feel so bad about what we did, go and
marry her. All we did was have sex and a bit of fun. It's not
illegal. It's allowed.'

Teddy had deliberately blocked out the two weeks they had
spent together. The vast quantities of alcohol, her constant
demands. At first she had excited him, then exhausted and
quickly repelled him. During their brief conversations over

dinner, he had discovered that she had been brought up in an orphanage and had never known either of her parents. All she knew was that she was born in Southend-on-Sea and that her mother had delivered her to the front door of the orphanage on the day of her second birthday. She appeared to be almost indifferent to her past, but Teddy had sensed that she was deeply resentful. He pitied her fiancé. He looked at her face as she wrote his details down in his notes. She was stunningly attractive and there was no doubt about it, she could pitch her frilled cap at almost any doctor she wanted. But he saw nothing but a rejected, motherless past that would haunt her future and, for the briefest moment, he felt deeply sorry for her too.

Mr Mabbutt appeared behind the curtains and looked at them both disapprovingly. 'Am I expected to wait all bloody day?' he asked tartly.

'Coming, Mr Mabbutt,' said Nurse Makebee.

'Where's Nurse Brogan?' Mr Mabbutt asked with a hint of surprise in his voice. 'She told me yesterday she would be bringing you over, Dr Davenport. Matron tells me she has been a bit of a hero where you're concerned. I hear you haven't been the easiest patient.'

'She is outside, waiting,' said Nurse Makebee.

'Well then, Nurse, I suggest you call her in. As the nurse who has put all the hours God has sent into nursing this young doctor better, she is the one I want to bloody well speak to.'

Nurse Makebee looked less than happy at this instruction and appeared to be about to object. But, thinking better of it, she turned and headed to the door. Teddy felt all the fight leave him in a rush.

Mabbutt glanced at the door and looked slightly agitated.

'I had better be quick,' he said. 'Look here, I heard all that and it sounds to me like you have been a bloody fool. Is there anything I can do to help? I haven't patched you up, you know, so that you can live a life of bloody misery.'

Teddy's fingers brushed across his lips as he looked down. The last time he'd cried was when he fell out of the apple tree when he was eleven years old and Roland had laughed at him for being a cissy. 'Thank you, sir, but I am afraid there is nothing anyone can do. It is a problem of my own making and one I have to sort.'

'Just because they call me the silver fox, don't think I don't know what you're going through,' said Mabbutt. 'Look, I will send Nurse Brogan back to her ward when we've finished and you and I can have a chat then. I will wheel you back. Two heads are better than one and I think we might be able to sort this between us.'

Matron had spent an hour of her morning talking to Emily Haycock about Nurse Dana Brogan and Dr Teddy Davenport. Sister Haycock wanted to give Nurse Brogan more flexibility in her shifts, so that she could continue caring for Dr Davenport, but Matron wasn't at all keen. Now that they were both back at St Angelus it wasn't seemly. 'News has reached me that Dr Davenport is less than grateful for the work Nurse Brogan has so far put into his recovery, or indeed, for my allowing her to nurse him in Bolton. Seems to me he needs to spend less time with Nurse Brogan, not more. Time for him to appreciate her efforts. What an ungrateful young man.' They were sat in Matron's office, on opposite sides of the large oak desk. Emily was taken aback. How did Matron know this?

'Of course, Matron,' Emily replied. If there was one thing she had learnt over the years it was never to argue with Matron when she had 'that' tone in her voice and it was certainly present today.

'Is everything well, Matron?' asked Emily as she folded her notebook and prepared to leave. Their meeting was now obviously over. Matron sighed and looked out of the window. 'I fear not. I had hoped to have received some news by now, important news, for St Angelus, but sadly, I have heard nothing and I fear I may have lost an important battle for the women on the dockside streets. I'm just not used to losing, Sister Haycock.' Emily was stinging from her request for Nurse Brogan to be given more flexibility in her shifts flatly refused and the words, 'You should try walking in my shoes for a day' were on the tip of her tongue. Instead, as she stood, she said, 'Never, Matron. You always win,' and with a warm smile to disarm her words, she took her leave.

Matron spent the rest of the morning deep in bed statements and pharmacy orders and could barely utter a thank you or raise a smile when Elsie arrived with her mid-morning tea. She heard the phone ringing just as she was about to take Blackie for his lunch-time walk. Having clipped on his lead, she attempted to walk back to the desk, but Blackie was clearly unimpressed. He dug his back paws in very firmly and had to be dragged across the carpet. 'No, Blackie, stop, I have to answer it, it is three minutes to one. We don't leave until one.'

A pitiful howl came from somewhere within his tartan coat. Matron picked up the telephone. 'Matron's office.'

Madge's chirpy voice came back down the line. 'Hello,

Matron, it's the MP Mr Marcus on the line, shall I ask him to call back after lunch?'

'Oh, goodness me, no, please put him through.'

'OK, give me two seconds then, please, Matron, while I speak to his secretary, Miss Jackson. We will both patch you through together.'

'Thank you, Madge.' Matron heard the click from the switchboard followed by a silence broken only by a light fizz of static on the line. Through the window, she watched two brown-coated porter's lads race past. They were obviously calling out to a group of nurses who were rushing back as fast as they could, doing the heel–toe walk without breaking into a forbidden run. One of the nurses turned and said something back to the lads and she saw one boy push another in the arm in a jocular manner. Matron smiled, something she rarely did in front of her staff. Out on the wards she was Matron, a woman with impeccable standards, and to smile would imply a weakness that would dent her authority.

Her eye was caught by something else: Dr Gaskell's son Oliver calling Nurse Harper to the side of the prefab building that housed the path lab. Her brow furrowed and she took a step closer to the window, as far as the telephone lead would allow. The fact that he had checked to see that no one was watching before they spoke, the clandestine manner in which their heads dipped close, and the way that Nurse Harper then set off before he followed a few moments later, having again looked left and right to confirm that the coast was clear, spoke volumes. The only other person she noticed who had witnessed the meeting was Bryan Delaney, standing at the window of the porter's lodge, and he looked almost as unhappy about what he had seen as Matron did herself.

She had no further time to reflect on this as the familiar tones of Maximillian Marcus crackled down the line from Westminster. 'Matron, good day, how are you?'

'I am very well, thank you, and delighted to take your call. How is the weather in Westminster? It must be better than here.'

'I'm afraid to say it is, Matron. I have already spoken to my mother this morning, in Hoylake, not so far from yourself, and she tells me the north-west is only just surviving under a tempest of gales and rain. A drifting of distant cumulus is about as bad as it has been down here for some time. We even have a sunny blue sky today.'

'Well, we do have our own spell of wintry sunshine here,' Matron replied, 'but I am sure it won't last long and no doubt whatever weather they're having over the water in Hoylake will be with us soon enough.' She actually loathed the way people who lived in the south were so smug about the weather. It was her own fault, she had started it, but wouldn't it be nice if for once she had a telephone conversation with someone in London who told her how awful the weather was down there while Liverpool basked in sunshine.

She gave a small cough and waited for him to continue. From here on in, the telephone call could go one of two ways. Success or disaster. For she was certain that if her eminently reasonable request for a new maternity unit was not granted, the reasons would be sinister and deep and, worse, would very likely not be shared with her. She was nervous for the future of St Angelus, for she was not deaf to the rumours about a brand-new hospital that were doing the rounds. She was worried not just for her patients but for everyone else who depended on St Angelus. First and foremost her staff and all those who relied on hospital wages, especially the families of the fallen and injured. She was the matriarch of the largest family on the dockside, the family of St Angelus. Her beloved family whom she would always put first, even if none of them ever put her first by way of return.

Mr Maxwell's deep baritone voice drifted back to her. 'Anyway, as I promised you, I have spoken to the secretary of state and indeed to the major as well. I have to say, Matron, you have a big fan in your Dr Gaskell. From what I hear, he has been immovable with regard to his position.'

She wondered what position that was. She was suspicious. Dr Gaskell had not mentioned a word to her about having held a conversation with anyone; in fact he had become rather distant of late. He had taken to bringing his golf clubs to work and sneaking off after his afternoon clinics rather than joining her for a cup of tea, as had always been their way. She didn't like to admit it, but she rather missed his company. Since he had stopped visiting, she had found herself retiring to her lonely bed without having had a single social conversation, to do with something that didn't relate to the hospital, in the entire day.

'I am very pleased to hear that, Mr Marcus. It would be a sad day indeed if Dr Gaskell did not support my aims and objectives for the hospital. We have always worked together closely on matters to do with providing the best care for everyone.'

'Indeed, Matron, you do have a formidable supporter and, may I say, not only in Dr Gaskell but in myself and my mother and, I would imagine, in the hundreds of patients who have had much to thank St Angelus for over the years. The hospital runs as well as it does because of you, Matron, and your exceptional organizational skills.'

Matron was silent, not knowing how to respond. As someone unused to praise, she feared the emotion she could feel stirring within.

Maximillian Marcus, clearly pleased that his words had had such an impact, continued. 'Matron, as impressive as your reputation is, and as good as the care is that is provided at St Angelus, I have met with considerable opposition to your plans for a new maternity unit. Far stronger than I could have imagined. There were some very strong forces working against me at a very high level.'

Matron's heart sank. This was it. The flowery words at the beginning of the call had been for no other reason than to lay a soft landing for the news that was about to follow.

He had failed. There would be no new maternity unit. She felt anger bubbling up inside. How could she have been so stupid to have fallen for his flannel? After all these years, to have allowed herself to be taken in in this way.

Blackie growled. He was becoming impatient for his walk. They were now almost ten minutes late and unlike many of the patients lying in beds in the wards, Blackie's bowels were very regular.

Matron took a deep breath. 'I am very sorry to hear that and very disappointed too. I thought that the powers that be would have had the interests of our local families at heart. Indeed, before the appointment of the major as chairman of the Liverpool District Hospitals Board and the strategic removal of every single female representative from that board – women who had until recently been considered irreplaceable and immensely valuable – what was best for the community, for local mothers, was very much a priority.'

This was something that made Matron blister with anger

and it was happening even in clinical settings. Male nurses were now almost immediately promoted to charge nurse once they'd qualified, whereas staff nurses could wait an entire career before being promoted to ward sister. And despite having removed the unmarried nurses rule at St Angelus, so that nurses who married could now remain in employment and were no longer forbidden from having contact with patients, Matron was certain that if Emily Haycock were to stand down as director of the school of nursing, the board would replace her with a male nurse who'd served in the medical corps.

'Now then, Matron, don't be too harsh. There are plans being formulated for the whole of Liverpool and how best to meet the needs of all, over a longer period of time.'

At Matron's elbow a cup of tea materialized on the desk and from the corner of her eye she saw Elsie retreating from the room. Elsie never brought her tea at ten past one. It was Blackie's walk time. She turned her head to whisper thank you, but Elsie had her back to her and disappeared through the door. She had no time to consider the peculiarity of the unrequested tea as the next words she heard took her breath away.

'I have managed to secure the new maternity unit for you on the basis that those who were initially opposed are to head up a feasibility team to appraise the needs of Liverpool over the next twenty-five years and produce a report. This in itself will take a number of years to complete and evaluate. However, given the current birth rate in Liverpool, the provision of a maternity unit cannot wait. They are calling it a baby boom apparently, and you have it bad in Liverpool.' Blackie growled and for the first time ever, Matron nudged him with her foot to silence him. She swallowed hard as she tried to make sense of what she was being told. 'And so the secretary of state and I have agreed on an incremental spend for improving existing services to meet the predicted and increasing demographic need, until such time as a decision is taken on when, where and how a new hospital is to be built. And indeed where and how it should link with the medical school and the university.'

Matron needed a second to allow the words to sink in. 'You mean we actually are going to have a new maternity unit?'

'Yes, Matron, you are. The decision is that St Angelus has a minimum shelf life of a further ten years, but we all know how the wheels of finance and town planning turn. My guess is it will take until the 1970s or even the 1980s before any substantial change takes place and by then, Matron, you and I... Well, it will no longer be our problem, will it?'

Matron was steadying herself against the desk now and was only half listening, but Mr Marcus was still in full flow. Blackie had wound himself and his lead around the leg of the desk and had become trapped. He whined and whimpered in order to attract her attention. Always so attentive to his needs, she failed to even notice.

'The world will have altered so much by then, Matron. Liverpool especially. Our job is to man the bridge until the country has truly moved on from the ravages wrought by the war. The rebuilding of our great city will take much longer than most people believe. The war was expensive and money is in short supply. Besides, the prime minister is prioritizing housing, which, I don't have to tell you, is in desperately short supply. And roads too, out to the places where new houses can be built as cheaply as possible. So, Matron, your maternity unit is approved. The paperwork is with the secretary of state, in his red box, waiting to be signed this week. All you need to decide is where you would like the unit to be situated.'

His words were met with silence.

'Matron, are you still there?'

'Er, yes, I am. I'm most terribly sorry, you have caught me unawares. I don't know what to say except thank you. Thank you. You have achieved something wonderful that will benefit many.'

'Well, Matron, don't thank me, thank Dr Gaskell. I understand that a great deal of pressure was applied to force the good doctor to disapprove of the unit and instead to back the plan for the hasty construction of a new hospital, regardless of a feasibility study, on the basis that St Angelus is no longer fit for purpose. I have no need to tell you I am sure that he steadfastly refused, even though he would doubtless have benefited in a personal capacity. The wheels turn in very murky ways.'

Matron felt quite ashamed. She had doubted Dr Gaskell and his commitment. After all these years. 'Mr Marcus...'

'Oh, Matron, please, it's Max, would you call me that? You virtually nursed my mother back to life. You returned her to me. She had all but given up, you know, because of the pain, the mountain she had to climb. You, you and your nurses, you made the difference. Mother is everything to me and I cannot imagine how my life would run without her. She and your mother were the oldest of friends. Isn't it about time you called me Max? Although I must admit, you will always be Matron to me.'

Matron remembered his mother, her own mother's friend, very well. They had both attended the same girls' boarding convent on the Fylde coast. Mrs Marcus had received a diagnosis of cervical cancer and Matron remembered that she had instructed the surgeon to 'take everything possible away because my son needs me. I have to see him established in his career before I go anywhere.' Her numerous post-operative complications had tested her resolve to the limit, but she had been determined not to succumb. Matron had spent many nights at her bedside, fighting the fever with nothing more than an army of sponges dipped in tepid water. There were no antibiotics freely available then. Nursing an infection equated to physical combat between the patient, the nurse and an unseen enemy. It had been touch and go a number of times, but Mrs Marcus had got through it, propelled by her maternal instinct to survive, and she was still here.

'Well, if I may... Max.' It sounded so strange, she could barely say the word and she knew that as soon as this conversation was over, she would revert to 'Mr Marcus'. 'I think your mother has had some input here. I can almost hear her fighting my corner. Would you please give her a personal thank you from me. She has very well repaid any debt she feels to St Angelus.'

Mr Marcus laughed. 'Matron, Mother tells me she hasn't seen you since the funeral of your own mother and she would like you to come and stay. You can thank her yourself. You and Blackie are warmly invited to spend a weekend in Hoylake with us. Would you do that?'

It was so long since anyone had invited Matron anywhere, she felt slightly overwhelmed. A knot formed in her diaphragm and as she breathed it slowly released a warmth within.

'Please, don't hesitate to say yes. Mother mentioned it again only this morning. I'm sure it is what your mother would have liked, so please say yes.'

This time Matron didn't pause. 'Well, yes, thank you. Are you sure about Blackie? It's just that I never like to leave him.'

'Of course we are sure. How about later this month? Can I tell Mother you've said yes?'

Five minutes later, Matron walked down the stairs, Blackie at her side, feeling as though she was floating on air. She had her unit. Dr Gaskell's loyalty had been put to the test and he had proved to be as good a caretaker of the families of the dockside as she was herself. She had been invited to stay at the Marcus home, her first social engagement since she could remember.

As she made her way to the front doors at the main entrance, various people called out, 'Afternoon, Matron.' The lady on the WRVS stall said, 'You will need your brolly today, Matron. The weather has turned quickly, pouring down out there, it is.' And everyone thought it was most odd when, instead of grimacing at the rain that flew in through the door on the tail of a mini tornado, soaking the front of her dress and cloak, Matron beamed from ear to ear as the umbrella shot out in front of her.

Chapter 15

As Noleen neared the hall, her step slowed and her heart beat faster. It was so long since she had been to the bingo, she thought that maybe she had forgotten how to play. She could just see inside. The women staffing the cloakroom were standing at the hatch, exchanging coats for little chits of grey paper on which they wrote numbers. The overhead light beamed down on them, and their cigarettes, which they only relinquished when they needed to hang up a coat, sent up plumes of thick smoke, making their faces barely recognizable.

Beyond the cloak hatch the hall was dark and Noleen could hear the murmur of excited chatter. The dockside mothers loved their bingo. It was the second religion of the streets. Chair legs scraped across the parquet floor as lucky seats were resumed in anticipation of a good win. Noleen smiled as she remembered nights during the war when players had almost come to blows if they'd arrived to find their own special seat had been taken by someone else.

The familiar feelings of doubt and anxiety began to take hold as she decided that maybe coming to the bingo had been a bad idea after all and she should give tonight a miss.

Return home to the kids, just in case Bryan wasn't managing. After all, Paddy hadn't been working for long.

She heard the sound of laughter spilling out of the hall and looked up. It was a sound she was unused to and she'd missed it. But although she felt the pull to join in with the women she had known for all of her life, the fear of condemnation drew her back. Yes, I'll go back home, she thought.

As she turned, she met the examining stare of Biddy, who was right behind her. 'Where do you think you are off to?' asked Biddy. 'Now you're here, you aren't leaving me to the rabbiting of that one.' She flicked her head back and Noleen saw Elsie, hurrying along behind her, swinging her lucky bingo handbag back and forth as she went.

'Noleen, well, aren't you a sight for sore eyes,' said Elsie as she stopped and caught her breath.

'Isn't she that. What a great night this is going to be. I have a feeling in me water that one of us is going to have a big win tonight.'

Noleen shook her head and smiled.

'No, Noleen, 'tis true. My bladder is better than any crystal ball, even with the pessary fitted. If anything, it's made it better than before, in more ways than one. Come on or Madge will complain that she's been left to keep the seats again. I would have been here ten minutes ago if it wasn't for that one.'

Elsie rolled her eyes heavenwards and smiled at Noleen. She was well used to taking the blame.

Once the coats were handed over, Noleen stood at the entrance to the inner hall, Biddy on one side, Elsie on the other. On the stage ahead and in between, rows of tables and chairs were being filled by women talking fast and furiously, getting all their news out before the serious business of the bingo began.

Because of the thick pall of smoke, it was difficult to see to the end of the hall and make out any faces. The chatter began to subside and Noleen blushed. She instinctively felt that they were staring at her, the newcomer. Although she knew the name of pretty much every woman there, she had been unable to join them on the bingo nights since the day Paddy had come back from the war.

'Oh look, would you? It's Noleen Delaney.' The voices faded to silence.

Noleen felt her heart somersault. It was as she'd expected. They were judging her to be a bad wife who sent her injured husband out to work while she came to the bingo. Someone was going to shout out any moment now, 'Who's looking after your kids now your Paddy has to work nights, Noleen?' The shame of it. She would have to answer, 'Our Mary.' And everyone knew Mary couldn't manage the kids. She couldn't say 'Bryan,' even though that was the truth. He would have seven kinds of a fit if she did, and he had given her strict instructions. 'Don't say I'm at home, Mam. I don't want the other women going home and telling their lads I'm a big cissy.'

The silence was broken by a single clap from Madge Jones, who had stood up and was smiling at her. One by one, all the women stood and began to clap and then someone cheered. Noleen was steered down the hall by Biddy and Elsie, deafened by the cheers. She could not make out who the individual women were who shouted their messages of good will as she passed them because a river of tears had filled her eyes and threatened to pour down her cheeks.

*

Lorcan had offered to work the night shift with Paddy and Paddy was delighted. He had become fond of the earnest young lad. 'Now, all of you, behave for Bryan until your mam gets back from the bingo,' he said as he prepared to leave the house. 'Do you hear me?'

Finn didn't respond. He was lying in his usual position in front of the fire. Jack was yet again waiting patiently for Cahill to finish the comic Bryan had bought him from the tobacconist.

Lorcan almost jumped in through the back door. 'Are you ready, Mr Delaney?'

'I am, lad. How's your mam?'

'She's awake and she's allowed to sit up tomorrow.' Lorcan beamed from ear to ear. It was a smile that was quickly removed by the next question.

'And what about that no-good brother of yours? Have the bizzies got him yet?'

Lorcan looked down at his feet. The thought crossed his mind that someone else might have seen and recognized J.T. at the hospital the other day. He had put it to the back of his mind. At times, he convinced himself that he was wrong, that it hadn't been J.T. at all. But the feeling in the pit of his stomach that hadn't left him since that day told him he had been right the moment he had seen him. It had been J.T.

'Da,' said Bryan, 'give Lorcan a break. He's not responsible for his brother.'

'Sorry, lad,' said Paddy. 'Just can't help thinking he has something to do with your mam's condition. The Bevan boys didn't just turn up with all those guns, did they? Someone must have told them it was OK to leave it all there and if it wasn't J.T., who was it?'

'The bizzies will pick him up soon and Lorcan will be as pleased as anyone, won't you, lad?' said Bryan.

Lorcan handed Paddy his coat from the back of the door. 'I will. I want to go home and get Mam home too. I don't think we can until the bizzies find him. I don't think Biddy will let us. Are you going in the chair, Paddy?'

'No, Lorcan, I'm going to try the leg. Your man at the prosthetics clinic has worked wonders.'

Bryan tied off the bandage he had been wrapping around the wood-and-iron end of the leg ready for the bandaged stump.

'No more padding,' Paddy instructed, 'or I won't be able to fit the stump in. Joe was very clear about that.'

'Are you going to be all right in that, Da? What if you need to move quickly?'

'I won't need to do that, Bryan. I just have to check off the dockets. It needs a man to deal with the drivers. Some of them are right hard cases. Any running around is done by the night lad, isn't that right, Lorcan?'

Lorcan nodded enthusiastically. 'If he needs to move quickly, I'll do it for him, Bryan.'

'Aye, Lorcan is one of the best,' said Paddy as he playfully swiped at Lorcan's cap. 'I never have to ask him twice.'

'Right, try this, Da,' said Bryan.

Paddy slipped his stump into the false leg and winced. Bryan grimaced in sympathy. 'Hang on a minute, it will pass,' said Paddy. 'I just need to get used to it.' After a few moments, his facial muscles eased. 'Right, let's tighten these new straps and tighten this girth and see if do they do the job.'

Ten minutes, two more painkillers and an even thicker bandage later, and aided now by a pair of carved wooden crutches, Lorcan and Paddy made their way towards St Angelus.

Lorraine and Mary came in through the Delaneys' back gate just after Lorcan and Paddy had set off.

'Where's Mam?' asked Mary as she walked into the kitchen and looked around in surprise. 'I thought she'd given up her weeknights and wasn't going to work two on the trot any more?'

'She isn't,' said Bryan. 'She's down the bingo.' He had sat down in Paddy's chair and was staring into the fire, his chin on his hand, barely noticing the girls.

Mary had commented to Lorraine earlier how miserable Bryan had been for the past few days, but there'd been no explanation why. 'Me mam said a smile hasn't cracked his face for ages,' she'd told Lorraine, 'and he wouldn't eat his dinner on Sunday. He's not laughed once since he helped Dessie and Emily with the house shopping at the Sunday market. He hasn't fallen out with them though because he's down there helping Dessie paint every moment he has.'

Lorraine had immediately grasped the situation. She wasn't Maisie Tanner's daughter for nothing. It had to be because he was having to do so much in the house, on account of Mary's laziness, even if he would never admit to it. Having worked this out, she was gobsmacked by what she heard Mary say next.

'Do you want to go down to the pool hall with the rest of the lads, Bryan?' Mary asked, looking directly at her brother. 'I'll stay here and look after the boys if you want.'

Bryan's head shot up. Someone was standing in their kitchen who looked like Mary and smelt like Mary but sounded like someone else entirely. 'Mary, is that you?' He was genuinely amazed that an offer of help had come from her lips.

Mary glanced at Lorraine, who was equally surprised. 'Bryan, you soft lad, of course it's me, who do you think it is? You are such a stupid eejit sometimes.'

Bryan looked suspicious. 'But I promised our mam...' He was half expecting Mary to laugh and reply, 'I was only kidding,' but instead she seemed put out.

'Bryan, I am here. You go out and do what all the other porter's lads are doing and I'll put the boys to bed. I'll lay the table up for breakfast in the morning.'

Even Finn looked up from his book. 'But you're our Mary,' he said. 'You don't do nothing, ever.'

Mary began clearing up the used cups from the table into the enamel wash bowl. 'Yes, well, you aren't as clever as you like to make out, Finn, because I can and I am. Bryan, go now because I want to do it and you're just after being in my way.'

Bryan met Lorraine's eyes, as if looking for confirmation. 'Is this your doing?' he asked.

Lorraine smiled back shyly. Her heart began racing so fast and loud, she could hardly hear her own reply. 'Er, well, I don't think so, no. I help me mam at ours, it's what all us girls do, isn't it? Mary and I had a bit of, er, a chat about it the other day. So I guess she's just come to it a bit later than the rest of us.' She forced herself to calm down and as she did so, her normal confidence resurfaced. The way Bryan assisted his mother without complaining pulled at her heart and she decided she would help. 'I tell you what, Bryan, if you go out, I'll stay and keep Mary company and while I'm here I'll dry-iron the boys' shirts and trousers for school tomorrow, then when your mam gets back, that's another job she won't have to do.'

'I've just done the ashes,' said Bryan, his voice filled with a mixture of hope and anxiety. 'I've filled the bucket, so that won't need doing again until tomorrow.' His voice trailed off as he realized there was nothing else standing in his way. He could join his friends.

It seemed that Lorraine had worked a miracle on their Mary. He imagined the look of pleasure on his mam's face when she came home to find that she didn't have a list of jobs waiting for her, that her Bryan hadn't missed out on his night out and that the house was clean and orderly. He smiled. Lorraine's instinctive understanding of the things that needed to be done and her desire to do something, anything she could, to relieve his mam's heavy load had made him see her through new eyes. It was as if the scales had fallen away. He thought his heart had been broken and his crush on Nurse Harper could never be replicated. But here he was, peering into the soul of a girl he had known since the day she was born, and what he saw made him want to know her more.

The first coal lorry had finished its delivery and Lorcan was hosing down the dust when Paddy called him into the hut. 'Right, according to Dessie's notes, the next one arrives with the coke from the gasworks at midnight, so that gives us time for a break now. I've put the kettle on the hob.'

Lorcan looked back towards the door.

'What's up, lad, have you not finished?'

'I have, Paddy, but the staff nurse on Mammy's ward, I saw her pass through and she told me I could pop in to say goodnight to Mammy at half ten.'

'Did she now? Nice, is she?'

Lorcan blushed and Paddy laughed. 'Go on then, I'll make the tea while you're gone, but hurry, the kitchen porter is bringing us a plate of jam toast. Oh look, here's that young Mr Gaskell, best wait until he's gone past.'

Oliver Gaskell was walking back to the doctors' residence from the Lovely Lane entrance.

'Looks like he's lost a pound and found a shillin',' said Lorcan.

'He does that. Although if I had to guess, I'd say there is a young lady somewhere giving that man the runaround. The kitchen porter was telling me that he was getting a hundred letters or more from Ireland from some young nurse and then they all stopped.'

Lorcan laughed. 'I don't think it was a hundred, Paddy, but he's not very happy, is he?' He slipped off the long overalls he wore for the hosing down. 'God, my hands are so frozen,' he said, 'I can't do the buttons up.'

'They will be, lad, with the cold water. Come here.'

Lorcan walked over to Paddy, who leant forward and fastened the buttons on his brown coat as he would have for one of his own children. 'There you go. You are respectable now.'

'Thanks, Mr Delaney.' Lorcan sprinted out of the light and warmth of the wooden hut and across the dark courtyard to the glorified Nissen-hut ward where his mother slept.

Staff Nurse was sitting at the wooden table at the bottom of the ward. 'Well, hello. What a busy evening your mammy has had. First her nephew and now you.'

Lorcan's mouth almost fell open. He instantly knew what this meant. There was no nephew. His worst fears had been realized: the figure he'd seen the other day must have been J.T.

and he'd obviously come back again today. He had visited their mam, but why?

Through the glass window, Lorcan could see that his mother was dozing. He approached her cubicle and as soon as he came through the door she woke and turned her head towards him. She was propped up in bed and although she was still on bed rest and bedpans and not allowed to even put her feet on the floor, it was clear that she was getting better. The ward lights were off and the red overhead night light flickered above her head.

She smiled when she saw him. 'Ah, Lorcan, 'tis you. I thought 'twas the man back again.'

'What man, Mam?' Lorcan stood directly at the side of her bed so that she could see him better. 'Mam, was it J.T. who was here? The man you saw?'

Mrs Ryan smiled vacantly at him and whispered, 'Sure, was that him? No, 'twasnt. It definitely was not J.T. He has never had a beard and this man, he had on him a very smart suit and hat and he wore glasses. He did look familiar now, though.'

A chill ran through Lorcan's body. Something wasn't right, but he couldn't put his finger on what. Maybe it hadn't been J.T. after all. But if not J.T., then who had been in pretending to be his mam's nephew and what did he want? He felt a flash of irritation. Why was his mother always so hopeless?

Staff Nurse popped her head around the door. 'Everything OK, Lorcan? Isn't she doing well? I've seen an improvement even since last night.' She walked over to the bed. 'We're coming along nicely, aren't we, Mrs Ryan? Is that because your nephew came today?'

'That was Lorcan,' said Mrs Ryan and she placed her hand on top of Lorcan's.

He almost froze with fear. What if she had said J.T.'s name? Someone might think that he was associated with J.T. and his break-out from Walton.

Staff Nurse smiled at Lorcan. 'Well, I'm not saying everything's perfect just yet,' she said and laughed. 'Especially with the short-term memory. Right, I'm off to do the medicine round. Will you be staying long? Night Sister will be here fairly soon.'

'No, I can't. I have to get back to the hut. There's another delivery due.'

'I'll see you tomorrow then.' She turned to go. 'I'll be back soon, Mrs Ryan, with your medication.'

'Do you want some water before I go, Mam?' asked Lorcan.

Mrs Ryan lifted her head and as Lorcan turned to get the glass off the top of her locker, he noticed that the cupboard door was open. He placed his hand inside to check that his mother's bag was still there. She went nowhere without it. It sat by her feet at home and hung from her arm when she was out. Suddenly panicked, he inched his fingers inside the bag to make sure the house keys were still there. What if the mystery visitor had stolen them, as he'd feared?

The bag felt different, fuller. Pulling it free, he moved it under the night light and recoiled in horror at what he saw inside. Wrapped up in rubber bands were bundles of bank notes. Fat wads of fifty-pound notes. Lorcan had never seen so much money in one place. His fingers trembled as his eyes widened in alarm. What if Staff Nurse had found it? What was all that loot doing in his mam's bag?

He had only seconds to decide what to do before his mam turned her head and made things a hundred times worse. The blood pounded in his ears and his breath came faster as he put his hand inside. He grabbed the bundles one by one and hurriedly stuffed them into the large brown pockets of his porter's coat. He was trembling so violently, his teeth began to chatter. He hurriedly pushed the bag back inside the locker and slammed the door shut and quickly looked through the window to check that no one had seen him. Staff Nurse was unlocking a large wooden trolley under the glow of another night lamp and whispering something to the probationer nurse who was with her. The other patients were all either dozing or chatting to each other. He was safe; no one had seen him. He quickly kissed his mother on her brow, bade her goodnight and, with his mouth dry with fear and his head bent low, he walked speedily out of the ward.

Paddy was sitting in the hut when Lorcan returned, stirring the leaves in the big brown pot with a screwdriver. Before him sat an enamel plate piled high with toast. 'Eh, what took you so long? The toast is nearly cold. I waited for you, see. I never knew your mam to be able to string, er, to be so big into the conversation before she was sick, let alone now. She getting on OK?' He'd been about to say 'string two words together', but he'd checked himself. He knew that Lorcan had taken his fair share of name calling from the other kids when he'd been at school. 'Anyway, you're back now. We have ten minutes. Take the weight off your feet and get this toast down you. You have to do the night round at eleven on the dot.'

On the hour every hour, the hospital had to be checked inside and out to ensure that all was well. A full circuit of the wards was made, along with the outbuildings and units. Paddy insisted on doing his share; he covered the outbuildings and stores nearest to the porter's hut and the night boy did the main ward blocks, the pre-fabs and the car parks.

Lorcan hadn't moved since he'd got back to the hut. He was almost literally frozen to the spot and his skin had turned a deathly grey. Paddy shoved the tin mug towards him and began to pile the sugar into his own. 'Come on, Lorcan, what's up with you?' He could see Lorcan's hands were shaking. 'What's up, lad? What's wrong? I've seen a marble statue with more colour in its cheeks than you.' He was worried now and he began to rise to his feet. 'Lorcan, come on, you're scaring the shit out of me. What is it?'

Lorcan's eyes were wide and unblinking, his bottom lip trembled. He attempted to speak, to move his mouth, but no words emerged. He looked down at his pockets and stared at them as though they had a life of their own. As far as he was concerned, in each pocket sat the Devil himself. They burnt into his leg and were weighing him down so much that his limbs refused to move.

'Lorcan!' There was alarm in Paddy's raised voice. 'What is it? For the sake of Jesus, tell me. Did you see a ghost? Did you go to the mortuary?' And then it dawned on him. 'Oh, Lorcan, is your mam... you know... has she...? Jesus, Lorcan, is she dead?'

Lorcan didn't reply. Couldn't reply. Instead, lifting his violently shaking hands, he took the rolls of cash out of his coat pockets and laid them on the table.

Paddy collapsed back down on to the seat. 'Feckin' hell. All the time you were gone, I thought you were visiting your mam, and Jesus, you went and robbed a bank? Did you?'

Chapter 16

Roland arrived at the Lovely Lane home at seven thirty on the dot. He hadn't eaten since lunch time and had been dreaming about the chip shop at the end of the lane. It served the best cod and chips that he had ever tasted. He mentioned this to Victoria as soon as she slipped into the car. 'Right, I am famished. It's the chip shop for me. Fish and chips. Lots of chips.'

'Do we have to?' asked Victoria, even though she had used Roland's visit as an excuse to Mrs Duffy when she couldn't face the gammon and eggs she had been presented with.

'We do. No ifs or buts. I love you dearly, Victoria, but I warn you, it is very dangerous to stand between me and my stomach.'

Almost an hour later, Victoria watched with mild amusement as Roland wiped the last of the sauce off his plate with a slice of bread and butter. 'Honestly, I have never seen you eat fish and chips in Bolton.'

'No? Really? They have great pie shops, but not as good as here. Anyway, what's the urgency? Has Teddy been behaving himself?'

'Well, actually, as you ask, no, I don't think so. He is a little sod, isn't he? Why do you think he is so horrible to Dana? Everyone is beginning to notice – except, it would seem, Dana herself.'

Roland picked up his tea mug and began to drink. As he did so, he made his decision. 'Victoria, I have something to tell you.'

'Do you? I have something to tell you too.'

'Can I go first?' said Roland. 'I am quite sure what I am about to tell you is far bigger and, frankly, I am glad you are sitting down.'

'Go on then.' Victoria began to sip gingerly on her black tea. 'What is it?'

'It's Teddy. He has, er, confessed something to me.' He paused, took a deep breath and launched straight in. 'Before his car accident, Teddy had been on a two-week holiday with Nurse Makebee. In one room, sharing the same bed.'

Victoria spluttered into her tea and sent it scudding into the air.

Roland grinned. 'There, I knew you would be shocked.'

'Roland, there's nothing funny about it.' Victoria was truly horrified.

'Oh, I know. You don't have to tell me that, my dearest. It is an appalling way to behave. It was just your reaction, it mirrored my own. I swear, the shock of it made me ill and confined me to my bed.'

'Nurse Makebee! Oh my goodness… Poor Dana.'

Roland nodded sympathetically. 'I at least have had a little time to get used to it. So, what to do? How do we deal with this? I can't even begin to know where to start.'

Victoria pursed her lips. 'You are asking a question to which there is only one answer.'

Roland wiped his plate clean with the last crust. 'And that is…?' he said as he stuffed the bread into his mouth.

'We tell Dana, of course. She has to know.'

'Really? Should we not weigh this up first, go over the arguments for and against?'

'Roland, you are not a lawyer here, you are Teddy's brother and I am Dana's friend. This is quite different.'

Roland stared out of the window. 'Hmm, nonetheless, there are considerations. Not least the fact that I promised him I would tell no one. If he finds out I have, my credibility as a brotherly confidant will be shot to pieces, and my relationship with Teddy could be permanently damaged.'

Victoria snorted her derision, but Roland carried on.

'My initial reaction was exactly the same as yours, Vic, but we need to think seriously hard and do the right thing, not just what our emotions compel us to do. There is also the fact that when we do tell Dana, as witnesses to her humiliation, we will leave her with only one option and it is an option she will take. She will leave Teddy then and there. We know what a proud individual she is and I cannot see her even staying at St Angelus. If I were as proud as she is, I would probably waste my training and head back to Ireland. Her reaction will be a hundred times greater than ours. We will be destroying her life too. So I will have lost a brother and Teddy will have lost the woman he loves.'

Victoria sighed, imagining how utterly distraught Dana would be. 'What a horrible mess,' she said.

'I could murder a drink,' Roland said. 'Let's go to the pub and you can tell me your news.'

*

Beth tapped on Victoria's bedroom door. She wanted to borrow her jade-green scarf. Victoria had the most extensive wardrobe of all the girls and was the most generous in lending things out. The agreement was that if anyone borrowed something, they left a note on her dresser saying what had been taken and by whom.

Victoria had the tidiest room. Even the maids enjoyed putting away her things, admiring her new clothes, smelling her perfume. But tonight, when Beth popped her head around the door, she was met with mild disarray and an unpleasant, stale smell that lingered despite the window having been left open. Beth was surprised, both by the state of the room and also because it was so unusual for Victoria not to have knocked and said where she was going.

The girls were like family to one another. They let each other know their evening plans and when they would be back and that was before they checked out with Mrs Duffy. Pammy was out with Anthony tonight, and Dana was still at work. In truth, Victoria's slipping of their self-imposed rule came as a relief to Beth. It meant she could go out too and would only have to tell one little white lie, to Mrs Duffy. After so many evenings spent staying in with just Mrs Duffy for company, it was nice to finally have somewhere to go.

There was an open bottle of lemonade with a glass next to it on the dresser and Beth thought this was also unusual. She had never known Victoria to drink lemonade before. She was a champagne girl and often sneaked a bottle back with her when she went home to Bolton and then called them into her room to share it. Afterwards she would bribe the maid with an eye shadow or some trinket to dispose of the bottle. Beth cast her eye around the room. It took less than a minute to find the scarf. It was exactly where she had last left it. Victoria has more clothes than she can wear in a month, she thought, as she took it down from the shelf.

Placing the scarf around her neck, she took a pen out of the pretty bone-china jug on Victoria's desk and looked for a blank piece of paper to write on. 'Hello, Vic, bringing work home?' she said out loud as she saw a path-lab report lying open on the dresser. All reports had to be punched and filed in the back of the patient's notes ready for the doctor to see during the morning ward rounds. Beth could not imagine why anyone would bring one home. Maybe Victoria had brought it back in her uniform pocket by mistake.

The words at the top of the form drew her attention. *Pathology Department: Hogben Test.* That was even odder. Victoria was working with her on theatre, and the only places the Hogben Test was used were on gynae on ward two, and maternity. Neither of them had been on gynae and nurses were only put on maternity for the last placement of their training.

Beth reached out and picked up the flimsy carbon-copy paper of the test report. She could not believe what she was seeing. She had to bring it closer to her face before her eyes could take it in. The name on the report said simply: *Mrs B Victor.*

'Mrs B Victor? B. Victor. Was this a play on words? Victoria Baker. No, it can't be, surely not?' Beth placed her hand over her mouth as if to stem her own words. It was surely too much like Victoria's name to be a coincidence. Next she looked at the box bearing the signature of the doctor requesting the test. When she saw that it had been signed by Pammy's boyfriend, Anthony Mackintosh, she realized the truth. The fainting, the sickness, the stale smell in the room, even the open bottle of lemonade – it all pointed to one thing. Vic was pregnant.

Did Pammy already know? Was Beth the only one who didn't? Were they all keeping secrets from her? Beth felt lonelier than ever. And here was I, thinking I had the biggest secret of all, she thought as she laid the path-lab report down, picked up the scarf and slipped out of the room to get ready for her evening out.

Oliver Gaskell had hounded her relentlessly for this date. He had asked her exactly fourteen times before she said yes; twice a day over the past week. He had sent notes, cornered her yet again in the clean utility room in theatre and outside the changing-room door. Most daringly, he'd sent another letter via Jake to the nurses' home.

It was only when she saw him outside the park gates on the opposite side of Lovely Lane when she was returning from a split shift that she thought she had better speak to him. He was becoming more foolhardy in his methods and she worried that the others would be bound to find out soon. He had obviously seen the off-duty and decided to wait for her.

'What are you doing here?' she practically shouted at him. 'I have told you, what happened was a once-only. It will never happen again. Mrs Duffy will see you if you hang around here. Now please go away.'

'Are you mad?' he practically shouted back as he grabbed hold of her arm. 'You can't do this, you can't just ignore me and refuse to answer my letters. I know you have been avoiding me. Sister Pokey told me you had requested off-duty on my list day and she almost sneered at me! It was like she was telling me to stick to the qualified nurses for my operations in future. Why are you doing this? Are you trying to punish me for something?'

'You know why. I told you. It was a once-only occurrence. You have a reputation for being a bit of a rake and it is not one I want to be associated with. Besides, you will only get fed up of me. I'm just boring old Beth. I am not your type.'

She glanced across the road to the nurses' home to make sure no one was watching. She thought she saw the net curtain in Pammy's room twitch, but it must have been the breeze. The sash was open at the bottom by a couple of inches, but there was no one there.

'If you don't at least agree to meet me for a drink and let me try to persuade you of my honourable intentions, I shall simply continue to keep asking you until you do.'

They were standing near the bus stop and Beth looked nervously over towards the front door. Mrs Duffy would be waiting to serve her her lunch before catching the bus home for the afternoon, but pretty soon she'd assume Beth had been asked to stay at work and would then come out for her bus and see them there.

Oliver Gaskell saw her looking and noticed her anxiety. 'Hello!' he shouted and waved his arms frantically in the direction of the home.

'What in God's name are you doing?' said Beth.

'I'm asking you for a date and it appears that the only way I am going to get you to agree is to embarrass you into it.'

'Hello!' He jumped up and down and continued waving wildly.

Beth shot him another look. There was someone in Pammy's room, was there? Could it be the maid? Or was Pammy at the home? She usually spent her days off with Maisie. 'Look, you are an idiot. Please, stop it. Where shall I meet you, and when?'

Oliver Gaskell grinned broadly. It was obvious he'd never faced such a challenge when trying to get a nurse out on a date.

As she walked back into the nurses' home, Beth headed straight to Pammy's room. 'I'm just going upstairs for a wash, Mrs Duffy. I can help myself to lunch. Don't miss your bus, just leave mine in the oven,' she shouted through to the kitchen as she ran up the stairs. If Pammy was home, if she had heard them outside talking or seen the way he had pulled her to him and planted a very firm kiss straight on her mouth, she would be furious. Beth knew she needed to speak to her and explain, before things went any further or Pammy told anyone else. Above all, Beth did not want that.

'Pammy, are you in?' she shouted as she opened the door. She looked around. The room was empty. Not a sign of her. She must have been imagining it. Maybe it had been the maid after all.

As the door banged shut behind her and Beth's footsteps receded down the hallway, Pammy slipped out of the wardrobe. She had not wanted Beth to speak to her. She wanted to tell the others what she had seen. This was serious.

Roland and Victoria had decided to go to the Grapes for their drink. 'Let's grab a seat by the fire,' Victoria suggested. They waited at the door to let several bowler-hatted gents out first, clearly on their way home having stopped in for a pint or two after work. Most of the rest of the clientele were younger, wearing Teddy-boy slicks, perms and kitten heels, and looked as if they would be there until closing. Victoria spotted a corner booth. 'Here we go,' she said as she slipped on to the red leather seat.

'Marvellous. What would you like to drink?' said Roland.

'Oh, just a lemonade, please.' She extended her hands towards the fire to warm them and waited for Roland to return.

'Here you go. I bought us some pork scratchings.' He popped one in his mouth before taking a big swig of his drink.

Victoria caught the whiff of the roasted pigskin and it took every bit of willpower not to heave.

'Have you had any more thoughts about what we should do?' Roland asked as he sat down. 'I'm depending upon you, darling. You are the wise one and you know Dana better than I do. You know, I can't stop thinking about my stupid brother. I am so worried for him. I almost suggested that he and Dana come out with us tonight and then, you know, I thought that might help us to make up our minds.'

'Roland, could you just forget about Teddy for a moment, as awful as it all is. I have something else I need us to talk about.'

'Oh yes, sorry, darling. Is something wrong? I can tell you aren't yourself. You look a little pale, if I am being entirely honest.' Roland placed his arm around Victoria's shoulders and hugged her into him. 'Tell me then. What is it?'

Victoria took a sip of her lemonade. She had discovered that this was one drink she could actually enjoy. She couldn't stomach anything milky and it seemed like an age since anything that could legitimately be classed as proper food had stayed down for longer than ten minutes.

Over the last few days she had thought long and hard about how best to tell Roland her news. She'd decided to ease him in as gently as possible. 'Roland, have you heard of the Hogben Test?'

He lifted his head and looked at her in alarm. 'No, but it sounds, oh, I don't know, serious, darling. Serious and scientific. Is it something you are stuck on for the exams? I'm not sure I am the person to help. Science wasn't my thing at school. It was Teddy's though. I suppose that's why he became a doctor. Have you asked him?'

This wasn't going in the direction she'd hoped. She was feeling weary and sorry for herself, but she knew she had to plough on. She tried another tack. 'Do you remember, Roland, telling me what a lot of fun you used to have with Teddy as children, in your garden at home, playing in the tree house and everything? Well...' She cleared her throat, less discreetly than she'd intended.

'Are you all right?' interjected Roland. 'You aren't sick, are you? You do look terribly pale.'

'Er, well, the thing is, Roland, that test I mentioned... I had it done because I thought I might be pregnant. And... I am. I'm pregnant.'

Roland did not say a word.

Victoria took another sip of her lemonade. 'Gosh, I needed that, my mouth was dry, I was so worried about telling you.' She turned to look at him. 'Roland, Roland, are you OK?'

Before he could answer, Roland fainted clean away.

'Is he all right, love?' the barman shouted over. Victoria let Roland's head collapse on to her knee. 'Not drunk after one pint, is he?'

'No, no,' Victoria shouted back. 'He will be fine in a moment. He's had a bit of a shock.' She remembered what Maisie had said when she herself had fainted at the Tanners' and she almost shouted back, 'He's passed the eleven-plus and forgot to tell me,' but she thought better of it.

'You're one of the angels from the hospital, aren't you? Live in over at the home?' said the barman.

'I am,' said Victoria, with a lift in her voice.

'I thought so. Well, he's in good hands then. If I'd spotted you when you walked in, I wouldn't have charged for those drinks. When miladdo wakes up, the next round is on the house.'

Victoria smiled. The barman was called away to serve another customer and she looked down at Roland and stroked his hair. The colour was slowly creeping back into his cheeks and soon he would open his eyes. 'From the moment you wake up, my love, nothing will ever be the same again,' she whispered. For the first time in weeks, she felt hungry. Leaning over Roland's slumped body, she picked up the packet of pork scratchings and began to munch.

Oliver Gaskell was already waiting outside the pub, pacing up and down. He seemed nervous. Beth smiled to herself as she watched him. He looked nothing like the extremely confident man he portrayed himself to be and was a sight for sore eyes.

'Ah, thank you for not letting me down,' he said as she approached.

'Really,' said Beth rather tartly, 'am I the sort to do that?'

'Gosh, you do take some winning over, don't you? I thought that the last time we were together… well, that it might have been the start of something more permanent. Didn't think I would have to fight this hard for a second date.'

'I am afraid that was your error,' said Beth. 'I am sure you have never let any nurse assume she was a permanent feature in your life after one date.'

'I had thought it was more than a date.'

Beth's resolve weakened. He looked downcast. The truth was she didn't know what it was she had fallen for: the excitement he offered, the status of being the girlfriend of a consultant, his reputation as the hospital Casanova, or one-uppance on her friends, who she was sure thought her life path was on a trajectory quite different from theirs.

'Now that you are here, shall we go inside for a drink?'

She softened. After all, she chided herself, this is the man who took your virginity. You spent the most exciting afternoon of your life with him. Throw him a bone, be nice. 'That would be most enjoyable,' she said. 'But please don't think that the evening will end up the way our last date did. And do not take this drink as evidence of any change in our relationship. I am not your girlfriend.'

His face broke into a grin, despite her words. He didn't care what she said, he was in with a chance. 'Message received and understood.' He mock saluted her and opened the pub door for her to pass through.

Beth's father always did that, mock saluted when he saw her, with the same look on his face. Even if in every other respect Oliver Gaskell was a million miles from her beloved army captain father. She grinned; he did make her smile, and that was something she could not stop happening.

'They have a nice fire in here,' he said, 'and they serve a good pint too. Shall I take your coat and lovely green scarf?'

Beth didn't reply. She was too busy staring at Victoria, who was holding Roland's head down between his legs.

Chapter 17

Since he'd discovered the money in his mam's handbag, Lorcan had become very nervous about what else he might find whenever he visited her on the ward. He continued to call in every evening, either before or after his shift, depending on whether he was on night duty or not. The doctor had told him it would be at least another month before she would be allowed home and Lorcan felt almost relieved. He could carry on staying at Biddy's, while the hospital cared for his mam.

As soon as he arrived at the ward he always asked the night staff nurse the same question. 'Has she had any more visitors today?'

The response was always the same. 'No, only yourself.' But tonight there was a pause before the nurse answered and it made Lorcan's heart thump. 'It says here that a Mrs Delaney came today.' She turned over the page. 'Pardon me, I forgot, but a Mrs Kennedy came yesterday. They both work here, don't they? Noleen used to clean the main corridor on nights. I only see her occasionally now.'

'That's right,' said Lorcan. 'She's Paddy Delaney's wife.'

Staff Nurse looked surprised. 'What, the new night watchman?'

'Yes, so Mrs Delaney only has to work two nights a week now.'

Staff Nurse picked up the charts at the end of his mother's bed as she spoke. 'Well now, isn't that great. He's the one grafting and bringing the bacon home. The poor woman always looked so tired. Is she putting her feet up now?'

Lorcan hadn't a clue. It was a reasonable assumption. 'I think so,' he said.

'Isn't it marvellous,' she said. 'He probably earns more than I do and I'm a qualified nurse, but you see, I'm not a man. Do you know, the charge nurse on ward eight earns exactly double what I do and yet I qualified five years before he did.'

Lorcan stared at her, eyes blinking.

'I'm sorry, Lorcan, I shouldn't go on at you. You have it tough enough already without listening to my complaints. Funny world we live in, though, don't you think? I know it's because we get married and stop work, so it doesn't really matter, does it, but that won't last for ever. They will want us doing two jobs soon, raising a family and working full time. Mrs Delaney should take the rest while she can get it.'

She wrote something on the chart and then looked up towards his mam, who was resting against the pillows with a contented half smile on her face. 'Are you in any pain, Mrs Ryan?' she asked.

Mrs Ryan shook her head. 'No, no pain, not now my Lorcan is here.' She turned to Lorcan and smiled.

'I have told her already once tonight, and I'm not going to mention it again in case I worry her, but you do know she's off to theatre again tomorrow? They have to fit a metal plate over where they removed the piece of her skull. She won't have to wear those enormous bandages any more then, not once it knits and settles, anyway. That will be there to protect her brain from any knocks or bumps in the future.'

Lorcan's eyes were wide with amazement.

'Don't worry, it's nowhere near as serious as what she had done before and not as dangerous either. She will have forty-eight hours of being groggy and you remember what that was like, don't you? We will have oxygen in here and she will be on a drip, but, honestly, after a few days she will be no different to how she is tonight. It's an operation to help put her right, not to treat anything.'

Lorcan let out a long sigh of relief.

'Don't you even think about a thing, there is nothing to worry about. Just come along as usual tomorrow evening. I just wanted to prepare you for what you will find when you get here, that's all.'

'There is nothing to worry about.' The words ran riot in Lorcan's mind as he made his way out of the hospital gates. Nothing to worry about? If only that were the case. He ran towards St Chad's and the sound of the Angelus bell. He gave thanks in church every day for Paddy and Dessie and everyone he now depended upon. He could not imagine what he would have done without them all.

As he turned towards the church steps, he noticed the ominous presence of a police car as it crawled across the top of the road. He had seen it by the hospital gates as he had left the ward. They were watching him and he knew why. He swallowed hard as his mouth became dry with fear.

Almost throwing himself into the pew, he clasped his hands together and pointed them heavenwards as they shook. He didn't bother to look for Noleen; he knew she was at the meeting in Biddy's house. The meeting about him and the danger he had put everyone in. That Noleen would miss Mass was a measure of how serious things were.

As he shut his eyes to pray, he replayed Paddy's reaction as he'd laid the rolls of money down on the table in the porter's lodge. Paddy had shot out of his chair and staggered backwards, catching his hand on the waist-high shelf that ran down the side of the hut.

'Where the feckin' hell did you get this?' he said. 'Here, quick.' Paddy reached up and pulled down a large brown cardboard box marked 2½" *Washers*. He shoved the rolls of notes in as though they were burning his hands and then quickly pushed the box back into place.

'Did you see that?' he said. 'Them's rolls of ponies.'

Lorcan had no idea what a pony was.

'Fifty-pound notes,' Paddy explained. 'Where did you get them, Lorcan? Where?' Paddy was looking anxiously out of the hut door, his voice raised and trembling.

The hut smelt like the chandler's shop Lorcan had known all of his life. The familiar scent of oil and rags and linseed gave him comfort. 'It was in Mammy's handbag. Someone came to see her today and put it there.' His voice trembled as he spoke.

'Who?' Paddy hissed, trying to keep his voice low and avoid attracting the attention of any passing domestic or kitchen porter. The two other porter's lads on duty that night were both out, transferring a body from ward seven to the mortuary.

'I don't know. Someone with a hat and a beard. I think I might have seen the same man running away the other day, when I was putting the flow meters away.'

Paddy had already reached for the phone on the wall and

was dialling out. At night, the porter's lodge was one of the few places in the hospital where you could call direct to the exchange. As he held the phone to his ear, he nodded towards the mug of tea and tower of toast. 'Eat, drink,' he said. 'We have a long night ahead of us.' After what seemed to be an age later, Paddy had made a connection. 'Rory, is that you?' Paddy was now speaking into the handset of the phone. 'I need Dessie Horton, is he there? Good, can you put him on now?' Paddy's voice had an urgency to it and Lorcan was sure that Rory, the landlord of the Silvestrian, wouldn't argue with him.

There was silence in the hut while they waited, broken only by the sound of Lorcan munching his toast.

While Lorcan prayed in St Chad's, Biddy was buttering the new Ritz crackers she'd bought specially for the meeting.

'We need to keep this one tight,' Dessie had told her when he'd come round the night before to arrange the meeting. 'Someone is using Mrs Ryan to fence money.'

'Don't we just give the money to the police?' asked Biddy. 'Sure, we know who it is, don't we? 'Tis J.T., he's still on the run.'

'No, we don't,' said Dessie. 'The police want someone to blame. They will be after taking Mrs Ryan in for harbouring stolen goods or some such claim, as if she even knew the money was there. As long as they get someone, they don't care who, and what is her defence? She's not certified as mad. The woman is just puddled. The police will run rings around her. She's already spent one night in a cell. She doesn't know what she is talking about from one minute to the next.'

'She's improving, I think. I popped in to see her the other day,' said Biddy.

'Well, that would be even worse. And this is a fact, if the bizzies have the money but no J.T., no matter who handed it in, they will go after Lorcan next. They will say he got scared or some such ridiculous cocked-up story. If they can't get J.T., they will take both Lorcan and his mam and pin it on them for colluding,' he said. 'They might even take Mrs Ryan in to flush out J.T.'

'Would they sink that low?'

Dessie raised his eyebrows. 'Biddy, we are the Irish. They would. And I doubt once they had used her they would admit a mistake and let her out again, head injury or not.'

'Over my dead body will that be happening,' said Biddy.

'We need a plan. This money, it is red hot and whoever put it there will be coming back for it. We can't put it back in her handbag. If a nurse finds it, Mrs Ryan is as good as spending the rest of her life in jail, especially as the notes and the rolls are numbered with a tape wrapped around them. It looks like they've come straight from a bank.'

Biddy's hand flew to her mouth. 'Jesus wept, do you think it's from the jump-over that was in the *Echo*?'

Dessie shook his head. Biddy could see he was worried that they might be out of their depth on this one.

'If the bizzies come after Lorcan, he won't stand a chance. He doesn't have to have been involved in any jump-over or whatever. The money has his fingerprints all over it already and it's in his hands, that's enough to put him away.'

Biddy slumped into the chair. 'Will we ever stop being Irish immigrants?' she asked him. 'I've been here most of me life and yet they still call us for everything.'

Dessie didn't answer. He didn't want to dwell on the fact that the legal system in Liverpool was none too friendly towards the Irish. That time after time they heard stories of gross unfairness and miscarriages of justice, some of which even made the headlines in the *Daily Post* and *Echo*. He had more pressing things on his mind than self-pity. 'Biddy, I can't keep this money in the porter's hut. I can't do that to Matron and look her in the eye. Is your tea chest still in the scullery?'

'It is.' Biddy leapt to her feet. 'And what's more, 'tis full. We had a nice little delivery from the *Cotie* only yesterday.' With J.T. now out of the picture, Biddy had found a new source for her black-market supply of tea from the ships in the docks.

'Grand. Let's dig down deep and hide it in the black gold dust then.'

At six o'clock on the dot, Noleen and Paddy slipped in through Biddy's back door.

'Would you get the cut of you, gadding about on your sticks and with the false leg an' all,' said Biddy as she took in the hobbling Paddy. It was the first time he had been in her kitchen since before the war and she was filled with pride at how he had come on since Dessie had sorted a job for him.

'I'm off to trial for Everton in the morning,' said Paddy with a wink. 'They have a position for a goalie. I thought as I'm doing so good, I might as well try.'

'Who do you think you are then?' asked Dessie with a grin. 'George Bargery? He was the best goalie Everton has ever had. Magnificent, they called him. To think that the bank he worked in told him he had to choose between his job and the footie. The day he gave up Everton for his job was a sad day indeed.'

'Yes, but he had kids to feed,' said Paddy. 'What was he supposed to do? They say that the goalie for Accrington Stanley used to try and throw a sickie when he knew they were playing Everton if George was in goal, he was that good.' Biddy shook her head, perplexed.

'Jesus wept, are we here to talk about the football?' she asked. 'I thought we had something much more serious to discuss.'

Emily was the next through the door. 'Dessie never stops talking about the footie, Biddy. I'm beginning to wonder if I've made a mistake.' She removed the scarf from around her neck as she spoke, then put her arms out to take Dessie's coat. As she did so, Dessie planted a kiss on the end of her nose and they exchanged a tender look. 'And by the way,' she said as she scooped his coat into her, 'there's a big bubble in the parlour wallpaper.'

Dessie put his hand to his head and groaned.

'That's an easy one,' said Paddy, 'just burst it with a pin, push the air out and then press it down with a bit more paste. Make a little cut if you have to.'

'What's this rattling?' said Emily as she ran the flat of her hand down Dessie's jacket.

'Oh, I nearly forgot.' Dessie grinned as he began to remove bottles of Guinness from the huge deep pockets in his coat. 'I've brought us all some light refreshments.'

Elsie barged through the door next, bearing paste sandwiches, followed by Branna, Madge, Betty Hutch, Maisie and Stan Tanner, Bryan, and then Lorcan himself, straight from church. There was lots of chatter and Stan Tanner held aloft a bottle of sherry. 'Here we go, ladies,' he said. 'Courtesy of Rory down the Silvestrian. I got it half price.'

'Oh, really?' said Madge. 'And which ship did that fall off the back of?'

'The *Cotie* is in, Biddy, which do you think? Get the tea, did you?' said Stan as he gave Biddy a knowing wink.

'Do you have enough glasses, Biddy? Shall I fetch some from next door?' said Elsie before Biddy had the chance to answer Stanley.

'I think you'd better. Before you go, Elsie, could your Martha spare Jake for an hour?'

'Of course she can. I'll get him to carry a couple of chairs through too.' Elsie headed out again.

Betty Hutch was looking with disdain at Stanley and Dessie, who were now flicking the tops off the Guinness bottles. 'I only want tea,' she said.

'One day I'll force a drink down you, Betty Hutch,' Biddy replied. 'I know you quiet types, and when that day comes, you'll be flinging your knickers off and chasing old Dr Gaskell down the wards.'

Everyone began to laugh, except Betty herself, though she almost managed a smile. She had held a torch for Dr Gaskell since 1927 and the mere mention of his name warmed her heart and brought the colour to her cheeks.

'She would have retired years ago if it wasn't for him, wouldn't you, Betty?' teased Biddy. 'She only comes to work to catch a word with him. That and waiting for his wife to pop her clogs so that she can jump straight into his bed. Eh, Betty, when you do, ask him to take a look at your varicose veins before he jumps on. He might be too knackered after.'

Biddy chuckled as Betty sat down unperturbed. She was inured to it all after so many years of being ribbed and smutty talk. In her experience, the women who worked at the hospital were worse than the men. As Biddy turned on the tap to fill the kettle, she saw Elsie open the back gate with glasses in her hand. Behind her came Jake, carrying four kitchen chairs stacked one on top of the other. Biddy's heart warmed at the sight. This is all for Mrs Ryan and Lorcan and it's what we do best, she thought to herself. We look after our own.

Jake crashed in through the back door and sent a chill through the room as he said, 'The police are out in the road. Parked at the end. Another car has just pulled up and joined them. Four men, two in each car.'

Emily cast a nervous glance at Dessie, who pushed his cap back and scratched his head. 'Have you still got that record player in your parlour, Biddy?'

'I have, but I only have a Glenn Miller to put on it.'

'Doesn't matter. Emily, come with me, quick. Let's light the fire in the parlour and pull the curtains half across. Stan, carry the drinks though. Lorcan, go and get a bucket of coal. Bryan and Jake, get back out into the entry and carry Biddy's tea chest into your scullery, Jake, just in case. But check no one is looking first. The bizzies obviously know Lorcan is living here. Tell Martha to come over here with the baby.' Dessie was in his element. 'This meeting is turning into a party. If they are watching the house, that is what they are going to see. Paddy, we are celebrating your being able to walk down the street for the first time without your crutches, isn't that right? Elsie, carry the butties through.'

Half an hour later, Maisie and Stanley took a spin around the parlour in step to Glenn Miller and his band playing 'In the Mood' and were followed by Dessie and Emily, then Jake and Martha as Madge danced with the baby and Biddy and Elise clapped along. To all intents and purposes a grand time was being had in Biddy's house. Fifteen minutes later, Bryan pretended he was walking back home out of the front door and down the street so that he could check on the police cars. He returned back down the entry at a run. 'All clear,' he said as he raced back in. 'They've gone. We fooled them.'

Everyone was visibly relieved. Dessie was the first to speak. 'Right, this is what we do,' he said. 'We need a rota of visitors for Mrs Ryan. Someone needs to pop a handkerchief or a few sweets into her handbag each day as a pretext for checking that no more money has arrived. Paddy, we need to keep all eyes on the back door to the ward. Someone will be coming back for that loot and we need to know who it is and get them while they are still in the hospital grounds.'

'And do what with them?' asked Paddy, wondering how he would manage that with one good leg and one wooden one.

'We need to let them know the money has been deposited in the Mersey, that's what. To make sure they know that there is no point in coming back and that it's lying on the bottom of a muddy bank and gone for ever.'

'Is that what we're going to do with it then?' asked Bryan as he looked up from the cup of Guinness Biddy had placed in his hands.

The room fell silent and then everyone began to laugh. 'Not on your nelly, lad,' said Stan.

'The next thing is, everyone needs to look out for Lorcan. Stick near someone at all times, Lorcan. Don't be alone. They may come straight for you first. We have to keep you safe. We don't know what they will resort to to prise information out of you.'

Lorcan looked terrified.

'And very importantly, no one, not one of you, breathes a word about this to anyone. Especially not to the likes of Hattie Lloyd or any of the gossips. Go to bingo tomorrow as normal. Lorcan, I'm keeping you on nights. Biddy, walk Lorcan to the Tanners' on your way to the bingo, and Paddy, make sure he sticks by your side all night. Keep the patterns the same and the lad safe. I will put an extra lad on nights for you as well. Right, everyone, one last drink and then we have to go and keep the biggest secret of our lives – so far, anyway.'

Stan began pouring drinks and Biddy proposed a toast. 'Raise your glasses, everyone,' she said. And much to Lorcan's surprise she continued, 'To Lorcan and his mammy.'

The room rang out with toasts. 'To Lorcan and his mammy.'

Lorcan felt more cared for, more wanted, more valued and protected than he had at any time before in his life. Tears pricked the backs of his eyes and he felt Biddy place her hand on his shoulder.

'No time for that, lad. You have to help me wash up when this lot have gone.' She smiled and patted his back, and Lorcan's tears melted away.

None of them could have known that things were about to move very quickly indeed. If Dessie had known just how fast, he would have stationed a lad at the back doors to Mrs Ryan's ward. But as he commented later, none of them could have guessed just how low a desperate man would go.

Chapter 18

Beth and Victoria were clearing up theatre following a dilatation and curettage when Oliver Gaskell popped his head into the clean utility room. 'Am I allowed to ask to date you tonight?' he asked Beth. Then he turned to Victoria. 'I have to ask permission to ask!' he said with a grin.

'It's Pammy you should be concerned about,' she replied tartly.

Oliver groaned.

'Well, as you ask so nicely, I shall say yes,' said Beth. 'But I want to be back at the home for nine. We have exams after Christmas and I want to begin revising now.'

Oliver saluted her and replied, 'Aye, aye, boss. I'll pick you up in the car straight after work then. I will be outside the door at six. Is that enough time?'

Beth smiled. 'Plenty, thank you. But no, not outside the door. I don't want to have to explain you away to either Mrs Duffy or Pammy.'

He placed his hands on the top of the door frame and looked as if he was about to swing himself back and forth. 'How long is that situation going to last?' he asked.

'Until I've decided whether or not you're going to be worth

explaining, with all the problems and aggravation that will bring me. That's how long. Now, will you please leave as we have a neurology op to prep for and the consultant who is doing it is visiting from Walton. The patient is the mother of one of Dessie's lads. Sister is in a flap and wants to make an impression on the consultant with our new theatre.'

A moment later he was gone.

Beth began to clear away equipment from the top of the trolley that Victoria was washing down.

Victoria was on the floor, wiping the wheels. 'Well, I take my hat off to you, miss. You have him wrapped around your little finger, don't you? I have to say, I thought he was quite charming at the Grapes the other evening and a great help with Roland. Roland is so embarrassed, though. He doesn't normally faint.'

Beth smirked. 'He did seem to be in quite a state when he came round. I'm glad we were there to help.'

Victoria sprang up with the cloth in her hand and threw it into the dirty wash sink.

'How is he feeling now?' asked Beth. She wondered when Victoria would confide her news and decided to probe. 'More to the point, though, how are you? Not so sickly any more?' She lifted the lid on the Little Sister steamer and placed the curettage spoon and the speculums on the tray inside. Raising the handle, she lowered the tray, fastened the lid and turned the timer to sixty minutes.

Victoria didn't answer straight away. She turned the tap on the sink, let the hot water rush into her enamel bucket, then threw in two sterilizing tablets. The air filled with the smell of chlorine and the sound of angry fizzing.

Beth turned her head, trying to work out what words she

could use to coax Victoria into sharing her secret. 'You look a bit better anyway.' Still no reply. 'Any news of wedding bells? I wondered if Roland had proposed or something and then fainted with shock that you'd said yes.'

'Oh, that happened a long time ago,' Victoria said. 'Actually, Beth, I do have some news. I'm going to tell everyone soon, but… I may have to be married a lot sooner than I planned and I may not be able to get through to finals.'

Beth turned to face her. 'You're pregnant, aren't you?'

Victoria half laughed, half cried her reply. 'I am. Trust you to be the first to guess, Beth Harper. Is there anything you don't know?'

Beth put out her arms to Victoria, who willingly fell into them and allowed herself to be hugged. She didn't see Beth's smile and she certainly couldn't hear her thoughts.

If this had to happen to any one of us, Beth thought, it is right that it is you, Victoria. No parents to disappoint. A man of means desperate to care for you. A home of your own to fall back on and money left over from the sale of the Baker estate to keep you in some degree of luxury.

Victoria lifted her head. 'I'm in such turmoil, Beth. Roland and I, we have had our first row and he won't support me and I've never felt so alone and everything is just too much,' Victoria let out a sob and her shoulders heaved as tears ran down her cheeks.

Beth held her by the shoulders and looked into her face, 'Goodness me, Victoria, having a baby isn't that bad. You can get married very quickly and no one will be any the wiser. You can say it arrived early, like everyone else in your position does.' Victoria almost pushed Beth away as she took her handkerchief out of her pocket.

'No, that's the point,' she shouted. 'This is the worst thing that could have happened to me. It is a dreadful mistake and, if Roland loved me, he would support me and not be as dreadful and as stubborn as he is. He refuses to listen to reason.' Her nose began to run and her tears showed no sign of abating. Beth felt stunned into silence. If there was one man anywhere she felt would have supported and stood by his pregnant girlfriend, it was Roland.

'Victoria, I don't know what to say. I am so shocked. I cannot believe that someone like Roland would be such a cad, I would have thought that at the very least, he would be wanting a wedding as soon as possible.' Victoria looked at Beth and furrowed her brow, as though she could not make out what Beth was saying.

'What? But, he does. It's not him, it's me, Beth. I have to get to the end of this, to pass my finals, to become a Staff Nurse. It's me, not him.' Victoria blew her nose and her voice dropped to a whisper when she spoke again. 'Beth, I want an abortion. I don't want to go through with it.'

Beth felt sick to the pit of her stomach. She swallowed hard, at first, not knowing what to say. Her arms fell from Victoria's shoulders as her mind scrabbled around for an appropriate response, and then it dawned on her. 'Do you see that woman in there on the operating table, Vic. She isn't just a D and C. She's having the retained products of pregnancy removed following a miscarriage, only, Sister Pokey said that it is as plain as the nose on her face it was a bad abortion and that the damage was awful. They are doing the D and C to remove infected tissue. That woman has been sick with a malaise and low grade temperature for over a year, too afraid to seek help because she knew, just like you and I know, it is illegal. Is that what you want? To become a criminal?'

Victoria wrung her hands in despair. 'Oh, I don't know. I am so confused. This is all wrong, everything is going horribly wrong.' Both girls heard Sister Pokey's voice as she approached the swing doors.

'Quick,' said Beth. 'Hands in the sink, I will talk to her. Let's chat on the way home, but Victoria, I will not stand by and watch you or even help you to commit a criminal act whilst you are in this distressed state. You have to make the decision calmly and with Roland – it is his baby too.'

Victoria stuffed her handkerchief back into her pocket and cast a nervous glance towards the door. 'I know, I know. I'm all over the place. One minute I agree with Roland. He says to pass my second-year exams and to finish off my training one day and when I am talking to him that seems sensible, but then, when I am on my own, I feel differently. I think of mummy and I wanted to make her so proud.'

Beth almost laughed out loud. 'Do you think your mother would not be proud of the match you have made with Roland? Of the wonderful mother you yourself would become? Of the wonderfully compassionate, capable and caring person you are now? There are so many reasons your mother would be proud of you, Victoria, so many. Don't get hung up on just that one and, I am sorry, I have to say this, if she were here now instead of me, what would she say? What would make her proud? The baby growing in your belly. The flesh of her flesh. Or would your thoughts of an abortion make her prouder?' Victoria paled and her lips wobbled. 'Not now,' whispered Beth. 'We will get into trouble. Come on, back to work. Think a little harder and we will chat later.'

Victoria, now composed, flicked the switch on the Little Sister as the sound of the buzzer filled the room. 'Well, I know one thing,' she said, 'If you and Roland get your way, Auntie Minnie will now have to stop trying to match me up to her friends' sons and she'll have to accept Roland once and for all.'

'Well, every cloud has a silver lining. You don't have to worry about me telling anyone. Cross my heart and hope to die, I won't tell a soul.'

'I know,' said Victoria. 'I will tell the others just as soon as I have made a decision. Mrs Tanner is going to be very disappointed in me. I don't think I can face the Tanners again. I'll feel too ashamed. She would never forgive me.'

'Well, there are secrets everywhere,' said Beth. 'Dessie Horton is organizing a big party for Sister Haycock's birthday, so let's just enjoy that for now, shall we? You and Roland need to talk face to face and to have a bit of fun.'

'I think we've had too much fun, Beth, that's part of the problem. I got my invitation this morning too, in the pigeonhole. It's for Roland as well, which is nice. I saw Dana's was still in her pigeonhole, I'll take it back for her later. Did you see her earlier, by the way? She seemed in a real hurry coming down the lane off her night shift. I hope she's OK.' Victoria sighed at the thought of having to tell Dana her news. 'I suppose she will disapprove, given her background. And I'll have to face Sister Haycock too, and Matron. You see, if I have the abortion, no one will have to know.'

She groaned and covered her face. 'Yes, they will Victoria, stop kidding yourself. You will know – you will and I don't think you will ever forgive yourself.'

Beth grabbed Victoria's hands and pulled them away from her face. 'Listen, I will go and see Sister Haycock and Matron with you if, and I hope you do, decide to keep the baby and to get married. If I'm not allowed in, I'll wait outside. You don't have to tell anyone anything alone, Vic. I'm right by your side.'

Victoria shot Beth a disappointed look. 'You are with me, if I throw my career away, but not if I want an abortion. It would seem that neither you nor Roland are with me there.'

Beth didn't have time to reply as Bryan's voice rang out from the doors. 'Mrs Ryan here from the ward, Nurse.'

There was always a sense of urgency when a trolley bed crashed in through the theatre doors. It was like the curtain going up on the first act of a play. Every thought and personal emotion was put on hold and the only concern was the case and the operation ahead. The porters, nurses and doctors all rushed into position, ready to act out their particular parts. Whatever the procedure, there was danger present; it was intimidating and everyone's heart beat a little faster.

Dana almost ran through the gate as she made her way to the bench by the park keeper's hut, opposite the pond. She was intrigued. Mr Mabbutt had told her not to mention to anyone that he'd asked her to meet him there. She had slipped back into the Lovely Lane home after her night shift to change out of her uniform and on her way out had called into the kitchen to beg some stale bread from Mrs Duffy so that she could feed the ducks.

She shielded her eyes against the low, wintry sunlight and scanned the pond to see if Mr Mabbutt had taken pity on the ducks and decided to feed them also. As there was no sign of him yet, she focused on the ducks nearest to the bench so that he could easily spot her when he arrived. She had been throwing the bread across the water for ten minutes or so when a voice from behind made her jump.

'Lucky ducks, living so close to the nurses' home. I only have a new dual carriageway opposite my front door.'

Dana smiled. She wasn't sure what to say in response.

'Come and sit down, would you,' Mr Mabbutt said. 'It's cold out here, I know, but I have something I would really like to discuss with you.'

Dana still didn't say anything, just sat down on the bench next to him. She guessed it had to be about Teddy, and she hoped it wasn't bad news. Was he going to say something dreadful about Teddy never being able to walk properly again? Or that he would need nursing care for the rest of his life? Well, so what if that were to happen, she thought resolutely. She would be there for him. She would stick by her Teddy come what may, even if he had driven her half mad over the past weeks. He had been grumpy and miserable, but Dana had complete faith once he returned to work, he would be back to his old affectionate, funny and charming self.

Mr Mabbutt pulled his plaid scarf closer around his neck and tucked it further down into his coat. He wore a dark grey felt hat pulled low over his brow and Dana noted that the wool of his coat and scarf looked of the highest quality and very expensive. It was nothing like what men wore back home in Ireland, which was more likely to be ripped and frayed donkey jackets and oversized caps. There was a nice smell about him too, of lemon and spice. She guessed he was about the same age as her da, who only ever smelt of peat and earth. She had been in Liverpool long enough now not to be goggle-eyed at the way some people dressed, but even so, she couldn't help taking note. She looked at his gloves. They were made of the softest-looking leather and she had an urge to touch them, but she didn't, she just slipped her hands inside her own pockets.

He turned towards her slightly and began to talk. 'Look, this is all a bit difficult and, I have to say, I wasn't sure how I should go about this. But I've talked it over with the wife. I always do that – sensible woman, my wife. She was a nurse during the war, you know. In the Queen Alexandras.'

He was talking fast now and staring at the pond. Dana had to concentrate hard to follow his train of thought.

'She was an excellent nurse and she was about to be made into a theatre sister, but she gave it up to marry me.' He gave a sharp little laugh. 'Clever as she is, she was very stupid to do that, don't you think?'

Dana managed a brief, polite smile by way of reply.

Mr Mabbutt slipped his hand deep inside the top of his coat and pulled out a pipe. Removing a tin from one of his coat pockets, he began to stuff threads of tobacco into the bowl.

While Dana waited patiently for him to finish, her mind raced ahead of her. Was he about to tell her that she'd need to give up her nurse training to look after Teddy? Just like his wife had, though for different reasons. The thought made her gut churn. That really would be a huge sacrifice. Her mammy had never stopped bragging to anyone who would listen about how proud of Dana she was. During her holiday home a few months earlier, she had almost laughed out loud at how everyone on the village appeared to have placed her on a pedestal. She had cracked the mould. She would never be a farm girl. Her life was to take a different path and if that was what he was about to tell her, she would be torn.

There would have to be another way. She could not let her family down like that. It wasn't as though she and Teddy were even married. Her parents would never understand.

Mr Mabbutt slowly replaced the tobacco tin and removed a silver lighter. Flicking the lid, he turned the flint until it ignited, then puffed and puffed on his pipe, enveloping them both in a cloud of the sweetest-smelling smoke. Rather than coughing, Dana inhaled deeply. Teddy had taught her to smoke cigarettes and it had made her feel very sophisticated, but this heavenly smell reminded her more of the fireside at home. The blocks of peat burning in their huge fireplace and her da in his chair, his feet stretched out before him after a long day of hard physical work on the farm, puffing slowly on his own pipe until he dozed off. Either she or her ma would then rescue the pipe from his lips, just as it began to slip.

Much as she loved seeing that familiar picture in her head, of her family at home, there was no sentiment attached. Life on the farm was hard and she was well aware how lucky she was to have had the opportunity to change her prospects and earn a decent living of her own, doing something she loved. Nurse training might be tough, but it was nothing like being a farmer's wife.

Mr Mabbutt was certainly taking his time. He'd now placed the pipe on his thigh and was holding it with one hand, cupping the bowl between his fingers. He was precise and slow in everything he did. Nothing was rushed.

She leant back against the bench and watched as the ducks swam towards them and fanned out across the water. The message had gone out that she had bread. The sun bounced off the ripples and reflected the pruned trees around the edge and the manicured lawns beyond.

'I know you are probably wondering why I wanted to see you. It's why I had to speak to my wife first, because this isn't really anything to do with the hospital.'

He shuffled on the bench and turned to face her. Dana noticed that his eyes were a very pale grey and that the lines around his eyes became deeper as he squinted to protect them from the sun.

'I didn't think I could go to Matron, and the wife told me not to. She said that Matron wouldn't understand because she's had no experience of affairs of the heart herself. Never known a romance, has Matron.'

Dana had no idea what he was on about. All she did know was that her heart was now beating faster and she was fighting off an overwhelming instinct to flee because she could sense by the graveness of his expression and the seriousness of his voice that he was about to tell her some very bad news.

'Shall we walk?' he asked and she jumped to her feet. 'I think there's a wooden tea hut or something over by the other gate, isn't there?'

'Yes, there is.' At last he was asking a question that she understood and could answer. 'We often call in there at weekends if we have an off-duty day. The owner likes it that he has nurses calling in. I haven't been for ages though,' she replied.

He nodded sympathetically, well aware that nursing Teddy had been a full-time undertaking. Dana wanted to ask him straight out what this was all about, but his seniority and her training prevented her. It would not have felt right, even given the extraordinary situation they were now in, walking around the duck pond towards the tea cabin. What would people think if they saw us, she wondered.

'You are probably asking yourself what this is all about, aren't you?' He didn't wait for her response. 'Well, I wanted to tell you my story. Or, should I say, our story, mine and my wife's.' He stared resolutely at his smart leather shoes as he continued, the words tumbling out almost faster than Dana could take them in. 'There was a time before the war when we were apart and I thought she would never want to marry and that nursing meant more to her than me. She was one of those who was destined to become a matron. Nothing frightened her and she never doubted her own ability. Scared the life out of me, she did. We weren't very good at communicating with one another in those days, you see. It wasn't really the done thing, to confide in each other.'

He gave Dana a wry smile and, stopping suddenly, bent down and banged his pipe against a bin with the back of his hand before slipping it back inside his coat.

'So I went off like a bear with a sore head and... I have to say that what I did, well, I am not very proud of.'

Dana looked at him with a quizzical expression on her face. This conversation was not turning out as expected. He appeared uncomfortable. It was as if he assumed she could read his mind, but she really had no idea what he was on about.

'Look, Nurse Brogan, I shan't beat about the bush. Fact is, I was not as faithful as I should have been to my future wife – not that I knew she was to be my future wife then, of course. Do you understand? There was a lady and I made a terrible mistake.' Now he was looking at her directly, as though to emphasize his point.

Dana blushed bright red until her face almost matched the colour of her hair.

'Quite. Good. You get my meaning, that's excellent. However, I very quickly knew what a foolish man I had been. An idiot. A numskull of the highest order. And this is something I would like you to understand: we men, we are not as clever as we like you to think we are. In fact, we're nowhere near as clever as we think we are.'

Much to Dana's relief, they had now reached the hut. Her thoughts were reeling and she was desperately trying to make sense of what she was being told and why. The vendor was setting up a wooden easel outside, advertising Cornish ice cream. Recognizing Dana immediately, he said, 'Hello, Nurse, haven't seen you for a while. How's that doctor of yours? The other nurses told me. Terrible business.'

Dana was grateful for the conversation and the change of subject. 'He's getting better, thanks. A bit cold for the ice cream, isn't it?'

'I know, I know, but you would be surprised how many buy ice cream in the winter. Bring your dad inside and I'll get you both a nice cup of tea.'

She looked at Mr Mabbutt and they both grinned. 'An honour, I'm sure,' he said as he opened the door for her.

Once they were sitting down with the tea and the vendor was outside cleaning the windows, they continued their conversation.

'Sorry, I didn't realize this place was so small,' he said. 'Anyway, what my wife said I should do was tell you our story.'

'But why on earth would she ask you to do that?' Dana had gone from scared to confused. She picked up her tea and held it in front of her as though to ward off his reply.

'Ah, well now, someone else will have to explain that bit. That's not for me to do.'

His cryptic answers were starting to exasperate her. But he clearly had more to say.

'My wife and I have had thirty years of joy. We have three fine sons who I hope will never make the mistake their father did. I nearly didn't have my wonderful wife because she very nearly treated me like the idiot I was. I deserved to be punished, but she demonstrated how exceptional she was by being understanding. She didn't take the moral high ground and that is a measure of the woman, of her intelligence. You see, she could have responded to me with her heart, in an emotional way, but instead she used her head. We talked and as a result we have led the most blissful life. But what my wife doesn't know is that I have never forgotten how close I came to losing her. Not a day goes by when I don't do some little thing to try and make it up to her. Maybe if we hadn't had our trials in the early days, things would not have been as wonderful. It could be that I needed to be forced to appreciate how special what I already had was. What I do know is that I should have talked to her long before I risked everything. I should have put my stupid male ego away, been more sympathetic and listened to my future wife.'

Dana sipped her tea and looked at him over her cup. This was all so bizarre. Had she been captured by a Martian and landed on another planet? There was no way Pammy, Vic and Beth would believe her if she tried to tell them about this conversation – with the fearsome Mr Mabbutt, of all people.

Mr Mabbutt lifted the sleeve of his expensive-looking coat and consulted his watch. 'Oh, bloody hell, is that the time? I'm going to be late for my bloody clinic. Oh, bloody Nora!' Then he looked at her shamefaced. 'I am so sorry. I told my wife I would try not to swear in front of you and now I have. Listen, my dear, you and your Teddy, you need to talk. Go to him. Talk to him. Not about his pain or his rehabilitation but about what is on his mind. Speak to him, not as his nurse but as his love.' Then he picked up his hat, placed a ten-shilling note on the counter to cover the tea and was gone.

The vendor came back in and, picking up the note, said, 'Your dad has left enough to pay for your lunch here, Nurse. Shall I cut you a sandwich? I've got some nice ham on the bone.'

'That wasn't my da,' said Dana distractedly.

'Sandwich then?'

She almost banged her cup down on to the saucer and her chair scraped back as she stood. 'No, thanks. I have to go and see someone.'

She just about heard the vendor shouting his reply as the wooden door clanged behind her. Outside the hut she emptied the last of the bread from her pocket for the ducks hovering nearby, then walked away, head down, lost in thought.

Mr Mabbutt called into the doctors' res on his way to the clinics and walked into Teddy's room without knocking. 'I can't stop. I did my best. It is down to you now. I'm in my car, but my guess is she will be right behind me, on her way here right now, I should think, in the hope that someone will let her in to see you. Keep away from bloody Makebee, Teddy. A woman like that nearly stole my wonderful life. You have been a bloody stupid fool.' He turned to go. 'Oh, by the way, your last X-ray was good. I'm happier with your recovery than I was. You can get back to work next week, for a few hours each day. I will let Matron know.'

Teddy stared at the patch of carpet where Mr Mabbutt had just been standing and for the first time his eyes filled with tears. To the closed door he said, 'But will she forgive me? Please God, let her forgive me.'

Ten minutes later, he heard her footsteps on the fire escape and she was with him, inside the door. Her face was flushed from walking into the wind. Their eyes locked.

Dana's were brimming as she said, 'Teddy, do you have something to tell me because I am very, very scared and whatever it is, I need to know, right now.'

Chapter 19

Lorcan was sitting in his mammy's cubicle in a side ward, waiting for her to return from theatre. It looked very bare. Dessie and Bryan had wheeled her up to theatre on her hospital bed, and while she was away various bits of equipment had been trundled in to stand around the periphery in anticipation of her return. An oxygen bottle had been placed to one side and an empty drip stand to the other.

Sister brought a trolley in. She pushed it against the wall and flicked open a white cloth to cover whatever was laid out on the top. On the bottom layer, Lorcan could see a glass jar with a thermometer in an opaque Dettol solution and next to it she positioned two large white kidney dishes and some brown rubber tubing.

'You are a lucky young man, having Matron's permission to stay here,' she said. 'Your mother should be back within the hour. Theatre will call to let us know when she is on her way back down. I'll ask the orderly to bring you in a cuppa.'

'I've had a word with Matron,' Dessie had told him. 'She doesn't know the real reason why I asked if you could stay with your mammy. I just said you were the only one and a bit upset. Thank God himself, she was in a good mood and happy for you to sit on the ward and wait for her.' He looked furtively about him and dropped his voice to a whisper. 'If whoever is behind this knows she's having another operation, it might be the moment they decide to come back and claim what they think is their stashed loot.'

'Will Matron remember she said that when she does her rounds?' asked Lorcan nervously. They were all scared of Matron and with good reason. She could reduce a porter's lad to a trembling wreck by dint of nothing more than a glare through narrowed eyes or a chilly stare.

'You don't have to worry about that, she was on her way out of the door with Blackie. Had a car waiting for her. Off to stay with some friends on the Wirral for a couple of days, she said. I've never known that before. You could have knocked me down with a feather. She called Sister before she left, said you could have unlimited visiting time with your mammy. Didn't ask me a single question, she didn't have time.'

Dessie had been gone for some time. It was now dark and the ward lights had been switched on. Out on the main ward, nurses swept in and out, pulled curtains around beds, carried washing bowls and bedpans here and there. The orderly had forgotten to bring Lorcan's tea, but he didn't mind. He watched her at her work as she wheeled a trolley down the ward dispensing tea, biscuits and kindly words.

He began to pace around the room. Dessie had told him he would be back in half an hour, but he still hadn't returned. He'd told Lorcan he wasn't to move and that he had to stay within sight of Sister's desk, but Lorcan was anxious and tense. His mother had been gone for what seemed like hours.

He rolled a cigarette and lit it. Lorcan had never smoked in his life, but he was desperate to fit in and every one of the porters' lads had smoked. He had asked Bryan to teach him and he had practiced, making Bryan's roll-ups for him. Now, his hands were shaking and the tobacco was spilling out all over the floor. He searched around for the ashtray, but one of the nurses had obviously taken it away when his mother had left the ward. He decided to step out of the rear ward doors to finish his cigarette and dispose of the stub. The doors faced straight out on to the railway line and to the side looked out over the delivery bay. Glad of the distraction from his anxious thoughts, Lorcan stepped to the side to see if any of the other lads were around. The oxygen lorry was parked alongside the porter's hut and in the orange light spilling out through its windows Lorcan could see that Jake was organizing the unloading. Jake and the driver appeared to be arguing about one of the oxygen bottles and the driver was gesticulating madly towards the inside of his lorry. Lorcan guessed that a valve was missing. He remembered how miserable the driver was and was half glad he wasn't unloading that delivery. Not tonight of all nights.

As he threw his cigarette stub on to the ground and crushed it with the heel of his boot, he remembered Dessie's instruction that he was to be within sight of someone else at all times. He turned back to the wide arched doors and thought he heard a noise, a shuffle. He looked down the side of the door, but it was nothing, a river rat burrowing down into a small hole between the bricks. It disappeared in a flash, but it had startled him and his pulse was racing. If Dessie saw him out here on his own, he would half kill him for having disobeyed orders. Dessie ran the porter's lads with a military efficiency and in his own way he could be as frightening as Matron.

Lorcan heard a shout from the lorry and looked round.

He could just about make out Jake, trying to wheel a bottle back on to the lorry, to the obvious agitation of the driver. Turning back to the warmth and light of the corridor, Lorcan had no time to see what hit him as a blow caught him on the back of his neck and felled him full length on to the brick floor. The impact winded him and he had no chance to breathe or speak or scream before a well-placed boot caught him square in the eye.

He turned his head, squinted through the curtain of red that was cascading down his eyeball and saw the familiar brown lace in the black boot. Kevin Bevan. The lace was frayed and partially untied, and it was trailing the floor dipped in his own blood. A bolt of pain seared through his ribs as he tried to pull in air, but it was no use, he was pinned down by the weight of his attacker straddling his back. One of his hands was grasped and his arm was yanked up his back. Lorcan wanted to scream at the burning sensation shooting up his arm, but he had no air to spare and the agony screeched about his brain, robbing him of any clarity of thought. He was almost blinded by what felt like a bomb exploding in his head.

'Where's the fecking money?'

He tried to turn his head to the side. He was confused. He knew that voice as well as his own. It wasn't Kevin Bevan, it was J.T.

Lorcan couldn't answer, all he could focus on was the fact that his arm felt as though it was leaving its socket.

The weight on his back lifted as J.T. leant forward. 'Tell me, where's the fecking money?'

Lorcan had just enough breath to gasp out the shortest reply before the pain in his ribs prevented him from saying any more. 'What money?'

'Don't you fecking "what money" me.' J.T. turned Lorcan on to his back with one pull of his arm and thwacked down hard with a stick across the top of Lorcan's thighs.

Now Lorcan did yell with the pain, but the yell was swept away by a passing train.

J.T. swiftly dropped to his knees and clamped his hand over Lorcan's mouth, the stick held high above Lorcan's head. 'Now you listen to me. See this?' He dropped the stick and removed something small and metallic from his pocket.

Lorcan squinted. It was a valve, just like the ones that fitted on to the tops of the oxygen bottles. Despite the pain, things suddenly started to make sense. The valve was probably the missing one that Jake and the driver had just been arguing about. J.T. must have stowed away on the lorry to get so close. There'd been an oxygen delivery the time before too, when Lorcan had seen J.T. running away.

As Lorcan stared at the valve, J.T. shoved his thumb into it. 'See this?' he snarled. 'I will turn it and turn it and turn it, and don't think I won't, until you tell me where the money has gone and who the feck has it. Because whoever it is, they are dead. Have you got that?'

Lorcan didn't reply. His left eye began to swell and close over as he watched the line of spittle on J.T.'s chin move downwards. He was not unused to the feel of J.T.'s boot or the force of his fist. His brother had beaten him many times before, but never with this much anger. In the last few weeks Lorcan had started to hate his brother, but now, with his ribs screaming out in pain and his arm dislocated, he felt a surge of something inside that caused him to appeal to him. He was all he had in the world. Lorcan needed him to help with their mam, to know that she was in the theatre. He made to speak, but no words came. He spat blood and a tooth on to the ground, and his head flopped back and banged against the brick floor. He pulled in the damp night air, the cold burning his lungs, and tried again. To his surprise, he found that he was sobbing, pleading.

'J.T., the Bevans, they hit Mammy, they near killed her.'

J.T. looked briefly confused and then he sneered in a way that was so malevolent and sinister, Lorcan began to tremble violently.

'The Bevans? You stupid bastard, 'twas no Bevan, it was me. The nosey bitch had her hands on my stash. I was being paid good money for that. The stupid cow would have given the bleedin' game away.'

Lorcan could barely take in what he was saying, but J.T.'s voice had dropped and his tone was menacing.

'Where is the fecking money? Who has it? Is it the big man, Dessie Horton? It was in the bitch's handbag, but some bastard's taken it. Where the fuck is it?'

Lorcan imagined his mother being wheeled back into the cubicle and Staff Nurse wondering where he was and he was seized with panic at the thought of her coming out there to find him. He couldn't bear the thought of J.T. hitting her too. He pushed the elbow he could still feel underneath him and tried to rise up, but it was no use. J.T. shoved him back down.

'You know where it is, you toe rag!' His eyes were bulging now. 'I know you do. You've been in 'ere every night, I know you have. Where the fuck is it? Some of that money is the Bevans', from a jump-over. It was too hot for me to keep on the run. If I don't get it back and I don't kill you, they will sure as hell kill me.'

Lorcan stared at J.T., but he was barely listening to him,

he was praying to God with every ounce of strength he had left. Please, God, don't let Staff Nurse come out. He was more worried about her safety than his own, but God wasn't listening because he heard her voice calling out, 'Lorcan, are you out here? Your mammy's back,' and then came the stifled scream as she opened the door and was faced with J.T. lunging towards her.

But then he realized that God must have heard because all of a sudden Dessie and Bryan appeared and raced in from the side of the ward. As he closed his eyes, terrified, he heard bodies collapsing on to the floor. Then blackness fell over him as though someone had covered him with a dark, comforting blanket that took away his pain.

Chapter 20

The party had been organized in one of the large rooms in the Silvestrian just off the main bar downstairs. Emily had no idea what was going on or what Dessie was really up to. As far as she was concerned, it was another Veterans' do and did not require her input. Dessie had told her it was a special night and that he would like her to attend. Everyone else had been told it was a surprise birthday party for Emily, whose birthday was the following week, but that Emily was not to be told. Dessie was providing two barrels of Guinness and the wives had each been instructed by Biddy Kennedy to bring along a plate of food. She and Elsie had spent the day brushing, mopping and polishing the parquet floor as an army of women carrying mops and buckets walked down the road towards the club. Skirting boards were scrubbed and windows washed with vinegar and rubbed with scrunched-up newspaper until they gleamed.

'Why did he have to come all the way up here?' Branna complained. 'What's wrong with the Grapes? They do a lovely wake at the Grapes.'

'Yes, but it's not a wake, is it. He says he wants it to be special, that's why, and we are going to make sure that it is special, spotless and special, so stop complaining, Branna. It's so nice. No one has ever organized a birthday party for me.'

'Ah, I'll do it for your next one, Biddy, if you don't make me get on a chair to clean those big windows. I won't be happy if I do, not with my vertigo.'

The kids had run up and down the streets excitedly for two days carrying messages from one house to the other. 'Elsie said don't make brawn, Noleen, Cathleen has done that already,' a child shouted through Noleen's back gate and into the kitchen. 'Biddy says don't make the scones because Madge is doing those,' another shouted an hour later, as Noleen stood there with the flour jar in her hand, about to tip it into the mixing bowl.

'God in heaven, there will be nothing left for me to make,' Noleen had complained to Paddy the evening before.

He looked up from his paper. 'Well, don't be asking me to do the baking. I might be walking, but there's no way I'm doing women's work.'

Noleen grinned and flopped on to his knee in front of the fire. 'Really? Was that not you emptying the washing out of the boiler this morning?'

'Oh, behave, Noleen. I emptied it, but you wouldn't see me hanging it out now, would you? Imagine. Hattie Lloyd would put an announcement in the *Echo*.'

'Lorcan hangs the washing out for his mammy. He does it every morning before he goes to work or when he gets back. He runs that house like clockwork, he does.'

Paddy slipped his arm around Noleen's waist and pulled her into him. 'I went round there last night while you were at the bingo. Stan and I helped him to put a shelf up in the scullery. Showed him what to do, just like his da would have done.'

Noleen felt the familiar sadness that settled on her heart whenever they spoke of someone they had lost.

'Mrs Ryan, she was just sat by the fire. Lorcan made us both tea and she didn't move, but she was chatty. What I couldn't get over, though, was that she never stopped talking about J.T. About what a lovely lad he is and do you know what, not once did Lorcan put her right. It's cruel the way she dotes on J.T. and yet it's Lorcan who cares for her and does all the work. He still can't see properly out of that left eye, but he's back at work and pulling his weight.'

Noleen laid her head on Paddy's shoulder. 'Well, J.T. has gone down for a long, long time now. One charge of attempted manslaughter and one of grievous bodily harm means Mrs Ryan might be pushing up the daisies by the time he does get out. And to think, the police totally believe that no one around here has a clue about any jump-over or where the money went.'

The fire roared and they relaxed, warm and content, both reflecting on the happiness each felt at things between them having improved.

'Shall we have an early night?' Paddy winked at Noleen.

'You have to answer me one thing first, if that's what you're after. What happened to the money? It didn't go to the police, so where is it?'

Paddy grinned and, pulling his wife down towards him, kissed her tenderly. 'You might have to try and persuade me to part with that information,' he said.

'Paddy Delaney, you cheeky bugger!' Noleen shouted, outraged.

But he was already leading her up the stairs, walking with the now familiar swing to his gait from the false leg he had finally accepted. Once in bed, Noleen collapsed into the arms of her man, the confident, passionate Paddy she had known before the war.

Afterwards, sitting up in bed, Paddy lit two cigarettes. 'Eh,' he said as he slapped her bare backside, 'put that away, aren't the kids due back?'

Noleen pulled the cover up over her, shuffled herself up on to the pillow and took the lit cigarette from him. 'Not for a while. The lads are playing footie on the wasteland and Mary is guess where.' She took a drag and turned towards Paddy with a smile as she made herself comfortable on her side.

He glanced sideways with a grin. 'The Tanners', by any chance?'

'Aye, but not with their Lorraine. She's helping Maisie with the bunting for the Silvestrian.'

'Our Mary, helping someone?' Paddy looked incredulous.

'Yeah, and that's not all. She did the ironing last night for me while we were out and did you notice when we got back that she had been making biscuits an' all?'

Paddy blew a smoke ring up into the air. 'Well, I've got news too, Mrs Know-It-All.'

'News? You? That'll be the day.' Noleen didn't bite. This was the old Paddy, who teased her, and she was remembering his ways. She laid her head back on the pillow and drew deeply on her cigarette while she waited for him to tell her.

He paused. He could feel her twitching; he knew her. Any second, her hand would come down and playfully tap him and she would demand to know his news. He stubbed out the dog end in the ashtray next to the bed and decided to put her out of her misery. 'Our Bryan is taking Lorraine Tanner to the do.'

Noleen handed him the last of her own cigarette. 'Quick, before the ash falls on the sheets,' she said. 'Well, fancy that.

I'm pleased. Who doesn't like Lorraine? You were away fighting, but it was touch and go with that kid for days after she was born. It felt like every one of us was holding tight until Nurse Heather said we could all breathe again. That was a terrible night, that, Paddy.'

'I know, love. We were doing our bit out there, you know.'

'I know you were, love.' She rubbed her hand on his stump. 'I know.'

He turned to her, a serious expression on his face. 'Noleen, I think it's best if the money is never mentioned again.'

Noleen gasped and made to protest, but Paddy put his fingers on her lips.

'Shhh now,' he said. 'Short of leaving it on the steps of the police station in the middle of the night, we had no option. We are Irish. The bizzies, they don't like us, some-one would have come a cropper. At the very least, the Bevan gang would have got to know and none of us on these streets would have rested. They are suspicious as it is. Dessie saw Kevin Bevan and two of his brothers hanging around only yesterday. The money is hidden, but from now on, just call it "the fund", OK? And don't ever speak a word about this to anyone. Do you understand that, Noleen?'

Noleen nodded, dumbfounded. 'What will you do with it?' she asked. Her voice had become a squeak.

'We have appointed a committee to deal with that. Dessie, Stan, meself, Biddy and Madge. It's to be used to help those in need. A coffin for a funeral. Flowers for a wedding. A bit of a do every now and then. Nothing so obvious that the Bevan boys will notice. Oh, and a school uniform, shoes and a satchel for any kid around here who passes the eleven-plus.'

Tears sprang to Noleen's eyes. 'Paddy, our Finn, he's in town in the library right now.' She imagined the look on Finn's face when she told him he would be able to go to Waterloo Boys' Grammar. 'And does Father Brennan know?'

'Don't be stupid, you daft bat. He would insist that every penny went to St Chad's and was doled out by him. But don't you worry, we have sorted the church out. You will have to go to St Acanthus for confession now that you know. I wasn't going to tell you for that reason. Don't ask me any more questions now. Keeping the Bevans away from here and looking after our own, that's what we're doing, and we have to do it in secret. Every penny of that money will be spent on helping someone, and that's all that matters.'

Noleen wrapped her arms around Paddy and hugged him into her. He was a changed man. Her important man. She didn't want him to see the tears in her eyes. 'I won't be going to St Acanthus,' she said. 'The Holy Mother will understand.'

She inhaled deeply the smell of smoke and sex and shared secrets and felt the burden of guilt and worry melt away. She had said her prayers to the Holy Mother every single day, over and over. She had begged her to find a way for Finn to take the place he had been offered at the grammar. She had sat by the range and sobbed. No matter how much she schemed, she could never afford even the shoes, never mind the uniform and everything else on the list that had arrived in the post and lived in her apron pocket ever since, for fear that Finn would find it. Now her prayers had been answered and that was all that mattered.

'I'm not coming,' Lorcan had said. 'I'm sure 'twill be a grand evening for you all, but count me out.'

Biddy swallowed the urge to thump him and from somewhere deep within found the most patient tone she could deploy. 'Well, that will be a great shame, Lorcan, because, you see, I'm not sure if you've noticed or not, but your mammy could do with a smile on her face. I was hoping that a night out would be good for her. The lumps have gone now, you have no excuse.'

Lorcan turned his face towards the fire and made no response. He was ashamed of what people would think of him, having been half murdered by his own brother, ashamed of the bruises that still stained his face and of his mammy telling everyone she met what a great son J.T. was and how he had the fastest legs in Liverpool. He would never tell her the truth about how J.T. had almost killed them both, but every time she spoke the name of his evil brother her words cut him like a knife.

His chest tightened at the prospect of people thinking that all the Ryans were cast in the same mould and that he might be anything like his brother. He was like his daddy, in looks, thoughts and deeds. He had tried so hard to turn everything around and he had done so well, until their luck had shifted, again. But, as Biddy often told him, it was his blessings he had to count. They were safe now that J.T. was in jail. Mrs Ryan was sleeping upstairs on a proper bed. Lorcan hadn't lost his job, in fact, Matron had asked after him herself and visited him when he was on the ward, having his injuries tended to. He had to admit it may hurt him to walk, but that was temporary. Everything at home was better than it had ever been before.

'Go on, Lorcan, come to the party. Besides, I need your help. I've so much to carry, I will need to be borrowing a crane from the docks at this rate. All the lads from the hospital will be there. Dessie has had a chat with you, hasn't he, about the fund?'

Lorcan nodded and whispered, 'He brought me a copper boiler, so I don't have to do the washing in the sink in cold water or go to the wash house. It's in the scullery.'

Biddy grinned and Lorcan knew he was lost. They would be going. He just couldn't stand up to Biddy.

The following afternoon, the noise of preparation and excited chatter could be heard coming from every street. Mary ran down the entry to Lorraine's house with her hair in curlers to attend the makeshift Maisie Tanner salon. Maisie had high standards and was never seen outdoors without make-up, nail polish and a pair of stockings.

'Come on in, Mary, love. Who's next to have their nails done?'

In the kitchen sat Pammy, Victoria and Beth. Lorraine was sitting on Pammy's knee, in the soft chair, having her nails done.

'She's nearly taller than you, you know, Pammy,' said Beth as she blew on the fingers Maisie had just painted bright red.

'Beth, where is Dana?' asked Pammy. 'She said she would be here by one.'

'Probably tending to her grouchy boyfriend,' said Victoria. 'I swear to God, that girl has been a saint the way she's put up with Teddy.'

'Pammy, will you take Mary's rollers out, love, now that you've done our Lorraine's nails. Vic, will you help me take all this through into the scullery.'

Maisie had been damping and ragging Victoria's hair. Victoria attended a very smart salon in Manchester when she was at home in Bolton, but it was nowhere near as much fun as having her hair done in the Tanners' kitchen. Now that she was there, she'd almost forgotten she was pregnant. But on the walk over from Lovely Lane, she had confided in Beth that she was nervous.

'Roland arrives at five. He has to work this morning and he said he is staying over. I'm off tomorrow and so it is decision time.'

'Have you made up your mind yet?' asked Beth. 'I have to admit, you know my thoughts, however, I cannot imagine living in Lovely Lane without you.' She cast a nervous glance towards Victoria. Tears had never been far from the surface since she had confided in Beth.

'Roland and I will be leaving straight after the party. He is driving me back to Bolton. We either have a wedding to arrange, or if I get my own way, something else altogether. At least because I am a nurse, I know what a sterile environment should look like and I will pick up on the first sign of infection. I have lots to do either way and if I keep the baby, I must get away from here before anyone guesses. Call me a coward, but I don't want to be here when Mrs Tanner finds out. It makes my heart heavy to think how disappointed she will be with me. I can't bear it.'

Beth had linked her arm through her friend's. 'Vic, don't worry about any of that now. Leave it to me. I will tell everyone for you, but not until you tell me to, once you're back in Bolton for your off-duty and you've made a decision.'

'Just put that bowl on the draining board,' Maisie said to Victoria now, as she sorted through the paraphernalia she'd been using to beautify half the girls in the street. She took a bottle of pink setting solution off the shelf. 'How are you feeling now, Victoria?' she asked.

'Oh, I'm fine, Mrs Tanner. I just had a bit of a sick bug that day.'

'Really.'

Victoria turned her head sharply. There was something about the tone of Maisie's voice that alerted her.

'You'll need a Silver Cross pram for that sick bug soon.'

Victoria's mouth dropped open at the same time as Maisie extended her arms and she fell straight into them.

'Vic, love, you need a mam at a time like this and God love yours, she's not here. Will you stop calling me Mrs Tanner and call me Auntie Maisie instead, and let me start knitting for this little bug you're carrying. Oh and by the way, I know that Anthony knows too.'

Victoria pulled back and looked Maisie in the eye. 'Pammy as well?' she gasped.

'No, not our Pammy. He would never betray the confidence of a patient.'

Victoria's brow furrowed. 'But he already has, if he's told you?'

'Oh no, love, he didn't. It was me that told him.'

Later that evening, over in the Delaney house, Paddy was having second thoughts. Having earned no money of his own for so long, he was now nervous about spending what little he did have. Noleen, on the other hand, having scrimped and saved and sometimes begged her way through their darker days, was ready to enjoy the fruits of his labour.

'No, I will not stay in, you cheeky sod. You think I'm going to miss Dessie putting on a do? Everything is sorted. Our Mary and Lorraine are coming over to put our Jack and Cahill to bed and then they are coming back to the Silvie. If all the other wives are going, I'll be there too. I don't want anyone thinking that just because I only work a few nights now, I can't manage to enjoy the craic.'

'But, Noleen, I don't think I can manage it all the way up that hill on my false leg and these crutches.'

'Yes, you can manage it, because Dessie sent a wheelchair home with Bryan. It's parked up by the outhouse. Now, sit in it and do as I say, Paddy. I'm in no mood for arguing tonight.'

Paddy knew that tone and didn't dare disagree. He slipped into the wheelchair with Bryan's help. 'It is a free bar, isn't it?' he said with an edge of nervousness in his voice.

'Of course it is, Da,' said Bryan. There was no need to add that there was no way they could go if there wasn't. 'It'll be the fund,' he whispered and Paddy winked.

The money had been hidden in Biddy's tea chest under a false bottom Paddy had fitted to it. Sacking had been placed on Biddy's kitchen floor and the tea tipped out while Paddy, with the help of Lorcan, had cut and fitted a piece of timber inside, with a small hinged hatch and handle at the back for access. 'There you go, Biddy,' Paddy had said as he screwed in the last hinge. 'Just make sure the chest is never less than half full so no one scrapes the bottom with a tin caddy and wonders what's going on. We don't want no nosey parkers digging around.' Everyone knew that Biddy kept an endless supply of tea in the chest, for anyone to help themselves should they need to. 'Black gold, that tea is now.'

'That must be why everyone is coming,' said Bryan. 'No one will be paying for drinks tonight.'

When Paddy was in the wheelchair and parked at the back gate, Noleen joined them. She was carrying a wicker basket.

'Now, do something useful,' she said with a smile. 'Carry this on your knee.' And she plonked the basket full of freshly baked meat-and-potato pies on his lap.

Paddy dipped his head into the basket and inhaled. 'They smell good,' he said.

'I know that. It will be the best plate of food there and the first to be emptied.' Noleen straightened her shoulders and puffed out her chest.

Paddy heard the note of pride in her voice before he saw the satisfaction on her face. The Delaneys were back where they should be, hanging on. Noleen could hold her head up once more and not be pitied. They would make their contribution and more than that, it would be the best. They had little to spare, but unlike in the past, there was nothing they needed either. Paddy was managing on his leg and holding a job down and Finn was going to the grammar.

The bar was already packed when they arrived and a blue haze of smoke hung over it.

'Here they come. The Delaneys are here. You made it!' said Madge as Bryan struggled to push the wheelchair through the door.

Madge was one of the most important members of the St Angelus mafia and not famous for her discretion. Noleen dreaded her making a fuss of Paddy and drawing attention to him. He was self-conscious enough about the wheelchair as it was. 'Just say hello,' she silently urged Madge in her head, 'nothing more.'

'Jeez, that lipstick looks nuclear,' muttered Paddy as she approached.

Madge had been widowed during the war and had clearly decided that it was at last time to find another man. She had seemingly dressed in a manner she felt would help achieve this.

'Evening, Paddy,' she said. She placed her hand on his arm. 'It's so great to see you walking about, but I knew that hill would be a killer. It wears me out.' She leant across him to speak to Noleen above the noise. 'Biddy, Branna, Elsie over there and meself are in charge of the buffet and dishing out the food.' Elsie waved at them from the food table. 'Can I take this basket, Paddy? Thanks very much, love.' Madge lifted the plate out of the basket on Paddy's lap without waiting for a reply. 'Did you write your name on the bottom of your plate, Noleen, so that one of the kids can bring it back tomorrow?'

'I did, Madge. It's my best, national issue, so don't let Elsie drop that.'

The two women laughed.

'Dessie said to take your da over to the table by the bar, Bryan.' And as quickly as she had appeared, super-efficient Madge disappeared in the direction of the long buffet table.

Noleen heard her shout to Branna, 'Lovely meat-and-potato pies coming over,' and she felt warm with pride when she saw Branna's eyebrows rise as she took the plate and then watched her mouth, 'Ooh, lovely,' back to Madge.

Bryan shot an anxious glance towards his mam. He couldn't see the table Madge had indicated for them to go to, or Dessie through the smoke. He handed Paddy his crutches and the two of them began to walk towards Biddy. If there was one sniff of someone giving them charity or pity, his da would want to leave and there would be no arguing with him. They would be out of the door quicker than they came in. Beads of perspiration broke out on Bryan's top lip.

He spotted Lorcan Ryan sitting on the corner of the lads' table, looking lost. Bryan hadn't told his da, but Lorcan had barely spoken a word since he had returned to work following the attack and J.T.'s second arrest. He'd asked Bryan just the one question when Dessie had sent him to help load the trailer with empty oxygen bottles from outside the theatre block. 'How's your da?' he'd said.

'He's alive,' Bryan had replied, 'which is more than you nearly were.'

Lorcan didn't say another word after that and Bryan had felt bad.

Finally Bryan heard Dessie's voice boom out from near the bar. 'Over here, lad.'

Others looked to see where Dessie was shouting from and as they turned, Noleen heard Paddy's name being called out by some of the men as they parted to allow him, his false leg and his crutches through.

'Paddy, mate, you're here! God help us, what a sight for sore eyes you are. Here, Dessie, a drink for Paddy!' That was Jake.

Noleen felt someone touch her arm and, turning, saw it was Maisie Tanner.

'Noleen, here, me and Stan have got a table and we've kept you seats. We're with Dessie and the bloody table is loaded with Babycham. We're gonna have a right laugh tonight, we are.'

Noleen smiled at her. Of all the women in the streets, Maisie Tanner was the most effusive and one of the happiest.

She made Noleen laugh just because her own laughter was infectious. Tears almost reached Noleen's eyes. They were being looked out for, cared for, because her husband was one of the walking wounded. Paddy didn't have a chance to object. He was too busy ensuring the pint of Guinness that had been thrust into his hand didn't spill.

'Bryan, leave your ma and da now, they don't want you hanging around. The lads, they all have their own table down at the stage,' Jake said. 'And there's a full barrel of Guinness just for the lads' table, laid on by Dessie. Even you lot won't manage to drain that dry.'

Bryan grinned from ear to ear, more with relief than pleasure. 'Oh, I don't know, if you give Lorcan half a chance...' He laughed as he tapped Lorcan on the back.

Jake had obviously taken on the role of master of ceremonies and he directed the crowd while his wife, Martha, sat with the other young mothers of the street, nursing their babies.

'Noleen, come on, get your coat off and take a seat.'

Noleen slid on to the chair Stanley held out for her and smiled her thanks.

Maisie noted that Noleen kept her coat on and almost kicked herself. She would have taken a frock down to the house herself if she had thought. There had been a bolt of turquoise satin that had found its way into Mrs Green's house from a ship and Maisie had made a frock and a skirt from it in exchange for a shilling. She refused to be intimidated by any fabric and made almost everything she wore. She would have happily loaned a frock to Noleen.

'Here you go, love.' Stan gave Noleen a wink as he poured a Babycham into a glass with a picture of a dancing deer on the side.

Noleen could not take her eyes off the glass. It was so pretty. Everything around them was changing. There was talk of sugar rationing ending altogether, and new things she couldn't afford were arriving in the shops every day.

Maisie giggled. 'Watch the bubbles, they fly up your nose.'

'Friends! Friends!' Dessie's voice boomed out from near the bar.

'Oh, good, there's our Pammy and the girls coming in through the door and they've got Anthony with them. Stan, look, she's got Dr Mackintosh with her.'

Stan was aware that Maisie was calling Anthony by his full name to show off in front of Noleen. Never once in conversation between the two of them had she called him 'Dr'. He lifted his pint and grinned at Paddy.

'Pammy, Pammy, over here, love,' Maisie shouted across the room.

Pammy smiled. Anthony Mackintosh had one arm protectively around her shoulders. Pammy, Victoria and Beth waved back at Maisie. The crowd parted with respect. The girls who nursed at St Angelus were treated as heroines, and a doctor was treated as if he was close to God himself and took direct instruction. The girls were all on their off-duty and they turned heads as they walked through. Maisie bathed in the reflected admiration as they wove their way through the tables. Having a daughter who was a nurse at St Angelus put her on an elevated footing in the community. It gave her status and she loved it.

'Where's Dana?' she asked straight away.

'She's back at Lovely Lane,' said Pammy. 'Said she will follow us on, but she is in such a funny mood, don't you think so, Victoria?'

Victoria didn't have time to answer as Stan placed a metal tray in the middle of the table.

'Thanks, Da.' Pammy grinned as he placed a glass of Babycham in everyone's hand and a pint in Anthony's.

'Oh, I say! Bottoms up, eh, girls,' said Pammy as she took a sip and then exclaimed, 'Oh, those bubbles! Straight up my nose.'

Stan started to drag over some more chairs, but people at tables nearby quickly gave up theirs for the angels of Lovely Lane. This act of rushing to give up seats now made Stan glow with pride. He was a happy man. How could he not be? A wife like Maisie, a daughter with lovely friends whom everyone admired, and a doctor who plainly adored their Pammy.

'Girls, it's great you could make it, and Anthony, well, we aren't used to doctors in the Silvie, unless they arrive in the back of the ambulance when there's a fight. I just hope your services aren't needed. Though I doubt anyone will be up for a punch-up tonight, what d'you reckon, Paddy?' Stan caught Maisie's eye and almost withered under her gaze.

'Stan, for pity's sake, why would you say something like that? Anthony will be put off us if you carry on like that,' she hissed. 'Don't you worry about anything like that happening, Anthony. We don't socialize with that sort, do we, Pammy?'

Pammy laughed and kissed her mother on her powdery cheek. If the Silvie was where Dessie wanted his do, it was good enough for them.

'I think it's great here,' said Anthony. 'Everyone is having such a laugh – listen to them all. I've never seen people so happy.'

Pammy looked around. She had never noticed it before, to her it was just a party night in Liverpool. High spirits were the norm. 'Do you all know Auntie Noleen and Uncle Paddy?' she said to the nurses. Everyone who was a neighbour was known as auntie or uncle. It was a mark of respect for the tight bond between them.

'I do. I know Mr Delaney from the prosthetics clinic,' said Beth. 'And I think you have started on nights at St Angelus, haven't you? Hello, how are you doing? Did the surgical spirit help in the end?'

Beth pulled her chair closer to Paddy, who seemed all at once to be flattered and happy and proud that a beautiful young nurse like Beth had sat next to him. He looked up at Noleen, who smiled. Paddy would be happy now, with a Guinness in his hand and someone from the medical profession to talk to about his stump. Poor girl. Noleen cast her eyes around the room. Lorraine and Mary had arrived and were standing near the lads' table. She saw Bryan carry a drink over to Lorraine and noted the smile that spread across his face when she looked up at him and said 'Thank you.'

The door opened and Roland Davenport walked in with Oliver Gaskell. Beth quickly turned to Pammy. 'Pammy, I have something to tell you...'

Dessie's voice rang out once again. 'Friends... Friends...' He was struggling to be heard. 'I have something special to say. Listen up everyone.'

Madge placed two plates of food on to the table in front of Bryan and the lads. 'Here you go,' she said. 'Make sure you soak up the alcohol. Lots of food, everyone, get the butties down you.' She raised an eyebrow as the lads leant in, grabbed a handful each and began to eat before she had finished speaking. 'We don't want no one off work tomorrow because of tonight, do you hear me?' She was mostly ignored and, shaking her head, she walked away. 'No good ever came from a free bar,' she said to no one in particular.

'Madge, stop serving food for a moment, please, love,' said Dessie across the crowd. 'Hush, lads. Hush, nurses. Dr Mackintosh, Mr Gaskell, welcome, welcome.'

The bell rang over the door and Dessie blushed as Oliver Gaskell's father appeared in the doorway with Matron by his side, Blackie in her arms. Just for a moment he was stuck for words. 'Matron, I didn't think you would come, it's so great to see you.'

A cheer went up around the room and people dragged chairs and drinks towards Matron and Dr Gaskell and someone produced a clean ashtray full of water for Blackie.

'I wouldn't have missed tonight for the world,' said Matron as she smiled and accepted a Babycham from Stan Tanner. 'Goodness me, can I drink this and live, Elsie?' she asked as she put it to her lips and sipped.

Anthony Mackintosh slipped his hand into Pammy's. He did that a lot. Just to make sure she was actually there with him and that he wasn't dreaming. After all his years as a bachelor, his funny, beautiful Pammy was his. When he squeezed her hand, she squeezed his back and, turning, gave him a smile that made him feel a foot taller.

'I had no idea about Beth and Oliver Gaskell,' she said.

'Do you care?' he asked, a note of concern in his voice.

'Not a bit. I don't care a jot.' She smiled and kissed him briefly on the cheek.

Dessie tried again. 'Hello everyone, quiet please.'

There were sounds of 'Shhh' from every table. Noleen accepted a cigarette from Maisie. She didn't often smoke and it was only one of Paddy's when she did. 'It's his only pleasure in. life,' she used to say when she sent Finn down to the tobacconist's with the last of their money. 'I can't leave him in all night with you lot without a ciggie, now can I?' Finn never said a word but always looked at her with disapproval in his eyes.

'Do you mind? I can't offer you one back,' she said as she looked down at the slim cigarettes with gold-foil tips. 'Not unless you want one of Paddy's Capstans anyway. These look gorgeous, so they do.'

'Don't be daft, Noleen, take one. Have as many as you like. Here you are, put some in your bag for after. Don't be worrying about giving me any. Where do you think I got these from, eh? They fell off the back of an American ship, queen. The landlord gets them and sells them behind the bar for a pittance. You have as many as you like. I'd be a bag of nerves if it wasn't for me fags.'

Noleen bent down to accept a light from the tip of Maisie's cigarette and began to laugh.

Paddy's head shot up. Noleen's laughter sounded to him like a peaty brook in Mayo tripping over weathered stones. It felt like an age had passed since he had heard it, and even longer since they'd been back home to Ireland. She caught his eye through the smoke as she sat back and relaxed. She smiled at her husband. He raised his pint of Guinness and smiled back. His leg and stump were beneath the table and for a brief second it felt like before the war: her good-looking man with the smiling eyes and she with her heart of gold.

Outside, in the street, Dana stood on tiptoes and peeped through the edge of the window pane that was free of frosting.

She could hear the muffled laughter and the clinking of plates and glasses, and through the fug of smoke she could see the backs of Pammy and Anthony, his arm stretched protectively around her. Beth was seated, with Oliver standing behind her, his hand on her shoulder, making sure everyone knew she was with him, and Victoria was leaning into her Roland. They all looked so happy.

Dana had felt like that once. Her eyes blurred with tears as she turned away. She felt lonely and isolated and standing out there on the street made it even worse. She took her handkerchief out of her pocket and blew her nose and wiped her eyes. She had been crying since the moment Teddy had told her what he had done. As much as he had pleaded and begged, in her heart she knew that she would not be able to believe him ever again. He had snapped their bond, betrayed her trust, deceived her. With one selfish act he'd destroyed the future that could have been theirs. Tucking her handkerchief back into her pocket, she let out a deep sigh. Picking up her suitcase, she made her way down towards the Pier Head and the boat back to Ireland.

Back inside, Dessie was still trying to gain the attention of his friends. 'Biddy, where's Emily?' he shouted.

'Here we go,' said Biddy to Elsie as the sound of the bar bell rang out, demanding that Dessie be heard. They piled brawn sandwiches on to a plate.

'Where the hell is Sister Haycock?' asked Branna.

'She's over there,' said Elsie. 'Sat with our Martha and the baby, having a sneaky cuddle. Let's hope there is time for them, eh, and they aren't too late. They deserve a child of their own.'

They all craned their necks and saw that Emily had moved back into her chair next to Dessie.

'Oh, doesn't she look lovely,' said Biddy as she knocked Elsie with her elbow.

'She does that,' said Branna. 'And you told the nurses about her birthday, Biddy? I bet they didn't take much persuading to come, did they?'

'No, not a bit of it. And they knew to keep it a secret, she herself had no idea the party was for her. They are good girls. Easy to see why they're her favourites.'

'Here, look, here he goes. Dessie's up on a chair.'

They shuffled across the floor with empty plates in their hands, back to the buffet table, where their drinks awaited them. Madge almost wobbled over on her high heels. The four ladies picked up their glasses and leant against the buffet table, nudging each other and exchanging knowing smiles. They were in on the secret. They wanted at least someone to notice.

'Look at that lot,' said Maisie as she nudged Noleen and nodded towards the buffet table. 'They all love a good do, don't they? We should have made a birthday cake, Biddy.'

'I heard about it from Frank and Lita in the fish shop,' said Noleen. 'When Dessie told me he was organizing a bit of a do, I didn't like to let on that I knew to anyone, bless him. I think everyone as far as Bootle knows it's Emily's birthday. Except Emily, of course. She seems to have forgotten.'

The room fell silent and anticipation filled the air as Dessie stood on his seat.

The voice of the barman rang out. 'Could everyone keep their glasses, please, as we've run out.'

Ribald jokes filled the air as the women pretended to cling

on to their glasses. 'Oh, you're not having ours,' said Maisie, hugging her Bambi Babycham glass to her chest.

'Thank you,' said Dessie. 'I just wanted to say welcome to everyone and thank you all for making the journey to the Silvestrian on what is a special night.'

'Why special, Dessie?' shouted someone who had taken full advantage of the free bar.

'Well, it is special, because...' Dessie looked down at Emily.

The three nurses gasped at the sight of her. She had swapped her standard knitted twinset for a cream A-line dress and her usually curly hair had been swept up on top of her head.

'Golly, she looks beautiful,' said Victoria. 'I've never seen her look like that before.' Victoria looked about the room, at the people she had come to know as well as family. She felt a pang of sadness and looked over at Roland trying his best to talk football with Stan Tanner.

'It must be because she's happy,' said Beth.

Maisie looked misty eyed. 'For the first time in a very long while,' she said. The night of the George Street bombing came to mind and a shiver ran down her spine. 'Imagine, Stan, if her mam and their lads could see her now. They were the same age as Jack and Cahill when the bomb dropped right on top of them.' Tears filled her eyes and spilt on to her cheeks. 'I just wish her mam could be here, to see her, you know.'

'I know, love.' Stan handed Maisie his handkerchief and Noleen picked up her hand.

'We are here for her,' said Noleen. 'We are her mothers. We know how her mam would have felt and we must feel it for her.' She squeezed Maisie's hand and they clung to each other, filled with motherly pride and love for Emily.

'Imagine, Noleen, who else would be in this room right now if that bomb hadn't fallen on George Street or if the war hadn't happened. I can almost see their faces.'

Stan reached out for Maisie's other hand and squeezed it. 'Don't think of things like that, love,' he whispered. 'We have to always look forward, not back, and this is a good night to remember that.' He cracked open two more bottles of Babycham with his back teeth and poured them into Maisie and Noleen's glasses.

'Lovely, this,' said Noleen as she took another sip.

Maisie handed Noleen another of the posh cigarettes. They both inhaled, sighed, squeezed hands and gave a little giggle, although neither was sure why.

God, I've missed this, Noleen thought to herself as Maisie complained about the American cigarettes. 'The bleedin' things are so thin, they've burnt down in seconds.'

Paddy's love for his wife filled his heart as he watched her commiserate and then laugh with Maisie. 'Women. I can't understand them, can you?' he said to Stan. 'Crying one minute, laughing the next.' You were a stupid, miserable git, he thought to himself as he turned to the sound of Dessie banging the table.

'I would like to announce...' Dessie's voice boomed across the room and a loud 'Woohoo!' went up from the tables. '... that I would like to ask this poor woman to be my wife. I say poor, because for some inexplicable reason, she might say yes.'

Dessie reached down and took Emily's hand. With one pull and some help from his friends, he lifted her through the air so that she was now standing on her seat. Everyone cheered so loudly, it would have taken a more-bomb-damaged roof straight off. He hugged her to his side and laughed so hard that the two of them almost wobbled off the chairs.

Emily's eyes filled with tears as she scanned the crowd of faces. She thought she saw Rita, her one-time neighbour and friend who had died in the bomb along with Rita's sons. She tried to raise her hand to wipe her eyes, but Dessie was holding on to her firm and tight. Her arms were pressed into her sides as he hugged her to him. 'Will you say yes?' he whispered into her hair.

She couldn't speak as her throat was thick with tears. She nodded her head and, looking up into his eyes, managed to mouth the words, 'Yes, I will.'

The cheers from the room sent the plasterwork on the ceiling in the room down below, crashing to the floor. Emily looked around her and cried tears of happiness but also tears for the loss of her parents and her brothers. She so wanted them to know. To tell them, to share her news. But, they were all gone, dead. Everyone in the room had known Rita, as they had her mam and Alf. Alf, the only survivor apart from herself, was now in the rest home, too far gone to join them. There was no one there that she belonged to, apart from Dessie. Despite the familiar pull of loss, for the first time since that awful night in the Blitz, she was truly happy. She blinked furiously as the cheering crescendoed and people shouted their good wishes.

'Don't let her go, Dessie. Taken you long enough, mate.'

'Start as you mean to go on, love, make him beg.'

Roland had slipped his arms around Victoria's shoulders. He had seen the tears flood into her eyes. He had hardly been able to bring himself to speak to her all evening. Her even considering aborting their baby had stunned him and he had felt anger towards her for the first time ever, but now, caught up in the moment, he had to ask her. 'Vic, when we leave for Bolton tomorrow, are you staying with me? Are you going to become my wife?' Everyone on their table was standing and cheering; they were the only two still seated.

Victoria's eyes met his and she had no hesitation when she responded. She felt her mother, close, urging her on. She only had to close her eyes and she knew exactly what her mother would want her to do. She would want Victoria to be the best mother, to finish a job she herself had only started and most of all, Victoria knew, she would want to see her grandchild. 'Yes,' she whispered. 'We will be married. I'm coming home with you to have our baby Roland. I'm sorry, I panicked. I was in a bit of a state, all my plans and dreams, they just came crashing down.'

Roland, unseen by the cheering crowds, kissed his Victoria. 'We are going to have the best life,' he said. 'I am going to make it my life's work to make you very, very happy.' And without question, Victoria knew, he would.

There were roars of laughter and Emily's vision blurred as she scanned the room. She saw everyone cheering, her nurses clapping, Biddy crying. Then she saw her, her mam, standing in the corner, near the door, with Richard and Harry. Her mother's hands were around her boys' shoulders and she was hugging them into her sides. The boys were jumping up and down and waving their arms and cheering her on. They were in the clothes they'd been wearing on the night they'd died, and they almost looked as if they'd come from another era. Her mother's smile shone with love and it said to her, 'We are ready to go now. Live your life, Emily. Be happy.'

Chapter 21

Sister Theresa was always the first into St Chad's, but this morning her steps were hastier than usual. She turned the polished brass handles and the large wooden doors creaked slowly open on to the familiar sight of the dark church and its huddled rows of pews. The smell of old oak, holy smoke and unanswered prayers assailed her senses. Lighting a candle, she made her way straight down the aisle to the statue of the Holy Mother.

Lorcan Ryan's prayer stool was half out of a pew and she stopped to bend down and push it back in. She was distracted because she had barely slept the previous night for worrying about a First World War widow who was about to be evicted.

It was Dessie Horton who had come to her and said, 'If there is a mother in need in this parish, leave a note at the foot of the statue of Our Lady and someone will look out for it. Don't ask me any more, Sister. Return to Our Lady first thing the following morning. Someone will help.'

Who, she had no idea. Dessie Horton wasn't the poorest man on the streets, but he wasn't rich either. And since he'd proposed to Emily Haycock not two weeks earlier and would doubtless be married soon, Sister Theresa couldn't think that he'd have much cash to spare. He had been adamant about one thing, though. 'If you tell one person, Sister, no more notes will be answered.'

She had racked her brains to think who it was who took her notes. There were no new worshippers attending St Chad's and church life had remained the same, except for one thing: the brown envelopes of money that miraculously appeared every time she left a note asking Our Lady to help. The church doors were never locked and Sister Theresa knew that the envelopes were taken during the night, for it was only after the last Angelus Mass that she left her notes. She had thought of asking Noleen Delaney whether she'd seen the mystery benefactor, but she didn't dare break her promise to Dessie.

The penny candle lit her way along the white marble floor as it reflected the light. There it was. The brown envelope, at the feet of Our Lady, always in the same place. Sister Theresa dipped her knee, blessed herself and tucked the envelope inside her habit. She looked up and the serene face of the Holy Mother smiled down at her. She wondered whether her serene expression had deepened since the day she had begun leaving small miracles for the mothers of Lovely Lane.

The doors opened and Sister Theresa turned around to see Lorcan Ryan entering the church.

'Oh, Lorcan,' she said in the hushed tones she always kept for church, 'are you on your way from or to work?'

'From, Sister. I thought I would just call in on my way home. I'll be back tonight for the Angelus.'

Sister Theresa smiled. 'You are a good boy, Lorcan. The best. Your mammy is a very lucky lady to have a son like you. Close the door on your way out, would you now? I'll be back across for Mass soon.'

Lorcan watched her leave, saw the envelope was gone, dropped to his knees and gave thanks. Once his prayers were said, he made his way to Biddy's house, to let her know the widow, the mother, was safe.

Acknowledgements

I can never write a book without saying a big thank you to my editor Rosie de Courcy. She inspires me and spurs me on. We fire ideas off each other and she understands what I want to write and achieve, often before I do myself. She's the best editor in the business – a legend who has worked with all the greats and not a day goes by when I am not truly grateful that, now, she is mine.

Thank you, Rosie.

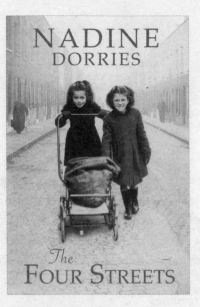

1950s Liverpool

In the tight-knit Irish Catholic community of the
Four Streets, two girls are growing up.

One is motherless – and hated by the cold woman who
is determined to take her dead mother's place. The other
is hiding a dreadful secret which she dare not let slip to
anyone, lest it rips the heart out of the community.

What can the people of the Four Streets do when a betrayal
at the very centre of their world comes to light?

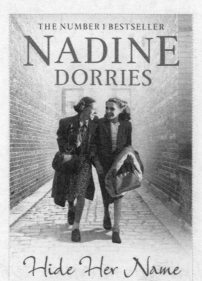

THE NUMBER 1 BESTSELLER

NADINE DORRIES

Hide Her Name

1950s Liverpool

In the Four Streets, a dreadful murder has been committed and fourteen-year-old Kitty Doherty is pregnant with the dead man's child. This secret is so dangerous that it is decided Kitty must go to Ireland to await the baby's birth.

But in Liverpool, the police aren't giving up their search for the truth. Somewhere, in this tight-knit Irish Catholic community, someone must know something. The streets are alive with gossip and rumour, and it isn't easy to keep a secret that big.

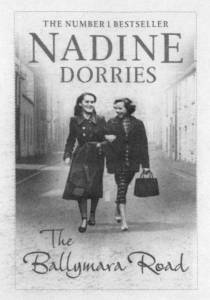

THE NUMBER 1 BESTSELLER

NADINE DORRIES

The Ballymara Road

Christmas morning, 1963

Fifteen-year-old Kitty Doherty gives birth in a cold,
unfriendly Irish convent. She knows her beautiful baby boy
presents a huge danger to her family's Catholic community
back in Liverpool's Four Streets. When he is adopted by
a wealthy family in Chicago, Kitty considers the problem
solved. But soon it's obvious the baby is very sick and only
his birth mother can save him.

In Liverpool, a charismatic new priest has arrived. As
the Dohertys cope with the tragic consequences of Kitty's
pregnancy, the police seem close to solving the double
murder which rocked the Four Streets to the core. But
now all that is about to be put at risk once again.

The final gripping instalment in the
bestselling Four Streets trilogy.

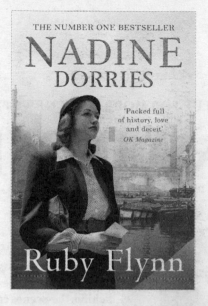

THE NUMBER ONE BESTSELLER

NADINE DORRIES

'Packed full of history, love and deceit'
OK Magazine

Ruby Flynn

County Mayo, Ireland, 1947

In the worst winter in living memory, Ruby Flynn is rescued from the tiny cottage on the Atlantic coast where her family has perished. She is one of the storm orphans, taken in by nuns to be educated for a life in service. Now she must find her own way in the outside world.

The FitzDeane family have a thriving shipping business in Liverpool and they also own beautiful Ballyford Castle in Mayo. When Ruby is appointed as their nursery maid, a dangerous attraction to the young Lord FitzDeane begins to grow. Soon the tragedies and secrets that link her family to his will threaten to overwhelm them.

The darkest sins cast the longest shadows…